"Though Scott Russell Sanders is best known today as an essay-ist and conservationist, he previously was one of the brightest science-fiction newcomers of the 1980s, and his incisive, playful, startling stories—which speak directly to our twenty first-centu-ry environmental and genetic concerns—were staples of *Omni*, *Asimov's*, and *The Magazine of Fantasy & Science Fiction*. To have virtually all this material back in print in a single collection is a joy. Whether you knew it or not, you've had a space on your shelf all these years, waiting to be filled by *Dancing in Dreamtime*."

ANDY DUNCAN, author of *The Pottawatomie Giant and Other Stories*

"Although the stories in Scott Russell Sanders's new col-lection, *Dancing in Dreamtime*, often portray futuristic worlds, they always hold a mirror to our contemporary society in a way that allows us to see ourselves and our present time more clearly. Wildly imaginative and haunting, these stories are the stuff of dreams, yes, but they also have much to show us about who we are in the here and now."

LEE MARTIN, author of *The Bright Forever: A Novel*

"*Dancing in Dreamtime* sparks with brilliant imagery, from a city where dreams roost in trees and the destruction of their habitat threatens the inhabitants' sanity, to a circus where robotic pandas play organ music and tigers blink with neon stripes. These are stories of people subjected to the dreams of others, reminders that our best fantasies have unintended consequences. They dream our doom, they dream our possible salvation, they draw us further into the dance."

TERESA MILBRODT, author of *Bearded Women: Stories*

"The stories in *Dancing in Dreamtime* are familiar enough to make your heart ache and new enough to feel fresh and wondrous. Here you will find people connecting and falling apart as people have always connected and fallen apart, but beneath a fantastical and occasionally terrifying sky."

CARMEN MARIA MACHADO

"These brilliant stories explore birds who've time-warped to avoid extinction on earth, and people who long for both tidiness and the wilds. Human innovation and destruction are at the center of all these tales, which leave reality in order to return readers to this planet we've ravaged, more awake to ecological catastrophe, and our earth and its peoples who are ravenous and yearning and not-yet ruined. These fictions both delight and warn."

ERIN STALCUP, author of *And Yet It Moves*

"As these enchanting stories examine how technologies and advancements disconnect us and create chaos, Sanders always shows that we will persevere with our own kind of hope, our own kind of love, and our own kind of heart."

"Scott Russell Sanders is certainly best known as one of our finest essayists. What is less known—and likely more surprising—is that he was once also an artful author of science fiction. We should all rejoice that these stories have at last been collected in *Dancing in Dreamtime*. Sanders is the Alice Munro of science fiction, and these quiet, lyrical stories covering his career in the genre offer all the necessary proof. Highly recommended."

ALSO BY SCOTT RUSSELL SANDERS

FICTION

Divine Animal
The Invisible Company
The Engineer of Beasts
Bad Man Ballad
Terrarium
Wonders Hidden
Fetching the Dead
Hear the Wind Blow
Wilderness Plots

NONFICTION

Earth Works: Selected Essays
A Conservationist Manifesto
A Private History of Awe
The Force of Spirit
The Country of Language
Hunting for Hope
Writing from the Center
Staying Put
Secrets of the Universe
The Paradise of Bombs
Stone Country

DANCING IN
Dreamtime

break away books

INDIANA UNIVERSITY PRESS

Bloomington & Indianapolis

DANCING IN
Dreamtime

SCOTT RUSSELL SANDERS

This book is a publication of

INDIANA UNIVERSITY PRESS
Office of Scholarly Publishing
Herman B Wells Library 350
1320 East 10th Street
Bloomington, Indiana 47405 USA

iupress.indiana.edu

The paper used in this publication meets the
minimum requirements of the American
National Standard for Information
Sciences—Permanence of Paper for Printed
Library Materials, ANSI Z39.48-1992.

Manufactured in the
United States of America

Library of Congress
Cataloging-in-Publication Data

Names: Sanders, Scott R. (Scott Russell),
[date], author
Title: Dancing in dreamtime / Scott Russell
Sanders.
Description: Bloomington and
Indianapolis : Indiana University Press,
[2016]
Identifiers: LCCN 2016019538 (print) |
LCCN 2016024281 (ebook) | ISBN
9780253022516 (pb : alk. paper) | ISBN
9780253022592 (e-book)
Classification: LCC PS3569.A5137 A6 2016
(print) | LCC PS3569.A5137 (ebook) |
DDC 813/.54—dc23
LC record available at https://lccn.loc.gov
/2016019538

1 2 3 4 5   21 20 19 18 17 16

FOR URSULA K. LE GUIN

The universe is made of stories,
not of atoms.

MURIEL RUKEYSER, "The Speed of Darkness"

Contents

The Anatomy Lesson

By the time I reached the Anatomy Library all the bones had been checked out. At every table, students bent over yawning boxes, assembling feet and arms, scribbling in notebooks, muttering Latin names. Half the chairs were occupied by slouching skeletons, and skulls littered the floor like driftwood.

Since I also needed to cram for the following day's exam, I asked the librarian to search one last time for bone-boxes in the storeroom.

"I've told you there *aren't* any more," she said, frowning at me from beneath a tangle of dark hair, like a vexed animal caught in a bush. How many students had already pestered her for bones this evening?

"Are there partial skeletons? Mismatched sets? Irregulars?"

The librarian measured me with her stare, as if estimating the size of box my bones would fill. She was young enough to be a student herself, yet shadows drooped beneath her eyes, like the painted tears of a clown. "Irregulars," she repeated. "You're sure?"

"I'll take anything."

A bitten-off smile quirked her lips. Then she turned away from the desk, murmuring, "Very well. I'll see what I can find."

I blinked with relief at her departing back. Only as she slipped noiselessly into the storeroom did I notice the beige gloves on her hands. Fastidious, I thought.

While awaiting the specimen, I scrutinized the vertebrae that were exposed like beads along the bent necks of students who labored over skeletons at nearby tables. Five lumbar vertebrae, seven cervical, a dozen thoracic: I rehearsed the names.

Presently the librarian returned with a box the size of an orange crate, wooden, dingy with age. The metal clasps that held it shut were tarnished green. No wonder she wore the gloves.

"You're in luck," she said, shoving it over the counter.

I hesitated, my hands poised above the crate as if I were testing it for heat.

"Well, do you want it, or don't you?" she said.

Afraid she might return it to the archives, I lifted the box, which seemed lighter than its bulk would have promised, as if the wood had dried with age. Perhaps instead of bones inside there would be heaps of dust.

"Must be an old model," I observed amiably.

Her plump lips curled.

I found a clear space on the floor beside a spindly man whose elbows and knees protruded through rents in his clothing like the humps of a sea serpent above the waters. The clasps, cold against my fingers, yielded with a metallic shriek, drawing the bleary glances of my fellow students. I shrugged apologetically, and the glazed eyes returned to work.

Inside the crate I found a stack of hinged trays, as in a fishing-tackle box, each tray gleaming with putty-colored bones. I began on the foot, joining tarsal to metatarsal. It was soon evident that there were too many bones. Each one seemed a bit odd in shape, with an extra flange where none should be, or a misplaced knob, and they were too light, as light as hollow reeds. Fitted together, they formed a seven-toed foot, slightly larger than that of an adult male, with phalanges all of the same length and ankle-bones bearing the sockets for . . . what? Flippers? Wings?

This drove me back to my anatomy text. Yet no consulting of diagrams would make sense of this foot. A scrape with a coin assured me these were real bones, not plastic or plaster. But from what creature? Feeling queasy, as if in my ignorance I had created this monstrosity, I looked around to see if anyone had noticed. Everywhere living skulls tilted over dead ones, ignoring me. Only the librarian seemed to be watching me sidelong, through her tangled hair. I hastily returned the foot bones to their various compartments.

Next I worked at the hand, which boasted six rather than seven digits. Two of them were clearly thumbs, opposite in orientation, and each of the remaining fingers was double-jointed, so that both sides of these vanished hands could have served as palms.

After examining fibula, femur, sternum, and clavicle, each bone familiar yet slightly awry from the norm, I gingerly unpacked the plates of the skull. Their scattered state was unsettling enough, since in ordinary skeletal kits they would have come pre-assembled into a braincase. Their gathered state was even more unsettling. They would go together in only one arrangement, yet it appeared so outrageous to me that I reassembled the skull three times, always with the same result. There was only one jaw, to be sure, though an exceedingly broad one, and the usual pair of holes for ears. The skull itself, however, was clearly double, as if two heads had been squeezed together, like cherries grown double on a single stem. Each hemisphere of the brain enjoyed its own cranium. The opening for the nose was in its accustomed place, as were two of the eyes. But in the center of the vast forehead, like the drain in a bare expanse of bathtub, was the cavity for a third eye.

I closed the anatomy text. Hunched over to shield this freak from the gaze of other students, I stared long at that triangle of eyes, and at the twinned craniums that splayed out behind like a fusion of moons. No, I decided, such a creature was not possible. It must be a counterfeit, like the Piltdown Man or the Cardiff Giant. But I would not fall for the trick. I dismantled the skull, stuffed the bones into their trays, clasped the box shut and returned it to the check-out desk.

"This may seem funny to you," I hissed at the librarian, who was rooting in her bush of hair with the point of a pencil, "but I have an exam to pass."

"Funny?" she whispered.

"This hoax." I slapped the box, raising a puff of dust.

"Not so loud, please."

"It's a fabrication."

"Is it?" She rested her gloved hands atop the crate.

"Nobody who knows a scrap of anatomy would fall for it."

"Really?" she said, peeling the glove away from one wrist. I wanted to hurry away before she could uncover that hand. Yet I was caught by the slide of cloth, the sight of pink skin emerging. "I found it hard to believe myself, at first," she said, spreading the naked hand before me, palm up. I was relieved to count only five digits. But the fleshy heel was inflamed, as if the bud of a new thumb were sprouting there. A scar, only a scar, I thought. Nothing more. Whereupon she turned the hand over and displayed another palm. The fingers curled upward and then curled in the reverse direction, forming a cage of fingers on the counter.

I flinched, and turned my gaze aside, unwilling to look her in the eye, fearful of what those snarled bangs might hide. Skeletons were shattering in my mind, names of bones were fluttering away like blown leaves.

"How many of you are there?" I whispered.

"I'm the first, so far as I know. Unless you count our friend here." She clacked her nails on the bone-box.

I guessed the distances to inhabited planets. "Where do you come from?"

"Boise."

"Boise . . . Idaho?"

"Actually, I grew up in a logging camp out in the sticks, but Boise's the nearest place anybody's ever heard of."

"You mean you're . . ."

"Human? Of course!" She loosed a quiet laugh. Students glanced up momentarily from their skeletons with glassy eyes. The librarian lowered her voice, until it burbled like whale song. "At least I started out that way," she whispered.

"But what about your hands? Your face?"

"Until a few months ago they were just ordinary hands." She wriggled fingers back into the glove and touched one cheek. "My face wasn't swollen. My shoes fit."

"Then what happened?"

"I assembled these bones." Again she tapped the crate. From inside came a muffled clatter, like the sound of gravel sliding.

"You're becoming one of *them*?"

"So it appears."

Her upturned lips and downturned eyes gave me contradictory messages. The clown-sad eyes seemed too far apart, and her forehead, obscured behind a thicket of hair, seemed impossibly broad.

"Aren't you frightened?" I said.

"Not anymore," she answered. "Not since my head began to open."

I winced, recalling the vast skull, pale as porcelain, and the triangle of eyes. I touched the bone-box gingerly. "What are you turning into?"

"I don't know yet. But I begin to get glimmerings, begin to see myself flying."

"Flying?"

"Or maybe swimming. I can't be sure. My vision's still blurry."

I tried to imagine her ankles affixed with wings, her head swollen like a double moon, her third eye blinking. "And what sort of creature will you be when you're . . . changed?"

"We'll just have to wait and see, won't we?"

"We?"

"You've put the bones together, haven't you?"

I stared at my palms, and then turned my hands over to examine the twitching skin where the knuckles should be.

Clear-Cut

"Have you noticed there aren't nearly so many dreams these days?" said the man who sat down next to Veronica on the park bench one April morning. He was about her age, mid-twenties, bearded, bespectacled, thin as a bird's wing, with the secretive air of a spy. "And the dreams that do come," he added, "are so threadbare you can see right through them."

When Veronica merely studied the black scuffed toes of her nurse's clogs without replying, the man leaned toward her and confided, "It comes from cutting down the old forest. There aren't enough places for dreams to roost in the daytime. I can remember when this whole ridge was covered in trees."

Ordinarily, when a strange man addressed her, Veronica either ignored him until he fell silent or else, if he persisted, she glared at him and walked swiftly away. But she was intrigued by what this stranger said, and reassured by his shyness. Accustomed to being stared at by men, she found it refreshing that he peered through his metal-rimmed glasses in every direction but hers.

"Yes," she said. "From the fire tower you could see trees all the way to the horizon."

The man nodded agreement with a wag of his chin. Veronica gripped the edge of the bench to keep her hands from trembling, wondering if she had finally met a kindred soul.

✳   ✳   ✳

Although she did nothing to enhance what nature had blessed her with, neither padding nor painting, wherever Veronica went men flung after her the lassos of their gaze. They saw in her wavy auburn hair and rosy complexion promises of offspring and delight. Her swaying walk set their hearts racing. Had they been moose or bison they would have battered one another to win her favor; since they were human, they invited her on dates. But Veronica found her suitors to be drearily predictable, passionate only about money and sex, perhaps with milder interest in cars or golf, without an ounce of imagination. Their idea of high adventure was to try a new restaurant or to shift the asset allocation in their portfolios. One after another she told them no, no, a thousand times no.

"You won't bloom forever," her mother warned. "One day the bees will stop buzzing around." Then I won't get stung, Veronica thought. "Would a doctor be such a bad catch?" her father asked. Caught like a cold, she thought, or like plague? She bit her tongue and let her parents nag. For how could they know what she longed for, when she had only the vaguest notion herself?

She chose to work the graveyard shift in the emergency ward because at night there were fewer doctors around to pat and pinch and ogle her. The bleary-eyed interns only gave her speculative stares, as if they were studying the menu but too tired to eat. The male nurses had learned to fear her wrath.

Night was the prime time for accidents and mayhem, as if people took leave of their senses with the onset of darkness. Husbands beat up their wives. Boys raped their girlfriends. Mothers with nerves rubbed raw by bawling infants took too many pills. Toddlers swallowed paperclips or mothballs or keys. Teenagers tried uppers or downers, sliced their arms with razor blades, wrecked their cars. Drunks tripped on curbs and broke bones. Muggers worked the sidewalks, car thieves worked the streets, rival gangs fought over turf with guns or knives. During the graveyard shift, wave after wave of sirens rushed toward the emergency room like storm-driven surf.

"It beats me why you keep working nights," her father said, in the tone of baffled affection he had used toward Veronica since her adolescent blossoming. "You've got enough seniority to work afternoons, maybe even straight days."

"Don't hide your light under a bushel," said her mother.

"Those surgeons you work with can earn a thousand bucks with a few flicks of a scalpel," her father said, "and you won't give them the time of day."

"You're so often asleep when your beaus call, I have to convince them you aren't sick," her mother complained.

"They aren't my beaus," Veronica said. "They're just men pestering me."

Her mother sighed. "You're punishing us, aren't you? As if it's our fault you're gorgeous."

"Okay," her father conceded. "Maybe all the doctors are creeps. But there's other fish in the sea. Right? What about that vice president from the bank? Or the bowling alley magnate? Or the tech entrepreneur? Or the contractor who builds pizza franchises? Those are decent guys, and they're rolling in dough."

"Snag a husband while you can," her mother advised. "Do you want to be a night shift nurse for the rest of your life?"

The answer to that question was no. Veronica did not want to be any sort of nurse forever. She was already nearing burnout from dealing with broken, bleeding, desperate people. But she could not decide what else to do with her life. No matter what path she envisioned—teaching, forestry, market gardening, graphic design—it led through a gauntlet of men. They would be her bosses, her colleagues, her students, her customers. Until her accidental beauty faded, they would value nothing else about her. With their rudimentary drives, men seemed to her a separate species, trapped in an evolutionary cul-de-sac, like plankton or horseshoe crabs, while women had evolved to higher levels of complexity.

For the present, Veronica stuck with her midnight shift despite the stress and gore. After supper she changed into her navy blue scrubs and sturdy clogs. Although her jacket and pants were a couple of sizes too large, chosen to fit loosely, when she arrived at the hospital men would still gawk at her.

She always arrived early and parked her car at the edge of the lot near a stand of big trees, mostly beeches and maples and oaks, the last survivors of an ancient forest that once covered the ridge now occupied by the hospital. From this vantage point, she could see skeins of streetlights stretching along the three rivers that converged at the heart of the city, the flashing red beacons atop bridges, the glare of blast furnaces, the jets of yellow flame above refineries, and steam drifting in luminous clouds above the mills. But her chief pleasure was to watch the dream creatures stir from their roosts in the high branches and go gliding down to haunt the bedrooms of sleepers.

Once she clocked in for work, time passed quickly in a siege of heart attacks, gunshot wounds, diabetic seizures, broken legs, collapsed lungs, third-degree burns, and sundry other afflictions, all accompanied by cries of pain. Among the few patients who lifted her spirits were the expectant mothers, too far along to reach the maternity ward, who staggered in and delivered their babies on a gurney, often into Veronica's gloved hands.

During the rare lulls between emergencies, she wrote lists in a small notebook she kept in her pocket—lists of proverbs, vegetables, rivers, constellations, titles of books, women scientists, famous painters, obscure actors, songs—lists of anything she could dredge up from her brain. While hoisting the bag for a blood transfusion or pressing defibrillator pads to a patient's chest, she might recall burnt sienna or Baton Rouge, Louisiana; then at the next opportunity she would add those items to her lists of colors or state capitals. Noticing her habit, one of the gawkers might ask, "What are you scribbling, baby doll?" "Poetry," she might answer, to discourage the man, or "Letters to a crazed world." Indeed, as the world sank into disarray, she would have written poetry if she knew how, but at least she could make little havens of order by writing lists.

Veronica's favorite moment arrived after she clocked out at dawn. In cold weather she sat in her car and gazed down at the incandescent city. In mild weather she watched from a bench under the creamy branches of a giant sycamore. As alarm clocks rang and sleepers awoke, dream creatures slipped away from bedsides and came wafting up out of the valley to roost in the old trees beside the parking lot. They filled every branch, crammed together cheek by jowl. Judging by their gaudy outfits, they might have been a flock of parrots. Yet they made little noise, only a dry rustling, like wind in leaves. The sound enchanted Veronica, who imagined they were exchanging notes about the dreams they had performed for sleepers in the city.

Of course dreams were also needed in daytime, though not so many, for napping babies and drowsy old folks and dozing workers home from the graveyard shift. On mornings when Veronica sat watching the flocks of characters returning to the ridge, a smaller number rose from the treetops where they had been roosting and swooped down into the city. Occasionally, she would meet in her dreams some dragon or soldier or crone whom she had seen gliding away on this daytime duty.

Back in her childhood, when the ridge was still part of a state forest, Veronica often came here with her parents to picnic or camp. At first she had been frightened by the flying specters, with their talons and fangs, their metal hooks for hands and barbed tails and tentacles. When she pointed them out with a shudder, her parents dismissed her worries. "Monsters in the trees!" her mother echoed teasingly. "Let's have a look," her father said, shining his flashlight into the branches. The beam swept over a white-bearded gnome, a scarlet devil, and a burly gorilla, all clear as day to Veronica. But her father merely said, "See there, kiddo, just empty trees. Nothing to worry your pretty head about."

She soon lost her fear of the creatures, and never again mentioned them to her parents. From the first she knew perfectly well what they were, these goblins and ghouls, these shaggy wolves, these hunchbacks and witches and mad scientists. Some she recognized from her own dreams, especially the nightmarish beasts, while others—the hunter, wizard, or drowned sailor—appeared in dreams recounted by her friends. It seemed reasonable to her as a child that these nighttime visitors would spend the daylight hours roosting in trees, like owls.

Back in those years before puberty, when girls still looked at her without jealousy and boys without lust, she would hike up to the forested ridge with friends at dawn or dusk to see if they noticed the specters swirling overhead. Only one of those friends—a languid boy with sunken cheeks and forehead pasted with sweaty hair—ever seemed aware of the chattering flocks. "Do you hear that?" he said to her one night. "Hear what?" she asked hopefully. "That whispery sound," he said, "like river rapids far away." Another evening he squinted up into the bustling air and observed, "The sky is full of colored patches." "What shape are they?" she asked. "I can't make them out," he said, "they keep shifting, like jewels in a kaleidoscope." Soon afterward, the boy took to his bed and died of leukemia, leaving Veronica alone with her visions.

And so when the bearded stranger sat down next to her on the bench one April morning and said with a secretive air, "Have you noticed there aren't nearly so many dreams these days?" Veronica neither glared at him nor fled. Instead, she gripped the edge of the bench to still her trembling and waited to hear what he would say next.

He recalled the hardwood forest that once covered this ridge where the hospital now sprawled amid parking lots and landscaped grounds, and then she recalled how as a girl she would climb the fire tower and gaze with wonder over a sea of trees. Of course the tower had long since been taken down, together with all but a scattering of trees that were spared to provide islands of shade on the groomed lawns.

"The city keeps on expanding," the man said, waving a bony hand at the horizon. "Any day you can hear chainsaws and bulldozers leveling another woods."

"It's worrisome," said Veronica. She stole a glance at the man, so pale and thin, his hair and sparse beard as blond as corn silk. His blue eyes, glinting behind the spectacles like pebbles at the bottom of a creek, shyly avoided looking at her.

"The fewer the trees, the fewer the dreams," the man went on. "Some people get only half a sleep's worth, others don't get any. That's why the hospital is so busy. That's why the city is boiling with anger and fear. People are going nuts from dream deprivation."

Veronica had been disturbed by the same thought, and was about to tell him so. But before she could speak, she burst out laughing, overjoyed to meet someone who shared her vision.

Abruptly the man stood up. "I didn't mean to bother you."

"Oh, you're not bothering me."

"You're laughing. You probably think I'm weird."

"No, no."

His scrawny frame swayed, as if caught by a breeze. "From the way you were watching the skies, I thought maybe you saw—" Without finishing his sentence, he bolted for his car.

Veronica rose from the bench and called after him, "Wait!"

But without looking back he hurried on to a mud-splattered Jeep, climbed in, and drove away. As the engine noise receded, she could hear the chatter of flocks rising from the ancient trees to go deliver daytime dreams.

That night as usual Veronica arrived early for work and the next morning she lingered afterward. Instead of going to the bench under the huge sycamore, however, she sat in her car to watch the flurry of dream characters arriving and departing, aware of the bearded man sitting nearby in his Jeep. They kept on like this for several days, cooped up in their cars. Then one morning she walked to the parking lot after a hectic graveyard shift, the food in her cooler bag still untouched, and there he was standing at the base of the sycamore, hands pressed against the trunk, gazing up through the branches where new leaves blazed like tiny green flames. Curious to see him touching her favorite tree, she continued on past her car and onto the lawn, drinking in the fragrant spring air. Eventually, as if by chance, she circled back to the bench and sat down, placing the bag beside her on the weathered slats.

With eyes closed, the man was embracing the great tree, his cheek against the massive trunk, his arms reaching perhaps a quarter of the way around. As if sensing her presence, he suddenly opened his eyes and stood back, brushing flakes of bark from his jacket. "I like trees," he said apologetically.

"I love them," said Veronica. "Especially this one, with its patchwork bark and creamy branches. It's like a dancing goddess with a hundred arms."

"Yes, a dancing goddess!" His beard parted with a smile. Gesturing at the bench he asked, "Do you mind?"

By way of answer she picked up the bag and placed it on her lap.

He lowered himself beside her, not too close, and kept his legs cocked as if ready to flee. "I didn't mean to spook you the other day."

"You didn't spook me." She hesitated, then decided to take a chance. "I see them, too."

He gave her a startled look, his eyes wide behind their lenses. "What do you see?"

She tilted her face toward the brightening sky and pointed. "There's a fox, a fat lady, a burglar, a tangle of snakes, a dwarf."

"And a peacock," he said, grinning broadly now, "an octopus, a two-headed calf..."

"A gambler in a green eyeshade, a lumberjack, a tattooed woman..."

"A beggar with a bowl, a child in a lab coat..."

They fell silent and stared at one another. His eyes watered, and Veronica could feel tears brimming from her own. After several deep breaths, she asked, "Have you seen them all before?"

He nodded. "All of them. I've cataloged several hundred characters, but I haven't added any new ones for years. In fact, lots of those on my list don't show up any more."

"I've noticed that. Many old standbys are disappearing. I suspect they're migrating."

"Searching for a forest that hasn't been clear-cut," he said, finishing her thought.

"That's why our city is suffering a drought of dreams."

"Exactly."

Veronica shivered. It was as if she had finally met someone who spoke her native tongue. "I've always wondered where the dream furnishings are kept," she said. "You know, bulky things like rockets and cupboards, or scenery, like mountains and castles and caves."

"I've wondered, too. Maybe they're dissolved in the air of bedrooms and only precipitate out when they're needed for a dream."

"So that's why if you sleep in somebody else's house or a hotel or in a tent . . ." she began.

"The scenery and props are different from the ones at home."

No longer pallid, his face shone, and Veronica's own cheeks burned. She squeezed the cooler bag with both hands to keep from reaching over to stroke his downy beard out of sheer gratitude. No man except her father had ever made her feel so safe, and even her father had never made her feel so deeply understood. While the chatter from the trees ebbed into silence and the sky turned from pink to blue, they sat there trading stories. His name was Martin. He was an X-ray technician at the hospital. Starved of dreams, he had recently volunteered for the night shift, so he could sleep in the daytime when the characters might be more convincing and the plots fresher. Living alone since his parents had retired to a golf course condo in Arizona, he taped notes on the refrigerator to remind himself to eat. As a boy, he had wanted to become a painter, but his parents refused to pay for art school, insisting that he learn a practical skill, and he gave in, studying X-ray technology at the community college. Now, after four years of capturing ghostly images of bones, he was beginning to doubt the substantiality of flesh.

"When I saw you sitting here on the bench," Martin said, "at first I thought you were a figment from dreams. But when I looked closer I saw you were real."

"How could you tell?"

"Your curiosity, your excitement, the intense way you watched the sky. I could almost see the rays cast by your eyes, like searchlights."

Veronica remembered the beam of her father's flashlight shining up through the branches, and his assurance that nothing was there. "When you sat down beside me that first morning," she said, "you didn't seem very substantial yourself. You made me think of birds, with gauzy wings and hollow bones."

"Birds," he muttered, then snapped his fingers and drew a notebook from his pocket and jotted something down. "Excuse me. I just remembered the name of a constellation."

"Cygnus, the Swan?"

"How did you know?"

Veronica smiled. "I've made a list of constellations."

"You keep lists?"

"Lots of them." She produced her own notebook and riffled the pages with her thumb. "They're something I can hold onto while the world's spinning out of control."

"Amazing. It's as if we're twins." He ran his gaze over her, head to toe, lightly, then blushed and looked away. "Not identical, of course."

She laughed. "No, not identical."

Gripped once more by shyness, Martin stood up and squinted at the sky. "Looks like the show is over for this morning. Time to go sleep. Maybe we'll see one another here again."

"I hope so," said Veronica.

Back home that morning, she received the customary grilling from her parents, who wanted to know if she had met any cute doctors at the hospital, and would she please return calls from the banker and bowling alley magnate, and why doesn't she buy some pastel outfits for work instead of navy blue. "Pink would bring out your lovely coloring," her mother said.

As soon as she could disentangle herself, Veronica filled the bathtub and soaked neck deep in the steaming water and fell asleep. She dreamed of spiders spinning webs between the stars to snare comets and spaceships. It was a familiar scenario, interesting the first time, grown tedious through repetition. The spiders seemed as bored with their work as the orderlies at the hospital. She was entering a second dream—this one about a flying man, not brawny Daedalus with his wings of wax melted by the sun, but a slender man with a blond beard and blue eyes, wheeling in thermals above a forested ridge—when a knock rattled the door and her mother barged in carrying a pizza that filled the bathroom with the smell of pepperoni.

"It's from that contractor," her mother announced. "He delivered it himself. He said he'd bring one by every week, except he doesn't want to spoil your perfect figure. Isn't that sweet?"

Veronica groaned. "I can't eat it. I'm a vegetarian."

"Since when?"

"Since right now. I just converted."

Her mother frowned. "What are we going to do with you?"

"You can start by taking that pizza out of here and letting me dry off. This water's cold."

As Veronica rose from the tub her mother surveyed her up and down and repeated a favorite remark: "You could pose for statues."

A museum specimen was what Veronica felt like much of the time, or a zoo animal, as if she were an exhibit rather than a person. But just now, buffing herself with a towel, she recalled the secretive turns of Martin's voice and felt warmth spreading through her body.

✳ ✳ ✳

The two of them began arriving earlier for work in the evenings and departing later in the mornings. In dry weather they sat on the bench under the sycamore; in wet, they huddled in Martin's Jeep, shivering with pleasure at the sound of rain on the roof. Thunder and lightning pleased them even more. He did not kiss her or touch her before asking, and well before he asked she was ready to say yes. Holding one another, they felt less need for keeping lists.

Martin rarely brought much to eat during his shift and often forgot to bring anything at all, so Veronica began carrying extra food in her cooler. Boiled eggs, walnuts, apples, turkey slices, blueberry muffins, yogurt, quiche—all these and more she offered him and he ate obediently. Before long the shadows vanished from his cheeks, his limbs filled out, and his skin took on an earthy glow.

"You'll ruin your figure," her mother cautioned one afternoon, when she noticed Veronica packing so much food.

Instead of bristling, Veronica mildly explained, "I'm taking extra for a friend at work."

"What sort of friend?"

"Human."

Her mother snorted. "You know what I mean. Man or woman? Young or old?"

"A young man."

"Tony!" her mother yelled into the den, where the TV was erupting with sounds of gunshots. "Come listen to this!"

Veronica's father shuffled into the kitchen, groggy from the tube. "Listen to what?"

"Our girl has a boyfriend at work."

Her father suddenly came alert. "Is it that brain surgeon who keeps calling?"

"No, Daddy."

"The cardiologist?" her mother asked.

"Not the cardiologist," Veronica said patiently. "He's an X-ray technician."

Her father whistled. "A radiologist!"

"No. He only takes the pictures. But he has a college degree and a wonderful mind and the kindest eyes."

Her parents exchanged a look that lasted several seconds, long enough for them to arrive at some realization that made them both smile. They turned their beaming faces to her.

"If you found your guy, Ronnie," said her father, running a hand softly over her hair as he used to do when she was little, "then bless you, sweetheart. All we ask is that you don't move in with him until you've got a ring."

"And it wouldn't hurt to keep him interested by wearing some lipstick and eyeliner, and clothes that show off your figure," her mother added.

＊　＊　＊

Without resorting to makeup or changing her wardrobe, Veronica became, if anything, even more alluring. In the corridors of the hospital, men interrupted their errands to watch her pass. Male doctors would sometimes look up from a patient to issue a command, snag their gaze on her, and forget what they meant to say. Female doctors no longer scowled at her as if she were seeking attention, but accepted her as another example of nature's prodigal beauty, like butterflies or waterfalls or the aurora borealis.

Several times each night, Martin slipped into the emergency room to deliver X-rays from one or another victim, casting a glance at Veronica that set her nerves tingling. There was never time for more than a glance, because the number of victims kept swelling as woodlands around the city were cleared. Bored with flimsy dreams and fangless nightmares, or deprived of dreams altogether, sleepers awoke feeling muddled and furious. There were wildcat strikes at factories along the river, explosions at the refinery, bomb threats in the courthouse, lockdowns in schools. Knife fights broke out on playgrounds, fistfights in public hearings. Turf wars erupted in the suburbs. Policemen pepper-sprayed anyone who gave them lip. A homeless encampment under one of the bridges was set on fire. The reek of teargas and smoke hung over the city.

The emergency ward overflowed with bruised children and battered women, wounded teenagers, confused elders, zonked out druggies, failed suicides, mangled survivors of car crashes, sufferers of heart attacks or strokes—a procession of shattered and bleeding, shrieking and moaning souls.

Following their shift, Veronica and Martin would collapse onto the bench under the great sycamore, almost too exhausted for talk. When they broke the silence it was often to complain of their shabby dreams, which no longer aroused them, no longer scared or inspired them. The wizards and crones lacked wisdom, the storm troopers and demons lacked menace, the saints and bodhisattvas lacked conviction. The specters that still roosted in the big trees atop the ridge were tattered, like letters that had been folded and refolded too many times. Their chatter was drowned out by the clangor of fire engines and squad cars and ambulances.

As spring gave way to summer, sweltering heat increased the turmoil. Loaded gurneys filled the hallways of the hospital, and then the lobby, and then the cafeteria. In August, the hospital board announced plans to double the capacity of the emergency facilities by adding a wing, and to do so with all possible speed. Within days, the site of the new construction was marked by red survey flags, a large rectangle that enclosed the bench, the great sycamore, and the entire grove of old trees. The trunk of each doomed tree was encircled by a strip of orange tape.

Men wearing hardhats and fluorescent green overalls arrived one morning as Veronica and Martin were leaving the hospital, wrung out from the siege of patients during graveyard shift. Two of the men picked up the bench and moved it to a patch of grass far from the sycamore, so the lovers took refuge in Martin's Jeep. They stared glumly through the windshield as a truck pulled up hauling a bulldozer, which the men in Day-Glo overalls set about unloading. Chainsaws began to snarl.

"This will finish things off," Martin said quietly.

"There's no future here," said Veronica.

They stayed long enough to watch several of the big trees come down, the huge trunks and branches gouging the dirt and sending out shockwaves the lovers could feel in their bones. The few returning dream creatures swirled in the air above the spots where the crowns of the trees used to be. The specters circled higher and higher, as if bewildered, and then set off toward the horizon, dwindling away like brightly colored leaves riding the wind.

The bulldozer roared back and forth, tearing out stumps. When the teeth of a chainsaw began ripping into the trunk of the sycamore, Veronica whispered, "Take me to your place," and Martin started the Jeep.

She took the first shower, leaving her drab clothes like a discarded chrysalis on a chair in his bedroom. Then while Martin showered, she waited in his bed. When he joined her there, smelling of mint shampoo, he spread her damp hair on the pillow, an auburn fan, and kissed her forehead, then her lips. The tremors she felt as his hands grazed her body were like those from the falling of the great trees. They lay with their limbs entwined through the daylight hours, wakeful, whispering, unvisited by dreams. Then all through the following night, and all the days and nights thereafter, the city rattled with gunfire and boomed with explosions, and sirens never stopped wailing.

Ascension

For weeks before the mayor put on her startling exhibition, the townspeople had trouble sleeping. At dawn on those restless mornings, when garbage trucks began their growling rounds, damp heads were still flopping on pillows like beached fish, and hands were still plucking at sweaty sheets. Children trudged off to school with squinted eyes, relying on crossing guards to defend them from traffic. The guards leaned on their portable stop signs and listened for the squeal of brakes. With eyes as empty as the mouths of canning jars, mechanics slouched off to garages, clerks to their banks, sellers to their stores, everyone wrapped in a fog of drowsiness.

"It's the heat," muttered some, while others insisted, "It's the humidity."

No one could remember a hotter July. Instead of cooling off at night when breezes swept in from the ocean, the land stayed warm. Despite the incessant groan of air-conditioners, houses were slow ovens. More than heat was keeping the citizens awake, however, as demonstrated by a butcher who moved his bed into a meat locker, risking frostbite, and still could not slumber.

Old-timers blamed the plague of sleeplessness on the erratic tides. At whimsical hours, the ocean lapped high at the pilings of docks or sank low to reveal the granite bones of the shore. "It's all topsy-turvy," the elders complained. "Even lobsters are confused." But youngsters, who rarely looked up from their screens to observe the ocean, blamed the sickness on poisons dumped in the bay from paper mills.

Alone among the townspeople, the mayor's wayward husband, Kenneth, dozed serenely. Early in the summer, before the heat became oppressive, he had ordered an astronaut's suit from NASA Surplus Inc., and now he spent his nights cocooned inside it, breathing bottled air. He would tumble into bed soon after supper and sleep until morning, oblivious as a baby. Initially, the mayor had rejoiced at his show of enthusiasm for space paraphernalia. True, Kenneth's previous enthusiasms had filled the basement with cameras, woodworking tools, fly-fishing gear, a potter's wheel, a make-your-own harpsichord kit, and sundry other items, all now lying untouched. Yet the mayor kept hoping that some new toy might lure him out of the gloom in which he had been mired since the early days of their marriage.

They had met on the operating table, she as patient and he as surgeon. Sally was not yet mayor back then, merely director of the waterworks. Her own waterworks had gone awry, somewhere south of her navel, and Kenneth was trying to repair them with scalpel and sutures. All she glimpsed before the anesthesia washed over her were the surgeon's blue eyes, which had about them the anxious air of a pilot recalling dangerous flights. When she came to, she realized he had bungled the operation, for the first thing she saw as her eyes fluttered open was his apologetic face, asking her to marry him.

"It's the least I can do," he explained.

"You needn't worry," she mumbled. "I'm not the litigious type."

His blue gaze softened. "I'd like to marry you anyway."

"Nonsense," she declared.

Six months later she went through with it, having tested his resolve, his cooking, and his taste in art. By then they had shared late night talk after he slouched home from the hospital, early morning talk before she slipped away to the waterworks, talk under umbrellas and over meals and in bed—talk about their miserable first marriages, their love of wildflowers and crosswords and TV mysteries, their fears and hopes.

The hopes, it turned out, were mostly Sally's and the fears were mostly Kenneth's. Not long after the wedding, when she was promoted to chief engineer, he bungled another operation, then another. Obviously he couldn't amend every mistake by marrying the victim, even if all the victims had been female.

When the patient lay muffled in green sheets on the operating table, a rectangle of skin exposed to the knife, Kenneth began thinking of solar flares, meteor strikes, ion storms. What if dark matter engulfed the solar system? What if the moon spiraled away from Earth, abolishing tides? He knew from browsing on-line that tectonic plates were lurching about, triggering earthquakes and volcanoes. Glaciers were melting. Sea levels were rising. Deserts were spreading. Species were vanishing at a thousand times the normal rate of extinction.

During surgery one day he lapsed into a meditation on ozone holes, and only returned to the here-and-now when a nurse remarked that he had opened a potentially lethal hole inside the patient. The patient survived but Kenneth's nerves were shattered.

How could he concentrate on the geometry of incisions while Earth unraveled?

After settling the malpractice suit for a hefty sum, he announced that he was hanging up the scalpel. Busy campaigning for mayor, Sally didn't quarrel with his decision, not even when he began shuffling around the house, wringing his idle hands like a mourner beside a crash site. Those hands were as firm and steady as ever, he was quick to point out. Unlike many surgeons who retire in their forties, Kenneth had not lost his touch. What he had lost was his ability to concentrate. When he made love to Sally he stroked her body with a harpist's delicacy, teasing melodies from her skin. Then suddenly his fingers would freeze, his eyes would roll shut, and his mind would wander off—to fret about killer drones armed with lasers, perhaps, or antibiotic-resistant microbes, or some other menace.

"Come back, space cadet," she would plead.

Kenneth used to be the one who couldn't sleep, while Sally, exhausted by her mayoral duties, dozed through the night. At breakfast, his eyes glazed from staying up reading bad news, he would tell her about polluted aquifers, dying corals, blighted forests, or gyres in the oceans swirling with millions of tons of plastic.

"Did you realize the sun is already middle-aged?" he announced one morning over English muffins. "When it uses up all the hydrogen it will swell out and roast the planets."

"Is that so?" she replied, without looking up from the crossword.

"Maybe it won't matter," he added. "If we kill the plankton, we're done for anyway."

"Would you pass the honey, dear?"

She filtered Kenneth's fears through the grid of her engineer's pragmatism. Sufficient unto the day are the evils thereof, she thought, stuffing her briefcase with notes on the current emergencies. One by one the town's troubles crossed her desk, and one by one she wrestled them into submission. She could prevent the explosion of a boiler in the basement of a nursing home, but she could not keep the sun from going nova. She could protect kids by ordering the removal of asbestos ceiling tiles from schools, but she could not save frogs from pesticides. If Kenneth saw fit to lie awake brooding on catastrophes, that was no reason for Sally to ruin her own rest.

Well before sunrise on the day the spacesuit arrived, Kenneth was propped up in bed, reading by the glow of his headlamp, muttering to himself. At last unable to contain his alarm, he blurted out, "Honey, do you realize that bacteria from ice in a comet's tail could set off a worldwide epidemic?"

"That's nice, dear," Sally murmured. She folded a pillow over her ears and dove back in search of dreams. She didn't find any, however, and wouldn't dream again until long after her husband disappeared.

When the spacesuit was delivered, in a carton large enough to hold a refrigerator, Kenneth unpacked the numerous pieces, laid them out on the floor, and studied the instructions. Then at bedtime he began donning his mail-order gear.

"Isn't it rather late to be trying that on?" she asked.

"I'm going to sleep in it," he said as he wormed his arms into the puffy white sleeves.

"You're kidding."

"Could you reach me those boots?"

"You'll swelter."

"It has a ventilation system." He pulled on the clumsy gloves. "Now the helmet."

"But you'll suffocate."

"Each air tank is good for eight hours."

Sally quit protesting and helped him into the suit, since it appeared to be lifting his spirits. After the bubble helmet was in place and oxygen began flowing through the hose, his voice emerged by way of a speaker, sounding like the drone of a pilot instructing his passengers. "If you ever notice this needle creeping toward the red zone," he said, pointing to a dial on his chest, "open the air valve a half turn. If you hear a beeping sound, call the ambulance."

That first night, squeezed to the edge of the mattress by the bulbous white hulk, Sally slept fitfully. The second night she dozed off for only an hour or two. The third night she gave in to insomnia and read a report on waste management. Meanwhile Kenneth slumbered blissfully, his face inside its bubble as tranquil as that of a newborn in a crib.

In the mornings, he didn't stir when she left for work. He still cooked supper, but hastily, for the hours he once devoted to fixing elaborate meals he now spent shopping at big box stores and hauling back carloads of supplies, which he stowed in the basement alongside the residue from his former hobbies. When she asked what they would ever do with all this stuff, he replied, "Postpone the end."

Well, she thought, the canned goods and freeze-dried foods would keep, as would the bottled water and toiletries and fuel. If stockpiling supplies and sleeping in an astronaut's suit freed him from gloom, she would indulge him. Her insomnia was bound to pass, as soon as she grew accustomed to the wheeze and purr of his life-support devices. There were, of course, some practical difficulties, one of which she mentioned in the opening week of his spaceman era.

"How are we supposed to make love while you're wearing this contraption?"

"NASA thought of that," he replied. "There's a strategically placed airlock."

"I'm talking about sex, sweetheart, not the docking of spaceships."

"It's been tested in the space station."

"Couldn't you go without the suit once in a while?" His look of dismay kept her from pressing the point. "Okay, okay," she added soothingly. "Suppose I skip my yoga class on Wednesdays and come home at noon, so we can frolic in the old-fashioned way?"

He frowned. "That's my prime time for shopping."

One of the qualities that made Sally a good mayor was a high degree of tolerance for human idiocy. But Kenneth's antics were straining her patience. At the town hall, where the eyes of her staff members began to resemble empty eggshells, she grew irritable. "I haven't been sleeping well," she apologized after scolding her secretary. "Neither have I," the secretary replied.

Everywhere the mayor looked, faces had been eroded by sleeplessness. Upon questioning the clerks who gathered listlessly at the drinking fountain like buffaloes at a waterhole, she discovered that a plague of insomnia had swept through town in the days following the arrival of Kenneth's spacesuit.

Winos hugging their rags curled up as usual in the waiting room of the bus station, but they could not shut out the blare of departures or the shuffle of feet. Children sat up watching midnight movies. Babies clamored for attention at all hours. Parents took turns hiding in basements, in barns, in parked cars, anywhere to escape the tantrums of exhausted kids. Teachers called in sick. Druggists sold out their supply of sleeping pills and began recommending warm milk to their bleary-eyed customers. Soon the dairy cases in grocery stores were stripped bare, and the smell of scorched milk filled the July streets.

Not everyone complained about the insomnia plague. All-night disk jockeys welcomed the dramatic rise in song requests. "Play us some crooners, quiet stuff, ballads and blues," teenagers begged. Bowling alleys and cafes and bookstores kept their doors open, and doubled their business. On the town square, where the mayor would perform her startling exhibition, the cinema began screening films in the wee hours. An abandoned gas station was converted into a thriving doughnut shop. Truckers cruising through town discovered they could drive all the next day without needing pills. Traveling sales reps contracted insomnia as soon as they checked in to local motels.

Sally was reluctant at first to attribute the plague to Kenneth's donning of the spacesuit. As an engineer, she knew quite well that correlation is not causation. Still, it was hard to ignore the coincidence. While the townspeople tossed and turned in their beds, he slumbered placidly through the nights. Then he began dozing through the afternoons, and eventually he slept around the clock. Now and again, without opening his eyes, he spoke in a scratchy voice. "Maintain oxygen pressure in the blue zone," he might say, or "Add serum every fourth day." Several times Sally heard him whisper, "Don't open my suit or I will die."

Despite her engineer's training, she wondered if Kenneth's unbroken slumber might be sucking sleep away from the town, as a black hole sucks in matter and light. Tapping on the helmet would not rouse him, nor would jostling his body in its pale husk. Perhaps there were narcotics in the bag of pink fluid that fed nutrients to him through a tube. But the label seemed innocent enough, and so did the sample that the police lab tested for her.

After Kenneth had slept for seventy-two hours straight, she called in the hospital pathologist, an old friend who could be trusted to keep mum about her husband's peculiar condition.

"Damn fool stunt, if you ask me," the pathologist grumbled when Sally warned him that they mustn't open the suit. He shone a light through the helmet, flexed Kenneth's legs and arms in their bloated casing, read pulse and blood pressure and other vital signs from gauges on the front of the spacesuit. "It looks like normal sleep," the pathologist concluded. "Has he been exceptionally tired lately?"

"He's been wrung out by worry for years," Sally conceded.

Now it was her turn to worry. Not so much about Kenneth, who seemed to be enjoying his hibernation, and not about the town, whose problems could be solved. What kept her awake now were the vast, irresolvable dilemmas that had so deeply troubled Kenneth. Nor was she alone in her anxiety. At the office her secretary began quoting statistics about rising greenhouse gas emissions. The county surveyor brooded over satellite photos showing the clearcutting of Amazon rainforests. The panhandler who used to pluck a banjo for loose change on the steps of the town hall now passed out leaflets condemning strip mining. Children playing video games fretted about radiation poisoning from nuclear reactors.

While replacing Kenneth's nutrient bag one morning, Sally muttered, "You're making me a nervous wreck."

She was surprised to hear him drowsily reply, "I'm almost finished."

"With what?"

"The dream work. The sacrifice."

She asked what he meant, but he would say nothing more.

A few nights after this exchange, when the sultry air of August smothered the town, Sally lay wide awake, twitching with dread. She could feel, as if in her own body, the sinews of Earth snapping, its flesh withering, its veins running dry. She could sense Earth's creatures perishing, like a galaxy of stars winking out. Her own species was tearing apart and devouring this once-abundant home, the only habitable planet within billions of miles.

Panic forced her out of bed, heart racing. The air in the room was stifling. Mummified in his spacesuit, Kenneth seemed to radiate heat. The air-conditioner whined continuously, with little effect. She took off her nightgown and let it fall to the floor. Why bother to hang up clothes? Why even wear them? Such habits now seemed pointless. She moved to the window and stood there a long while, looking out, wondering how many experiments in life the cosmos had tried, how many had flourished, how many had failed.

When she turned around, Kenneth was floating a foot above the bed. Rushing over, she touched his booted foot, which set him gliding across the room until he bumped helmet-first against the sliding door to the balcony.

"Kenneth!" she cried.

He did not reply. The helmet thumped against the glass door. She needed to call for help—the police, paramedics, firemen— someone, anyone. But her phone wasn't on the nightstand, where it should have been. So she hurried downstairs to check her briefcase in the kitchen, but the phone wasn't there either. Rattled, she searched countertops and cupboards, pulled out drawers, flung pillows from the couch. She was rummaging through the pockets of coats hanging in the closet when she heard the rumble of the balcony door sliding open.

She raced back upstairs and into the bedroom, just in time to see Kenneth floating out over the balcony railing and into the muggy night.

How she passed the next two hours Sally herself would never be able to recall. Nearly everyone else in town did recall, however, and in gossipy detail, for no public official had ever before done anything half so remarkable.

The mayor ran screaming down the front steps of her house, as naked as the day she was born. She kept pointing skyward and yelling. At first no one understood what she was saying. The late-night strollers were too distracted by her appearance to notice the ghostly white figure gliding overhead. The sight of her body amazed the men, who had always assumed that beneath her severe workaday suits she was an iron maiden. Even the women found themselves captivated by the spectacle of their naked mayor. Such intelligence, such drive, in flesh so like their own! Anything was possible, the women reflected. Girls thought of running for office or becoming engineers. Matrons vowed to take up yoga and stick to their diets. Young children wriggled out of their clothes and ran after the mayor, who rushed ahead, baying like a hound.

Sally reached the town square just as the cinemas, churches, and dance clubs were letting out from their midnight sessions. Her grief hushed the buzzing throng, which parted to let her through to the courthouse lawn, where she climbed onto the equestrian statue commemorating a Civil War general. Clinging to the general's uplifted sword, she stood on the bronze rump of the horse and shouted at the sky.

No one knew what to do. Call her husband? Nobody had seen him for weeks. Call the sheriff? Wrap her in blankets and carry her to the hospital?

While the townspeople crowded about the statue, stunned into silence by her shrieks, the mayor kept gesturing skyward. At last the onlookers followed her pointing finger and spied the astronaut floating above the courthouse trees. Now the people found their voices and cried out in surprise or delight or bewilderment. Children glanced at their parents to see what they should make of this apparition.

Balanced precariously on the bronze horse, the mayor lifted both arms, fingers splayed, as if imagining she could pluck the astronaut from the air.

"Kenneth!" she yelled, her first decipherable word. "Please don't go!"

Feeling her anguish, many onlookers thrust their arms into the air in sympathy. Toddlers waggled their small hands at the darkness. Soon all of the onlookers, from babes in arms to oldsters in wheelchairs, were reaching for the sky.

The glint of the spaceman's helmet and the glow of his chalky suit reminded young and old of when they had first glimpsed the full moon, and had begged their parents to pluck it down for them. Their parents had merely laughed or frowned or shaken their heads helplessly no. The townspeople felt once again the tug of infinite longing and infinite regret as the astronaut spun slowly in the moonlight like a tethered balloon.

"Stay, Kenneth, stay!" pleaded the mayor. She teetered on the horse's back. "Don't give up on us! We'll survive! We'll come through!"

At that moment the onlookers felt a tug on their uplifted arms, as if the threads of desire they had flung into the sky were actual strings of gossamer. Instinctively they squeezed their hands into fists, and for an instant their feet lifted clear of the ground. The mayor let out a piercing cry. Then with a barely audible whisper every fist opened and the townspeople settled back to Earth. High overhead the spaceman swung about and began to rise. As he ascended, he appeared at first like a small cloud, then dwindled to the size of a minnow, a needle, a star. When at last he vanished, the townspeople slumped down on the courthouse lawn, and for the first time in weeks they slept, and dreamed, and scarcely heard the mayor's wailing.

Sleepwalker

I awake from feverish dreams to the thunder of jets overhead, which reminds me that I must report to the airbase this morning for X-rays. The daylight world knifes into me. In my nightmare I was captured, put on trial, and sentenced to be hanged for refusing to serve in the war. Awareness of the slaughter in Africa rises in my stomach like nausea.

I roll over to find Sharon watching me, her chestnut eyes slick with tears. I kiss her on each wet cheek, but she refuses to smile. Her worried expression has become so habitual that I almost forget how serenely happy she was—how happy we both were—during those early weeks of marriage before the draft summons arrived.

"Gordon," she says, "I can't bear to think of you in jail."

"Let's not start on this again." I've run out of reassurances for Sharon, just as I've run out of appeals for the draft board. It seems more and more likely I will have to choose between prison and exile, if I am to avoid putting on a uniform and crossing the ocean to kill strangers.

"Tell them your ankle's ruined. Tell them it aches all the time."

"I'm not going to lie." I throw off the covers and begin to dress.

"They'll never let you do civilian service." Her voice cracks. "If they honored your conscience, they'd have to question their own."

"Can we just drop it? I've got to catch the bus." I wrench a shirt from its hanger and button it quickly as I huddle over the radiator. Water gurgles in the pipes, circling round and round through the system, as I keep circling through this quarrel with Sharon.

"Maybe the X-ray will show your ankle's still a mess," she says.

"It works fine." I tug on my jeans, parcel keys and coins and wallet among my pockets, lace my boots.

Lying on her side, head propped on one bent arm, she follows my movements with her tear-slick gaze. "You're forgetting to limp."

"Limping won't fool the doctor."

"You promised you'd at least *try*."

"Maybe the war will end before they arrest me."

"They'll start another one."

"Got to go." I bend down to kiss her, but she rolls away to face the wall. Pulling the bedroom door closed behind me, I realize she's right, which maddens me. Right that war has become perpetual. Right that I could try using my rebuilt foot as an excuse for a medical waiver. But a year has passed since the climbing accident shattered my ankle, and the artificial joint no longer gives me pain. The mended bones and tissues have become as numb as the metal and plastic lodged under my skin.

Descending the stairs, I am gripped by the chill of prevision. I can see the next few seconds of my life laid out before me as if in time-lapse photography—my stumble on the stairs, my grabbing the banister, the phone ringing in my pocket. When I answer, I hear the voice I expected, saying words I expected.

"Gordon," says my sister, "if you think the doctor would fix this report for a fee . . ."

"Not a chance," I answer, hearing my words before I utter them.

"Then go to Canada. Go to Argentina. They're accepting resisters."

"I'd never be able to come home." I mean to stop there, but I hear myself adding, "Besides, Sharon can't go with me."

"Why not?"

"Because she's pregnant . . ."

"My God, that's wonderful!"

". . . but the fetus isn't implanted well, so she might miscarry if she travels."

"Oh, I'm sorry."

"We just found out."

There is a pause, but I know what my sister will say next, and the words duly follow: "That's all the more reason to bribe the doctor to declare you unfit."

"I can't buy my way out."

"Can't, or won't?"

"Okay. I won't."

Even her peevish sigh I recognize before it hisses into my ear. "You're stumbling into this like . . ." While she searches for the word, I hear *sleepwalker*, and then she says, "like a sleepwalker."

"Good-bye, big sister." I want to say more, but I see myself ending the call, and that is what I do.

This clairvoyant spell persists through my hasty breakfast. Then as I wash my dishes, I settle once more into the present moment, no longer foreseeing what will come next. The smell of coffee, the feel of suds on my wrists, the glint of snow-light through the kitchen window—every sensation comes to me fresh.

＊　＊　＊

On the bus ride, as the snowy countryside slides by in stark shades of black and white, I try to read the book I have brought along, Frantz Fanon's *The Wretched of the Earth*. But I keep being distracted by recalling those moments of prevision. I have experienced *déjà vu* before, but never for so long at a stretch. When the spell comes over me, it's as if a switch has been thrown, and suddenly I foresee everything that will happen in the next moment, and then just as suddenly I slip back into my ordinary mind. I've read the explanations offered by psychologists and mystics—neurological asynchrony, epilepsy, reincarnation, spirit possession—but the phenomenon still baffles me.

When the bus reaches the county seat, I realize I've gone more than an hour without thinking of the war. At least my seizures, whatever their cause, have distracted me from this constant fret.

The moment my boots touch the salted pavement, the switch is thrown again, and I am possessed by foreknowledge. As I crunch over the snow toward the highway, I feel split in two—one version of myself walking ahead, and a second version following, as if dragged along. I shake my head, trying to clear the illusion. But even this gesture I see before I make it.

Standing by the roadside with my thumb jutting in the direction of the airbase, I sense each car a moment before it approaches, foresee its make and color. After twenty minutes or so, when the cold has made my undamaged foot as numb as the reconstructed one, I realize that the next vehicle to appear—a battered van, reeking of paint—will stop for me. I hear what the driver will say as I open the passenger door.

"Damn fool day to be hitching," he says.

"You going near the airbase?" I ask, knowing his answer.

"That's exactly where I'm going. Hop in."

"Much obliged."

The man turns to me a face already familiar, right down to the broken front tooth and the bruised skin under his left eye. "What business you got at the base?"

I tell him about my synthetic ankle, and the X-ray that will decide whether it is healed well enough to suit the army.

"Got a titanium rod in here," he says, tapping his gas pedal leg, "thanks to a roadside bomb in Afghanistan."

I wince. "It must hurt in this cold weather."

"Hurts like hell," he says. "Every twinge makes me cuss the sons of bitches who sent me over there."

Hearing his words, I am delivered back into ordinary time, not knowing what will come next. We talk about his folks and mine, about where each of us played high school basketball, about truck stops and hunting dogs. Just as I am preparing to ask him what he thinks of the war in Africa, we draw abreast of a chain-link fence topped by razor wire. I swallow the question. The fence I have seen countless times while traveling past, but this time I am going inside. We turn in at the main gate, which is flanked by two vintage fighter jets.

"Shame to see those planes rust like that," the driver says. "Give them a good paint job, they'd look like new."

Abruptly the switch is thrown again. I know the guard will recognize the painter, ask to see my papers, check my name on his list, and then will say, "Physical, eh?" before waving us through. His gruff voice reminds me of the water gurgling in the radiator, circling time and again through the closed circuit of pipes.

"You figure that bum foot will keep you out of the war?" the painter asks as we ease forward.

"Not likely. But I'm hoping my conscience will."

He snorts. "Conscience? Good luck with that, kid."

Black pipes mounted on posts snake along beside the road. The painter tells me they carry steam from the heating plant, and I imagine the vapor circulating from boiler to barracks to warehouse to machine shop and eventually back to boiler.

"What are you painting today?" I ask.

"The gym in the officers' quarters. It's a bear. Walls thirty feet high."

"How does that titanium leg do on ladders?"

"Hurts like hell!" he says again, and his laugh rattles through the van.

We pull up in front of the hospital, which might have been blue once but is now drab gray. As I climb out, the painter says, "Don't think killing foreigners makes you a patriot."

"I won't," I say. "Thanks for the lift."

"You bet."

The van pulls away, trailing a stench of burnt oil mixed with the tang of paint.

I spend most of the day in the hospital, waiting for my exam. Every now and again a clerk calls my name, only to direct me to another waiting room. Meanwhile, I nearly finish *The Wretched*

of the Earth, a disturbing book, with its advocacy for violence by colonized people, but it helps me understand the history behind the current turmoil in Africa.

Eventually, I am summoned from the last of the waiting rooms. As I make my way down a corridor toward the X-ray lab, I can already see the caramel-colored face of the technician, already make out her name on the badge pinned to her white coat, already hear the southern drawl in her voice.

"Enjoy that beard while you can," she says cheerfully. "They'll shave it off first thing."

I lift a hand to my chin and pinch a tuft of whiskers. My smile feels as if it has been drawn on my lips from outside.

At her instruction, I pull off my boot and peel away the sock. She has me lie down on the examining table and positions the snout of the X-ray tube over my bare foot. "Now hold quite still," she says, before disappearing behind a screen. A moment later I hear a brief hiss. She returns, repositions the foot, takes a second X-ray, and then repeats the cycle a third time. Then she escorts me to another room, where a doctor is studying the images of my ankle on a screen.

He turns when I enter, asks me to sit on the paper-covered table with my leg extended. There is a whiff of peppermint on his breath. With gloved hands, he manipulates my foot, rotating it left and right, up and down, testing the range of motion.

"How does it feel?" he asks.

Thinking of Sharon, I am tempted to give the painter's refrain—"Hurts like hell!"—but I feel compelled to answer, "Numb."

"No pain at all?"

I shake my head—or rather, it shakes of its own accord. I see myself as if from the outside, sitting on the table, my naked foot cradled in the doctor's hands. It is as though I am watching a film of myself, every word and gesture already scripted.

He lets go of my foot and turns back to the ghostly X-rays on the screen. "It's an elegant piece of surgery. This ankle should hold up better than your natural one. Nothing here to bar you from service."

Leaving the hospital, I walk back toward the main gate. The last light is fading from the sky. I hear the sizzle of pipes overhead, the steam cooling as it circulates from building to building. At the guard shack I pause to show my papers once more, and once more I am waved through.

Near the rusting fighter jets, their engine cowlings clogged with snow, I wait for a ride. As cars and trucks pass, their headlights pick me out of the obscurity for a moment before sliding by. My thumb grows stiff as I wait for the Chevy pickup that finally stops, as I know it will. Likewise, I know beforehand that baby shoes will dangle from the rearview mirror, that the driver, a woman in her fifties, will tell me I remind her of her son, who was killed by a sniper in the Congo, and I know before I speak what I must answer. Hurtling down the tunnel bored through the darkness by the headlights, we exchange our lines, for the film will not stop.

On the bus I am granted a few minutes of freedom. These periods of lucidity occur less and less often, as the spells of foreknowledge lengthen. The view through the window might be of an alien planet, everything in shades of gray, silent and bleak and cold. The focus of my gaze shifts and I see my dim reflection in the glass—empty sockets where my eyes should be, my mouth a dark slash.

At the final stop before my own, an old woman boards the bus. As she teeters along the aisle, her bag of groceries lurching side to side, I know she will ask to share my seat, I will nod *yes*, and she will settle beside me with a wheeze. As I expected, her bag smells of cinnamon and garlic, and so does her black wool coat.

"No night to be alone on a bus," she says.

"I'm almost home," I reply. "My wife's waiting."

"Count your blessings. My husband died when he was about your age." She fishes a snapshot from her purse and holds it out for me.

Reluctantly I peer at the photograph in the dim light. It shows a man in white Navy dress uniform, with a woman in a wedding gown clinging to his arm. I feel certain I have seen this image many times.

"Believe it or not, that's me," the old woman says, pointing to the bride.

I am startled to feel tears welling in my eyes. Hoping she won't notice, I turn away to blink at my reflection in the window.

"A Chinese missile blew up his ship in the Indian Ocean," the old woman continues. "Where is the war now? I can't keep track. It's been going on since before I was born. Took my father, both my brothers, and my husband."

I want to ease the hurt I hear in her voice, but I can't speak. So I put on my knit hat and gloves in preparation for my stop.

She lays a hand on my forearm. "Here, let me give you a pomegranate for your wife."

"That's kind of you, but really—"

"It's full of vitamin C," she says, drawing the plump red fruit from her grocery bag.

"For good health, then," I say, accepting the pomegranate and stuffing it in my coat pocket.

As she turns in the seat to let me slip by, she adds quietly, "It also brings fertility."

I mutter thanks and hurry down the aisle. From the sidewalk, I watch the bus drag its rectangles of light into the darkness.

The snow on our street sounds brittle under my boots. My breath fumes, glistening with daggers of ice. The winter's chill will not let go, nor will the sense of *déjà vu*. I can read the script but cannot change it. Our front door opens without my key, and I am upset with Sharon for leaving it unlocked. I take off my hat and gloves and boots in the hall before going to the kitchen, where I know she is sitting at the table over a mug of tea.

She flashes me an anxious look. "What did the doctor say?"

"I'm fit for war."

Her lips crimp tight.

I shrug free of my coat, drape it over a chair back, and lift the pomegranate from the pocket. "A woman on the bus gave me this," I say, offering the fruit.

Reaching out hesitantly, Sharon cups it in her palm. "A woman on the bus?"

"An elderly lady, returning from the grocery store."

"Why would she give you a pomegranate?"

"She said it brings fertility."

"Did you tell her I'm pregnant?"

"Of course not."

"How odd." Slowly a smile breaks over Sharon's face. "How lovely."

Before she has a chance to ask, I fetch a bowl and knife and spoon, and set them before her. She slices the pomegranate and spoons out a mouthful of seeds, each one coated with ruby pulp. Her lips take on the color of the juice as I tell her about my sense of prevision, how it began as brief episodes and eventually became an unbroken awareness.

"Even now?" she asks. "You know what's going to happen next?"

"Yes. Each moment is already laid out. I see the two of us here at the table, watch you lift the spoon, hear our voices, as if we're speaking lines in an old film."

"Well, get up and dance. Stand on your head. Do something crazy to snap the illusion."

"I've tried. But every time I think I'm doing something truly free, I realize it's what I'm required to do."

"Required by whom?"

"By whoever wrote the script."

Although Sharon faces me across the table, her chestnut eyes don't look straight at me. All day other people have focused their gaze a few degrees away from where I imagine myself to be, as if I really am split in two, and my second self is drawing their attention.

There is caution in her voice as she says, "Gordon, this is a textbook case of paranoia. Don't you see? For months now you've been feeling caught up in the military machine . . ."

"I *am* caught up."

"But it's not a machine. It's just a big bureaucracy. It's not running your life."

I realize I should try to reassure her. But I feel compelled to insist, "*Something* is running my life. I've lived this day before. Maybe many times. In fact, this may be the only day I've ever lived."

"That's nonsense. Think about other days. Remember our wedding . . ."

"What if those memories are the illusion? What if they're planted in our minds to hide the fact that we're doomed to keep repeating this one day?"

Her gaze rakes across me, then swivels away. "You've been under stress—"

Unable to stop, I push on. "Sleep makes us forget today, so we can wake up and live it again as if it were new. But I've seen through the scam. I know I've lived this day before."

"You need to rest," she says carefully. "Let's go to bed."

"I tell you, I *know*!" I slam the table, scattering pomegranate seeds. One version of me looks on, appalled, as the other self pushes back from the table, upsetting the chair, then jerks his arm free from Sharon's grip and grabs his coat and lurches away.

"Gordon, you're not going out."

"I have to."

She follows me into the hall and crosses arms over her breast, shivering. "Sweetheart, you're scaring me."

I should take her in my arms, this woman I adore, and I should whisper in her ear a prayer for our coming child. But I cannot. I knot the laces in my boots, swing the door open, and step outside.

"Please don't go," Sharon cries after me.

"I *have* to."

The door slams.

I blunder forward into the night. Snow is falling, large flakes that sway as they tumble. I tilt my face up to feel them settle on my cheeks, but they make no impression. My feet convey nothing about the ground I walk over, my ears capture no sounds, my nose discovers no smells. My whole body is numb, as if all of me, and not just the artificial ankle, were made of metal and plastic. Only my eyes keep me bound to the world.

I must do something crazy, as Sharon says. For her sake, for the baby's. So I step into the street just as a snowplow turns the corner and heads my way. In the glare of the truck's headlights, I cannot make out the driver, cannot tell if he sees me.

Should I stand here, or should I leap aside?

At the last moment I leap aside. Without slowing, the truck rumbles on, spewing snow. My heart thuds. My senses revive. Did I choose to live, or was the choice made for me?

I must go back indoors to comfort Sharon. I will hold her until she sleeps, then I can sleep, forgetting this day, so tomorrow will come as a surprise.

I awake from feverish dreams to the thunder of jets overhead, which reminds me that I must report to the airbase this morning for X-rays. The daylight world knifes into me.

The First Journey of Jason Moss

One October day, an accountant from Buddha, Indiana, decided the time had come for him to travel around the earth. Although Jason Moss had always felt a passion for women, as a man might have a passion for bowling or pies, a profound shyness had kept him a bachelor, and so he had no need of explaining his journey to any wife or child. No goodbyes were needed for his kinfolk either. They all lived elsewhere, mostly in trailers on the coasts of Oregon and Maine, where they hunted mushrooms and carved figurines out of tree roots. Every Christmas they would write to him—Box 12, Buddha, Indiana—and send him photographs of a woodstove they had built from an oil drum, or a packet of seeds for growing foot-long cucumbers, or a newspaper clipping about the extinction of Siberian weasels. He would answer these letters promptly, saying that business was good, the weather bad, and his life ticking on as usual.

And so things had kept ticking along until his forty-seventh birthday, which fell in the middle of apple season. To mark the day, Jason always drove out to Burley's Orchard, where he picked two bushels of Granny Smiths, enough to keep him in fruit until spring brought rhubarb. On this particular birthday, after his baskets were full, he was standing tiptoe on the highest rung and reaching for one final apple when the ladder slipped. During the split second of his fall, he remembered the last glimpse of his father waving from the door of a boxcar, remembered helping his mother drag home from an auction a tombstone bearing the family name, and he realized he was utterly sick of adding up columns of numbers, sick of hearing doors slam in his rooming house, sick of living womanless in Buddha, and he vowed that if he survived the landing he would set out on a journey and not stop until he had circled the planet.

Jason hit the ground without breaking a bone.

That night he reviewed his catalogs of backpacking gear. Since he had been poring over the various editions of these catalogs for years, he already knew which items to order. As many things as possible should be green, because that struck him as the proper color for traveling: a green rucksack and sleeping bag, green tent, green shirts and trousers and waterproof jacket, a slouch hat of green felt, and green nylon laces for his boots. Along with the order for boots he enclosed a sheet of paper on which he had carefully outlined his stockinged foot.

Packages arrived for him all winter.

"Setting up a store?" the deliveryman asked.

"Just some things I've been needing," Jason replied.

When all the gear had been delivered he practiced stuffing it in the rucksack. The loaded pack weighed forty pounds, one-quarter as much as Jason himself. Dressed in green and propped on the walking-stick, which blossomed into an umbrella at the flick of a button, he posed before the bathroom mirror. Hardly an imposing figure, he knew. Skinny, bespectacled, a clerical sag in the spine. No one could mistake him for a voyageur. But he had never much cared what other people thought of him.

All winter he studied maps, planning his route. Wherever there was land he would hitch rides or walk, and when he reached the edge of a continent he would sail. About the walking he felt no qualms, because every weekend he ambled through the woods near town. His legs were bony, perhaps, and bowed, yet quite sturdy. Sailing might present more of a challenge, for Jason had never set foot in any craft larger than the canoes he paddled on Syrup Creek. He had visited Lake Michigan, which was too wide to see across, and had watched cargo ships docking in Chicago, but such experience would hardly prepare him for crossing the sea. Prepared or not, he felt certain he would find a way, once he set out, to keep going.

Of course he could not set out immediately, not even when the last of the hiking equipment arrived with the warm weather in April. First he had to inform his clients that he would no longer be able to keep track of their money. Breaking the news to his landlady, who hated changes, took a week.

"That's a cockamamie idea if I ever heard one," she railed at him. But eventually she grew reconciled to the scheme, and advised him to rub alcohol on the soles of his feet, which would toughen them, and always to wear wool socks.

There were forms to fill out at the insurance company and post office. His savings, which after decades of shrewd living were substantial, had to be invested in such a way that even five years from now, even in Tasmania, he would be able to pay for whatever he needed. Delivering his clothes to the Salvation Army kept him busy for an afternoon. He had to find homes for thirty-four houseplants, including some finicky African violets and a rambunctious aloe that had won a red ribbon at the county fair.

Having at last cut himself free of people and having reduced his possessions to what could be carried in his pack, he still had to decide in which direction to begin his trip, whether east or west. If west into the prevailing winds, he could be guided by the sounds and smells of things. In Illinois he might sniff the pigs of Iowa. In Utah he might hear the purr of rain on the Sierras. Ever since Marco Polo revealed how long and toilsome were the eastern routes, the great explorers had journeyed west, Hudson and La Salle and Daniel Boone, Lewis and Clark, the men whose travels Jason had studied since childhood. But if he set out eastward, he would not have to squint into the afternoon sun. Most days the wind would be at his back, helping him along, and his steps would be aligned with the spinning of the earth.

In the end he chose sunrise over sunset and headed east. He was accompanied to the edge of town by his Vietnamese laundress, his Argentine barber, several former clients asking final questions about their money, a boy whom he had once helped with algebra, and by the landlady, who presented him with a handsome pair of green wool socks. "Remember," she said, "there's always a home for you in Buddha. And rub your feet with alcohol."

Jason hoisted the walking stick to wave back at them. Then he faced the rising sun and took his first true step.

Each of these steps was, on average, thirty inches long, which meant 2,112 paces to the mile. At three miles per hour, eight hours a day, every week he would take 354,816 steps and cover 168 miles. In just under six weeks he would lift each boot a million times. If he maintained the same pace on the oceans as on land, he would circle the earth in a thousand days. The land portion of this circumambulation would require 16,727,040 steps, assuming he walked the whole way.

With these numbers buzzing in his head, Jason made his way down the Cincinnati highway. His calculations were soon in need of revising, however, for within an hour he accepted a ride in a chicken truck. On its side was painted BUDDHA'S BETTER BROILERS. The chickens were so crammed in their cages that a deaf person seeing the truck from a distance might have thought it was loaded with snow. A person with good working ears could have made no mistake. Jason heaved his rucksack onto the seat and climbed in. The driver was a bear-shaped woman with skin the color of wheat bread and eyes that made him think of pirates.

"Where you headed, bowlegs?" she roared above the noise of the chickens.

"Around the world," Jason shouted back.

"Lucky dog. Wish I was. But I've got to come on home after dumping these squawkers in Cincy. Listen to them. You ever hear such a racket? It's all I hear seven blessed days a week. Chickens! As dumb as an animal can get without expiring. Shoot, if I didn't have the four kids I'd buy me a backpack and go with you." She glared across at him. "Say, you married?"

Jason admitted that he was a bachelor. The woman's presence filled the cab like the smell of fresh biscuits, and filled him with yearning. Could he stand to meet and leave a woman each day for a thousand days?

"That's pure waste, if you ask me," she said, "a healthy gent like you and no wife. There's not enough men to go around as it is, when you get up in the neighborhood of fifty. They die off right and left. My old man walked under a concrete chute, arguing with the foreman about a baseball game, and that put out his lights. Made himself into a statue."

"I'm sorry to hear that," said Jason.

"He wasn't much account. Warm in bed, though, and a set of ears at the dinner table." Without warning, she slammed her fist against the cab's rear window, yelling, "Stupid birds!" Jason leapt, but the chickens never hushed. Then she added gruffly, "Travel the world, you ought to find a sweetie somewhere."

"One never knows," he answered.

"Hey, listen, do me a favor. They say the Japanese have bred up this mute chicken that lays three eggs a day. Would you check that out for me?"

"I'll certainly inquire." Jason scribbled the query into his pocket notebook. "And to whom should I address my reply?"

"Doris Wilkins. Rural Route 3, Buddha."

Be bold, he thought, and asked her, "Why haven't I ever seen you in town? I'm an accountant, and I thought I knew all the business people."

"My farm's four miles out. I only go into the burg for groceries. What few bucks I make I can add in my head."

"Do you raise the chickens yourself?"

"With my own little hands." She lifted both meaty fists from the steering wheel by way of illustration.

"I've never met a chicken grower before."

"And I never met an accountant. So we're even."

"I suppose somebody has to raise them," Jason observed.

"They don't just wander into the supermarket from the woods." With her hands once again on the wheel, she turned those piratical eyes on him. "Before you get through traveling, you're going to meet a lot of things you never bumped into before."

On a wharf in Cincinnati, Doris Wilkins gave him a crushing bear hug and introduced him to a barge captain who was bound for Pittsburgh with a load of coal. "Give this guy a lift," she told the captain. "He's going around the world."

Driving away, the chicken truck left a swirl of white feathers in its wake. Jason watched the spiraling fluff a long while after the truck had disappeared.

         ✺   ✺   ✺

The captain could answer none of his questions about sailing, but he was an expert at stamp collecting. All the way up the Ohio River, while Jason gazed out the window counting smokestacks and dumps and huddles of trees along the banks, the captain talked about first-day covers, plate blocks, cachets, mint-sheets. Hauling album after album down from a shelf and spreading them across Jason's knees, the captain showed him stamps triangular and hexagonal, stamps depicting butterflies and biplanes and dead dictators, stamps in a rainbow of shades.

"This one here," the captain said, fingering a thick album, "has got an uncanceled stamp in it from every country in the UN except Upper Volta. You wouldn't be going through Upper Volta, would you?"

"I just might," said Jason, writing the name of the place in his notebook. "If I do, I'll be sure to send you some stamps."

"It's right in there between Mali and Dahomey." The captain began drawing excitedly with his finger on the steamy pilothouse windows. "Sierra Leone's down here, see, then Liberia and the Ivory Coast, then Ghana, Togo. You can't miss it." Saying the names, he seemed about to lapse into song. "If I could go to just five countries I've got stamps from, I'd die happy. I've never in my life been any place where if you pissed on the ground it wouldn't run into this river."

"The beautiful river," Jason murmured.

"To you, maybe. What I see is a thousand-mile sewer. An oily highway."

"That's what Ohio means in Iroquois. Beautiful river."

The captain grunted. "You read a lot, don't you?"

"Life would be awfully pale without books."

"I know what you mean," said the captain vaguely. "Tell me, how'd you get started in this traveling business?"

Not used to answering personal questions, Jason was slow to respond. In Buddha, people thought of him as a two-legged calculator, without concern for anything but numbers. "When I was nine years old," he said at last, "the librarian gave me a book about world religions. In it, I discovered that a famous Indian holy man had been named Buddha about a thousand years before anyone ever heard of America or Indiana, let alone our little town. And right then I realized how big a place the world is."

"You ought to collect stamps," said the captain.

"I tasseled corn in the summer and saved up enough money to buy an atlas. And I started planning this trip."

"So if you'd come from a place called Jonesville or Gnawbone you might never have stirred from home?"

"Quite possibly."

Rain had turned the barge loads of coal as slick and lethal-looking as obsidian. Studying the captain's stamps, each one opening like a tiny window onto jungles and snowy mountains, Jason already felt a long way from home.

"Aren't you afraid of getting lost?" the captain asked.

"I have a keen sense of smell," Jason said. Realizing this might not explain why he felt confident of finding his way, he added, "And I've studied nature's signs on the weekends."

"Nature's signs?" the captain muttered.

Jason would not be daunted. He knew what he knew. Spiders build their webs in line with the wind. In deserts at sundown flocks of pigeons will lead you to a waterhole. Termite hills in Australia are topped by sharp ridges that point unerringly north and south. A dark patch in the clouds above an ice-covered sea betrays open water. From walking in the Hoosier National Forest and from reading the journals of great explorers, Jason had learned such things and a thousand things more. Over his brownbag lunch, every working day for twenty-six years, he had studied *National Geographic* and *Natural History* and *Smithsonian*, so he knew how various parts of the world should look. He would be certain of recognizing a place when he came to it.

In Pittsburgh, Jason thanked the captain and continued eastward. Wishing to give his new boots a test, he refused all rides. He stopped shaving and his beard came in pale yellow, the color of old sheets. Every few hours, crossing Pennsylvania by the National Road, he consulted the map to see how far he still had to go to reach Philadelphia. The map, which he had picked up free at a gas station, was devoted to the Eastern United States. Being so ambitious in scope, it lacked details. For example, it made no mention of the Allegheny Mountains, over which he had been laboring for three days, and it neglected all rivers smaller than the Susquehanna. The atlas was too bulky to pack, but fortunately Jason had committed most of it to memory.

A rainstorm drove him to shelter on the porch of a farmhouse near Gettysburg. The only person home was a teenage girl who wore an actual bonnet. She reminded him of a girl he had secretly adored in high school. While brewing him a pot of sassafras tea, this bonneted girl told how her pony had died from eating green apples. "Just swole up and keeled over," she said. Ever since that death, she had been looking for another pony just as small, as shaggy, and the same rusty color. A person could find such ponies on the Shetland Islands, or so she heard tell.

"If you pass by that way," she said to Jason, "and if you'd pick me out a mare that's less than ten hands high, with bushy mane and forelock down over her eyes, the color of this corduroy," giving him a scrap of cloth, "my daddy would pay for it and I'd put you in my prayers from now till eternity."

Jason wrote all the details in his notebook and tucked the piece of cloth in his pocket. As he was leaving, the girl handed him a corn bread muffin. He carried away with him the smell of her hair, like newly cut pine boards.

Before he reached Philadelphia, where he stood on Penn's Landing beside the Delaware listening to a brass band play salsa tunes, three more people had charged him with missions. In addition to the chickens in Japan, postage stamps in Upper Volta, and pony in the Shetlands, there was a grave to be located in Belgium, a prison warden to interrogate in Mongolia, and a debt to collect in Malaysia. Jason was beginning to feel as though he had undertaken this journey on behalf of a multitude.

When the brass band crashed to its finale, the conductor, a dark-skinned man in a shirt emblazoned with parrots, noticed him listening with rapt attention.

"If you think that was good," said the conductor, swaggering up to Jason, "you should hear the stuff we play on the ship."

The ship turned out to be the *Mexico* from Venezuela, a sailing schooner with three masts, bound on a training cruise to Europe. The musicians had been packed along to shorten the days with their playing. Jason arrived there with the band after an interlude in a seaman's bar, where he drank only apple juice.

"Not even a little beer, the man is so incorruptible!" the band leader proclaimed, introducing him to the first mate. "He will go with us to Portugal, no? A moral influence!"

The mate had no objections. Jason unrolled his sleeping bag on the deck, between two coils of rope.

Aside from the conductor and first mate, no one on board spoke English. Jason managed quite well with gestures. His hands wove pictures in the air, and his face, once he relaxed a bit, had a mime's expressiveness. Drawn by his sympathetic way of listening, the men approached him one by one, cooks and trombone-players and cabin boys, each one telling his life story in patient Spanish. Occasionally Jason would understand one of their questions well enough to record it in his notebook. Much of the time he simply nodded, absorbing their griefs and desires.

"You have kind ears," the conductor crooned. "I can tell by the way you listen to our music."

They docked in New York, to replenish their supply of remedies for seasickness. Jason was glad of the stopover. He wanted to see the Empire State Building, because the limestone for constructing it had been quarried just down the road from his home in Indiana. Half a dozen sailors insisted on going with him, to protect him from thugs. They wore white, dazzling in the sunshine, and Jason dressed in his usual green. The ascent in the elevator made him dizzy. From the top of the Empire State Building he looked down at the lesser skyscrapers, the maze of streets, the hurry of people, and thought of the quarries near Buddha. It seemed a strange thing, to dig so much limestone out of the earth, drag it halfway across the country, and stack it so high in the air. The sailors dared one another to throw coins from the roof. Jason cautioned them against it, for he had read that a penny dropped from such a height could pierce right through a person's skull. The sailors understood his gestures, if not his words, and held onto their coins.

On a street near the docks a barefooted woman asked Jason to help find her baby. The sailors joined in the search, peering through gratings in the sidewalk, turning over heaps of rags in doorways, but they could discover no baby, and at length the woman went sniffling away. Even lacking several teeth and smelling of cough medicine, she made Jason's heart ache.

After three panhandlers had shuffled up to him begging money and a wino had asked him for advice about delirium, the sailors perceived that Jason was a man who drew other people's needs to him as a magnet draws the inner spirits of iron. Once this was clear, they formed a barricade around him and let no one through. And so they arrived back at the ship, the sailors in white suits encircling him like a picket fence, green-clad Jason in the middle like a rare plant.

Sight of the Atlantic Ocean made even Lake Michigan seem humble by comparison. During the first night at sea, Jason lay awake thinking about the spaces between stars. Matter was so thinly scattered through the universe, it was a wonder how any two atoms ever rubbed against one another. That all the stuff necessary for making his body had joined together within this immensity seemed to him wildly improbable. And yet here he was, flesh and bone, nauseous from the heaving of the sea. He sniffed avidly at a land-breeze, which carried the reek of an oil refinery and a hog farm. So long as he could smell the shore he was not utterly adrift in this emptiness. During the day he gained comfort from watching gulls and terns cruising in the ship's wake, but eventually these birds reached the border of their fishing territory and swooped back.

Whenever the sea was calm enough the band set up folding chairs on deck and played music, either feverish dance tunes or mournful ballads, depending on the mood of the conductor. The off-duty sailors hunkered down beside Jason and resumed their life stories. Every now and again he would scrawl a memorandum: "Greetings from Juan to Esmerelda in Istanbul," it might be, or "Price garnets in Turkestan." When the sailors arrived in bunches and were reluctant to speak of what pressed on their hearts, Jason entertained them by calculating the hour of moonrise and moonset. At night he would estimate the time by the position of stars. Of course they had tables for predicting the movements of the moon and they had luminous watches for telling the time, yet they were fascinated by Jason's ability to compute such things in his head.

"What kind of sailors are you?" he scolded. "What if you were cast adrift, with nothing but your wits to guide you?"

With his odd notions about sea craft, his habit of sheltering beneath a fern-colored umbrella, and his energetic pantomimes, this gringo was the most engaging performer they had ever brought on board. He made the band seem dull. The conductor soon grew jealous, and regretted having offered Jason a ride. But the other musicians were secretly pleased, for they would rather confess their miseries to Jason in the shade of his umbrella than blow on their horns in the sun. They were glum when he strode down the gangplank in Lisbon. Even the conductor, repenting of his jealousy, wept a few tears. The cook chased after him with a savory parcel. Jason tipped his green slouch hat to them and headed off walking across Europe.

If he kept on course as far as the Bering Straits, he would cover twelve thousand miles before reaching another ocean. To keep track of his progress he stuffed a handful of pebbles into his left pocket. Each time his left foot struck the ground for the hundredth time, he moved a pebble to the right pocket. For every ten pebbles thus transferred he would have walked about a mile. After two days he grew weary of such counting, however, and decided to walk on in ignorance of distance.

His dramatic gestures served him well in Portugal and Spain. Three days out from Lisbon, a peasant gave him a ride on a donkey, unlashing a brace of water pots to make room. Jason had never sat astride a beast before, not even at the Lawrence County Fair, where he went each July to admire the champion rabbits and pigs. Riding the donkey was a bit like sailing, and inspired in him the same glee, as if he were playing a trick on the laws of physics. He slept in a hut with the peasant, staying an extra day in order to figure the man's income taxes. For supper each night they ate a flat bread which reminded Jason by its smell of the chicken lady,

Doris Wilkins. One of the man's children asked him in textbook English if he would kindly secure the autograph of a soccer star in Brazil. To be certain of the spelling, Jason had the boy write the hero's name in his notebook.

For several days, as he trudged across the desolate plains of northern Spain, the Pyrenees loomed out of the north like a bank of thunderclouds. Jason rode across the mountains in the truck of a painter who was smuggling marijuana into France. "With the stink of turpentine," the painter confided, "the dogs cannot smell my weeds."

Neither dogs nor border guards had any chance of sniffing this delivery, in any case, because the painter veered off the road on the French side of the mountains and bounced the last few miles across a rutted field. "Is it true the Colombian gold leaf is sweeter than our Spanish?" the smuggler wanted to know. Jason explained that he had never smoked any variety of leaf, but offered to seek the opinion of experts.

The smuggler's family turned out to be Loyalists who had been hiding in the south of France since the Spanish Civil War. They gave him the names of other old guerrillas, with addresses ranging across Europe from Toulouse to Bucharest. "Kiss Vladimir in Odessa for me," said the smuggler's wife.

In order to accommodate the names and addresses, Jason had to buy a second notebook. By the time he reached Vienna he was writing in his third. For many of the questions gathered along the way he had already found answers. These he wrote carefully on postcards, which he mailed to the questioners. Although the drift of his travels had carried him past Africa, he had found in Geneva a packet of stamps from Upper Volta, a present for the captain of the coal barge. He bought a Shetland pony of just the right color from a circus in Lichtenstein and had it shipped to the girl in Pennsylvania.

Every day or so he would knock at a door—in Berchtesgaden, say, or Zagreb, sometimes at a farm in the middle of nowhere—to pass along a message. A seamstress in Milan was so astonished to find this green apparition on her doorstep that she knelt down and uttered a prayer. When he delivered news of her son, who was earning good money at a fish cannery and had given up drink, she made Jason stay with her for three days so that all her relatives might hear from his lips these revelations about her wandering boy. "You see," she crowed, "he doesn't take after his good-for-nothing father!"

As Jason was leaving she hung a silver whistle on a thong about his neck. "If you're ever lost or in danger, blow this like fury and God will save you."

The only danger he encountered in Vienna was the loveliness of the women. He could not understand how their husbands and boyfriends managed to stroll beside them without breaking into shouts. He would have shouted, if he had been permitted so much as to hold one of those women by the hand. Watching them feeding seals in the zoo or tying the knots of kerchiefs beneath their exquisite chins, he was struck again by the improbability of the universe. Nothing in books explained how the sight of a face could set up these enormous tides in his heart.

The women had so disturbed his equilibrium that he nearly forgot to buy a pound of chocolate from a certain confectioner in Vienna for a policeman in Madrid. The main post office happened to be across the street from the confectioner's. While he was mailing the chocolate, he decided on an impulse to ask the postmistress if there were any general delivery letters for him. No one on earth knew he would pass through Vienna—or even cared, for that matter—and yet asking for general delivery seemed the sort of thing a serious traveler should do. The woman soon returned with a postcard. On one side it bore a photograph of the limestone pyramid under construction in Bedford, Indiana, right near his hometown, and on the other side a printed message: MR. MOSS, I'LL MEET YOU IN TOKYO, IN FRONT OF THE ASSYRIAN EXILE CHURCH, MAY FIRST AT NOON. WE'LL CHECK OUT THOSE JAPANESE CHICKENS TOGETHER. HOPE YOU'RE HAVING A GOOD TRIP. YOUR ITCHY-FOOTED FRIEND, DORIS WILKINS. In the upper left corner a forceful hand had written, "Number 212 of 500."

Jason recalled with perfect clarity jouncing in the truck beside the bearish widow who ranted in rage and affection about her four children and her farm mortgage and her fool husband who had died under five yards of concrete, and behind her voice the groan of the engine and the squawking of chickens, and her nearness filling the cab like the aroma of hot biscuits. Merely thinking about it, here on the tile floor of a Vienna post office, he was pierced by longing.

Of course he could not possibly meet Doris Wilkins in Tokyo. Would she expect him to shake hands? Kiss her? Buy her lunch? He was too old for learning the do-si-do of courtship.

Yet he held off replying to her message. Each time he entered a post office, instead of mailing the letter of apology which he had laboriously composed, he inquired at the general delivery counter. There were postcards waiting for him in every capital and in many of the secondary cities. One side invariably showed the limestone pyramid, the other carried the familiar message from Doris Wilkins. The only change from card to card was the number.

By the time he reached Ankara, where he collected his twenty-seventh card, Jason realized that he could not mail his letter of apology. He would have to meet the chicken lady. She had gone to so much trouble, and had perhaps already begun studying Japanese in preparation for her trip. Even now, browsing through catalogs, she might be circling the photographs of items she would need. Thinking about her preparations, he recovered some of his own early excitement, almost as if he himself were setting out on a journey once again.

For the truth was, his knees throbbed, his boots had worn thin, his umbrella was springing leaks. After tramping only a quarter of the way around the world, his joints were beginning to sound like old staircases. At least he remembered to rub alcohol into the soles of his feet. This not only prevented blisters but also mitigated the smell, a welcome side effect, for he was often forced to go long stretches without a bath.

In Kabul, a shoemaker to whom he had delivered a recipe for mutton pie rewarded him with a pair of ox hide boots, and also mended his umbrella. "To protect you from the murderous sun," the shoemaker signaled in gestures.

Jason had chosen to contend with sun instead of snow, taking a southerly route through Asia in order to avoid the Russian winter. This forced him to neglect a good many of the memoranda in his notebooks, including that troublesome kiss which he was supposed to award in Odessa. But what more could he do? How was one man to run errands for the entire world?

The new ox hide boots and the restored umbrella—as well as, he had to admit, the prospect of meeting Doris Wilkins in Tokyo—stirred up his spirits. He crossed northern Pakistan in a jeep with an army patrol, thus saving his legs a good deal of stony walking. The soldiers advised him against entering India. The beggars and fake holy men in that land would nibble him to nothing. "There is a glow about you which the needy can detect from miles away," said the lieutenant, who then asked Jason if he would mind carrying a blood-stained handkerchief to an old war comrade in Tibet. "He will know what it means," the lieutenant added darkly.

Although Jason kept taking on small items for delivery, such as this handkerchief, or a comb from a matron in Damascus, a pair of false teeth from a fisherman in Beirut, a harmonica from a street sweeper in Sofia, he also gave away to urchins some of the equipment he had brought along, and so the weight of his backpack did not vary much up or down. As soon as he delivered anything—the goblet for a Greek Orthodox priest in Baghdad, for example—someone else was sure to give him a new parcel.

The beggars and holy men did indeed flock to him in India, but instead of asking for handouts they asked for advice. They perceived that he was a battered pilgrim, a veteran of untold miles, and wanted to know what visions seized him when the winds turned wicked or rains filled the sky or the sun balanced on a mountain peak. Jason gave the best answers he could. Children toyed with his compass, squealing and leaping about to avoid the magical point of its needle. Old men solemnly tried on his felt hat, sniffing the headband, examining the sweat stains as if they were some obscure calligraphy.

Here in the land of the original Buddha, Jason shrugged off his weariness. He climbed through a mountain pass into Tibet, in company with a band of refugees from Bangladesh. All night they sang folk songs as they walked, and Jason hummed along. One by one they sidled up to him and showed him an old scar, a tattoo, a talisman, or merely tramped beside him in deep silence, occasionally brushing their fingers against his sleeves. When an avalanche threatened to bury their little party, he remembered the silver whistle hanging round his neck and gave it a powerful puff. As the snow crashed down harmlessly behind them, the refugees decided that Jason was indeed a wayfaring saint. How else explain the odd parchment color of his skin, the unruly beard, the walking stick that became a tent, the tamed avalanche?

Runners carried the news ahead into the hinterlands of Tibet. In the villages, children made him presents of flowers. Elders pressed their foreheads to his and clasped him gravely by the hand. Girls fed him fragrant beans wrapped in leaves. Word of him traveled ahead to the Chinese border guards, who gave him a bamboo flute and escorted him to the nearest communal farm. There he was examined minutely by dozens of curious eyes. Very little in his appearance fit their notions of how a man should look. They did not believe in saints, but knew all about wandering wise men, and took him for one. To entertain them, Jason recounted his entire journey in mime. The old people as well as the children clapped with delight and laughed.

When it was time for him to leave, a doctor on a bicycle led him to the next commune, and from there two girls led him to the next, and thus he was guided from settlement to settlement across China. In each place he performed the story of his travels. The number of companions escorting him between villages kept growing, until by the time he reached Lanzhou, where another card from Doris awaited him, he was marching at the head of a parade. Although he could not play any musical instrument, he boldly whistled along on his bamboo flute. His followers imagined that the awful noise he made was music in his native land.

In Xi'an he delivered a paper fan, in Nanjing a pair of sandals encrusted with seashells, in Shanghai a drop of amber enshrining a flea. As he completed each errand he placed an X in the margin of his notebook. No sooner did he complete a task, however, than somebody would set him a new one. Even as he began inscribing memoranda in his seventh notebook, Jason thought back with pleasure over his modest labors, which had now been scattered halfway around the world.

The throngs who accompanied him into Shanghai gave the local authorities a fright. Was it an invasion? Refugees from some disaster in the interior? Spying Jason, they were reassured. Such a man could not march at the head of anything dangerous. The mayor, learning that this serene stranger was bound for Tokyo, asked him to deliver a copper thimble to her cousin. Since the mayor's brother piloted a fishing boat, Jason's passage to Japan was quickly arranged.

In the waters off Kyushu the Chinese rowed him to a Japanese trawler, which carried him into Tokyo Bay on the last day of April. The sea journey restored him completely. He drank jasmine tea and mended his gear. While the fishermen labored, he studied the flight of birds and the motions of clouds and the patterns of waves, regaining his bearings in the great wheel of things. To keep his joints limber he stood up from time to time and danced on the deck, or acted out some portion of his travels for the fishermen.

The woman in Tokyo to whom he delivered the thimble put him up for the night in her paper-walled house. "The honorable sir is truly around the world going?" she asked in polite disbelief.

"Yes, indeed," said Jason, "and I'm on the homeward leg."

The woman's knowledge of English stopped short of allowing her to grasp how a trip could be divided into legs, and so she merely smiled, and the warmth of that smile left Jason wondering how he could possibly gather up enough courage before tomorrow noon to meet the chicken lady.

That evening he counted his postcards: sixty-three photos of the Indiana pyramid, sixty-three identical messages from Doris Wilkins. Nothing in the whole journey so amazed him as his arrival here for this rendezvous. He was sorely tempted to blow on his whistle; and indeed that night, in the midst of a dream about flower-covered islands, he did so, waking not only his hosts but also the neighboring families, all of whom shuffled into his sleeping alcove to see what was the matter.

"A dream," Jason apologized.

Staring down into his eyes, as if surveying a pond for turtles, an old woman declared, "It is loneliness." Everyone in the room nodded agreement.

Next morning, as he walked the last few blocks to the Assyrian Exile Church, Jason felt himself laboring uphill, even though the land was perfectly flat. He reached the spot five minutes early. Doris was already there, gazing about at the pedestrians as if they were migrating caribou.

"You don't look half bad," she cried on catching sight of him. "In fact, you look like you've ripened up. I like your sun-roasted color, and I flat out admire that beard. Who'd ever think it would come out like new butter? How're the legs?"

"Still kicking," said Jason. He was trying to decide whether to doff his hat or shake her hand when she seized him in a mighty hug and planted a kiss on his chapped lips.

"So you got my card?" she said, releasing him.

"Oh, yes. Several times. Sixty-three times, in fact."

"I sent five hundred. Didn't want to miss you, and God only knew where you might be headed. You were pretty vague about your itinerary, back when you hitched a ride in my truck."

She was dressed in gear to match his own, except in yellow instead of green: floppy hat and windbreaker and baggy trousers, a rucksack with sleeping bag strapped on, a walking stick that doubled as an umbrella, a canteen slung round her neck. Out of respect for her stout build and raucous manner, the pedestrians gave her a wide berth as they passed.

"Who's looking after the chickens?" Jason inquired.

"My brother. He owes me a favor for pasturing his goats."

"And the children? Four of them, if I remember correctly?"

"Four is right. Seems like forty, some days. They're with my other brother, who promised to keep them until school starts in September. I've been feeding him and his family free eggs ever since Adam and Eve got kicked out of the garden."

Jason reflected on dates for a moment, then asked, "You're planning to be away from home until September?"

"I don't see how we can get back to Buddha any sooner, not if we're going to really see South America."

"Right," said Jason, after the shock had worn off.

Before shipping to South America, they walked and rode the length of Japan, investigating numerous breeds of chickens along the way. Although some varieties were indeed quieter than the ones Doris raised, none were mute, and none laid as well or put on flesh as quickly, and so she decided to stick with what she had.

"There's no substitute for looking into things yourself," she declared.

Among the other things they looked into while traversing Japan were volcanoes, about which Jason had often read in *National Geographic*. He felt some kinship with these quaking mountains, for ever since joining company with Doris he had been feeling as though a pool of lava bubbled in his own depths.

Although Doris rode guard beside him, people still approached him daily with petitions. Would he carry a deathbed message from a grandfather to a grandson? Would he give a wedding certificate to a plumber? Would he pass along a poem to an estranged sister? Filled with these missions, his notebooks occupied the lower third of his pack.

"Folks know a soft touch when they see one," said Doris.

"I can't help it," he said.

"Don't try. I've lived too long around people you couldn't rouse with a poker."

She made no bones about anything, eating out of the same bowl with him, unrolling her sleeping bag next to his at night. She treated their journeying together as such a matter of course, a thing as natural as summer lightning bugs, that after a while Jason began to treat it so himself. In fact, the second night of their passage from Japan to Argentina, he was the one who finally zipped their sleeping bags together. They rode on a freighter as guests of the bosun, to whom they had delivered a family watch. Although loaded now with automobiles, the freighter smelled of the cattle it routinely carried on return trips from Argentina.

"For warmth," Jason said, explaining the joined bags.

Doris required no explanations. She crawled in beside him and hooked a brawny arm around his shoulders, as though dragging him to shore, then she led him down into the lava depths of his body and back up again, up into the avenues of birds, up into the moon's path, up where the edges of galaxies brush against one another in the invincible darkness.

"I'm not looking to marry," said Doris, as they started their hike northward from Buenos Aires, "but I sure need company, especially the adventurous kind. I got to feeling closed in and smothered, the way I was living. And it wasn't only from breathing feathers. If you want, I'll handle the chickens and you can do your bookkeeping in the dining room."

Jason needed to savor the vision only for a moment before replying, "That sounds good to me."

"How do you feel about kids?"

"I've met some amazing ones on this trip."

"Good, because mine would amaze a zookeeper." She heaved a sigh. "Someday maybe they'll quit going to university and get jobs. They've been collecting degrees like T-shirts."

Jason and Doris traveled the length of the continent, through swamps and deserts, with gauchos and priests and tax-collectors, sometimes in the cabooses of trains, in pirogues and panel trucks, once on a cart drawn by llamas, twice on mules, moving steadily northward until they reached the jungles of Central America. From there they took ship to New Orleans and then worked their way up the Mississippi Valley, Jason distributing messages and presents. They hiked from Illinois into Indiana, then rode the last fifty miles into Buddha with a bus full of gospel singers who were on their way to a contest in Fort Wayne.

The town was unchanged by the passage of a year, but Jason surveyed it now with altered eyes. Gas station, liquor store, corner grocery, rival churches—nothing had budged an inch. Some of last year's posters, faded by sunlight, still hung in windows. The same yard flowers were in bloom. The money he had counted for others still swam like fish from pocket to pocket. Familiar voices complained of familiar ailments, or shouted with familiar joys. It was a spot on earth. Just one spot. He had dozens of errands still to run, parcels to deliver, questions to answer.

"I don't think I'll be able to stay here long," Jason confessed.

"I didn't expect you would," Doris answered, "not after seeing the world."

He stared at the buckled sidewalks and potholed streets, the pathways of his old self. Beside him, Doris seemed to glow in her yellow traveling clothes.

"Are your kids big enough to fend for themselves?" he asked.

"If they aren't now, they never will be," she replied.

"Then you're free to go?"

"Free as a blue jay."

"Where to next?" he asked her.

That night they hunched over the atlas and studied maps, their shoulders rubbing together like the curves of continents.

The Artist of Hunger

It was not a convincing dawn. The eastern horizon resembled chicken liver simmering in butter. Flocks of chocolate birds wheeled overhead. Banks of fog rolled in from the North like a tide of mashed potatoes, and popcorn clouds dotted the South.

Edible, yes, but one could hardly call it persuasive. Gripping a lightbrush in one hand and a mug of malto in the other, Sir Toby Moore reclined on a couch and brooded on his wretched painting. The image shimmered on the vaulted ceiling of his studio, a miniature of the version that would later be projected onto the domes of shopping malls in five continents. With the lightbrush he added another touch of butter-yellow to the sunrise. Rather a vulgar mixture of foods, he had to confess, what with chicken giblets and chocolate. Why could he paint nothing but banquet skies? They had become a fixation with him, these firmaments stuffed with carbs and candies, poultries and pastries. He took a chilly swig of malto, then lay back on the couch and set the mug upon his prominent belly.

Sir Toby's belly was prominent in two respects: it was large and it was famous. Its conspicuous bulk was due to his zeal for eating, his distaste for exercise, and his steadfast refusal to undergo a slenderizing operation. His rotund profile had achieved fame because it belonged to one of the world's most celebrated mall-artists, whose sponsor, MEGA Corporation, owned The Sleek of Araby, the leading chain of slenderizing shops. He was not a sterling exhibit for their services. Nonetheless, he considered himself to be only physically fat, not metaphysically so. In his heart and mind he was svelte. Indeed, for the first twenty-odd years of his life he might have passed for willowy. Only after moving into the Wabash River Mall six years earlier had he begun putting on weight, and now he kept swelling, season after season, like a glacier adding a layer of snow each winter. While global warming had melted the glaciers, it had not diminished his bulk.

Journalists christened him Sir Tubby Roly-Poly. Video crews delighted in catching him in the company of his petite lady-friend, Lyla Bellard, whenever the two appeared together in public. On screen he loomed beside her, huge and pale, like a domesticated polar bear.

One such video aired while Sir Toby was engaged in perusing his chicken-liver sunrise. He was informed of this new publicity by a MEGA vice-president, whose bony face materialized on the phone screen. "You just can't stay away from the cameras, can you?" said the woman in an exasperated voice.

"It's not my fault the paparazzi hide in the shrubbery and ambush me every time I stir from my apartment," replied Sir Toby.

"Not only do we see you from all angles, with your tiny mistress standing next to you as if to represent the human scale, but the news anchors have fun estimating your weight and life-expectancy." The vice-president forced a smile, like a doctor trying to cheer up a terminal patient. The taut skin of her cheeks reminded Sir Toby of trampolines. "We're being flooded with complaints from stockholders," she noted.

"Are they requesting my head on a platter?"

"They'd prefer the sacrifice of your paunch and half of each buttock. Enough to slim you down to respectable proportions."

Knowing, or at least hoping, that he was too valuable a property for MEGA to lose, he ventured: "So fire me. I'll sign on with another weight-loss outfit tomorrow."

"Don't be rash. I am simply appealing to your dignity."

Sir Toby half-lifted the mug from his stomach, and then, bethinking himself, lowered it again. He was famished. The woman on the phone screen kept smiling grimly. All these marketing people had too many teeth. "My dignity?"

"When people think of our brand, Sir Toby, we want them to *think thin*. We want them to imagine fashion models, not Sumo wrestlers."

"I rather fancy being compared to those agile giants," he bluffed. "If I may say so, you bring to mind a praying mantis. What is there for your male friends to grasp?"

The vice-president's grin froze, an expanse of teeth floating on the screen like a crescent moon. "Listen, our competitors are displaying posters of you in their shops, identifying you as The Sleek of Araby mascot. As our *symbol*."

Sir Toby sighed. He was only too familiar with those competitors and their revolting names: Fat-Away Farms, Rub-a-Dub-Tubby's, The Beauty and the Feast, The Incredible Shrinking Man, Ipso Fatso, Gorge Us George's, each of them with outlets in malls around the world, vying with one another in the lucrative war against obesity. The mere thought of these shops, with their needles and vaporizers, made Sir Toby queasy. On several occasions he had gone so far as to deposit himself on the slenderizing couch in a Sleek of Araby parlor, only to flee in terror once he caught sight of the fat-extraction devices. The whole enterprise struck him as an unholy alliance between modern electronics and medieval torture.

"I can't help the way your competitors decorate their shops," he said.

"But you can. A series of operations . . ."

"Out of the question."

"MEGA would raise your fee."

He lurched upright on the couch and glared into the screen. "Madam, I'm an artist, not a rack for displaying clothes. Nor a video star. It so happens I am content with my present shape. I have no desire to resemble a weasel or a lightning rod. If MEGA doesn't approve of my physique, then I'll get someone else to sponsor my skies."

The professional smile faltered. "I only meant to suggest a possibility."

"An impossibility."

"You won't even consider it?"

"I have considered, and the answer is no. I won't have my body shriveled by machinery."

"Could you at least find a larger mistress? Miss Bellard makes you appear so—"

Sir Toby flung the empty mug at the screen. Plastic bounced harmlessly against plastic. With the angry punch of a button he erased the grimacing face in mid-sentence.

He longed to gather all these corporate image-makers, tie them in a sack, and dump them in the Wabash River—assuming one could still *find* the river, down in its concrete channel beneath the mall. They would never quit meddling. When they insisted on changing his name from Thurgood Moranski to Toby Moore, he had been annoyed, but he could see their point. Adding the "Sir" had struck him as comical, given that he had never set foot in England, let alone been knighted. But next they ordered him to shave his beard, give up wearing plaid, and take up wearing square-framed spectacles, at which point he rebelled. To spite them, he now wore plaid coats and trousers at every opportunity, allowed his blond beard to sprout defiantly, and banished his glasses. Once they offered to hire a stylishly thin actor to make his public appearances, but Sir Toby threatened to strangle the reedy wimp on sight.

Now this really was too much, when they began dictating the size of his mistress. He adored Lyla, every cubic centimeter of her. The less of her there was the more affection he could invest per gram. She was the only woman who had ever succeeded in making him feel graceful. "It's not a matter of bulk," she told him early in their friendship. "It's how the soul moves." The way she said it made him feel that his soul was as tangible as his fleecy beard. When their friendship had matured sufficiently to afford him an opportunity of examining her naked body, he searched her belly for the telltale puncture scars from slenderizing operations. He had seen the scars on so many others, on men in saunas and shower rooms, on women in swimming pools and more intimate settings—tiny puckerings of skin like pursed lips marking where the needles had done their work. But the skin on Lyla's midriff was as smooth and unblemished as a freshly laundered sheet. "However do you manage to stay dainty—and, may I add, sexy—without subjecting yourself to those barbarous operations?" he asked her. "I only eat when I'm hungry," she told him. "So do I," he said. To which she replied, "Ah, yes, but you're hungry all the time."

This was unfortunately true. Hunger gnawed at him relentlessly, like a rat in his guts. Even while recollecting that marvelous first perusal of Lyla's body, he was munching pretzels. He could only stop thinking about food when he was sleeping or, strangely enough, when he was at Lyla's apartment. She refused to live in the mall, or even to visit him there, complaining that its hives of bedrooms and clanging shops made her ill. Instead she lived in the wilds of southern Indiana, on a military base devoted to psychological warfare. "Why don't you come live with me?" she kept urging him. But he always refused. Since childhood, he had dreamed of growing rich enough to live in the Wabash River Mall, where every conceivable need, from cradle to grave, could be satisfied. That childhood vision still gripped him so firmly that nothing less than Lyla's potent allure could persuade him to move outside.

After the irksome phone call, Sir Toby was too stirred up to resume painting. So he left his unfinished sky shimmering on the roof of his studio and trundled into the mall. Some piece of romantic trash was playing overhead on the dome, featuring a hero with chiseled chin and a heroine with heaving bosom. A close-up of the damsel's moist lips showed them parting to admit a soda straw, giving way seamlessly to an ad for Giga Gulp, "The Juice Full of Joy." He knew all the slogans by heart.

Dodging a pack of kids who were hurtling toward him in a zip cart, Sir Toby clutched a plastic tree for support and uprooted it, setting off an alarm. One of the hazards of being fat in a world of skinny people was that you could never count on railings or chairs or other props to bear your weight. Presently a guard appeared to find out who was assaulting the vegetation. Before Sir Toby could explain, a look of recognition wiped the scowl from the guard's face. "Hey, you that painter?"

"Certainly not," Sir Toby insisted, stepping onto a pedbelt and gliding away.

A blast of music announced a change of program, and he made the mistake of looking up. An ad showed before-and-after photos of a young man, in the first of which he appeared grotesquely bloated, his eyes mere slits, his jowls bulging over his collar, while in the second portrait, taken after the slenderizing operation, he looked as lithe as an otter. "LET THE SLEEK OF ARABY REVEAL YOUR TRUE SELF," the announcer boomed. The ad agency had taken pains to make the slenderized young man appear handsome, but in Sir Toby's eyes he looked sadly withered, like a helium balloon, abandoned at night in robust plumpness near the ceiling, discovered next morning in a shriveled heap on the floor.

As he rode the crowded belts through the mall, he noticed other riders drawing away from him, their scrawny bodies encircling him like a stockade about a blockhouse. He was painfully accustomed to this isolation. The space they left around him bore less resemblance to the aura of respect surrounding a king than to the buffer zone surrounding a plague victim, as if obesity might be contagious.

Most of his fellow passengers were nibbling snacks and guzzling drinks. As the belt slithered past food shops, the non-eaters stepped off to replenish their supplies, and new riders hopped aboard with jaws grinding and lips slurping. Sir Toby was feeling virtuous amid all this gobbling until he realized he was holding a half-empty bag of salties in his hand. He stopped in mid-chew. Where had they come from? Probably his pocket. Food seemed to hide in his garments, even though he rarely remembered stashing it away. After hesitating briefly, he shook the remaining salties into his mouth. Then he stuffed the bag into a pocket of his plaid sport coat, where he discovered lumps of hard candy, stored there like a squirrel's acorns. With an effort of will he forced himself to leave the candies in place.

Suddenly he was jolted by such an intense craving for sugar that he lost his balance and staggered a few steps along the pedbelt. The other riders cleared away, lest he should fall and crush them. He felt panicky with hunger. The sound of chomping reverberated in his ears. He had to escape from these stares, go somewhere to eat in secret. Glancing up, he saw the neon lights of a Rub-a-Dub-Tubby's. Beyond that shone the marquees of Fat-Away Farms and Gorge Us George's. Sir Toby teetered on the edge of the belt, unwilling to let the skinny riders think he was going into one of those shops for an operation. But someone jostled him with an elbow—or perhaps a sausage or baguette, he imagined in his hunger—and he stumbled onto the pavement, nearly bumping into an emaciated woman who was emerging from the door of Fat-Away Farms.

"Sir Roly-Poly!" the woman exclaimed.

"Moore," he answered stiffly.

She grinned up at him with her newly shrunken face. A series of fresh scars along her throat and jaw stood out like scarlet stitches. "I just saw your picture," she breathed.

"Picture?"

"That poster they've got hanging inside," she said, brushing past him to hop on the belt.

And it was true; there on the rear wall of the slenderizing parlor hung a life-size portrait of him, in corpulent profile and lurid color. He stood transfixed in the doorway. His unflattering likeness dominated the shop like some evil totem designed to frighten passersby into the clutches of the fat-removal machines. The caption below read: REPRESENTING THE SLEEK OF ARABY. One of the operators glanced at him, then at the poster, then back again at Sir Toby, eyes widening, needle poised above the beefy thigh of a carefully draped customer.

"You're all a pack of leeches and ghouls!" Sir Toby bellowed through the open door. "Fat-suckers and walking cadavers!" A dozen operators glared at him now and a dozen customers twitched beneath their draperies. As an after-thought, backing away, he shouted, "May every needle strike a nerve!"

Fuming, he avoided the pedbelt, with its cargo of chomping scarecrows, and ambled down the walkway past Gorge Us George's and Ipso Fatso's. He stole a glance through the window of each shop, and in each he saw his unbecoming portrait.

He walked hurriedly on, feeling morose and hungry. Within moments he was puffing. At least, in his unhappiness, he was burning calories. Lyla would be proud of him for exercising like this. She despised pedbelts and elevators, insisted on using her own legs. And such legs! Too shapely to be described as thin, they were delightfully proportioned, like the rest of her, as if she had been designed for a world more elegant than the one other mortals inhabited.

Outside the window of a Cravin' Haven his exercise came to a halt, and he stared in like a tramp at the diners seated along the counter. His mouth opened and shut in sympathy with theirs. At about the third bite he tasted chocolate, having unconsciously stuffed his mouth with a joybar, which he had fished from some hiding place in his voluminous suit. The taste of chocolate always dissolved his last vestiges of self-restraint. Watching the diners, he pulled from his pockets and devoured in rapid succession the hard candies (butterscotch), a box of raisins, a stale pastry, and a packet of crushed soy-chips. After the last hiding place had been ransacked he went on thrusting hands into pockets, opening and closing his coat, slapping his thigh and rump, in search of more food. He gave up searching only when he noticed that the diners inside Cravin' Haven were watching his pantomime with great amusement, pointing at him with drinking straws and half-eaten burgers. Several of them appeared to be mouthing his name, or some slanderous variation on his name.

He resumed his trek through the mall, sunk in gloom, wondering how far he would have to trudge in order to burn up all the calories he had just consumed. It was hopeless. His exertions would never catch up with his eating. He could sympathize with people who sank ever deeper into debt by adding a bit more on the charge card each month. Still he felt ravenous. It was absurd, it was humiliating, to be so thoroughly a creature of one's gut.

"What provokes this ferocious appetite?" he had asked Lyla early in their acquaintance, imagining that as a neuroscientist she might know the answer.

"It comes from living in the mall, where you're surrounded by food and bombarded by ads," she said. "That's all the more reason to move in with me."

She had something there, he conceded, as he shuffled past eateries, taverns, snack shops, and sandwich carts. Even the eros parlors, feelie booths, and game arcades sold food and drink. The incessant dome shows beamed down mouth-watering ads, alternating with weight-loss promos.

Thinking of dome shows, he glanced up, and was startled to see one of his own vintage sky-paintings. Thunderheads that actually looked like surly clouds instead of mashed potatoes and gravy; dragon kites playing against a lavender haze; a flight of Canada geese beating their way across the face of a late-afternoon sun;

around the horizon a rim of hills topped by trees. He had painted that sky at least a dozen years earlier, while still a teenager, before moving into the mall. It already showed his characteristic strokes with the lightbrush. Yet by comparison with his recent work, over-stuffed with allusions to food, this early painting seemed to him fresh and powerful. Every detail in it was authentic, something he had *seen* rather than vaguely hungered for. It was a creation of the eye, not the belly.

Had he lost so much power? he wondered, standing outside a Never Say Diet store ("Open for Eating 25 Hours a Day"), a pudgy silhouette so familiar that shoppers paused to gape at him. He was surprised by tears slithering through his beard and over his multiple chins.

For such misery there was only one antidote—Lyla. He barged straight for her, like a draft horse headed for the barn, rid-ing the shuttle through its translucent tube out to the military base in the Hoosier National Forest. She would scold him for bothering her at work, something he had never done before. But this was an emergency. Most likely she would be dousing rats with exotic rays, turning them into spies or torpedoes, and how important was that by comparison with restoring her lover's self-esteem?

He did not fully grasp Lyla's research, and was not certain he wanted to. It involved poking about in the brain with vibrations, or perhaps devising ways of preventing enemies from poking about in the brain, or some such business. Her scientific jargon might as well have been the language of dolphins, for all the sense he could make of it. Never having progressed beyond arithmetic and

Bunsen burners in school, Sir Toby drew a blank when confronted with equations or graphs. He was grateful that he did not need to understand electronics in order to use a lightbrush or understand holograms in order to have his skies broadcast in malls.

The shuttle quivered to a halt. He glanced at the signboard: Old Bloomington. Two more stops to go. Ads beckoned from walls and ceilings, sales patter oozed from speakers. During the lull at the station, the sounds of chewing filled the air like subdued applause, reminding him that he had emptied his pockets in the mall. There were vending machines two cars down, but he could not bring himself to squeeze through the aisle past all those staring faces. Lyla would have nothing to eat in her lab. She seemed to subsist on air, like the wispy plant she had given him to brighten his bathroom. He would have to endure the hunger. Only two more stops. Surely there would be a snack bar at the base. Or perhaps he could persuade a guard to sell the contents of his lunch-bucket.

First the guard must be persuaded not to arrest or shoot him. In his haste, Sir Toby had not sufficiently pondered how to gain admission to this ominous facility. Perhaps he could introduce himself, note that he paid substantial taxes, and declare that he wished to evaluate Ms. Bellard's research. But what if they required a security clearance? And wouldn't he be doubly suspect as an artist? Allow him inside, and he might discover military secrets and paint them into his next sky, which would be broadcast in malls around the world. Spies would stop in the midst of shopping, gaze up at his revelations, and snap photos to smuggle back to hostile governments.

No, they would never let him in.

Another quiver of the shuttle. His stop. He might as well try. He could propose that Lyla vouch for him and lead him blindfolded to her rat maze lab. He stood up, smacked his jacket and trousers into a semblance of neatness, and stepped onto the platform. No one else left the shuttle and no one boarded. In fact, there were no people visible, no vending machines, no benches or ticket booths. The Fort Hoosier station consisted of a windowless building, painted porridge gray and surrounded by razor wire. The blank steel door was plastered with warning signs.

Before he could budge, a camera mounted above the door swiveled to focus on him and a voice boomed: "STATE YOUR BUSINESS! CLEARANCE CODE! PASSWORD!"

Sir Toby blinked at the camera. "I've come to see Dr. Bellard on urgent business."

Evidently this answer flummoxed the guard, for several seconds of electronic hum ensued. Presently the same male voice, but considerably less belligerent, inquired: "Excuse me, sir, but you wouldn't be the guy who paints the skies, would you? Sir Toby Something?"

"Moore," Sir Toby answered, bowing slightly. "May I speak with Dr. Bellard? I promise not to steal any secrets."

A moment later the combined breathing of several onlookers, who had evidently gathered near the monitor, was audible through the speakers. "Look," whispered a female voice. "It's really him." There was a muffled discussion, of which he could decipher only two words, *Toby* and *Lyla*. This conference was terminated by a round of laughter, and then the guard's chastened voice: "One moment, sir, while I page Dr. Bellard."

Sir Toby, who was beginning to feel like a zoo exhibit, turned from the camera's scrutiny to wait. Out of habit, he searched his garments once again for provisions. To his surprise, he discovered a joybar in the watch pocket of his plaid vest. To his even greater surprise, he felt no desire to eat it. Indeed, he felt crammed to the gullet, as if he could go a month before his next meal. With a shiver of revulsion, he slipped the joybar back into its hidey hole. What was happening to him? He studied the oatmeal-colored walls suspiciously. Maybe they were beaming rays at him to quench his hunger. They did such things at these labs. Poking about in the brain.

He felt woozy. There being no seat, he propped himself against the wall. Lyla would make them stop experimenting on him. He closed his eyes and took deep breaths. In his dizziness, he did not hear the door open or footsteps lightly approach.

"Toby, darling," came a gentle voice, "whatever's the matter?"

It was as if birds had begun singing in his heart. He opened his eyes and engulfed her in a hug, murmuring, "Lyla, dearest, they're tormenting me."

"Who?" she demanded, pulling back to gaze at him with luscious brown eyes.

"Everybody. The paparazzi with their videos. The Sleek of Araby bosses with their teeth and needles. Gawkers in the mall. And even here," he protested, gesturing at the camera's glass eye, "the guards are beaming some kind of—" he groped for a word, "*fullness* rays at me."

"Fullness rays?" she repeated skeptically.

He explained to her about the uneaten joybar, the loss of appetite, the faintness.

"Nobody's messing with your brain at the moment," she assured him. Her small hand played like a mouse in his beard. She wore an olive-green uniform, with her name and rank stitched on the breast pocket, instead of the white coat he had expected. It was always disconcerting for him to be reminded that this tiny woman, with her ponytail and mice-size hands, actually worked for the Psy-Ops division of the Pentagon.

"I just feel strange," he said.

"Why don't you take a vacation from the mall?" she suggested, as she had so often suggested before. "Stay at my place."

"The evening news would love that."

"What more can they say about us than they've said already?"

He wavered. "Yes, but I've got a sky-mural due in two days."

"I'll bring a lightbrush and projector from the lab."

"But I've already got a painting started on my ceiling."

"Then zip the file out here." She looked at him intently, a slight smile on her face. "Have you run out of excuses?"

He shrugged, and returned her smile. He had always offered the same excuses. Publicity. Work. Deadlines. Yet, in his heart of hearts—or perhaps in his stomach of stomachs—he had been reluctant to leave the mall itself, with its eateries and domeshows and pleasure arcades. Now the mere thought of food filled him with loathing. As for pleasure, there was always Lyla.

"The change might do me some good," he agreed at last.

"Delightful!" She took one of his great paws in her tiny one, and with her other hand she waved at the camera. The featureless door clicked open. Of course someone had been watching.

The partially finished sky glimmered on the ceiling of Lyla's apartment. After prolonged frowning at the chicken-liver sunrise, chocolate birds, and mashed-potato fog, however, Sir Toby could not bring himself to add another stroke of the lightbrush. Lyla had dubbed it "the great floating smorgasbord." Only a starving man could paint such toothsome skies, and Sir Toby, lounging like a walrus upon his lover's couch, was not the least bit hungry. He still had cravings, but not for food. With the flick of a switch he erased it all, the popcorn and giblets, the gravies and syrups, the sugary constellations. He closed his eyes and waited for inspiration.

He was still waiting when Lyla summoned him to the guest bedroom. Ordinarily he avoided this room, for it housed a colony of white rats, which had retired here after finishing their careers in the lab. "Come," she said, "I have something to show you."

With foreboding, he shuffled down the hall, but only after tucking his trouser cuffs into his socks as a precaution against inquisitive rats. He was relieved to see that a stout gate sealed off the lower half of the guest room doorway. Lyla stood just outside.

"Closer," she insisted, drawing him to the threshold by his elbow. He peered into the room, where perhaps a dozen rats were nosing through mazes, working out on rodent-scale exercise equipment, or otherwise frolicking, apparently indifferent to the food heaped in a trough along one wall. "Here goes," said Lyla, pushing a button on a control wand.

The ceiling was suffused with a rose-colored glow, which darkened to the color of tomato soup. Within that goop, creamy pasta-shapes slowly congealed. Sir Toby recognized this as the overture to one of his recent skies, broadcast within the past six months. "How did you get hold of it?" he asked.

"Military channels," she answered. "Now watch what happens."

He knew only too well what would happen. After the tomato soup would come lasagna, eggplant Parmesan, and so on through a five-course Italian meal, all smeared across the ceiling in shades of catsup and cheese. A scrabbling noise made him look down, afraid the rats might be assaulting the gate. But they were scurrying toward the food trough, fighting for position, gorging themselves. Bits of kibble flew as the furry jaws snapped. Watching them made his skin crawl. The rats nipped one another in their frenzy to get at the food. They hauled themselves from dish to dish, their bellies sagging.

"They'll kill themselves," he said with horror.

"Some of them would if I left it running long enough."

"My art is doing that?" Standing in the doorway, he realized that a feeling of hunger was mixing with his nausea.

"Not your art, but what your sponsor blended with it." Lyla pressed a hand against his back. "Stick your head inside the room and see how it feels."

Fascinated, frightened, he leaned over the threshold, and was immediately seized by an overwhelming craving. He clutched his stomach, screaming, "Turn it off!"

Lyla quickly extinguished the painting, drew him back into the hallway, and put her arms around as much of him as she could encompass. "I'm sorry, sweetheart, but you wouldn't have believed me if I'd only told you about it."

"What the devil—" he began, but he was too dazed to formulate a question. He sympathized with the rats, which now lay on their sides, paws outstretched, bellies swollen.

"MEGA programmed into your sky-show a vibration that stimulates the hypothalamus—the hunger center in the brain," Lyla explained. "You get a more concentrated charge in here than you would in a mall, but this gives you an idea of the effect."

"They can *do* that?"

"Oh, yes. They've been doing it for nine or ten years, with the government's blessing."

"To keep everybody hungry?"

She nodded. "Twenty-four hours a day. In every mall, shuttle, stadium, and dome."

"But not at the base?" he said, thinking of the windowless buildings at Fort Hoosier.

"No, our heads must be clear. Protecting national security, you know."

He surveyed the engorged rats. After a few weeks of such eating, they would all need slenderizing operations. From trough to needle. Then back to trough. With a stab of insight, he understood—food shops and slenderizing parlors, Cravin' Haven and Sleek of Araby—a closed circuit of gluttony and shame to make the cash registers ring.

"Do you know how it works?" he demanded.

"I'm afraid I do," said Lyla. "I helped develop the technology."

"You? For the malls?"

"No, for the military. It was supposed to be used in war. But the Pentagon decided it wouldn't incapacitate enemies. So they licensed hunger to the merchants."

"What did they come up with instead?"

"Lust, anxiety, paranoia, depression, and hallucination proved to be more disruptive."

"All of that came from your research?"

"Indirectly. It turns out by modulating the beam you can play the brain like a piano."

"That's *evil*." He backed away in disgust and hurried down the hall.

"Thurgood," she called after him, using his real name, the one she sometimes whispered when they were making love. He did not stop. She caught up with him in the living room. "I could be court-martialed for showing you my little demonstration with the rats," she said. "But I needed to share this with someone outside Psy-Ops, and you're the only person I can trust."

Without answering, he slumped onto the couch.

"Maybe I should have left you in the dark," she said.

He glared at her. "How can you go to the lab every day, knowing what your research is doing to people?"

"I have no say over how my research is used."

"Then you should have quit."

"Maybe so. Maybe I will." She sat beside him on the couch. "But hasn't your art been used to manipulate people?"

"I had no way of knowing," he objected.

"You didn't know the technical details, but you knew MEGA owns both ends of the food-and-fat cycle, all those franchises with their stupid names. You knew your paintings were helping to lure people into food shops and slenderizing parlors."

"I never—" he began. Then he faltered into silence, for Lyla was right. He was as much a captive of MEGA as she was of the Pentagon. She had chosen to look the other way when her science was misused, and he had done the same with his art.

"Thurgood?" she said, cuddling against him, sobbing. "Sweetheart?"

He drew her close and spoke quietly. "It's time for both of us to quit what we've been doing and find work we can believe in. Meanwhile, I'd better get out from under those appetite rays and move in here with you."

For supper there was kale salad, falafel, and yogurt. Though the meal was scrumptious, Thurgood—as he now thought of himself—could not clear his plate. Every bite reminded him of those rats and the munching passengers aboard the shuttle and the chewing faces at the counter in Cravin' Haven. As he toyed with the last of his food, Lyla said, "Keep this up, and you'll melt away to nothing."

He laughed, relieved that they still loved one another. "Sure, like the Arctic sea ice."

The image reminded him of the MEGA branding executive, her teeth glistening like tiny icebergs, and he was pitched into gloom once again. He wouldn't do any more Sleek of Araby skies. But what could he paint instead? Where could he get his murals shown?

Sensing this change in mood, Lyla said, "Never fear. We'll find ways to use our talents and brains that don't involve manipulating people."

"It's scary, though. I wonder if I can still paint anything besides food."

He rose to clear the table and load the dishwasher. He was handling the last plate when he noticed hairline cracks in the glaze. Immediately he set down the plate, rushed into the living room, grabbed the lightbrush, and began sketching a feathery lacework pattern on the ceiling.

Lyla drew close to him and gazed at the emerging design. "It looks like crystals of frost."

"Right you are!" he cried. The cracked glaze had reminded him of frost-covered windows in his grandparents' farmhouse.

He could have shouted for joy. There were paintings in him still, preserved by memory and affection. Suddenly he thought of an idea so delicious that he began prancing around the living room, hooting with laughter.

"What is it?" Lyla spun about as he circled her in his lumbering dance.

"I want to broadcast one last sky!" He pointed at the ceiling. "Lovely, innocent frost. Only you'll doctor it up with your voodoo vibrations. Not hunger this time. No, no. This time it's going to be sex. The Sleek of Araby brings you an orgy! Think of it. The dome lights up, ice crystals thread across the screen, and people in malls around the world strip off their clothes, grab the nearest warm body, and tumble onto floors and countertops. Shoppers, gawkers, guards, teenagers, geezers—everybody coupling wildly! What do you say? That would put MEGA and the rest of them out of the brain-tampering business, wouldn't it?"

As he danced, his arms waving and beard wagging, Lyla gaped at him, like a bear-handler whose pet had gone berserk. "That's utterly crazy," she said, laughing.

"So you'll do it, right? A little subversive science." He whirled to a stop, bent down, and painted her face with kisses. "We could try it on the rats first, in case you need to work out any kinks. Or work in any kinks. Better yet, we could try it on ourselves. What do you say?"

For a moment her smile was uncertain, and then it brightened into glee.

The Engineer of Beasts

Orlando Spinks meant no harm. You could have searched that dilapidated organ, his heart, without discovering any murderous hankerings. You could have shone searchlights into the basement of his brain without finding the least cobweb of malice. His intentions were as innocent as shoelaces. He merely wished to inject an element of wildness into the beasts he constructed for the Oregon City Disney.

Wildness, or at least the simulation of wildness, had been the Spinks family business for generations. Orlando had learned the trade of beast-engineering from his father, who had learned zoo-keeping from *his* father, who had stuffed animals for a living back in the days before the Enclosure when there had still been animals to stuff. Once the domes clamped down over the cities, and the travel-tubes bound the cities together in a global web, and extractors began mining the oceans and recyclers began filtering the air, and the Enclosure was sealed tight in all its manufactured perfection, Grandfather Spinks, who was inside, could no longer stuff the cadavers of animals, which were forever shut outside. He therefore abandoned taxidermy as a doomed craft, like blacksmithing, and went to work for the Oregon City Disney restoring moth-eaten bears and crocodiles. Tiring of the jovial owls and congenial tigers that Grandfather left behind, Father Spinks introduced frankly imaginary beasts, such as unicorns and griffins and mermaids. By the time Orlando became chief engineer, the visitors who ambled through the disney no longer knew or cared which of the animals had once lived on Earth and which were imaginary.

Orlando's initial problem was in deciding what constituted wildness. He brooded on this question while puttering in his workshop, where Grandfather's collection of stuffed animal heads gazed down at him from the walls like a glum and moldering board of trustees. Was it simply filth that distinguished wild creatures from his robots? Shaggy fur swarming with vermin? Or was it stupidity, the inability to reason and talk? Viciousness? Unpredictability? A yen for howling in the night?

He discussed these conjectures with his apprentice, a mop-haired girl of twelve with ingenious fingers and foxy eyes.

"I'd vote for filth as a starter," the girl suggested.

"But what shall we use for dirt?" said Orlando.

"Don't you worry, I'll find some."

Before he could object, she was off in search of dirt, pulling a wagon. Today her honey-colored pigtails were coiled into the shape of a beehive, and convincing bees zipped in the air about her head. She had painted her face and arms with raspberry splotches to simulate stings. The pedbelt riders—who would never have seen actual bees, but who could recognize eccentricity from a kilometer away—shouldered aside to give her room.

If anywhere in this immaculate floating city a bucketful of dirt had escaped the cleansers and recyclers, Orlando felt confident she would retrieve it. Her name was Mooch. He had first encountered her one Sunday in the lion's den, her lower half protruding from the alpha lion's mouth. The jaws were programmed to open and shut in synchrony with recorded roars, but the girl had jammed the mechanism, and the lion's rubber teeth clamped tight about her midriff. Instead of hanging slack or jerking in terror, her legs—clad in baggy purple trousers—stood firmly planted on the cage floor. In place of the lion's voice, there issued from the cavernous throat a child's bemused humming.

When he pried her loose she lambasted him for having stuffed the lion's gut with gears instead of lungs and bowels. "You've even got him saying silly speeches between roars," she griped. "Don't you know lions couldn't talk? And if they could, they'd have talked about sunlight or the taste of antelope, not about safaris. You need a helper, somebody who knows the beasts. Somebody who's read all the animal books, watched nature feelie films, tromped through hologram jungles. Somebody like me. Make me your apprentice and we'll turn this disney into a place that will stand people's hair on end."

At this point in their initial interview the girl extended one small hand, greasy from the lion's jaw. Instinctively grasping it, Orlando felt the nimbleness in the fingers, saw the shrewd eyes measuring him as if he were one of the mechanized exhibits.

"Then it's a deal," she said. "Call me Mooch."

In fact Orlando had been searching for an apprentice, whom he could teach the art of beast robotics. Since he had scored too low to qualify for breeding, he would never father a child, so he was content when the girl emerged from the lion's jaw and ensnared him in her dizzy speech. Officials at the city orphanage were glad to let him claim her, for Mooch was the slipperiest foundling they had ever tried to corral. She would sneak from the dormitory and ride the belts or creep through engine rooms in the deepest levels of the city or poke about the disney, as she had been doing on the day when the lion bit her.

Thus Orlando was not surprised when she returned from her dirt search with the wagon full of dust, grit, straw, balls of hair, and sundry obscure items of filth. While Mooch plastered the animals with this grime, Orlando posted messages on the electric signs explaining to visitors that such squalor was typical of beasts in the wild. He also took the occasion to rearrange the exhibits. Father Spinks had displayed the beasts alphabetically, so that dragons stood next to dinosaurs, griffins next to giraffes. However beasts used to array themselves in the wilds, Orlando felt certain they would not have done so alphabetically.

"Why don't we put the forest creatures with other forest creatures," Mooch proposed, "and all the river beasts together, the snow leopard with the abominable snowman, and so on?"

"You tell me what goes with what, and I'll shuffle them," agreed Orlando, who was a genius at engineering but rather in the dark in matters of biology.

Since there was no distinction between workday and playday within the Enclosure, the disney never closed, which meant Orlando had to shuffle the exhibits while patrons watched. The temporary separation of beasts from their labels led to confusion. He might be wheeling a polar bear onto a foam iceberg, say, while Mooch danced alongside smearing the fur with goo, and a tourist would holler, "What did that skunk used to eat?"

Indeed, as the filth began to ripen, many of the beasts were mistaken for skunks. More than one school child yelled out rude variations on the question, "Why do these mechos stink?"

"That was their general custom in the wild," Orlando would answer politely.

Fortunately, the Overseers, who cruised through the disney several times a day on their rounds, knew even less of biology than he did, so they permitted him to rearrange the exhibits and besmirch the beasts to his heart's content—provided, of course, that calm was preserved.

How to relocate the imaginary beasts was a puzzle, because in most instances their habitat was ill-defined. Dragons and trolls could be placed in caves with bats and bears. But where would you put a griffin? Among the eagles, in keeping with its front half, or among the lions, in keeping with its rear? Should centaurs graze with zebras, or should they be assigned to the ape house out of respect for their human torsos? Sasquatches had been reported everywhere from the rainforest of Colombia to the airless heights of the Himalayas, yet none had ever been captured; so where did you exhibit this hairy shambling monster? Orlando was beginning to understand why his father had opted for the alphabetical display.

In the end he and Mooch herded all the unclassifiable beasts— the feathered serpents and snake-haired gorgons, the whiskered growlers and long-fanged snuffers—into a huge pit, where the creatures milled around like a nightmare stew.

This monster pit soon became a favorite haunt for visitors, who poured through the gates in undiminished numbers, wigs and mood gowns gleaming in the fluorescent light. Many of them now wore breather masks, to shield themselves from the stench.

No sooner had the soiling and shuffling been completed than Mooch declared, "How about we do over the voice boxes? Erase the goofy speeches and make them sound like animals?"

"There's quite a collection of howls and hisses in the archives," Orlando said by way of agreement.

"Sure, and whatever we can't find there I'll do myself," said the girl, whereupon she launched into a hair-raising chorus of snarls and grunts and whistles. "And I can do gnawing on bones, death-rattles, panting, and fights. Just listen."

The girl's demonstration convinced Orlando that she had animal blood in her. The goose bumps on his skin did not smooth out for a long while after.

Modifying the voice boxes took just over a month. The brown bear no longer told stories about forest fires, but merely snorted or growled. The monkeys now gibbered instead of reciting jingles. The elephants ceased ruminating on philosophy and began simply ruminating, quietly munching plastic hay. The giraffe stopped bantering jokes about the inconvenience of a long neck and kept silent. Following what Mooch had gleaned from old books, Orlando programmed the other beasts to remain silent most of the time. The woods must have been eerie, he decided. Quiet as tombs except for wind and water and birds. And even birds kept mum half the day.

Visitors who complained about the silence or about the sporadic bestial sounds were provided with headphones that played all the old malarkey.

Continuing the search for wildness, Orlando and Mooch asked themselves what else could be done to make the mechos act more like beasts and less like humans dressed up in fur suits. Well, rhinos should not balance balls on their nasal horns, rabbits should not consult pocket watches, gorillas should not play drums, and flamingos should not play croquet. Deciding what all these creatures should *do* was a more difficult matter.

"Mostly they just slept and ate and hunted," said Mooch.

"Who'll pay to watch beasts snoozing?" Orlando objected.

"Suppose we make half of them hunt while the other half sleep."

"What will they hunt?"

"Each other."

This alteration required another two months of labor. Frogs now gobbled dragonflies, mice pounced on frogs, rabbits gobbled mice, owls murdered rabbits, and high-leaping wolves snatched the owls. At the end of each murderous cycle, the victims were restored to life, put to sleep, and the former sleepers awakened for hunting.

Despite some muttering, the visitors generally applauded this new regime. There was plenty of action. Wherever they turned, some beast was always slaughtering some other one. Even the cows and sheep, stupidly chewing their cuds, would sometimes be attacked by a mountain lion or a pack of beavers.

Undeterred by grungy hides and this new show of aggression, people still crowded up to pat the beasts. "Nice kitty," they would purr to the tigers. "Sweet little pooch," they would lullaby to the jackals. They climbed on the centaurs and ostriches and kicked them in the ribs, shouting, "Giddap!"

All this familiarity struck Orlando as unseemly. "Should I put up glass to keep people out?" he wondered aloud.

Mooch withdrew a well-chewed pigtail from her mouth. "No, don't. Beasts never lived behind glass. How about we paint a line between the crowds and the exhibits, and program the critters to bite anyone who crosses it?"

"Bite the visitors?" he repeated incredulously.

"Only a gentle munch on the arm, and maybe a lash or two with the tail." When he hesitated, the girl added, "You want them to respect the beasts, don't you?"

They converted the jungle exhibit first. Chimpanzees would now hurl plastic fruits at intruders, cheetahs would leap on them, pythons would coil about their legs, spiders would crawl through openings in mood gowns and probe with needle teeth. The warning signs declared:

DO NOT CROSS SAFETY LINE

LIKE THEIR WILD ORIGINALS,

THESE BEASTS ARE DANGEROUS

Anyone invading the barnyard exhibit would now be kicked by mules, butted by pigs, pecked by chickens, and battered by the stiff wings of geese.

Inevitably, some patrons ignored the warning signs. When this happened, Orlando and Mooch had to shut off the power and go pry the trespasser from the grip of a giant panda, as the case might be, or from beneath a squatting stegosaurus. More than once they had to fiddle with the programming, when an overzealous beast ripped a gown with its claws or bloodied a visitor's nose.

Gate receipts swelled. Apparently the citizens enjoyed being terrified out of their wits. As news of the beast attacks spread through Oregon City, visitors crowded into the disney, edging beyond the warning lines, provoking assaults from squirrels and moose and pterodactyls.

Catching wind of these developments, the Overseers sat Orlando down in the control room for a lecture. There were two officers, one a brawny great lug and the other one even brawnier, both in silver jumpsuits covered with bulging pockets, their faces hidden inside mirrored helmets. In voices like the rumble of a bowling alley, they reminded him that humanity had withdrawn into the Enclosure to be shielded from the grab-and-gobble of nature. And here he was unleashing mechanical marauders indoors. All their talk added up to the warning that, if anyone got seriously hurt in his diddly amusement park, Orlando would be in the deepest, darkest trouble.

After they left, he prophesied bleakly, "Somebody's going to get hurt."

"I wouldn't be surprised," Mooch agreed.

The way she twisted her mouth, Orlando could not tell whether she was reluctant or eager to see the first mangled body.

❋　❋　❋

The first mangled body turned out to be Orlando's. He forgot to switch off the beam one day before entering the alligator pool with his oil can. By the time Mooch heard his yelps and cut the power, the gators, with their slashing tails, had broken one of his legs and three of his ribs.

"You see what I mean about respecting the beasts," Mooch pointed out.

While he was laid up recuperating she spent a good deal of time, he noticed, tinkering with the beasts. On the monitors in the control room he could see her moving from exhibit to exhibit with her tool cart, and often he would hobble into the workshop to find her performing surgery on mother boards.

"What's up?" he asked her.

"Improvements," was all she answered.

As soon as he was sufficiently mended to roll about the disney in a wheelie, Orlando painted a second warning stripe at a safer distance from the exhibits. Crossing this new line would trigger sirens. He was afraid to think of what crossing the old line would trigger, now that Mooch had fiddled with the controls.

In addition to the new warnings, the sight of the engineer gimping around in an invalid's chair, his leg in a cast, had a chastening effect on the visitors.

Several weeks passed without further mishap. Then a gang of teenagers dared one another into invading Monkey Island. They soon regretted the venture. Inflated coconuts rained down on them, followed by monkeys with flailing limbs. The strength of these little manikins astonished even Orlando, who after all had built them. Their ferocity could only have come from Mooch. For some reason he could not shut down the power beam, so he had to rescue the battered teenagers with ropes. All were bruised, and three were hospitalized with mild concussions.

The Overseers wheeled Orlando to the local station, where they read him the laws regarding public hazards. They could revoke his license right now, without further ado. But instead they gave him ten days to clean up his act. At the end of that period, a squad would come round to make sure everything was perfectly safe. In the meantime, the disney would be closed.

"I'm afraid we'll have to tame them after all," Orlando told Mooch later.

"Good luck," she muttered darkly.

Against doctor's orders, he abandoned the wheelie and heaved himself onto crutches. Mooch grumped along at his heels. He would begin by disarming the monkeys, which peeled back their lips and gibbered at him. "Cut the power," he said to Mooch.

"It isn't on," she answered.

He gazed across the moat toward Monkey Island, where a baboon was shaking a fist and a gorilla was torturing a tire.

"Then how are they running?" he asked.

"I've been meaning to tell you about that."

"About what?"

"Well, you see, it didn't seem right that we could turn them off and on anytime we felt like it. I figure a creature's not free so long as you can flip a switch and shut it down. So I rigged them up with batteries."

"Batteries!" he shouted. From a palm tree on the island a chimpanzee regarded him soberly, like a scholar perusing a footnote. Orlando tried to recall the fatal moment in which the yearning for wildness had blossomed in his heart. Was it before or after he liberated Mooch from the lion's jaw? Sighing, he told her, "Well, I'm going to have to unplug them."

"I wouldn't try that."

"Why? What will they do?"

"I don't know."

"You don't *know*?"

"That's the point. Nobody knows. Nobody *can* know. They're wild."

Staggering on the crutches, he turned his back on Monkey Island and glanced across the way at a sullen water buffalo, which was idly demolishing its manger. "You mean they might tear me limb from limb?"

"I wouldn't be surprised."

Orlando thought hard. The squad of Overseers would be making their inspection in little more than a week. If they found even one hazard in the place they would put him out of business.

Scowling at Mooch, he said, "How long before those batteries run down?"

"Five years, I figure. They're the best you had."

"Five *years*!" He closed his eyes, then quickly opened them again as he lurched dizzily on the crutches.

"You want your wheelie?" she asked.

"I want my *disney*. My calm, peaceful, poky old disney."

"But I thought we were turning it into a wildlife sanctuary," said Mooch hotly.

"I didn't want to go this far." He gazed around forlornly at the growling, pawing, sinister brutes. "The place is too dangerous to keep open. But I can't afford to close it. Can't you see? It's my livelihood. It's my *life*. And now you've ruined it."

The girl appeared to chew on this verdict as if it were the first bite of the worst food she had ever tasted.

The gates remained locked, with a sign out front explaining that the disney was closed for renovations, while Orlando tried every trick he could think of to disable the mechos. Fortunately, Mooch had not altered their territorial imprints, so they did not stir from their pools and caverns and dens. Thus he could ride his wheelie up and down the aisle without being attacked, so long as he did not cross the warning stripes.

Jabbing the beasts with poles only upset them, and resulted in the loss of poles. Surrounding the exhibits with energy shields had no effect, nor did he have any luck with neutralizing rays. He was soon at his wits' end.

Mooch, all this while, holed up in her room. Orlando had to work alone, muttering to himself in a fury that gradually changed, over the course of the week, to despair. He scarcely slept. On the appointed day, the Overseers turned up at the gate and blared through a bullhorn to be let in. There were six of them, big hulking bruisers, with meltguns and truncheons dangling from their hips. In their silver uniforms and mirrored helmets, they towered above Orlando, who met them in his wheelie, the game leg jutting before him in its cast like the masthead on a ship. "Gentlemen," he pleaded, "I haven't quite whipped things into shape. If I could have just a few more days . . ."

"You've had a few days already, Mr. Spinks," the lead officer growled.

"I don't think it's wise, just now, to go—" Orlando began.

The officer cut him off: "We'll decide what's wise and what isn't, Mr. Spinks."

"But, sir—"

"Shut up and keep out of the way."

When Orlando still protested, the officer waved his gloved hand. One of the Overseers grabbed the handles of the wheelie and shoved Orlando roughly against a ticket booth.

Holding his breath, Orlando watched them divide into three pairs and scatter among the exhibits, their helmets gleaming, truncheons in their fists, meltguns swinging.

Soon the first scream tore through the disney. Within minutes, four of the six men came staggering back to the gate, their jumpsuits torn and bloody. They dumped Orlando on the ground, hurled the wheelie aside, and pounded him with truncheons and questions.

"I don't know *how* they got that way!" Orlando cried, wanting even then to protect the child. "It just seemed to happen! I lost control over them!"

Meanwhile the lead officer was shouting instructions into his wristphone, summoning riot control. Soon a flight of shuttles would glide overhead, melters would spew their vaporizing beams, and everything Orlando had made would turn to mist.

He writhed on the ground and wailed. A boot landed in his ribs, on top of the old fracture, and other boots were drawing back to kick when suddenly one of the Overseers yelled, and they all took off running for the street.

Wincing with pain, Orlando sat up to watch them go, then snapped his head round and stared back down the main aisle of the disney. A tide of beasts came surging toward him, snakes and leopards and ostriches, lumbering gorillas, monkeys shuffling arm in arm, a pride of lions and a family of dragons, one-eyed monsters and monsters with two heads, pandas and camels and goats, and right at the front was a phalanx of elephants, and perched atop the largest of these, like a diadem, sat Mooch.

The ground shook from the thud of feet. Orlando scrambled into the ticket booth to keep from being trampled, and the flame in his ribs made him whimper. "Mooch!" he bellowed. "Stop!"

She did not speak or wave or even look his way as she went riding out through the gate.

Just then shuttles appeared overhead, melters zinging. Orlando shielded his eyes and blinked up at the sleek machines. The pilots cut down the laggards at the rear of the troop, then started blasting their way forward through the ranks.

"Not the elephants!" Orlando hollered.

The shuttles glided relentlessly onward, erasing the beasts with sweeps of the melters. Mooch did not slow down, her knees tight around the swaying neck.

Orlando dragged himself into the wheelie and rolled in pursuit. The people who had been riding the belts or strolling in the plazas when the beasts broke out had all fled into buildings. Awestruck faces gazed from every window.

The air tingled from the melters. Here and there a paw or tail escaped the annihilating rays and lay among the rubble like discards from a costume shop.

"Don't hurt the child!" Orlando screamed, his voice drowned out by the whine of engines.

The pilots vaporized every last creature except for the lumbering elephants, then briefly held their fire. The shuttles hovered a few meters above Mooch's head like blind fish that had blundered into the air. Then one by one they picked off the outriding elephants, until only hers remained. Still she kept on, leaving Orlando farther and farther behind.

"Mooch!" he screamed. "Give it up, child!"

Far down the avenue he could see the elephant lean its vast, wrinkled forehead against the wall of the city. The beast reared on its hind legs and slammed against the translucent dome, reared and slammed, while Mooch held on to the flapping ears. The city's very foundations seemed to shiver from the blows. The girl stared ahead, as though trying by the force of desire to pierce the barrier and see, beyond a stretch of ocean, the lost green hills of Oregon.

At last the melt-beams sliced into the elephant's heaving buttocks and hacked through the spine and knocked out the legs, and down Mooch tumbled, still clinging to the huge gray ears.

Wheeling along, the stiff leg thrust forward, Orlando barged through the crowd of medics and Overseers and buzzing onlookers to where she lay. She was sitting up, dry-eyed. When he reached for her, she sagged into his arms, but did not make a sound, her quivering jaw firmly shut, as if she had caught some rare bird of grief in her mouth and meant to keep it safe.

✷ ✷ ✷

Waking later that night to the sound of clinking tools, he rose from bed, scrabbled for the crutches, and hobbled through the darkened shop. He found the girl leaning over a workbench, where a ropy monster was taking shape. It was made of flexible conduit, and looked like an enormous snake. Where the fangs would be, she had mounted one of his diamond cutting-wheels.

"Mooch, you know we're forbidden to make any more beasts."

"It's not a beast," she said.

"It looks like a python. Big enough to swallow you."

"It's just a machine. A tool."

He fingered the cutting wheel. "A tool for what?"

"Don't worry," she said, "I'll drill above the water line. I don't want the city to spring a leak."

The misery swelling in him felt so enormous he imagined his skin tearing. "Mooch, there's ocean out there."

"It'll be water-tight," she explained, slapping the conduit. "And I'll install a motor and propeller."

"But even if you make it to shore, you'll never survive in the wilds."

"I'll take my chances."

"Child, you can't go!"

She turned on him a look so dark it was as if two holes had suddenly opened in the roof of the city and the fathomless night were staring in. She said, "Are you going to stop me?"

Orlando retreated from her glare, lay down again on his bed, but could not sleep. The clink of tools played through the empty hours. The sound made him think of teeth clacking against bone, and he remembered his father telling him that wolves caught in traps would gnaw through their own legs to get free. After lying awake the rest of the night, thinking about Mooch and wolves and the numberless ghosts of wild things, he decided to let her go.

The Circus Animals' Desertion

Alone in his minibus after tucking the beasts in their lairs for the night, Orlando Spinks was stitching a tear in the lion's mangy hide when the monkey sidled in to announce that the lion itself had vamoosed.

"Without its skin?" said Orlando, forlornly raising the shabby pelt from his lap.

"You got the number on that ticket, chief," said the monkey, which picked up slang from street kids.

Orlando closed his eyes and thought about the skinless lion slouching through the spick-and-span avenues of Oregon City, its naked chassis gleaming in the fluorescent light, the wires in its belly snarled like spaghetti, computer chips encrusting its forehead like jewels. Blinking his sad eyes open, Orlando asked, "Where did it go?"

The monkey turned its palms toward the ceiling and hoisted its shoulders. There was a faint whining of motors, a gritting of metal on metal, and the monkey froze midway in its shrug.

"We're getting old together." Orlando sighed. He was feeling more rheumatic than ever. This news about the lion only made his joints ache the worse. Opening a door in the monkey's belly, he fiddled with the controls. When this did no good, he slapped it between the furry shoulder blades, and the monkey finished its shrug. An amnesiac fog dimmed the glass eyes.

"What's happening, chief?" the monkey said.

"You were telling me the lion's running away."

"I was?"

"Yes, you were," said Orlando wearily, knowing he was losing the tug-of-war with entropy. He could almost see the circuits unraveling in the monkey's brain. "Now please go back to the trailer and keep watch on the others."

There were not many others to watch—the kangaroo, anteater, musk ox, boa constrictor, crow, and twin pandas. These seven, plus the monkey, were all that remained of the three dozen beasts he had constructed for his Spinks Animal Circus. One by one they were leaving him, slinking away in the night. Where could they possibly go? He imagined the grizzly bear shouldering its way onto the pedbelts among the commuters with their briefcases, the python coiling its great length into elevators, the elephant blocking the doorways of shuttles at rush-hour, the gorilla swinging from balcony to balcony. None of them had ever been caught and returned to him, even though his name was clearly stamped on the control panels. He was afraid to ask the Overseers for help, because he had run afoul of the authorities several times already—and all on account of Mooch.

❋　❋　❋

Now Mooch was a sore point for Orlando. In fact, she was several sore points. He had encountered her eight years earlier, back in the glory days when he was engineer of beasts for the Oregon City Disney. When he came upon the girl, her top half was stuffed inside the jaws of his principal lion, the predecessor of the lion whose tattered skin Orlando was now holding in his lap. Rescued from the rubber teeth, the girl began scolding him for having made the animals so prissy and jovial.

"They ought to be wild, like in the old days," she said, "so they could eat people."

"If Lion was wild," Orlando pointed out, "you'd be well chewed by now."

"If this bag of gears was alive, I wouldn't be fool enough to stick my head in his gullet."

Her name, she said, was Mooch. "Rhymes with pooch. An old name for a dog. You ever heard of dogs?" She lived at the Serenity Orphanage, where she had been dumped as the fruit of a genetic experiment gone wrong. "Shoot artificial sperm into an artificial egg in a synthetic womb and—shazam!—you get a baby without parents." At birth her orange hair stood out from her scalp in unruly curls. Her eyes were a startling green and turned up at the corners like the eyes of a fox. Her ears were shaped like teacups and her nose was vanishingly small. Despite her peculiar looks, she might have been adopted had she not begun talking when she was four months old, and walking a month later. She spooked everybody who came shopping for a baby at the orphanage. As soon as she could hack the digital locks, she began escaping. But the cops always brought her back. Now age twelve, she would be stuck there until she turned eighteen. To her way of thinking, the ancients had been a good deal kinder when they dumped orphans on a hillside for the wolves to raise. Now, if somebody would take custody of her—some old man, say, with a steady job and a clean record—the orphanage would be glad to get rid of her.

"As a matter of fact," she said, surveying the disney, "I wouldn't mind staying here, helping you out, livening up this place."

Orlando knew right then he was in trouble. He had never found the nerve to ask a woman to live with him, and had never been permitted to breed, so he had no offspring and no mate. The children who came to romp through the disney set up currents in his heart like the motions of fish. At night he had only the machines to talk with. He often wished that the stuffed animals he had inherited from his grandfather, the taxidermist, would climb down from the walls of his workroom and rub their shaggy flanks against his knees.

So when Mooch popped out of the lion's mouth and offered to let him adopt her, Orlando promptly, if unwisely, agreed. The orphanage had him filling out forms for six weeks before they surrendered the girl into his care. He framed the certificate that declared him to be Mooch's guardian, and hung it on the wall of his workroom between a moose head and a swordfish.

Thinking back on his year with the girl, as he did now while mending the lion's pelt, a year of wonders and miseries, Orlando still could not bring himself to regret a minute of it. First she had persuaded him to make the beasts more natural, which meant smelly and shiftless. When this failed to impress the visitors, she urged him to make the beasts vicious. He was one of the first victims of this new regime, getting a leg broken in the alligator pen. While he was recuperating, Mooch programmed the beasts to attack anybody who put a foot in their territory. When the Overseers tried to shut the place down, four agents were mauled, and in the hubbub Mooch rode an elephant out through the gates of the disney, leading an exodus of beasts down the shocked avenues. Every last beast was vaporized. Only the girl was spared. While Mooch and Orlando were awaiting trial, she built a drilling machine, bored a hole through the wall of the city, and escaped. Waking up to find her gone was the worst pain he had ever felt.

The Oregon City Disney was torn down while he sat in prison. In its place rose feelie-farms, eros parlors, game arcades, a thousand-and-one delights. Orlando spent the three years of his sentence fixing gadgets for the warden and thinking about Mooch. The warden tried to get him to stay on past his allotted time and live rent-free in her guest room, since she had a houseful of appliances and one gismo or another was always breaking down. But Orlando wanted out. "If you ever change your mind," said the warden, sorry to see him go, "come back here and I'll put you to work."

He would need work, all right, since the authorities had confiscated his meager savings and auctioned off his possessions to pay for the damage wrought by Mooch's beast parade. Only his grandfather's collection of stuffed animals, protected under the law as family heirlooms, had been saved for him. When he crammed these moldering trophies into the minibus which he had bought with his prison-leaving bonus, there was barely room enough inside for his bed, stove, and workbench.

The city gave him a job repairing robocops. Although he frequently bungled his dealings with people, Orlando was a wizard with machines. Within a few months he was foreman of the maintenance crew, and had a private shop where he could tinker in his off hours. First he built the lion, in memory of Mooch. Next he built the monkey, rigging it with all the smarts he could program into it, so he would have somebody to talk with during his lonely hours. Then he went on to construct a rhinoceros, a gorilla, the two pandas, a Komodo dragon, an abominable snowman, a unicorn, a griffin—every beast, in fact, for which his grandfather's taxidermy collection provided suitable materials.

He left the monkey running all the time, for the sake of its chatter. The other beasts he fired up only one or two at a time, because there was so little space for them to do their tricks inside the bus. "Not room enough to swing a cat in," his grandfather would have said. Certainly not room enough for a gorilla to beat on its chest without hammering dents in the neighboring animals. As soon as he had saved enough money, Orlando bought a trailer to hitch on behind the bus, then a second trailer and a third.

"You ought to take that show on the road," advised his assistant, also an ex-con, who was angling for the foreman's job, "and see what you can milk out of the rubes."

"That's exactly what I'm going to do," Orlando replied.

He painted SPINKS ANIMAL CIRCUS in scarlet on the sides of the bus and three trailers. He furnished the trailers with grass-colored rugs and plastic trees and inflated stones, to give the effect of wildness. When everything was ready, he quit his job at the robocop shop, charged up the bus with a six-month supply of electricity, and set out to astonish the populace.

The populace—chiefly gawking youngsters and hawking oldsters—was intrigued, if not astonished. When the yellow bus and blue trailers rolled to a stop, loudspeakers blaring with circus tunes, a skeptical crowd gathered. The spindly, whitehaired man who climbed down from the bus and announced himself in an age-cracked voice to be Orlando Spinks, ringmaster, did not promise to be much of a showman. But once he got cranked up, hooting and hollering about the wonders of his mechanical beasts, he wasn't half bad. He wore white boots, white tuxedo, white top hat, and purple bowtie.

One by one his beasts lumbered down the ramps from the trailers, ambled onto the sidewalk, and did their turns. Bears sat up and begged, lions roared, elephants chomped bales of seaweed, dragons blew smoke rings, rabbits did cartwheels. "All authentic!" the ringmaster yelled while skipping among them, prodding the beasts with his whip.

But no sooner had the sidewalk show begun than the white-suited ringmaster was herding the beasts back into the trailers and crying, "See the whole show inside! Tonight at eight! Tickets only a hundred C's!" When no one stepped forward to buy a ticket, he lowered the price to ninety—then eighty, sixty, forty—all the while bellowing, "Wildness on stage! Animal secrets revealed!" Only when the price dropped to fifteen, and the ringmaster in despair began climbing into his bus, did a few people step forward to buy tickets.

These rare customers later reported to friends that there wasn't much more to see at the inside show than they had already seen for free on the street. The liveliest part of it was the skin-and-bones ringmaster, this Orlando Spinks, who cavorted among his sluggish beasts, balancing on a zebra's back, wrapping himself in a boa constrictor, making a tiger dance. The audience yawned. The more they yawned, the more frenetic the ringmaster became, revving up his beasts until they twitched through their routines in seconds. When the rhino thrust its horn through the trunk of a plastic tree and stopped dead, as if shot in its tracks, and the wolf began gnawing on its own hind leg, shorting wires and producing a billow of acrid smoke, the audience stood up. "Wait!" the ringmaster yelled, "there's more to come!" Ignoring him, the customers shuffled outside to find juicier entertainment elsewhere.

Orlando loaded up his bedraggled menagerie and drove the caravan to a new neighborhood. There he met with pretty much the same reception. "My kid's got fancier dolls than that!" somebody might yell during the tease performance on the sidewalk. "When's the show gonna start?" somebody else might yell halfway through the gala performance inside the rented hall. It was discouraging. People had no eye for art, and even less of an eye for nature. On his first swing through the precincts of Oregon City, Orlando earned just enough to pay for recharging the battery on his bus and restocking his larder.

Early in his second season, a heckler cried, "Is that all they do, jump around and growl?" Orlando shouted back, "Did you expect them to juggle? Do backflips? Tell jokes?" After weeks of such heckling, and after wrestling with his conscience, Orlando reprogrammed his beasts to perform such foolishness and worse. The pandas now played duets on the organ. The cheetah's spots and the tiger's stripes now blinked on and off like neon signs. The dragon swooped through the air, puffing smoke. The orangutan sped about on a motorcycle. With its long snout, the anteater tossed rings at the unicorn, which caught them on its horn. And so, in one way and another, all three dozen beasts were turned into buffoons.

Even though the audiences grew, attracted by these antics, Orlando took little joy in his success. Mooch would despise him for what he had done to the animals. She was a great believer in wildness, and a terrible scold about dumbing down nature. His ears burned from imagining what she might say about these shenanigans.

❋ ❋ ❋

"There's grumbling back in the trailers, chief," the monkey reported to him one night during that second season.

"How can there be grumbling? They're all turned off."

"I hear what I hear," said the monkey sagely.

Limping back to investigate, still wearing his white ringmaster's tuxedo, which was beginning to fray, Orlando placed an ear against each of the trailers in turn, and sure enough, through the aluminum walls there came a low rumbling.

"What are they saying?" he whispered to the monkey.

"You got me, chief."

"Who turned them on?" The monkey shrugged. When Orlando flung open the door of the first trailer, a hush fell over the beasts. "What are you all chattering about?" he demanded. No answer, only a heavy shifting of limbs. Angry and more than a little frightened, he rushed down the aisle throwing switch after switch until every beast was stilled. "You keep a sharp eye," he told the monkey, "and if anybody comes messing around with them, give a howl."

"Right you are, chief."

Later that night the tiger slipped away, the first of his animals to desert him. Swearing that it never saw the great cat slink off, the monkey advised, "You want things watched, you ought to build a dog."

"I might just do that," Orlando threatened.

He made inquiries in the neighborhood, referring to the escaped tiger in the vaguest terms, to avoid scaring people, but nobody had seen anything prowling about on all fours. Orlando was stumped. How could a tiger, even a mechanical tiger, meander through the streets of Oregon City without being noticed?

A few days later the mystery multiplied, for the gazelle and griffin vanished during one of Orlando's afternoon naps.

"Could be they eloped, hey chief?" said the monkey, trying to cheer him up.

Orlando was not cheered. He was downcast. He was mystified. It could only be a judgment on him for having made fools of his animals, who were abandoning him like sailors jumping ship to escape a mad captain.

He doubled the locks, shortened his naps, and slept at night sitting up on a recliner in the middle trailer.But still the beasts stole away. While Orlando was counting up the skimpy gate receipts after an evening performance, the gorilla and sasquatch disappeared. Surely this was a judgment. Mooch had warned him against trivializing nature to put on a gaudy show. Repentant, he began reprogramming the animals, erasing their tricks.

The audiences dwindled. Who wanted to pay to watch a herd of furry robots sit around and scratch imaginary fleas? After a while, only hecklers showed up, mocking the fidgety little ringmaster in his threadbare tuxedo. They flung taunts at him, and he flung them back. While the circus animals lounged and gaped and snored, the ringmaster danced. He juggled plastic coconuts. He twirled his baton. He performed tricks of derring-do with knives and torches. At the conclusion of his act he removed the top hat to bow, and his white hair blazed in the house lights, sweat stains showed beneath his arms, his legs trembled. Occasionally a few onlookers clapped halfheartedly. But more often Orlando heard only the scuffle of departing feet.

After his performances, he would put his animals away in the one remaining trailer—he had sold the others to pay his bills—and go sit on the bus, worn out, heartsick. He didn't bother locking up the beasts; if they were so eager to go, let them go. When he thought of the future, he saw only a black hole—his entire menagerie run off, the rented halls echoing to his solitary voice.

In the weeks following the lion's departure, all the remaining beasts except the twin pandas and the monkey stole away. Orlando sold the last trailer and moved the remnants of his circus into the minibus. He couldn't do anything flashy with two lethargic pandas and one sassy monkey, but he tried putting on a show anyhow. Four drowsy bums made up the entire audience, and they only sat through the performance because Orlando had given them bags of popcorn along with free tickets. Once they had gobbled the popcorn, all four began snoring. Orlando shut off the lights and left them in peace. The pandas and the monkey shambled out behind him, nylon joints and aluminum ribs showing through rents in their hides.

Later, he was soaking his feet in a tub of hot water, staring down at his bunioned toes, when the monkey scampered in to say, "You were dynamite tonight, chief."

"Sure—that's why they fell asleep," said Orlando

"Only at the very end, chief. You had them fagged out from clapping. You razzled and dazzled them. You wore down their buzz buttons."

"Buzz buttons?"

"What I'm saying, chief, is when you slung those lariats and noosed the pandas, why, the crowd was wowed. You ironed out the wrinkles in their tickertapes."

"It's kind of you to say so."

"Nilly dilly," proclaimed the monkey, which exited by swinging from the light fixtures.

Perhaps he was only getting old, but Orlando could understand less and less of the monkey's lingo. It was spending too much time jabbering with kids on street corners instead of watching over the menagerie. Mooch would have been able to translate for him. She always possessed an uncanny sympathy with the beasts. Thinking about her, Orlando felt a cold wind whistling through his heart. She had kept him young, right up to the moment when she made her escape. He couldn't stop wondering what had become of the girl. After drilling through the wall of the city, she might have found shelter in one of the outlaw domes that floated on the ocean nearby, or she might have made her way to the mainland. He liked to think of her living in one of the rebel communities on the Oregon coast, orange hair in defiant pigtails, feet bare, roaming the forests, tracking real animals. When he tried to imagine the wilds, all he had to go on were impressions gleaned from videos and old books, and from tales his grandfather the taxidermist used to tell about life before the Enclosure. Orlando hoped the atmosphere was no longer poisoned, the water no longer foul, the soil no longer radioactive, for Mooch's sake. She would be twenty now, primed for life. If she ever thought of him, which he doubted, she might assume he was still locked up, or dead and gone.

Orlando gazed down at his pink toes. Water dripped from his chin into the tub. He was sitting in this mournful posture when the pandas sauntered up from the rear of the bus. They drew near the tub and sat on their haunches. He had never rigged them to speak, and so they gazed at him in silence, four dark melancholy eyes.

"What are you two after?" he asked, to break the silence. The twins gathered into their faces the primordial sadness that pandas seem to have been designed to show. "You can't be after juice, you rascals. I just charged you up yesterday."

Orlando was on the point of calling the monkey, which could often interpret these melancholy silences, when the pandas turned away and shoved out through the front door of the bus into the alley. Orlando hurried to the window, his wet feet squishing on the floor. He drew aside the curtain to spy the monkey stooping beside an open hatchway in the alley and beckoning to the pandas. As they waddled to a halt beside the hatch, the monkey opened the control panel on each panda's chest and punched buttons. Their sorrowful eyes suddenly shone with yellow lights. Orlando's own eyes opened wide with a sense of outrage. The monkey bent over to whisper in their ears, and then down the pandas went, through the hatchway, beneath the pavement into the bowels of the city.

The monkey was creeping back toward the bus when Orlando flung open the door and charged into the alley. "You traitorous pile of scrap metal! You double-crossing babble box!"

The monkey covered its skull with balled fists to ward off blows. "What's wrong, chief?"

"Wrong!" Orlando yelled, circling the monkey, looking for an opening where he could smash the devious beast. "Didn't you just help the pandas run off? Is that how they've all disappeared?"

"Lay off! Listen a minute!"

"I'll lay you out!"

Just then a robocop rolled into the alley, headlamp fixing Orlando and the monkey in its glare. A vision of how he must look—bare feet, trousers rolled up, suspenders dangling, white hair spiked about his gleaming pate—sobered Orlando immediately.

"Problem?" said the robocop.

"My chief's going to turn me into scrap," the monkey cried.

Orlando gave a dismissive laugh. "We were just having a little disagreement."

"Then have it indoors," the robocop said. "It's 0200 hours."

"Is it, indeed? Time we were in bed." Orlando grabbed the monkey by one paw and dragged it after him toward the bus. Once inside, he peeked through a window to make sure the robocop was rolling away.

Meanwhile, the monkey wriggled free and clambered onto the workbench. "I can explain everything, chief. Just promise you won't undo me."

Orlando turned around, the anger draining out of him. He felt old, loose in his skin. So what if they were deserting him? He would hold nothing against its will, not even a mechanical beast. "Come on down," he said quietly.

"You won't turn off my juice? Won't tear me apart?"

"I won't. Promise."

Orlando sagged onto his bed. The monkey swung down from the workbench and squatted beside him, its fuzzy, triangular face wrinkled with concern. "Hey chief, don't blubber like that."

"It would take more than a bunch of mutinous machines to make me cry," said Orlando.

"They made me spring them loose, chief. They threatened me."

"The pandas?"

"The pandas, the lion, the griffin—all of them. They said if I breathed a word to you, they'd shred me into little bitty pieces and feed me to the recycle chute." The monkey crawled onto Orlando's stomach and clung to his shirt. "You won't let them do me that way, will you chief? I never told on them. You figured out the truth for yourself."

"Nothing's going to hurt you." Orlando ran a hand over the monkey's small skull. "Did they all go down into the tunnels under the city? Even the elephant?"

"We had to dismantle the elephant and hippo and other big bruisers. The gorilla carried them down in pieces. Even then it was a tight fit."

"What do they plan to do down there? Who's going to juice them up? Who's going to keep them running when their gears freeze and their circuits short out?"

"Oh, *she* will, chief."

"Who will?"

"The girl, you know. She's about as handy with tools as you are."

Orlando lifted his head from the pillows. "What girl?"

The monkey slapped both paws over its mouth. Orland peeled the paws away and repeated, "What girl?"

"They'll rip me apart if I tell," the monkey whimpered.

"I'll rip you apart if you don't!" Sitting up with a lurch, Orlando grabbed the monkey by its frail shoulders and squeezed.

"The Liberator! The one who led our ancestors out of the disney!"

"Mooch?" said Orlando, incredulous.

The monkey trembled, jerking its head up and down. "She's what they all ran off to."

Orlando heaved up from the bed, tossing the monkey onto the floor. He limped about, put on his socks and shoes, straightened his suspenders, knotted his purple bowtie, ran a hand through his hair. "Where is she?" he demanded. "No—don't tell me—show me!"

"You mean we're going to Mooch? Right now?"

"Right this minute."

"It's a long way, chief, and hard."

Orlando slipped his arms into the sleeves of his tuxedo jacket. "If those fat pandas can make it, I can make it."

"You're going to get your duds all filthy."

"Who cares? They're rotten anyway."

Mind awhirl, Orlando stuffed some food and a few tools into a satchel. He put fresh batteries in his headlamp and put extras in his pocket. Everything else he would leave in the bus. All that mattered was finding Mooch. After the monkey was recharged, it led the way, slithering through the hatch. Orlando followed, dragging the cover back in place and easing down the ladder. They set off along the echoing passage, the monkey skipping ahead with eyes ablaze, Orlando trudging behind with headlamp glowing. He thought of the yellow bus parked above, SPINKS ANIMAL CIRCUS painted on the side, its doors unlocked, and he hoped somebody would steal it or the robocops would haul it away. He could let it all go, and gladly, for now he was on his way, the last animal to desert his own circus, headed for Mooch.

* * *

Every now and again during that long meander through the maze beneath Oregon City, Orlando's body recollected its age and sat him unceremoniously down. While on the floor, he noticed a murky breeze flowing in the direction of their travels. It smelled of exhaust fumes and clothes dryers and neglected refrigerators. He decided the passageways must be drains for sucking away the city's used-up air. Fortunately, there was a thin current of fresh air near the ceiling, so by walking tall he could avoid gagging. The monkey had no use for air, foul or pure, so it pranced along. Whenever Orlando sat down to rest, it fidgeted about, darting glances forward, its eyes casting spears of light into the gloom.

"How did you ever find her?" Orlando panted during one of these dizzy halts.

"She found us, chief."

"She found you?"

"One night at the show, there she sat, wearing a black wig and welder's goggles, trying to go incognito. But we could see through that get-up. We knew her face from the photos all over your bus. The Liberator! Mooch the magnificent!"

She came so close without letting me know? Orlando thought. But then, what had she seen? An old man in a dirty tuxedo making a fool of himself. "Then what?"

"When she saw we got her ID, she beat it for the exit. Tiger trailed her, though, and then came back and growled the directions to me, and I've been passing them to the other mechs."

"Tiger made it clear to the mainland and back in one night?"

"Oh, no, chief. Mooch isn't camped in the wilds. She's down in the rag-and-bone shop."

"Where the devil is that?"

"The dump for burned out juice-jewels and frazzled magic boxes."

Translating his monkey's chatter, Orlando said, "You mean where they salvage electronics junk?"

"You got it. Mooch runs the whole shebang. She's got a shop that makes your old operation look minor league. After Tiger snuck back to the circus, I fired up all the beasts—to chew it over, you know—and we talked about how Mooch would goose our gears and smooth our circuits and set us all purring."

"Of course, of course," said Orlando absently. "She was a goddess to you. You'd heard me talking about her from the day I made you."

"Mooch ran in us like electrons, chief. We knew all the stories about how she'd sprung our ancestors from the disney. I mean, compared to her doings, your circus was Podunk city."

"I see," said Orlando. He had filled them with his own loving legends about the girl. No wonder they had run away to her. He sighed. The air near the floor where he was resting seemed to be congealing. Soon he would have to take out his pocket knife and slice his way through.

"You got a hitch in the get-along, chief?"

"Nonsense. I'm fit as a fiddle." Orlando heaved himself upright. "Lead on," he said, panting in the stale air. He wished he had a few spare parts for his own chassis—two knee joints, say, and a new ticker and a pair of air-bags for his wheezing chest. But he figured the original equipment would last him as far as the electronics dump. He had been there once on a field trip during school, and he remembered conveyors heaped with defunct devices, robots sorting through the junk and testing each scrap, cubbyholes crammed with salvaged parts, the teacher lecturing them on the text of "Waste Not, Want Not." Imagine little Mooch reigning over all that.

Would she even want to see him? he wondered, limping down the tunnel behind the monkey. She must have recognized him at the circus. And she must have known whose beasts kept arriving at her door. Yet all this time she had never said boo to him. But, then, why should she? What was he to her? Just a chump who had let her run loose in his disney for a year when she was a child. He was probably a joke to her, a pitiful old man, and she had come to watch him in his silly circus merely to confirm her judgment on that score.

Orlando's steps began to drag. His chest burned. Feeling more and more a fool, wishing he had never seen the pandas escaping down the hatch, he said to the monkey, "So you all conspired to steal away, one by one, and desert your maker?"

Over its shoulder, the monkey muttered, "A bunch of pure-D ingrates, right chief?"

"But you stuck around. Why?"

The monkey beamed its eyes at him, a blinding glare, and then looked ahead down the tunnel. "Oh, I thought about high-tailing it, but I knew you'd croak if we all ran off."

"You could have told me about Mooch long ago."

"Like I said, the others threatened to shred me if I squealed."

"But why did they care?"

"They figured you'd lasso them and stick them back in that rinky-dink circus."

"It *was* pretty wretched," Orlando conceded. Wanting reassurance, he added, "But you were going to stay with me, even if that meant being cut off from Mooch forever?'

"Not forever, no. Just until you cashed in your chips."

Orlando shuffled painfully along, his feet growing heavier with each step. "Mooch never sent back word that I should come?"

"Only word she sent back, chief, was don't any of us dare tell you her whereabouts, because she was afraid to see you."

"Afraid? Of me?" Orlando ground to a halt.

"She told us you hated her because she'd messed up your life. We swore you'd never breathed a mean word about her, and she said you were just hiding your feelings."

"Me hate Mooch? How could she imagine that?"

Orlando slumped to the floor of the tunnel, where the air seemed thick enough to chew. It smelled of parking lots, overheated circuits, spoiled food. He imagined that millions of people had already breathed this air and left in it their hearts' poisons and worn-out thoughts. The monkey jumped around him, tugging at his arms, jabbering. When Orlando's headlamp played over his outstretched legs, he noticed the stains, the ragged patches, the holes where his knobby knees showed through. It used to be quite a fine tuxedo. He couldn't remember why he had bought it. Sitting felt so good that he slid further down and lay flat. The monkey's malarkey played about him like a gang of kids yelling, and then it was gone. Orlando gulped for air, which came laden with whispers, kisses, curses, murmurs, and lies.

When light divided momentarily from darkness, the first object Orlando could make out was a woman's face, screwed up with worry, fox eyes peering from within a halo of orange hair. "Mooch?" he muttered. He felt a hand on his chest, where the burning had been so fierce, and the darkness washed over him again.

Mooch it was, all right. The monkey had fetched her—Orlando had passed out within a hundred meters of the dump—and she had come running with a cart and oxygen tank. She was amazed, lifting Orlando first onto a stretcher and then onto a makeshift pallet in her shop, at how little of him there was. She remembered him as bulky, a filler of doorways, and she found it hard to believe that this scrawny man was Orlando, who had offered to become her father and whom she had scorned.

"He made me show him the way," the monkey whined from its redoubt among the packing cases. "He's a holy terror when he's riled."

Mooch laughed, but softly, leery of waking her patient. Orlando was the most peaceable soul she had ever met. Whatever else might have changed in the eight years since she destroyed the disney and doomed him to prison, his deep sea of gentleness could not have evaporated.

"I'll jerk a knot in your tail later, Mr. Mud," she said to the monkey.

She gave Orlando a few more whiffs of oxygen, to wash the poisons from his lungs, and then pulled the blanket up to his chin and let him sleep. His old face, as cracked and stained as an antique leather purse, was beautiful to her. The rim of white hair encircled his bald scalp like frost-covered bushes around a winter pond.

"The show kept getting worse," the monkey said.

"You hush," said Mooch.

"It was bush. An old clown and his fagged-out beasts."

I reduced him to that, thought Mooch. To the monkey she whispered, "Why don't you go mess around in the warehouse with the rest of the menagerie?"

"They'll hammer me into a cookie sheet."

"No they won't. I told them to leave you alone."

"I want to see the chief when he wakes up."

"Go," Mooch hissed, "or I'll turn you into a squirrel."

The monkey scrambled away into the storage bay, where the refurbished circus animals were milling about. Mooch bent over Orlando and stroked his forehead, which was creased as if the skin were a letter that had been folded too many times. His eyes twitched beneath the lids but did not open. She felt ashamed, thinking of the pain she had caused him. During the year she had lived with him in the disney, loving him and afraid of loving, straining against the strange new bonds of affection, she had tormented him in every way her adolescent mind could imagine.

Despite the shame, Mooch looked back on that year as the brightest chapter in the gloomy tale of her life. The years before had been spent in the orphanage, and the years since had been spent first in the wilds, which turned out to be poisonous and murderous; next in a reform school, after she had surrendered to the Overseers; and finally here on parole in the bowels of the city, supervising the electronics dump, and living among machines, which she found more reliable than people. A single bright year amid twenty dark ones—a single kind man amid legions of the heartless—and she had been too stupid, back at age twelve, to realize how blessed she was.

Now here he lay on a pallet in her shop. Why had he come? For years she had longed for and feared such a reunion. Once, she had worked up the courage to go in disguise and watch him from the crowd during a circus performance. It was all she could do to keep from leaping into the ring and wrapping him in her arms. But she feared he would turn a cold eye on her, for he had good reason to hate her, and she couldn't bear such a rebuke. These past two years, each time one of his animals had come to her, shabby and confused, telling her stories about Orlando's pathetic circus, a new layer had been added to her guilt. Once the beasts found her, they refused to leave. They possessed an elaborate mythology about her, in which she figured as a savior, a mechanical genius, a comforter.

Orlando stirred, mumbled, and then resumed snoring. The smile on his battered face reminded Mooch of sunsets from her time in the wilds. She waited nervously. When he'd called out her name a few minutes earlier, he was still groggy, and she could read nothing in his face. Soon he would come fully awake, and she would feel his gaze on her, and find out whether she might be forgiven.

Orlando, meanwhile, was dreaming of his beasts. One by one they were returning, crowding around him, their pelts shiny, their eyes lit up with a secret they could not wait to tell.

Mountains of Memory

The mountains of Oregon City closed each night between 22:00 and midnight to allow for cleaning. Even in this spick-and-span metropolis, where dirt cost more per kilo than sugar, a mountain could become remarkably filthy in a day's time. Children climbing the flexiglass trees shook down a litter of twigs. Cups and wrappers spread about the vending machines like glacial moraines. Deltas of metal shavings accumulated at the ends of pedbelts. Hikers who refused to ride the belts, toiling instead uphill with the aid of trekking poles, often punctured the inflatable rocks, which then cluttered the mountainside like cast-off skins. Idlers on benches pared their fingernails and some even blithely spat on the walkways.

There were three such mountains in Natureland Park, out near the edge of the city where the curving, translucent dome met the sea. The summits rose high enough to offer views into the upper windows of skyscrapers. Molded with quickfoam over aluminum skeletons and named for the corporations that sponsored their construction, they were supposed to make up for the mountains of stone from which the citizens had been cut off by the move into the Enclosure. These days only old-timers, gazing at the fake peaks, could remember the Appalachians or Rockies or Sierras.

Each night, as the last of the idlers and gawkers withdrew at 22:00, detergents gushed from nozzles on the mountaintops and scoured the slopes. Drains siphoned the run-off into recycling vats down below, where the muck was reduced to its pristine molecules, which would be refashioned eventually into some new doohickey or other.

Mt. Texxon, tallest of the three, was honeycombed with caves. Stalactites dangled from the ceilings, mushrooms sprouted from the floors, albino crayfish speckled the walls, bats glided through the dank air, every feature having been made out of rubbery gunk. Hidden tubes dripped water into murky pools. The hollow chambers echoed with the grunt of circulating pumps. The psycho-architects who had designed Natureland Park, as they had designed every last nook and cranny of the Enclosure, believed that even space-age citizens would need some place for making stone-age retreats. The citizens thought otherwise. Each year fewer of them ventured into these clammy pits, and those who did often returned gasping from the gloom. So the caves were slowly filled by the groundskeepers with outmoded vegetation, deflated rocks, broken trees, shattered creek beds, sacks of frogs, tangles of snakes. These shaggy and bulging items only rendered the darkness more frightening. After a few spelunkers lost their wits in the labyrinths, the Overseers closed all entrances to the caves, leaving open only the ventilator shafts.

If, like Humphrey Tree and Grace Palomino, you were looking for a hidey-hole where you could stash away tons and tons of junk, then Mt. Texxon was just the place. The elderly couple had been collecting rubbish for years in the streets of Oregon City, not from any habit of tidiness, but, on the contrary, from a desire to spring a messy surprise on this oppressively neat hive. The two old scavengers usually reached the foot of the mountain at 24:00, an hour they persisted in calling midnight even though midnight looked no different from noon under the dome's eternal blaze of lights.

Tonight they arrived a few minutes early, while cleaning fluids were still pouring down the slopes. So they sat in their zip-carts talking over old times, which in their case stretched back nine decades. They had known one another since kindergarten in the suburbs of Old Portland. They married right after college, then served in the Pollution Corps, moving around the country as, bit by bit, the whole of North America was declared uninhabitable. They knew the history of one another's wrinkles. Over the years they had come to smell alike, a blend of fish oil and wintergreen. The sum of their weights hardly varied, so when Humphrey put on a kilo or two, Grace lost the same amount, and vice versa. By now they had loved one another so long that the edges of their personalities were fuzzing together. When either one began a sentence, the other could finish it.

Peering up the flank of Mt. Texxon, Humphrey sighed. "Won't be long now—"

"—before it's filled up," Grace added.

"Seems like only yesterday—"

"—when we started hauling."

At ninety-seven, Humphrey had a face that brought to mind a crumpled brown sack. Fortunately, Grace never gave a hang about looks. After his stint in the Pollution Corps he became a chip inspector, a tedious job from which he was now blessedly retired. His eyes and heart were electronic and one hand was synthetic, but otherwise he got by with his original joints and organs. Due to his monumental appetite, he had accumulated a big man's body on a small man's frame, so the flesh now sagged over his bones like a garment he would never grow into. Grace was three years younger, a retired dance therapist, not so quick on her feet since acquiring new hips and knees. Shriveled now, she possessed the antiquated beauty of a palace awaiting restoration. When she was feeling her oats, she still ran circles around Humphrey.

"What'll we do with ourselves when it's full?" he mused.

"Move on to Mt. Pepsicoke and start over," said Grace.

"Remember Pepsi?"

"Remember Coke? My mother would shake all the fizz out of it and feed it to me with a spoon when I had a fever."

Their youth was so far in the past it had taken on the blurry contours of myth. Grace was half convinced that her mother, an oceanographer, used to ride whales. Humphrey was persuaded that his coal-mining father had brought him ingots of goblin iron hot from the core of the earth.

At length the cleansing of the mountain was finished and the gates opened. Driving their zip-carts, which as usual were heaped with junk, Humphrey and Grace climbed the glistening slope. Everything shone as if newly made, the quickfoam gullies and hillocks, the flexiglass bushes and trees. Below, the avenues were marked out in a grid of lights, orderly, immaculate, as if Oregon City had just that moment crystallized out of the air like a snowflake. This geometrical perfection, false to everything they knew about the funk and mess of living, made the old couple grit their teeth.

While they had the peak to themselves, Humphrey and Grace climbed out of their zip-carts and peeled back the tarps and showed one another the treasures they had collected on their separate rounds that day.

"Twenty-seven cans," Humphrey announced, pointing out the highlights in his cargo bin, "five rags, two zippers, a pair of boxer shorts, a melted joy stick, and volume three of *The Anarchist's Handbook.*"

"Don't we already have the first volume?"

"It's down there somewhere." He thumped his foot on the roof of Mt. Texxon.

"Lord only knows where," said Grace. "Look here at this hubcap and this perfectly good catcher's mitt." She put on the mitt, which swallowed her tiny arm halfway to the elbow. "Chuck it in here, babe!" she sang, smacking a fist into the pocket.

Humphrey tossed her a doorknob, which she caught deftly. "Any spoons?" he asked. Because of his appetite, he coveted spoons above all other loot.

"No," said Grace, "but here's a fork."

"Ah, there's my sharp-eyed lass!" Humphrey kissed her full on the puckered lips. That was one of the fringe benefits of growing old—you could smooch whenever you liked and tell any busybody who objected to go take a flying leap.

"And would you believe four wigs?" said Grace.

"Isn't that a record for wigs?"

"I think it is. And they're good thick ones, too."

The blue wig that Grace was wearing had been acquired in this manner, as had the videocap worn by Humphrey, as indeed had the better part of their wardrobe. Her calf-length boots, for example, had been salvaged from a trash can beside the wading pool in Marconi Plaza.

They did not scavenge as a way of making ends meet, but as a hobby, almost an art. Unlike Old Portland, whose streets in the latter days had swarmed with bums and beggars and dumpster-pickers, Oregon City fed and housed every last soul. Collecting junk was not easy in such a sanitary city. Along with the moun tains, the streets and plazas were flushed daily, each quarter of the city at a different hour; and the recyclers down below gobbled ev-erything. No space station gliding in orbit, no ship cruising to the stars could have been tidier than Oregon City afloat on the Pacific. By timing their rounds, however, Grace and Humphrey scoured the avenues just ahead of the detergents, and thus managed to find, on most days, a cartful of trash: items of clothing, broken heels, foam cups, ad flimsies, toys, depleted batteries, electronic gizmos, belt buckles, even spare body parts.

People sometimes left stale food or wounded furniture in their path, imagining these old geezers had somehow fallen through the welfare net into poverty. Most people, however, encountering the two scavengers, looked the other way. The Overseers regarded them as harmless eccentrics. What did it matter if they hoarded rubbish?

After the day's discoveries had been admired, Humphrey and Grace rolled aside one of the pumped-up boulders, disclosing a ventilator shaft, through which they dumped their junk into the hollow crown of Mt. Texxon. As they listened to these new prizes clattering onto the hoard of rubbish below, they exchanged the sly prankish looks they had been sharing since kindergarten.

Once the boulder was back in place, they sat for a while atop the mountain, basking in fake sunlight, gazing down at the city. The icy glitter of the streets reminded them of the winter when the

Columbia River froze hard and they skated from Old Portland to Vancouver and back. That ice had gleamed with the same sinister perfection. The freeze would have played havoc with the spawning of salmon, if those marvelous fish had not already vanished.

"Will you look at that yucky color," said Grace.

Indigo vapor had begun spurting from vents on the nearby peak of Mt. Pepsicoke, forming imitation storm clouds that would never drop rain or snow but would merely hover beneath the dome like bruised angels.

"I don't like these sickly purples they're using on Tuesdays," Humphrey agreed.

"The old clouds used to remind me of purple iris," said Grace, "a color so thick you could spread it on toast."

"Toast," Humphrey repeated dreamily.

"Iris," Grace said, trying to get him back on the track of the conversation. "A flower so sumptuous it made me envy the bees."

"Marmalade on toast. Rhubarb preserves. Honey." Humphrey's tongue slicked across his lips as if he were prospecting for these vanished foods. "Apple butter. Watermelon pickles."

Once Humphrey began reminiscing about bygone foods, Grace had to let him run down. While he drooled through his epic of jams and jellies, she recalled her own vanished pleasures: the kiss of cotton on skin, the smell of dung from police horses, the raspy summer sound of locusts, the ooze of hot tar between her toes on a country road, the squirm of a kitten. So the two old people ambled on separate pathways back to the days before the Enclosure. They ended up gaping at one another, startled by the length of their memories, measuring how old they were by the remoteness of these things.

"All the same," Grace declared, "I wouldn't go back to those days for love or money. If we were still living outside, we'd be dead."

Humphrey nodded. "Killed thirteen different ways by poisons and radiation, starved to death, and shot full of holes in the bargain. Not to mention getting fried by ultraviolet rays and sizzled by microwaves and eaten up by acid rain."

"One of those alphabet chemicals—DDT or PCBs—would have rotted our bones."

"Druggies would have bonked us over the head."

"Warlords and bankers."

"Greenhouse effect."

"Smog."

They clicked their tongues in unison. At this point the first visitors of the day were gliding up the slopes on pedbelts or dawdling up on foot, toddlers tugging at leashes, kids wearing the masks of their favorite video stars, occasional elders as barefaced as Humphrey and Grace, all of them so fresh-looking they might have just been taken off a shelf and unwrapped.

"Here come the drones," said Grace. She stood up, beating the dust from her jumpsuit, stamping her boots on the mountain's pliable skin. The nearby trees wobbled and boulders bounced.

Humphrey laughed. "That's my Gracie, more powerful than an earthquake!"

"You'd better believe it," said Grace.

Day after day, the old scavengers wheeled through Oregon City, filling their zip-carts with refuse, castoffs, and lost articles.

Then at midnight they buzzed up the slopes to dump their haul. Eventually they decided it was time to see how much more rubbish the mountain would hold.

As the son of a Kentucky coal miner, Humphrey insisted that he should be the one to climb down the ventilator shaft. Grace protested, but he said, "No, no, ducky. Your flexy joints might give out. You stay up here and keep an eye peeled for the fuzz."

"Don't get your belly stuck down there," she warned.

He sniffed indignantly. "I am as svelte as an otter."

She snorted. "And don't go snapping your brittle old bones."

"And don't you be such a worrywart."

Fortunately, there was a ladder, or Humphrey would never have managed the descent. After some noisy reconnoitering, he surfaced again to declare, between labored puffs, "I figure we've got space for about another month's worth of junk."

"Only a month, and then no more scavenging?" Grace lamented. They had been working toward this moment for years, but now, having nearly reached it, she felt glum. Her face, pale and wrinkled, had the look of a snowy field crisscrossed by animal trails.

Humphrey, who loved every one of those wrinkles, was old enough to remember snowy fields. "Give or take a week," he said.

"When I was a girl, I never dreamed I'd grow up to be a bag lady!" She broke into a fit of laughter. "Remember how the scruffy old crones lugged their bags from one dumpster to another, picking up leftover pizzas and moth-eaten sweaters?"

Flowing easily into his wife's memories, Humphrey said, "And the winos near the Lighthouse Mission browsed in the gutters for cigarette butts, their eyes like holes in rusty pails."

"At night they'd wrap themselves in newspapers and sleep on benches."

"Or in cardboard boxes."

"Thank goodness nobody has to live on the street these days," Grace said. "You could, though, in a pinch. It's a regular cornucopia out there. Seems like the more stuff people have the more they throw away." She drew up her sleeve to peruse the gadgets strapped to her arm. A few of them kept time, although no two kept the same time. Out of old habit, she put one of them against her ear. But there was only silence—the vibration of crystals, the lunge of electrons. It was an overly tidy world, she thought, where time could slide by without ticking.

"What I'll never understand is the lost socks." Hoisting his trouser legs, Humphrey displayed two plump ankles, each one sausaged into multiple layers of socks. "How do people lose them, just riding around all day or sitting on their tails?"

"You've got me," said Grace. She gave a bewildered shake of her nearly hairless old head, which was adorned at the moment with a blond wig. "A body could fill up a closet after one day on the streets."

"Shoes I understand," he said. "You can slip out of them without thinking. Your hat could fall off in a crowd. I've seen people lose false teeth. I've seen tires fall off wheelies. No mystery there. But socks?"

"Remember when that lady at the lunch counter dropped her nose in the soup?"

"And she fished it out, snapped it on, and kept right on eating!" Humphrey's brown bag of a face crumpled with disgust. "I don't know what the world's coming to, Gracie. First we all move inside these bubble cities to get away from bugs and sunburn and poison rain and radiation. Live without threats from nature! And now everybody's redoing their faces, rewiring their nerves, replumbing their organs, replacing their joints. Where's it going to stop? With brains quivering in jars?"

"Who are we to talk?" said Grace, rubbing her knees. "I'm thankful for my new joints. And if you didn't have that ticker," tapping him on the chest, "your blood would turn to sludge and they'd make fertilizer out of you for the farmpods."

"You've got a point there." Humphrey lowered his eyes—his electronic eyes, he could not help remembering—and laced the fingers of his prosthetic hand into those of his natural one.

They lapsed into silence, feeling the full weight of their ninety-odd years. Entropy, they knew, was gaining on them.

✻　✻　✻

On the following nights, after dumping their debris, Grace kept watch atop Mt. Texxon while Humphrey drudged below in the caverns, laying out wires and relays and fuses. They had left passages through the rubbish for just this purpose. Over the years, they had pilfered the materials from demolition sites, including charges of plasty, which would go in last of all.

Here and there in the grottoes the shoring had collapsed, barricades of cardboard had given way, towers of cans had tumbled down, and so Humphrey had to proceed cautiously. As he crawled along, trailing wires behind him, he often found his way blocked by a rubbish-slide and had to backtrack. Twice the walls caved in on his very heels, and he was forced to grope his way out by side-tunnels.

After the second of these escapes, he slumped beside Grace on the mountain crest, gulping air. "If I don't make it out one of these days," pant, "I want you to go ahead," pant, "and throw the switch."

"With you inside? And me out here all by my lonesome getting grilled by the Overseers? Not on your sweet life."

"Forget I said it," he added quickly.

Her lips puckered and her face darkened under the blond wig. "I don't plan to go on living without you, Hump. So you stick around."

"All right, sweetums. Simmer down." He stroked her trembling hand.

"I can't stand the thought of staying on alone. You know that. With you gone, I'd be the only sane person left alive."

"Never you worry. We've got a lifetime hitch, you and me." He pecked her on the cheek.

Their minds running in parallel grooves, the two ancient scavengers thought of death.

"You know," said Grace after a spell, "when we lose our wits or our spunk, we ought to hold hands and jump down a recycle chute."

"Okay by me," said Humphrey. "Mingle our molecules."

She lifted the wig to scratch her scalp. "It still seems unnatural to me, dissolving people in a soup of acids, instead of burying them like they used to."

"Even when they planted folks in pine boxes, the worms eventually recycled them. Acids are just quicker."

She patted the wig back in place. "I'd rather feed worms."

"I wonder if there's a single worm inside the Enclosure. Maybe somebody raises them for experiments. To make protein burgers, say. We could donate our corpses to the lab."

"I don't know about you, kiddo," said Grace, bouncing to her feet, "but I'm not a corpse by a long shot. Let's go scavenge."

❋   ❋   ❋

In keeping with Humphrey's prediction, one midnight just four weeks later they found that Mt. Texxon would not hold all the rubbish they had collected. When Grace tried to mash in the left-overs, she could hear junk shifting ominously inside the caverns.

Humphrey was down there, crawling through the passage-ways, uncoiling wires. Headlamp bobbing, he squeezed into the deepest recesses of the mountain. He would have been glad right then for a pair of syntho knees. His natural joints were killing him. He wondered how his father had endured the pain and claustro-phobia during all those decades in the mines. A pack of hungry kids at home would make a man put up with just about anything, he supposed.

After depositing the last charge of plasty and hooking up the detonator, Humphrey sucked in his gut and started the long scramble toward the surface. Whenever he bumped the sides of the tunnel, the mass of junk shuddered above him. He made his way gingerly, thinking of his father crushed in that Kentucky mine, remembering his promise to Grace. From the walls on either side protruded the necks of bottles, rims of cans, strings, sleeves, artificial limbs, the edges of books, the corners of pic-tures, all compressed into strata like the mud of an ancient sea, but Humphrey scarcely looked at them, he was so intent on escap-ing. Then he noticed the bowl of a soup spoon jutting out. How could he have missed it? Gracie must have tossed it when he wasn't looking. Without thinking, he yanked the spoon from the drift of junk. A small quake buckled the props in front of him, lowering the ceiling.

That was royally dumb, he thought. Sinking to all fours, he crawled forward. He could hear other props giving way as the mass of debris shifted.

A few meters above him, Grace perched on a boulder, listening to the mountain as if it were a colicky baby. Each time it grumbled and heaved, she groaned. The quakes sent tremors up through the aluminum slope, through the elastic boulder on which she sat, through her bones.

"You all right, Humphrey?" she whispered into the talkie strapped to her wrist.

His reply seeped through the plug in her ear. "Little queasy down here, ducky. But I'll make it."

"You're not prospecting? Hunting for socks or spoons?"

"Heavens, no!" he panted. "Now hush."

She lowered the talkie from her lips. The Overseers could hear you blink your eye, if they happened to be listening in your direction. They could monitor your heart, and tell if one of the valves was sticking.

Grace kept an eye on the park gates, where early visitors would begin arriving within an hour or two. Most young people would ride the belts up the side. But many of the oldsters would climb on foot, mouths groping for air like stranded fish. She understood why they labored up these metal slopes, their hearts thumping, spots dancing before their foggy eyes. She was one of them, youthful in spirit despite her battered carcass, which had been mended with electronics and plastic. The artificial portions of her were numb, as if the surgeons had implanted lumps of emptiness in place of her knees, her liver, her right foot and left shoulder, all the failed organs and bones. Her own original flesh ached about these empty spaces, and her soul moaned through them like a ghost flitting through a crumbling house. There was nothing like a jaunt up the mountainside to revive the spirits.

She checked the most reliable of her watches. 01:20. "Hurry it up, kiddo," she whispered into her talkie.

For a moment only gasps leaked through the earplug. Then Humphrey muttered, "Going as fast as I can. Got to rest a bit."

"How's your ticker?" By way of answer, the thump of his heartbeat came slushing into her ear. "Sounds too fast!" she hissed. "How far do you have to go?"

A rasping noise smothered his reply as a quake shook the mountain.

"Humphrey?" she whispered.

"It's all right. A little slide. I'm digging through."

"Where are you?"

"The golf-and-garter tunnel. About midway."

"Here I come," said Grace.

"You stay put."

"Not on your life."

She donned a helmet and headlamp, pushed the boulder aside, and waggled down the ladder. If someone discovered their secret, so be it. Plan or no plan, she was not about to lose Humphrey. At the base of the ladder, where the rubbish tunnels began, she switched on the lamp and shuffled away into the gloom. From Humphrey's description, she recognized the mouth of his tunnel by the golf club elbowing out from the wall and the garter belt dangling from the roof. She crept on, careful not to touch anything but the well-packed floor. Another slide, she thought, and we'll both be sardines.

Within a few paces she came to a blockade where the ceiling had collapsed. Through the jumble she could hear the sound of Humphrey's quiet scratching, like a mouse trapped in a heap of cans. She began carefully working from her side, removing a pot, a crushed hat, a slipper.

His voice quavered in her ear. "Gracie?"

"You were expecting a troll?" She pried loose a clump of masks, a bag of hair clippings. "I hope your daddy was better than you at shoring up mine shafts."

"His mountains were made of rock," Humphrey wheezed, "not skittery junk."

The sound of his scratching drew closer. Grace clawed her way forward. A chunk of roof fell on her, but she wriggled free and kept going. Presently she cleared away the chassis of a wheelie, and there was Humphrey's light. In a moment his hands appeared through the opening, the fleshy one bleeding and the synthetic one leaking oil. Then his lovely crumpled face appeared. She squirmed forward and hugged him fervently, ignoring the spoon in his breast pocket.

It was nearing 02:00 when they rode their carts down Mt. Texxon. They stopped at the light-fountain in Marconi Plaza, too excited to fret over their aches. They sat on the fountain's edge, with colored lights swirling around them. Up in Natureland Park, the three mountains gleamed, still deserted, for the new day's visitors had not yet arrived. The entire city looked as though it had been hatched that very minute, the pure architecture of thought.

Humphrey drew the switchbox from his pocket and asked, "You want to do it?"

"Let's both," said Grace, placing her hand on his.

Together they released the safety and pushed the button.

There was a deep rumble. The sides of Mt. Texxon bulged and the top burst open, spewing smoke and ash and clots of junk into the enclosed sky of Oregon City.

Traffic stopped. Riders leapt from pedbelts and stood gawking as the air filled with shoes, wigs, spinning bottles and glinting cans, snarls of wire, printed circuits, posters, all the leavings of their lives. Gobs of plastic settled on walkways. Grease filmed windows. Scraps of metal pelted awnings and roofs. The citizens were struck motionless, gaping at the ruptured mountain, their avenues grown suddenly hazardous, while a blizzard of forgotten things blanketed the city.

Holding one another's hands, Grace and Humphrey rested solemnly on the fountain's lip, two old-timers with long memories, recalling the real mountains and volcanoes of their youth.

Oregon City ground to a halt. Gears and switches seized up, pedbelts froze, lights flickered whimsically, fountains spewed at crazy angles, smoke alarms wailed, fire sprinklers doused offices and stores, overturned wheelies blocked the avenues. The Overseers' shuttles could barely navigate through the soupy air. Their cones of light shone down on chaos. Cleaning robots made little headway against the mess, their tires skidding on oil smears, their brushes gumming up, their pincers snagging. In the end, soldiers were called out to deal with the emergency using those primitive tools, shovels and buckets and brooms.

Terrarium

Phoenix thought of her as the barefooted walker. On a day when the pressure inside Oregon City and inside his own head seemed no greater than usual, no more conducive to visions, he emerged from his apartment and there she was, pacing in the wrong direction on the pedbelt. By matching her stride to the speed of the conveyor the woman managed to stay at the same point in the corridor, just opposite his door. Bustling along, yet never stirring from her chosen spot, she reminded Phoenix of the conjoined whirl and stillness of a gyroscope.

This prodigy backed him rump against his shut door. He looked down, but not before catching a glimpse of red hair escaping from the woman's hood, cheeks glowing through a skim of cosmetics, green gown actually darkened with perspiration below the arms and around the neck. The corridor trapped her smell, the reek of a hot animal. She was a throwback, he told himself, aroused and ashamed. By lowering his gaze he hoped to give the woman a chance to withdraw from his life. Sight of her naked feet sent his gaze skidding back up to her face, and so he had the misfortune to be staring into her luminous green eyes when she turned on him and said, "It's called walking, you idiot."

Abruptly she stopped her pacing, and the belt carried her out of sight, bare feet and all, beyond a curve in the hallway.

Phoenix emptied his lungs. The ventilator soon banished her smell, but the image of her face, flushed and naked beneath the film of cosmetics, stuck fast in his memory. He went on to work, easing from pedbelt to escalator to elevator, and eventually to the roller-chair that carried him to his desk, where he bent as usual over satellite monitors. But rather than hunt for solar flares, hurricanes, ozone gaps, storm fronts, or the thousand other signs of nature's assault on the human system, his eyes kept tracing the shape of the woman's face in the cloud patterns, the bulge of hip and breast in the contours of continents.

After work, instead of gaming or chemmie-tripping, he went straight home. There was no barefooted woman pacing outside his door, of course, since the pedbelts were crammed with riders. He pressed a thumb to his lockplate, then stood for a minute in the opening, watching the double stream of riders. Their feet were shod, their legs still, their heads properly hooded or wigged, their bodies hidden beneath gowns, their faces masked. No one returned his wary glance.

It pained him to enter the apartment. The room's neatness suddenly oppressed him. Nothing invited his touch—not the sharp angles of his furniture, not the glinting console, not the wall murals that were just then shifting their designs to mark a new hour. The air smelled of nothing, tasted of nothing. He tossed a pillow on the floor, left a cabinet standing open, dragged a few costumes from their hangers, but without any real hope of disturbing the order of the place. Slumped in the softest chair, burning his lips on a cup of narco, Phoenix scrutinized the geography of his life, seeking some wild place that might accommodate the longing aroused in him by this barefooted woman.

Days ticked by. Each morning before work he peered out through the spyhole in his door, but with less and less fear—or was it hope?—of seeing her. Just when his life was composing itself again, when clouds on the Earthsat monitors were beginning to resemble clouds again instead of lips and ankles, one day he looked out and there she was, pacing along in sweat-darkened green. The lens of the spyhole made her appear swollen. Her naked feet churned and her bulbous head, fringed in red curls, bobbed ridiculously. Wondering how such an unappetizing creature could have enthralled him, Phoenix opened the door. It was a mistake. Her full stare caught him. Moist cheeks behind the glaze of makeup, long-boned feet, swim of legs beneath the gown.

This time she pronounced the words icily: "It's called walking. You should try it. Melt away some of that flab."

By reflex, he smoothed the cloth over his cushiony stomach. Flab? How dare she refer to his body. The chill in her voice implied that, while he had been moping around with her image spiked into his brain, she had forgotten him entirely.

"Do you mind?" she said, never breaking stride. "There's less traffic here. Fewer zombies to compete with."

He shook his head no, then in confusion nodded yes, unsure what he was answering. The woman kept up her treadmill stride. Phoenix shilly-shallied in his doorway, immobilized by a snapshot view of himself as he must appear to her: bouffant wig of iridescent blue, face painted to resemble the star of Video Dancers, every inch of flesh cloaked in a moodgown. He could not bear to look down at the garment, which was doubtless a fireworks of color, reflecting his inner pandemonium.

"I don't mind," he said, his nostrils flaring with the scent of her. "Why should I mind?"

"There are lots of drecks who do," the woman said.

She smiled, and he winced. The smile, the private sharing of words, the eye contact, the exposed face—it was all coming in a rush, shattering the rules of sexual approach. Unwilling to name a body part, he stammered "Do your walking things hurt?"

"Never. That's why I go barefoot, to keep them tough."

"And why have them tough?"

"So I can walk barefoot."

"But why walk at all?" he demanded in vexation. Before he could slice into her circular reasoning, passengers trundled around the curve, and the woman, with no attempt at disguising her smile, crossed to the other belt and rode away out of sight.

For a long time Phoenix stood in his doorway, hoping. But traffic thickened in the corridor and the woman never reappeared. Or maybe she did pass again, duly costumed and painted, lost in the crowd. Passing, she might even have seen him, but without being able to distinguish him from the hundred others who were decked out this morning in iridescent blue wigs and the painted face of that video star. Phoenix felt paltry, lurking there on his threshold, at once conspicuous and invisible.

Finally he surrendered to the day, to work, an afternoon of lightshows, an evening of brain-puzzles at the gamepark, and then a restless night on the waterbed. The barefooted woman stalked through his dreams. An extra dose of narco failed to soothe him. A bout on the eros couch, with the gauge spun all the way over to visionary delight, offered only mechanical relief. Neither drugs nor electronics could blank the screen in his mind where the woman's image kept burning and burning.

Desire melted away what little order remained in his life. The apartment grew shabby. Friends stopped scheduling daykillers with him when he failed to show up a second time or a third. His costume suffered, at first from neglect, and then from a striving for idiosyncrasy. Phoenix wanted to be visible to the woman when he met her again. So he hauled out unstylish clothes and flung them on in outrageous combinations. His wigs grew increasingly bizarre. His face paint appeared slapdash, as if applied in the dark by a vindictive cosmetician. Wherever he went in Oregon City the glances of passersby nipped at his heels.

At work the satellite photos looked more than ever like a collage of lips and ankles and trailing hair. His supervisor made him rewrite a third of the eco-warnings, and advised him to cut back on the narco. But Phoenix was not applying narco or any other balm to his inflamed heart. Nothing half so vivid as this love-ache had ever seized him before, and he was in no hurry to escape the exquisite pain.

Days off work he spent trying to discover some timetable in the woman's exercise. But he had no more luck than the ancients had at predicting sunspots. When she did loom into sight, he kept indoors, not yet ready to meet her again. Every night he paced with naked feet around the perimeter of his room. Five steps and then turn, five steps and turn; blisters multiplied on his soles. After two weeks of this, questioning his own sanity, he could walk for half an hour without panting, and his feet began to leather over.

Training on the pedbelt was more risky, only possible late at night, when anyone else traveling through the corridor would most likely be as eccentric as he. Soon he was able to stay abreast of his room for an hour. Laboring to counter the belt's motion, he did not feel like a gyroscope—he felt like a lunatic.

On one of his 3:00 AM training sessions, he was puffing along, oblivious, when her voice broke over him from behind:

"So you tried it?"

Glancing back, he met the achingly familiar stare. "Yes. I wondered what it was like."

"And what do you think of it?"

"It's interesting." Witlessly he repeated, "Interesting."

They paced side-by-side, two lunatics out for a stroll. From the corner of his eye Phoenix enjoyed the woman's profile, her skin showing more nakedly than ever through the paint, her legs kicking against the loose fall of gown.

"Good for the heart and lungs," she said.

"I suppose so," he replied, shocked by her language.

"And legs."

He loosed this sexual word without thinking: "Legs."

The woman blithely continued, as if she were in stage four of the mating ritual. "My name is Teeg Passio."

He could sense the expectant twist in her body as she waited for a response. "My name? Oh. Sure. It's Phoenix Marshall."

"You're not offended? About exchanging names?"

"No. I don't really accept all the . . . well . . . the formalities."

"They're stupid, aren't they?" She dismissed the mating code and his lifelong decorum with a stroke of her arm. "All this business of when you can look in another person's eyes, when you can swap names, when your little fingers can touch! Idiocy."

Phoenix heard himself agreeing. "Yes, it's like a web."

"Cut loose, is what I say."

"Loose?" He stilled his tongue, alarmed by the turmoil she had stirred in him. Sweat trickled down his face, no doubt streaking the paint, dampening the collar of his moodgown.

"How often do you walk?" she asked.

"Oh, every day. Sometimes twice a day."

"Any special time?"

His eye was caught by the surge of flame-colored hair along the borders of her hood. His fingers twitched. "Morning," he said, quickly adding, "or night, just about any time. My schedule's flexible. And you?"

Her smile seemed to raise the temperature in the corridor several degrees. "I don't keep a schedule. But maybe we could set a time, meet for a walk. That is, if you—"

"I would. Yes, very much," he said hastily.

"I know places we can walk without these conveyors."

"Anywhere's fine."

"Shasta Gamepark, then, south gate, at 1600 tomorrow." She lifted a palm in farewell.

"Wait," he begged. In a panic he cast around for ways to keep her, fearing that such an improbable creature might not survive until tomorrow. "Do you live in Portland Complex?"

She jerked a thumb domeward. "Seven floors above you."

"And what brings you through here for exercise?"

"Looking for a walking partner."

"Oh." Again he scrambled for words. "And why do you walk?"

"I'm in training."

"For what?"

"For going away."

※　※　※

Unlikely as it seemed to Phoenix, Teeg did meet him at the gamepark, where they strolled for an hour on the glass pathways, avoiding chemmie guzzlers and merrymakers. "Remember skating on these," she asked him, patting the scuffed walkway with her foot, "back when kids used their legs?"

Legs again. She would say anything. "Like so," he replied, assuming the bent-knee stance he had perfected as a boy on skateboards.

Teeg laughed. "There's hope for you yet."

On the following day, they ventured down into the bowels of Oregon City, along pipelines marked EXPLOSIVE, through tunnels pungent with brine. His thighs quivered from the incessant thrum of pumps and extractors. "You forget the whole city's afloat," she told him, cupping a handful of ocean water to sniff, "until you come down here. We forget a lot of things."

Other days, as they wandered among the green vats of the hydroponics district or between the huge whirling energy-storage wheels of the power zone, Phoenix discovered parts of Oregon City he had known about only from hearsay, and, in his anarchic talks with Teeg, he discovered parts of himself he had never known about at all. Signals kept arriving from neglected regions of his body—aches at first, then pleasures.

She was a squall of questions. What work do you do? Who are your parents? Any children? Ever go outside?

And so he told her about his training in meteorology, his job studying satellite images ("Because I have a good eye for patterns," he boasted, "something the computers still can't match."), and he told her about his mother's death in the 2067 fusion implosion at Texas City, about his father's three-year drug coma; told her his sperm was duly banked away but remained unused; told her he had never stuck so much as his nose outside the Enclosure; told her, in a voice that surprised him with its urgency, how restless he felt, how lonely, how trapped.

All the while Teeg was nodding yes, yes, that is truly how it is, and between questions she was telling about herself: most of her life spent in the wilds, shifting about the Northwest with her mother, who had been in charge of dismantling Anchorage, Vancouver, and Portland; her own work now back outside the Enclosure, in the wilds, fixing communications terminals; her eggs used for nine—or maybe eleven, she forgot—babies, all of them grown inside other women; mated three times, never happily, never long, twice with men and once with a woman.

"You're licensed to go outside?" he asked.

"Why so surprised?" she answered. "You think all those pipes and tubes and transformers maintain themselves?"

"But aren't you a risk, having grown up outside?"

"Not many people will take the work. Too messy in the wilds, too dangerous. And those who do, except the suicidal maniacs, know enough about the Enclosure's defenses to forget sabotage. The most I could do is stay out there after some job and never come back."

Phoenix pretended to be absorbed in watching his brazenly naked feet scuffle along beside hers. She had him so rattled, he had given up trying to calculate which mating rules they were breaking. "Do you think about that sometimes—staying outside?"

"Sometimes," she confessed, then after a few more steps she said, "Often. All the time, in fact. I've only lived in the city maybe five or six of my twenty-seven years. Here's the place that seems alien to me," arms sweeping overhead, the loose sleeves fluttering like wings, "and outside is home. Coming back inside is exile."

One moment the dome seemed to Phoenix impossibly high, higher than the unroofed sky, and the next moment it seemed a cruel weight pressing down on him.

"Coming back in," she added, "is like crawling inside a huge sterilized bottle."

A wave of claustrophobia nearly choked him, like the bitter taste of food long since swallowed. He stopped walking, halfway across Marconi Plaza, and the city snapped tight around him. Glide-rails sliced the air into hectic curves; towering offices and apartments shimmered with the trapped energy of a million lives, tower after tower as far as eye could see. The sudden pressure of the city was so intense that he did not notice for several seconds the lighter pressure of Teeg's hand on his arm.

"You never felt that before?" she asked gently.

"I guess I did," he answered, "I just never admitted it before. The frenzy—it's always there, like death, waiting. But I shove it out of mind."

"Keep things tidy."

"Exactly. Tidy, tidy. And then at night I lie in bed and a crack opens in my heart, and blackness creeps out, engulfing me." He stopped abruptly, ashamed of his passion.

"Yes?" she urged.

But he was too shaken to say anything more.

They parted without planning their next walk. Phoenix rode the belts home, aware for the first time in weeks of the alarmed glances provoked by his haphazard costume and bare feet. People must think he was crazed, afloat on chemmies, reverting to hairy beasthood. Somebody would report him to the health patrollers, for rehabilitation. But he could rehabilitate himself, could fight down the chaos that Teeg had loosed in him.

Safely back in his room, he put everything in its place, ran the sanitizer, gulped a pair of balancers. He scrubbed himself, dressed in his most fashionable moodgown and wig, then applied a fresh mask, painting carefully, copying the face of a crooner whose poster hung beside the dressing mirror.

All that day and the next he rode through the city, catching a lightshow, visiting eros parlors, simming a basketball game, clinging to his old entertainments. He played 4-D chess with one friend, designed murals with another, resumed lackadaisical mating rituals with two women who had nearly forgotten him. And yet he still felt the print of Teeg's hand on his arm, still heard her voice, so confident in its anarchism, still saw around him, not a city, but a smothering bottle.

After three days of this charade, he gave up and called Teeg. She gazed boldly from the screen, her face unpainted, her mouth a grim slash. "I've been sick," he lied to her.

"Sick." She echoed the word as if it were a place he had gone to visit.

"How about a walk today?" he asked.

"No walks. I'll come to your place tomorrow. Bring a map disk from work, okay? Thousand-to-one scale will be fine."

"What for?"

"I'll tell you tomorrow. Make sure it's got the Oregon coast between latitude 43 and 46," she went on in a voice as tough as the soles of her feet. "You'll do that, won't you?"

"Sure, but—"

Her face hovered on the screen like a forbidden planet, then vanished, leaving him to wonder what drove her to ignore the mating rituals, what urgency in her burned through all rules.

※ ※ ※

The relief map shone upon the wall screen as a snarl of dunes, cliffs, inlets, and river beds, each landform a distinct hue. The disorder of it made Phoenix feel slightly nauseous.

"You don't carry your own maps on repair trips?" he asked.

Teeg was crouching near the screen, tracing the shape of a bay that hooked into the coast like a bent finger of blue. "No. My shuttle's programmed to go wherever the job is. I climb out and work on transformers, maybe, or solar dishes, or travel tubes. I look around, but usually have no idea where I am."

"Usually?"

"I recognize a few landmarks from knocking around with my mother, especially on the coast near Portland, the last place she dismantled." Teeg crooked her finger to mimic the blue hook of water on the map. "This bay, for instance. Mother called it Wolf's Leg. We used to go wading there."

"In the ocean?"

Her eyes turned smoky, with the sudden anger he had glimpsed that first day after gawking at her bare feet. "Yes, the ocean. The stuff we're floating on, the stuff we're mining and tapping for energy and growing food in and pumping through the city every day in billions of liters. What's wrong with wading in it?"

Phoenix forced himself to look at the muddle on the screen. The only straight lines were the tube routes, angling north to Alaska and south to California or trailing away eastward, where further maps would show them reaching the land cities of Wyoming and Iowa, the float cities on Lake Michigan and Ontario, then further east to the pioneer float cities along the New England coast. Every line not showing a feature of the Enclosure was crooked, jagged, bent. Queasiness finally made him look away from the screen.

"You're moving out there someday? To stay?"

"I might."

"It's madness. Sure death."

"If you don't know what you're doing."

"And you know, do you? A few childhood memories, and you think you know how to survive in the wilds?"

"I can survive."

"Alone?"

Her fists unclenched, her body relaxed. "If need be."

For the next few days her answering tape informed him she was meditating, or at the clinic, or on a mission, somewhere tantalizingly beyond reach. When he finally did track her down, overtaking her at the base of the fire stairs as she began her daily climb, she told him she was about to leave for a seminar in Alaska City. Something to do with thermionics.

Casting aside restraint, he pleaded, "Can I go with you?"

"Phoenix—"

"I can arrange leave. We can talk after your classes. Walk around. See the sights. The disney's got mechanical beasts—"

"Phoenix, no. This trip I'll be very busy. Understand?"

Breathless from the stairs, he halted at the next landing and let Teeg climb on ahead. The determined swing of her hips and the angry strength of her climbing, so alien to everything he had been raised to believe about the body, convinced him that she really would slip away from Oregon City one day, enter that chaos of the map, and never look back. That would mean annihilation—first of the mind, cut off from civilization, then of the body, poisoned or broken or devoured by the wilds. Dizziness sat him down upon the landing. The metal felt cold through his gown. With eyes closed he listened to Teeg's bare feet slapping on the stairs above him, fainter and fainter as she climbed.

Yes, the work coordinator assured him, Teeg Passio was on a two-week leave. Yes, the Institute informed him, a Teeg Passio was signed up for the thermionics seminar. But when Phoenix reached Alaska City, driven there by his desire to see her, he found that she had not registered with travel control, nor with the health board, nor with the Institute. His return to Oregon City was delayed by a leak in the sea tube—one of his colleagues may have failed to warn about a tsunami—and by the time his shuttle was on its way he felt crazed. The curved walls, the molded seats, the loudspeaker babble: everything squeezed in upon him. Bottle, he kept thinking, glass bottle.

Back in Oregon City he could discover nothing more of her whereabouts. He was tempted to call the health patrollers and report her missing, but that would only get them both in trouble. Nothing to do but wait, and turn over the possibilities one-by-one like cards in a game of solitaire: She had lied to him about going to Alaska? She had been mangled in some piece of machinery? She had gone outside to stay? Perhaps all she wanted from him were the maps. Discovering he was a meteorologist, she might have lured him into walking just to get hold of them. But no, that was foolish. How many people would have opened their doors to find her pacing, barefooted, and felt only revulsion? She couldn't have predicted this craving the sight of her would trigger in him.

In those two weeks of fretting he discovered how little presence of mind his ordinary life required. He traveled through the city, performed the requisite bows and signals in conversation, processed skeins of images, fed himself, even played mediocre chess, all without diverting his thoughts from Teeg. He was convinced she had gone outside, into the chaotic world of the map. At odd moments—while a lightshow played or the eros couch worked its electronic charms—he would visualize the map in all its unruly colors, and imagine her as a tiny laboring speck lost in it, wandering through mountains, wading in the blue hooked finger of water.

If she came back—when she came back—he would find some way to keep her from ever again putting him through this agony. Make her take him along next time. But not outside. Somewhere human, safe, the inland cities, the spas. Anywhere but the wilds. He would beg her to change jobs, never leave the Enclosure. And if she insisted on going, he would inform on her as a health risk, get her wilder-license revoked.

Then she would be trapped in this bottle as surely as he was. Trapped, but alive, shielded from that disorder out there, from disease, from weather, hunger, beasts, pain. This yearning for the wilds was simple nostalgia, he told himself, a mix of childhood memories and old books. Yet part of him was not persuaded, the part that trembled when he was in her presence.

His fingers shook as he punched the health hotline number. He explained his concern to the rubbery, passably human face of the mechano on the screen, but without giving Teeg's name.

"Only licensed wildergoers are permitted to leave the Enclosure," the mech told him, its jaw slightly out of synch with its voice. "Such personnel must be sanitized before re-entry. Any persons breaking this code, either by leaving without authorization or by returning without decontamination, constitute an infection threat, and will be treated as beasts."

"What does that mean?" Phoenix asked.

"One who deliberately endangers the human system becomes a part of Earth—a beast," the mech explained. Within seconds a form headed INFECTION ALERT slithered from the printer.

Fingering the sheet, Phoenix said, "And if a wildergoer breaks the rules?"

"First offense, revocation of license. Second offense, quarantine. Third, exile. Fourth, execution." The mech paused for what seemed to Phoenix a carefully measured interval, before asking, "Do you wish to report name and circumstances?"

"No. I'm just curious. I have no evidence."

"Very well." Again the measured pause, the scrutiny by a counterfeit face. "Infection from the outside is the gravest threat to the human system. You do not wish to report?"

"Not at the present time."

Only when the mech vanished did Phoenix realize that he had been addressing it in polite mode, with face turned aside, eyes lowered, body rigid, as if this digital phantom were the most appealing of human strangers. Two weeks without Teeg, and already the web of inhibitions was tightening around him again.

❋　❋　❋

The messages he left on her answering machine pleaded with her to call, yet when Teeg did finally appear it was not on the phone but at his door, hood thrown back to reveal an unkempt blaze of hair, face bare of paint yet reddened in a way he had never seen before. It was like having a bomb delivered.

"You're just back from the seminar?" he asked her carefully.

"I never went to Alaska City," she admitted.

Watching her pad familiarly about his room, Phoenix looked for some taint of wilderness. Her ankles and wrists, jutting from the hem and cuffs of her gown, were the same uncanny shade of red as her face. Did the sun do that? Her smell ran like a fire in his throat. He sensed a lightness in her movements, a thinning of gravity, as she pranced and fidgeted.

"So where did you go?" he said.

She yielded him a faint smile. "Away."

"Outside? For two weeks?"

"Wolf's Leg Bay, to be precise. Look." From the pouch in her gown she tugged the map, now tattered from repeated folding. Cross-legged on the floor, she spread it across her lap and eagerly pointed where he expected her to point, at the blue finger of ocean that hooked into the Oregon coast about 44 degrees. "It was the place Mother and I used to go, all right. The water's colder than I remembered, and the beach is narrower, but it's still lovely."

"You were there all by yourself? With beasts and poisons?"

"The only beasts were a few bedraggled sea lions and gulls."

Illustrations recollected from childhood began streaming through his mind. "You saw actual sea lions?"

"Not only saw them—heard and smelled them. And the rock flowers! The spray! You've got to come see."

And so she went on and on, in a delirium of talk, tracing her explorations on the map, pulling at his hands as if to lead him there that very moment, looking up occasionally to read his face. The desire he felt for her, and the dread, swelled to encompass the sea lions, the gulls, the ferns and flowering bushes she described in her rapt voice.

"Fossils!" she cried, as if the word alone should convince him to share the delirium with her. "Leaves and shells and even— once—a three-toed footprint between the layers of slate. And in the shallows of a drowsy river I found some tall reeds. Cattails, Mother used to call them. Isn't that a name? And birds! Why doesn't video ever show any landscape with birds and trees? Oh, just come look!" And she grasped both his hands and tried to dance him round the room. But his legs would not bend, his whole body was rigid. He wrenched his hands free.

"Teeg, promise me you'll never go outside again."

She laughed once, harshly. "How can you say that? Haven't you been listening to me?"

"You can't recreate the old world. You can't crawl back into your mother's lap. All that's finished."

"I don't need to create anything. It's all there, waiting. All I have to do is walk into it."

"To a brute's death."

Stretching her arms wide, she spun in a circle, gown and hair aswirl. "Do you see any wounds?" He shrugged, avoiding her stare. But she tugged him around until he was facing her again, looking into her inflamed eyes. "Hasn't your body taught you anything after all these months of walking? We were made to live out there, shaped to it," she said, her voice softening. "Humans have lived in the Enclosure thirty years. And before that our ancestors lived outside for hundreds of thousands of years."

"In misery, sickness, and fear."

"Not always, not everywhere. Some people lived well, in peace and plenty."

"In Eden, I suppose."

"Listen, Phoenix, I know what I'm doing. I've been stashing supplies and equipment outside one of the stations ever since I went to work on the repair crew."

"You can't go back."

"Who said anything about going back? I'm going forward."

"No!" He clapped hands over his ears, frightened by what she was offering.

"Phoenix, please listen—"

"No no no!"

When at last he looked up, she was gone, the door standing open. On the threshold lay a hand-size wedge of grey stone. Stooping warily over it, he could see the faint imprint of a leaf in the surface. With a stiff tablemat he scooped up the stone, held it near his face. There was a damp, dusty smell. The veins of the leaf formed a riotous maze of lines that reminded him of the map's labyrinth of rivers. Had it been decontaminated? Where had she found it, in what mire out there? For a long time he hesitated, fingers poised above the stone. Then at last, gingerly, he touched the mazy ridges. The delicate lines of the fossil proved hard, harder than his cautious fingers.

❋ ❋ ❋

The stone felt cold in his palm, slick with perspiration, as he shifted from foot to callused foot before her door. This was her doing, the calluses, the twitching in his legs, the yearning for escape. Passengers streamed by on the belts, whipping him with glances as he debated what to do. But he ignored them, and that also was her doing. Should he report her, get her license revoked, then try to talk her into sanity again? Could he betray her? Or should he let her make those journeys outside, each one longer, until, one day, she failed to return? Could he actually go out there with her? His heart raced faster than it ever had from their walking or stair-climbing.

At last he rang, and the door clicked open. For the first time he entered her lair, smelling her, but unable to see anything in the dim light. He groped his way forward. "Teeg?"

"In here," she called.

Her voice came from a second room, visible only as a slip of blue light where the door stood ajar. With halting steps, hands raised to fend off obstacles, Phoenix picked his way through the darkness toward the stroke of light. As he approached, the door eased open, forcing him to shield his eyes. In the brightness he could make out Teeg's silhouette—not naked, surely, but with arms and legs distinctly outlined.

"I found this," he said, lifting the fossil in open palm.

"That was for you to keep," she said. "A gift for parting."

"I didn't come to return it. I want you to tell me what it means . . . what you want . . ." He halted in confusion. The hard edge on her voice, the blue glare, the inner turmoil made his eyes water. "You've got to be patient with me."

"So you'll have time to file that infection alert?"

"I didn't mean for you to see that."

"No, I'll bet you didn't."

"I won't file it. I can't."

She studied him. "Why did you get it, then?"

"I wanted to keep you safe, keep you inside."

"Well, I won't be kept inside, not by you or the healthers or anybody else."

His eyes still watered, but he could follow her swift movement as she paced about the room gathering vials and cassettes and food capsules into a suitcase. It was a shimmersuit she wore, silvered to reflect sunlight, skin-tight to allow for work on the outside. Even in stage five of the mating ritual he had never seen a woman so exposed.

"You're not going back outside?" he demanded.

"I'm not waiting here to be arrested."

"You're going right now?"

"I hadn't planned on it. Not yet, not alone. I wanted a few others, to build a little colony." A shove from her boot sent the case skidding. "But I'm tired of explaining. You're the fifth one I've tried, the fifth walker, and you're all the same. Maybe you want your body back, I tell myself, maybe you want out of the bottle. But no."

"You never asked me to go with you."

"I didn't want to spell it out. I wanted you to hunger for the wilds the way I do." Her anger drove her prowling back and forth in front of him. Beyond her, under hanging blue lamps, he could see a glass tank filled with a writhing mat of green. Could they be plants? In the city?

Her glimmering figure drew his eyes. "But how can I want what I've never had?" he protested. "This is all I know." His gesture was meant to include the domed city, the travel tubes, and the other nodes of the Enclosure he had visited, always inside, always insulated from the beast world.

She stopped her prowling in front of him. In the clinging suit her body trembled like quicksilver. Her stare no longer made him wince. Her eyes were the same grey-green as the slate he still held stupidly in his hand. "All you know," she murmured, grasping him by a wrist, "then come look at this."

She led him to the tank, drew him down to kneel with her and peer through the glass wall. Inside was an explosion of leaves, tendrils, stems, dangling seed pods, bright blossoms like concentrations of fire, all of it in colors so vibrant they made Phoenix quiver. His eyes hunted for a leaf that would match the fossil she had given him, while his thumb searched out the imprint in the stone. But there was too much activity in this amazing green stillness for him to see anything clearly.

"It's a terrarium," Teeg said. "A piece of Earth."

He ran his fingers along the glass, expecting to feel heat radiating from these intense creatures. But the tank was cool, sealed on all sides. "They're alive?"

She laughed at what she saw in his face. "Of course they're alive. That's dirt, the brown stuff."

"But how—closed in like that?"

"Wise little beasts, aren't they?" And she used the word "beasts" tenderly, as he had never heard it used before. "There's your chaos," she said, "that's what you're saving me from."

Phoenix started to protest that this was only a scrap of Earth, without animals, without tornadoes or poison ivy or viruses, without winters. But his tongue felt heavy with astonishment. He could not shift his gaze from this miniature wilderness, at once so disorderly and harmonious.

"Well," she said, her fingers tightening on his wrist, "will you go?"

"I might," he answered. And then, uncertainly, "I will."

Quarantine

The only troublesome items Zuni had not allowed the surgeons to replace were her eyes. Both lungs, one kidney, various joints, even the valves of her heart, those she had been content to let go, for they did not seem to be intrinsic parts of her. Let the doctors fiddle with her ears or pancreas, she would not care. But if she ever gave up her eyes, the ones she had used to design the Enclosure, to memorize the contours of Terra, to trace the shifting tones of daylight, then she would no longer be Zuni Franklin. Would surgeons consent to be fitted with new hands? They should have realized that an architect lives in her eyes.

So when drugs no longer cleansed the blight from her retina, she had to put up with dimming vision. And when she announced her plans to retire from the Institute for Global Design at age seventy-six, nine years early, everyone assumed her balky eyesight was to blame.

"Are you afraid blindness would spoil your work at the Institute?" an interviewer asked her on *Meet the Magicians*, a show that treated the ability to understand mathematics as akin to wizardry.

"It is true that I no longer see things as I once did," Zuni answered.

"You mean you can't see well enough to work on blueprints?"

"I mean that vision changes with age."

The interviewer gave up trying to straighten out her replies. He knew that better minds than his had been stymied by Zuni Franklin's ambiguities. They were seated in her office, surrounded on three sides by display screens and consoles. The room was as stark and impersonal as an operating theater. Zuni had deliberately kept any trace of herself from showing, for fear of giving away her masquerade. The fourth wall, of glass, overlooked the towers, plazas, and pedbelts of Oregon City, a dazzling metropolis she had largely imagined. The sky show for the afternoon was an electrical storm, so projectors flashed sullen clouds upon the inside of the dome and loudspeakers muttered with thunder.

"So what are your plans for retirement?" the interviewer asked.

"My plans would be puzzling to you, I'm afraid," Zuni said.

"But surely you won't abandon your lifework?" The interviewer gestured overhead at the suspended model of the Enclosure, a spherical web of tubes and nodes. Each tube represented a transport artery, each node a land- or float-city, and the emptiness inside the sphere stood for Earth.

Zuni pressed fingertips to fingertips and gazed at the earnest young man. They were all so earnest, these children of the Enclosure. "My mission is accomplished," she declared.

"And now you'll write a book about your career?" When Zuni waved the idea aside, the interviewer tried again: "Perhaps you'll travel?"

"I have a journey to make," Zuni conceded.

"To the lunar colonies? The asteroids?"

"Not so far."

"Ah, then you'll be traveling on Terra, exploring the Enclosure?"

179

"On Terra, yes. Where else but Earth?" Her white hair was braided and neatly coiled into a bun; her replies were neatly bound in a smile. Like the antiseptic room where she spoke, everything about her was scrubbed clean of self.

"Will you be lecturing? Teaching young architects?"

"No, I will be learning again, from the wisest instructor."

"From Rosenbarger? Chu? Sventov?" The interviewer named the only Terran architects whose fame rivaled Zuni's.

"None of those." She guessed the man's age. Under thirty, certainly. He would have been born in the 2050s, after the Enclosure. "You wouldn't know this teacher at all."

For a week or two the media poured out rumors concerning her future. Zuni Franklin, dismayed by blindness, would have herself vaporized and blown into the air of her beloved Oregon City. On the contrary, she would have her face rebuilt and begin life over as an eros parlor hostess. No, no, she would disguise herself and lurk through every dome and pipeline of the Enclosure, like a queen incognito, inspecting the empire she had helped construct.

Perhaps, some commentators reflected, she was merely impatient to get on with the business of evolution, to push Homo sapiens further from its animal origins, toward the realm of pure energy. She might stow aboard a lightship. She might experiment with chemmies, with trances, with psi-travel. Or she might even be the first person to have her brain transplanted into a cyber-field, and thus liberate mind entirely from the entanglements of flesh.

Zuni was content to let them guess away, so long as they did not guess the truth. There was little chance of that, since the truth ran counter to everything the public knew about her life. For wasn't her name synonymous with the Enclosure? Hadn't she fought harder than anyone else to move humanity inside the global network of cities, to shelter our species from the dangers of the wilds? During the middle decades of the century, when climate chaos and accumulated toxins were threatening humankind with extinction, she tirelessly preached the idea of a global shelter. She constructed models of the Enclosure, drew up detailed blueprints, described the safety of life inside that perfected world. If Terra is inhospitable, she argued, let us build our own habitat, as we have done on the moon and Venus and the asteroids. We can mine the ocean for materials. We can suck energy from sun and wind and tide. We can purify everything that enters our system, admitting only what is useful to us. The Enclosure can be the next home for our race, a waystation on our road to transcendence, and everything in it will bear our mindprint.

Knowing such things about Zuni, how could they ever guess her true plans?

Amid the speculations, Zuni quietly went about severing the ties that bound her to the Enclosure. She delivered the last of her scheduled lectures on the psychology of disembodied mind, and declined all further speaking engagements. She resigned from boards of directors, taskforces, committees. For a week she sorted through her files, assigning to the archives whatever she thought might be of use to future planners, erasing the rest. There were hundreds of blueprints, ranging in scale from greenhouses, designed as refuges for nature, to the global skein of cities, designed as refuges for humans. Had she lived in less troubling times, she would have preferred imagining cabins, gardens, backpacking tents, stone walls.

The only blueprint she chose to take away with her was for a twelve-person geodesic dome, and the only mementos she kept were drafting pens and rulers.

She assigned her apprentices to other master architects. One of those apprentices, a woman named Marga, wept on hearing the news.

"Don't fret," Zuni told her. "You will learn as much from Sventov as you would from me."

"But I haven't modeled myself on Sventov," Marga protested. "I've modeled myself on you."

Zuni interrupted her sorting of blueprints to study this young apprentice. The face was a cinnamon-colored blur, the hair a swatch of black. Solemn and reproachful, another earnest child of the Enclosure. "And are you certain you know what I am?"

Marga seemed startled by the question. "You're the architect of humanity's liberation from Terra," she said, repeating a catchphrase from the media.

"And you will carry on that liberation after I am gone?"

"Of course. But why should you leave us, with your head still full of visions?"

"My eyes are failing."

"I'll be your eyes. I'll draw your ideas." In her excited gesturing, Marga thumped the model of the Enclosure, setting the fretted globe swaying.

"That is kind of you," said Zuni, "but I have other work to do now."

"What can be more important than Project Transcendence?"

"In old China," Zuni began patiently, "before the Enclosure, it was the custom for a person to devote her youth to learning and her adult years to community work. When she reached a certain age, however, she was free to withdraw from the world and pursue her quest for enlightenment."'

Marga pondered this. "And you have reached such an age?"

"I have."

"Nothing will make you change your mind?"

"No, my dear." Zuni longed to tell this solemn young woman the truth, revealing the private self who had been kept secret during decades of public work. But the habit of deception was too old now to be broken. She would be freed from it soon enough.

"Enlightenment?" Marga repeated the word quizzically.

"Getting back in touch," Zuni translated.

"With what?"

"With the source of things."

"Isn't that where we're all headed? Back toward the state of pure energy?"

Zuni smiled, knowing it was foolish to speak of spiritual matters. "Sventov will teach you well."

"I suppose he will."

When Zuni busied herself once more with the stack of blueprints, Marga asked shyly, "Do you suppose I could have something of yours to keep?"

Zuni withdrew from her modest trove of mementos one of the drafting pens, and this she pressed into Marga's hand. The touch was obviously a shock to the young woman, but not so great a shock as the kiss Zuni brushed on her cheek. "Now go on, leave me alone," Zuni said, "and be sure you draw beautiful cities with that pen."

After Marga left, Zuni sat for a long time at her desk, staring out over Oregon City, wondering if she could have made it more beautiful. Nothing lived in it except people, the human microbiota, and experimental animals. Old-timers reminisced about the abundance of life in the wilds, about hickory trees and strawberries and kangaroos, but they did not reminisce about typhoid and famine, about mercury poisoning and radioactive dumps. At least within the Enclosure people were shielded from toxins and drug-resistant germs. The apartments were stacked a thousand feet high, nearly reaching the dome, but no one lacked shelter. The algae-based food tasted like pap to anyone who could recollect dirt-grown vegetables, but it was abundant and pure. The young people, those born inside the Enclosure, had never seen dolphins or potatoes, had never seen anything except what humans had fashioned. The young did not reminisce about a lost world. Their parents and grandparents had quit the wilds, as irrevocably as their evolutionary ancestors had floundered up out of the seas.

At least Zuni hoped the move inside was irrevocable. Had she betrayed her species? No, no, she had settled that doubt long ago. To reassure herself that the move inside had been the sole path to survival, she needed only to recall the decades before the Enclosure, when more than a billion people died from heatwaves, hurricanes, flooding, drought, famine, epidemic disease, and other consequences of ecological breakdown. Besides, how could this indoor life be a betrayal if it was what people had always longed for? Wasn't the Enclosure just a cave, a hut, a walled village, a shopping mall carried to its logical extreme, stretched out over the globe, hermetically sealed?

Before closing her office for the last time she looked carefully about to make sure no trace of her was left behind. Satisfied, she gave the hanging model of the Enclosure one last swing and shut the door.

Because Zuni replied to speculations about her future with vague smiles and crooked answers, the media soon decided she was not the proper stuff of news. Her face and name vanished from the celebrity columns. Before long only her friends and her colleagues at the Institute still wondered what was going on beneath that meticulous coil of white hair. Even they couldn't pry the secret from her. She had clutched it for so long that her will had sealed over it, like bark grown around a nail.

Left in peace at last, Zuni went about erasing herself from the city's records. She could have settled her accounts at the bank, the housing office, the clinic and elsewhere electronically, but she chose instead to go in person. More often than not, when she arrived at an office she had to deal with mechanoes rather than people. She didn't mind. The mechs were fun to puzzle, and they had no feelings to hurt. The glittering bulbous heads, like chromium balloons, purred ritual greetings at her. Was she certain she wished to close her accounts, terminate her insurance, cancel her lease? the mechs wanted to know. Yes, Zuni declared. Was she leaving Earth? No, she was returning. Perhaps she was planning to die? What human is immortal? Zuni countered. That answer never failed to silence the chromium heads.

"I am perfectly clear about what I am doing," Zuni would say firmly. "Now kindly settle this matter as I have instructed."

At that the glittering balloon head (or occasionally a human head, modishly wigged and painted) would nod obediently and comply with her requests. Her lease, her insurance, her media subscription, her allotment of food and energy were set to expire in a week. For seven days more she would remain a citizen, secured to the Enclosure by digits in databases, but then the numbers in every account bearing her name would go to zero, and so far as the human system was concerned, Zuni Franklin would cease to exist.

She spent much of those seven days riding pedbelts and gliders, tracing French curves through Oregon City. She had drawn those curves, once upon a time: And this was what kept her running errands in person through the city, this fascination with the glass and alloy shapes her blueprints had taken on. Many others had worked on the design of Oregon City, to be sure, but she had usually been given the final say. Her pen had moved armies of builders. So each soaring tower, each fountain, each plaza encircled by arcades, each sculptured facade echoed shapes that had lived inside her since childhood. The entire city bore the familiarity of an obsessive dream.

She could journey by tube to Bombay City or Arctic City or anywhere else within the Enclosure, and see much the same dreamscape. Once disease and weather had been eliminated, once the Enclosure had been sealed tight, once travel throughout the system had been made free, there seemed little point in concocting a different design for each city. The problems of feeding and housing millions of people did not change from place to place. The ocean yielded up the same materials everywhere. Media spread the same shows, ideas, products, and language around the globe.

The simulated weather during that last week was halcyon blue. Yet Zuni felt certain the weather outside the float city was stormy. When water trembled in drinking glasses, authorities blamed the extraction pumps or tidal generators, but she knew the shudder came from the ocean. As a young woman, she had stood atop cliffs on the Oregon coast watching storms, and had felt the stone tremble beneath her. Waters that could shake the basalt margins of a continent could easily shake a glass city.

Outside it would be March, a time of riotous green, a time for bursting out of shells. During all her years inside, where seasons did not matter and weather played out as electronic shows, Zuni had still kept track of the turning year. And now it was spring.

She went about saying good-bye to her friends beneath this virtual blue sky, knowing that the real sky, far above, would be changeable, now surly, now serene. Her friends had never been numerous, and several of the dearest had already taken the journey she was about to take. They had never been numerous because she was a difficult woman to draw near, at once passionate and aloof. "Like fire inside an icicle," was how one of the draftsmen had described her.

Coyt, the draftsman, was old enough to remember seeing icicles, for he had grown up with Zuni in one of the Oregon lumber towns, back in the 2020s and 2030s, when the last of the North American rainforests were being clear-cut. He had studied forestry with her, and when she switched to the study of architecture he tried to switch as well. But exponential calculus baffled him, so he had to settle for becoming a draftsman in order to stay near her. Over the years he had trailed her from project to project, a timid shadow. Once he even worked up the nerve to ask her to mate with him, and she agreed. Much of her remained hidden, however, a cold inaccessible depth, and when they separated amicably after two years he was relieved. Living with her had been like walking in limestone country, where at any step one might plunge into a sinkhole or cave. Indeed, three mates had vanished after spells of living with her, and she had merely noted each disappearance with a hazy smile. All in all she was a woman to admire from a distance,

Coyt decided. Still, no one inside the Enclosure knew her better than he did, or brooded more about her inscrutable plans.

So Coyt was the last person Zuni called on to wish good-bye. If he did not guess the truth, no one would. She found him at his studio, working on a design. Even though the details were blurry, she recognized the drawing as Project Transcendence, a space-going version of the Enclosure.

His palms kissed hers in greeting. "You leave tomorrow?"

"Bright and early." Zuni sat next to him at the drawing console.

"And you won't tell me where you're going?" he asked.

"Do you really want to know?"

Images of the colossal orb of cities glowed on the screen. Fitted with sails and great flaring scoops, the gauzy sphere was designed to voyage through space, gleaning energy and materials from interstellar dust, freeing humankind from Earth. *Transcendence*: Zuni repeated the word to herself as she waited for Coyt to answer.

Finally he said, "I've always respected your secrets."

"Then indulge me this one last time."

"Are you contemplating suicide?"

"Many people would think of it that way, yes."

"Would I?"

"No."

"Then I can see you again?" Coyt asked, suddenly hopeful.

"Probably not." Her fingers traced the outlines of the space habitat on the screen.

His hands reached toward hers, and then shyly retreated. "You and your secrets. You're like a robin building a nest in a bush."

Coyt's habit of speaking in the archaic language of nature endeared him to her. Robins in bushes! She longed to ask him what else he remembered from those childhood years in the Oregon forests. But no, those were the wilds, taboo. "Promise," she said, "you won't sniff around when I'm gone?"

"Like a hound dog after a raccoon?"

"Promise?" she insisted.

"Yes," he answered glumly. Then he stammered, "I just don't understand. You've never given up before."

If he wanted to believe she had been defeated by the complexities of the new space architecture, then let him. That might be the kindest illusion she could leave with him. "So that's the future you want?" she said, gesturing at the diagram of Project Transcendence.

He looked puzzled. "What other future is there?"

She kept silent. The gauzy construction of interlacing filaments brought back memories of spider webs, dew-soaked, each strand beaded with water diamonds. Were there still spiders?

"That's where we're bound to go next," he said. "It's where you've been pointing all these years. Escape from Terra."

"Escape," she echoed.

"Merge with the cosmos."

"Finally go home," she said.

He clapped with pleasure. "That sounds like my old Zuni. You've never lost your vision."

"No, I haven't," she assured him.

Packing her few remaining things in the apartment that night, she thought regretfully of Coyt. Once she had imagined he might go with her. But gradually she had realized his mind was too brittle. It would have snapped if he had tried to follow her. So she must go alone.

She selected from her library two of the rare paper volumes, Carson's *The Edge of the Sea* and Lopez's *Elegy for Whales*. The other paper books she tagged as gifts for the archives. The remaining volumes, all flexies and discs, she heaved by the armload down the recycle chute. The appliances were all standard issue, and so were the furnishings, so Zuni scrubbed them clean and left them in place.

She snugged the two books into her beltpack, along with the drafting materials from her office. That left just room enough for a first-aid kit, dehydrated food packets, a compass, and the much-folded map. The health-security pass would pin to her traveling gown. After some hesitation she tucked Coyt's gift into the pack as well. It was a model of the Enclosure, small enough to fit in her palm, with threads of silver to represent the transport tubes, silver beads for cities, and, inside, a blue-green sphere of glass to represent Terra.

As she strapped the pack to her waist, with its tiny cargo of mementos, she recalled how the ancients had loaded graves with tokens for the journey to the other world. Instead of miniature boats, dishes, and icons, she carried totems from her own days.

From vacuum storage she recovered the cotton shirt, wool trousers and leather boots that she had saved for this journey. The boots were cracked but serviceable. Although the shirt's color appeared to have faded (or perhaps her eyes could no longer perceive colors as brightly as her mind recalled them), the cotton still felt soft against her neck. She would cover these garments with a moodgown, which would also hide the beltpack. The rest of her clothes she dumped into the recycle chute. From the top shelf of her closet she retrieved a scarlet wig and a face mask meant to resemble an Aztec sun goddess. They had been given to her as a joke years earlier by fellow architects, who knew she wouldn't even paint her face or tint her hair, let alone wear such a frightful get-up. When the closets were empty, the cupboards bare, every surface in the apartment antiseptically clean, Zuni lay down to wait for dawn.

Next morning the screen of her phone refused to glow when she spoke to it. The food spout yielded nothing but a faint sucking noise. Bank, clinic, every agency replied with zeroes when she queried to see if they remembered her.

She felt a fool, donning the wig and mask, enveloping herself in the flashy moodgown. On her way out she paused at the hallway mirror to see if she recognized herself. A grotesque stranger gazed curiously back at her.

Outside the apartment she pressed her palm against the lockplate, to make sure it had erased her from its memory. The door made no response to her touch.

The pedbelt was jammed with riders. Towering headdresses, wigs of every hue, phosphorescent robes, sequined bodysuits— the usual office-going crowd. When Zuni stepped onto the belt (scarlet tresses wagging, gown flapping over the cracked tops of her boots) no one looked up to notice her. No one paid her any attention as she rode across Oregon City past the honeycombed towers, beneath the curving guiderails, to the shuttle terminal.

The ticket machine quizzed her when she requested passage to shuttle stop 012. Did customer know that 012 was a repair terminus? Yes, Zuni replied. Was customer authorized to enter a vulnerable zone? For answer, she waved her health pass at the scanner, and a ticket wheezed out.

The sea must have calmed, for the shuttle raced through the tube without any hint of turbulence. As Zuni rode toward the mainland she tried not to think of all she was leaving behind. Medicine, for example. Her least reliable implant—a kidney—was probably good for another twenty-five years or so, time enough for her to reach 100, if none of her original organs failed first. To wish for a longer life would be greedy.

When the shuttle began decelerating for 012, the other passengers glanced up in mild puzzlement. There shouldn't have been any stops before Rocky Mountain Nexus, another hour away. Zuni called reassuringly, "Just routine maintenance," as she ducked out of the car onto the platform. The doors clapped shut behind her and the shuttle whooshed away down the tube.

The repair station was deserted. At each turn, locks read her health pass before they would let her through. Near the last checkpoint she tossed her mask and wig and gown into a vaporizer. Then she entered the sanitation chamber, a gleaming white sphere that was the Enclosure's outermost defense against the wilds. After the security locks were satisfied, a round hatch swung open and she stepped into the damp green tangle of an Oregon forest.

She stood for a long time with eyes lowered, smelling the mosses and trees, listening to wind sizzle through the needles of new-growth firs, feeling the sponginess of soil beneath her feet. She ached.

After a spell she unfolded the map and blinked at it. Tears made her vision even hazier than usual, blurring the lines, so she tucked the map into her beltpack and set off through the woods along a pathway of memory. When she had last walked these slopes, fifty years earlier, they had recently been clear-cut. Raw dirt, oil cans, bone-white slash. Even though the fir and hemlock and spruce had grown back abundantly since then, she still recognized the contours of the land. Without pausing to rest, she continued past remembered outcroppings of granite, past waterfalls, over sand dunes, until the ocean was in sight. Even the spectacle of breakers didn't slow her, and she kept on, trotting now, down the last slope into the cove where the domes clustered. She laughed aloud at the sight of the colony, at the timid way the windmills and greenhouses and gardens huddled together. Yes, what this place needed was a good architect.

And she laughed at the sight of former lovers and students and colleagues hurrying from the meditation dome to greet her. Zuni! Zuni! they cheered. You've taken your turn at last!

"I thought it was time for me to join you," she answered, "before I'm too old to climb mountains and swim in the sea."

Welcome! Welcome! they cried in all their familiar voices, and their lips brushed her face, their fingers stroked her hair, their arms encircled her.

"And haven't things grown wondrously?" Zuni crowed.

Yes, the conspirators agreed. The wilds are coming back. Not everything. A fair number of birds, some butterflies, even a few of the big predators. Bears, lions, wolves.

"And the whales?" Zuni asked.

We don't know yet, they answered. There are seals and otters, herring and krill, a couple runs of salmon. So there might be whales.

Zuni touched their cheeks, their foreheads. "You've managed to stay healthy?"

Well enough, they replied. Some cancers from the lingering toxins, but so far no deaths. The health patrollers know we're here but leave us alone, watching to see how we get on. We're afraid if we thrive, people will come pouring out of the Enclosure.

"There's little danger of that," Zuni replied. "They're likelier to launch out into space. The dread of the wild runs deep." Gazing around at the humped green hills of the Oregon coast, the lichen-starred cliffs, and wildflowers glimmering on the beach, she added, "They're paying a terrible price."

But there was no choice, the conspirators objected. Without imposing quarantine, how else would Earth have recovered?

"Yes, of course," Zuni murmured. "Still, it grieves me to think of all they've lost."

Touch the Earth

The nine conspirators fled from Indiana City along separate paths. On the night chosen for the escape, Marn zigzagged through avenues and alleys, carrying her fear as if it were a dish of mercury. The last lights she passed were the neon signs at the gamepark, where the pedbelts ended and revelers caroused. Every step pushed her deeper into the unlit ruins of factories, over buckled pavement, past abandoned machinery ticking as it released the day's heat. This was how she had wanted to flee, carrying nothing from her old life except the mask and clothes she wore, without even a flashlight to burden her.

Smell told her when she had reached the abandoned refinery, for the scent of dust gave way to the tang of oil. In the glow from a fading sunset projected onto the dome she could make out soaring chimneys, a snarl of pipes, and giant pumps. The storage tanks echoed back the *grit grit* of her boots on gravel. She pressed her ear to the fifth tank, but could hear no murmur from inside. What if no one else had come? What if, after months of secret meetings, after gathering supplies for the colony, after vowing to risk their lives together in the wilds—what if the others had been seized by fear?

Her face felt hot behind the mask. Paint flaked away with snicking sounds as she brushed her gloved hands over the tank, searching for the drain valve. When at last she found it she hesitated, a fist clenched on the spoked wheel. After spending every hour of her twenty-two years inside the Enclosure, she could not resist taking one last look back at the city's dazzle of lights. Nearby, the gamepark glowed orange. Farther away the bio-gas plants and agrifactories flared yellow. And farther still, at the core of the city where her own chamber hummed to itself, the towers blazed toward the dome like mountains afire.

With a shiver, she turned back to the tank, opened the valve, and peered into a tunnel of blackness. "It's Marn," she called. "Marn-arn," the tank echoed back. "Code word harmony," she added, and the tank echoed, "Harm-arm."

Then light flared inside, and Jurgen's shaggy head filled the opening. "It's about time," he called gruffly.

She crawled through the valve and emerged, blinking, inside the tank, her gloves and suit smeared with oil. The other eight stood there waiting, muffled in worksuits and masks. Among the voices lifted in greeting, she noticed Hinta's throaty whisper.

After one last glimpse of the city lights snared in the opening like stars in a telescope, Marn cranked the valve shut. Safe here with the others, surrounded by crates and tools for the settlement, she began trembling. The fear she had balanced so carefully now threatened to spill.

"How's our chemist?" Jurgen asked. "No problems getting here? No one followed you?"

Marn shook her head. "I was careful."

"Good. We can go as soon as you've checked your crates."

Chagrined at being the last to arrive, Marn lowered her eyes until the man's bulky shape withdrew. From a pocket she took the inventory of medicines, catalysts, acids, and chemical reagents they expected to need on the outside but would not be able to synthesize right away. While she checked her supplies, the others began pushing loaded carts into the pipe, headlamps glowing. Jurgen went first, since he had discovered this exit from the city and had marked the spot fourteen kilometers out from the dome where the pipe broke ground. As usual he wore no hood, so his black hair flared out in an unruly mane. Sol went next, walking with an old athlete's cocky spring, then slouching Rand and gliding Hinta, each conspirator in turn with gait and posture unique as a thumbprint. Marn went last, disguising the tremor in her hands by tightly gripping the handle of her cart.

They slogged along for hours, gasping stale air, taking gulps from an oxygen tank when they grew lightheaded. Their headlamps struck rainbow reflections from the curving walls. Like the refinery and storage tanks, the pipeline had been abandoned when climate chaos forced the banning of fossil fuels. The slap of footsteps and grating of wheels reverberated, kilometer after kilometer, until they reached the spot Jurgen had marked with a phosphorescent red X. He unholstered his laser and began to cut an opening. The others rested, close together in the gloom. Marn could smell them, could smell herself—an animal pungency. She had never been this hot, this wet, this lost in her body.

When the laser finished its cut the section of pipe tilted outward. Cool, damp air rushed in. Daylight blinded her. Tears seeped around her closed lids, yet she wanted to look out, to see the wilds. The dome's filtered light had given her no hint of this brilliance.

No one spoke, no one moved. Marn squinted through a film of tears at blurred trees, bushes, stones. She had scant language for this outside world, only what she had picked up from reading. It was a muddle of browns and greens. She fixed her gaze on a single plant, its twin leaves canted upward like awnings, a bud sheltered underneath, brown-tipped, potent. If she stared long enough the bud might burst into flower, proving that she really was in the wilds.

Jurgen broke the silence by murmuring, "Great God in the morning."

Hinta swayed at the lip of the opening. "Just look! Listen! And the smells!"

Marn let out a breath, as if she had come to the surface after swimming underwater. She knew it was April, a month no different from any other inside the Enclosure, but out here it was a season of growth.

With a shout, Jurgen clambered through the opening. The rest followed, dropping gingerly to the ground. Marn stared down at her boots, amazed to find herself actually standing on the planet. She took a few cautious steps, saw the others doing the same, all staggering about as if they were toddlers again just learning to walk. The littered soil yielded beneath her feet and sprang back, resilient. No pavement or floor had ever felt so alive. Her eyes still watered from the raw sunlight. But she could see well enough to tell it was a young forest they had reached, few of the trees thicker than her waist, the ground a tangle of briars and brush.

Jurgen lumbered back to the pipe, pawing the greenery aside and yelling, "Let's get the stuff unloaded. Let's find some water and set up camp. Let's go."

Rand and Sol were the ones who found the lake, a blue bowl rimmed by trees with arching branches laced in white.

"Dogwood," said Jurgen, expert on the names of wild things.

By late afternoon, working with hoods thrown back, masks clammy from sweat, they had cleared a space on the shore, spread a layer of polyfilm, and inflated the dome. Long after everyone else had taken shelter inside, Jurgen kept lugging gear from the supply crates. Through the dome's translucent skin Marn watched his burly shadow pass.

"We've got to take this in small doses," she called out to him. "Leave it for tomorrow."

Jurgen only grunted as he trudged back for another load.

Beside her, Hinta lay with milky white hair spread in a halo against the somber brown floor. "He told me once that he feels most alive when he's aching," she said.

"He'll kill himself," Marn said.

"Not Jurgen." Hinta rolled onto her side, propped her head on a bent arm. A shining rim of skin showed beneath the edge of her mask. "He'll be around to bury the rest of us."

"Let's hope we don't bury anybody soon," said Marn.

"Let's hope."

Lying on her cushion, Marn stared up at the apex of the dome where the arched sections came together, like a map of travel tubes converging on Indiana City. She imagined the city as a vast printed circuit, its millions of people so many nodes. She would already be fading from the memories of the few who knew her back there, displaced by videos or holos, flushed away by chemmies. "Did you leave anyone behind?" she asked Hinta.

"Everybody I care about is right here," said Hinta. "And you?"

"I miss a few people."

"Anybody whose face you ever saw?"

"A couple," Marn admitted.

"Did you just look, or did you touch?"

Marn flushed. Her tongue felt prickly. Before she could answer, Hinta quickly added, "I'm sorry. That's a rude question."

They lay quietly on their cushions, Marn's heart pounding. She was ashamed to admit she had never touched anyone, skin to skin, unless perhaps in infancy, back before memory.

Jurgen was the last to retreat inside the dome, well after nightfall. He took his place among the others, who lay in their sleeping bags, their bodies arrayed like spokes with feet pointing toward the center of the dome. Because his cushion was next to hers, Marn turned away from him before removing her work mask. She paused, the night mask in her hand, feeling the breath-moistened air on her face. Then she covered herself and lay down, became a spoke in the wheel of bodies.

Tired but not yet drowsy, she listened to the others murmur and wheeze. She had never shared a sleeping space with anyone before, and at first their snorting and rustling disturbed her. Then as they drifted deeper, their breathing calmed and their limbs grew still. No electronic hum, no whirr of pedbelts, no blare of loudspeakers, no human clatter. Marn felt she could almost gather it in her hands, this downy silence. She imagined the wheel of bodies as a seed encased in the dome, the dome encircled by forest, the forest by continent and oceans, and so on outward, beyond Earth and solar system and Milky Way, circle beyond circle.

For the next week Marn would not leave the dome. She mixed a starting brew for the bio-digester, and ran tests on samples of water and soil the others brought in. But she would not remove her gloves or throw back her hood or venture outside. She took showers in distilled water. At night, she dosed herself with histaphones and immunies. Groggy from the drugs, she slept behind a screen, her ears plugged against the sound of other sleepers, dreaming of her own solitary chamber back in the city.

She woke in the mornings with the unsettling taste of the wilds in her mouth.

Hinta left her alone. But Jurgen tried to soothe her in his bearish, rumbling way. "It's wildershock, same as health patrollers and sea miners get. We've all suffered from it."

"I'm okay," Marn insisted. "I run the lab, right? Isn't that enough?"

Then on the seventh day, at sunset, she forced herself to go out. The countryside was luminous. For a long time she lingered near the dome, fighting her dread. Maybe she should throw off her clothes and dive into the lake, drown her fear by yielding completely. The thought made her shudder.

She turned her back on the lake. But the forest was equally troubling, with its drool of vines, maze of branches, explosion of leaves. Only the brand-new works of the settlement reassured her. Overhead, solar panels swiveled to catch the last rays of sunlight. Wind turbines spun, the whir of their blades barely audible against the rustle of leaves. Everywhere she looked, blueprints were coming to life: hydroponic tanks, methane generator, smaller domes for work and meditation clustered around the large central dome like a ring of bubbles, the whole settlement stitched together by graveled pathways.

Marn chose the widest path and followed it with head bent down, so as not to see the anarchic green that pressed in from all sides. When at last she looked up, she found herself at the pipeline. The slab that Jurgen had cut still lay in the weeds, its unpainted inner surface dull with rust. She scuffed at the redness with her boot. Nothing rusted inside Indiana City.

She pressed her hooded ear against the sun-warmed pipe, listening, unsure what she wanted to hear. The purr of patrol shuttles coming after them? The ticking gears of the city? The hum of her own abandoned chamber? But she heard nothing. Nobody would come for them, so long as they stayed outside, never broke the seal around the city. You could escape into wildness, if you were clever enough, but you could not return, lest you poison the Enclosure.

"Thinking about going back?"

Startled by the voice, Marn jerked away from the pipe. Hinta stood on the path, her mask askew, gloves crusty with dirt.

"I was just listening," Marn said.

"It's tempting, isn't it, to go back inside where everything is measured and predictable?"

"Yes," Marn admitted.

"It's scary out here." Freed of the hood, Hinta's pale hair sprang into a curly ruff. "But isn't it beautiful? Doesn't it make you feel like you've finally come awake?"

Studying her, Marn felt that Hinta might be the first person she could touch, a woman like herself, less alien, less coarse and brutish than a man. The flounce of her hair seemed as uncanny as the dusk-lit trees.

Later that night, when all nine sat in the dome planning the next day's work, Marn spoke for the first time of her dread. The others nodded, admitting their own fears, even Jurgen.

"I still have to squint every time I go out through that hatch," he said, "so I see only a bit of the wilds at a time. We've got to learn everything all over again. It's hard work. But we can do it. We belong out here."

A murmur of agreement ran around the circle.

"We've got to get back in touch with Earth," Jurgen said. "Back in touch with our bodies." A surge of emotion jolted his big frame, and he yanked the mask from his face.

Marn was too dazed at first to realize what was happening. Then Hinta removed her mask, revealing a pale, delicate face, and blue eyes as quick and bright as Marn had guessed they would be. A moment later Sol stripped his mask away, then Norba and Jolon, and so on around the circle until Marn found herself pushing aside the molded husk and gaping at the others with naked face. In her entire life, she had reached this stage of intimacy with only seven people, and only after lengthy rituals of preparation. Now suddenly here were eight more. Amid the confusion of lips and cheeks and gleaming eyes, she felt at last that she was truly outside, in exile from all she had known.

That night, a purring sound woke her, a soft drumming on the roof of the dome, and after a moment of unease she smiled. Her first rain.

Gradually, Marn began to trust the wind and rain, the dirt and sky, and the expressions on bare faces. Sometimes as she worked outdoors she would find herself in a drowse, saturated with sun, her mind gone out.

One afternoon, she helped Jurgen search the nearby hills for a spring to supply earth-filtered water for the fish tanks. Eventually they traced a brook to its source at the head of a ravine, where someone long ago had walled in a pool with stones. The walls had slumped, and from the jumble of stones, velvety with moss, water seeped downhill in glistening threads. The pool was fringed by blue flowers, their clusters of trumpet-shaped blossoms bobbing from tall stems. Jurgen had a way of stooping over any new plant, screwing up his black eyes in an effort of memory, and then declaring its name.

"Virginia bluebells," he announced. "Just like the pictures, only they're alive. Amazing."

Marn felt her own face mirroring his pleasure. She had not gone without a mask long enough to gain control of her features, so emotions swirled across her face as wind stirred the surface of the lake. "It seems a shame to disturb the stones," she said. "The flowers are so pretty."

"Call them bluebells," Jurgen insisted. "We need to recover the old names."

"Yes, bluebells."

A grin cracked his black beard. Turning to her, his arms spreading as if to enwrap her, he bellowed, "And look at that!"

She flinched back, but he lumbered past her, arms swung wide, and scrambled up the slope to the base of an immense tree. The gray bark of the trunk had flaked away in fist-size chips to reveal a creamy bark underneath, as if the tree were shedding. Higher up, where the branches canopied against the sky, the smooth under-bark showed through like the skin of something newborn.

"It's a sycamore," Jurgen cried, almost singing the word. He slammed his chest against the rough trunk and hugged the tree.

"You look silly," Marn said.

"Silly?" he roared. "How could anybody come across a great tree like this and not wrap arms around it? A sycamore! I never thought I'd see one." He leaned back and gazed up the trunk. "The old-timers used the wood for water troughs and wagon wheels and butcher blocks."

Marn turned away in disgust, thinking of knives, meat, blood. Her stomach churned. That was the way with Jurgen. One minute he made her feel easy in the wilds, the next minute he shocked her.

Noting her disgust, he growled, "City girl."

"I'm trying. It's a lot to get used to."

His mouth quirked into what she took as a smile, although she could not be sure. Only his teeth showed through the bristling fur.

"Sorry. I get impatient. Let's work."

They leaned their packs against the scabby trunk of the sycamore. Scrabbling down the bank, avoiding the frail blue flowers, Jurgen was the first to reach the spring. He grabbed a stone, then another and another, heaving them to the side. Marn slid after him, wary of his flailing elbows. As he hefted the next rock, there was a blur of movement, like a rope snapping and recoiling, and he cried out.

"What is it?" she asked.

"I'll be damned. A snake." He stared at his arm. "I've just been snakebit."

"A snake? But they're extinct."

He gave a harsh bark of laughter. "This one didn't get the message."

He loosened his cuff and folded back the sleeve. Marn forced herself to look at his bare forearm, which bristled with the same coarse black hair that covered his jaw and skull. The muscles were thick and netted with veins. Near the elbow were twin rows of puncture-marks, like pin-pricks, leading up to a pair of larger purplish holes, oozing blood.

She pressed a hand over her mouth. Words dried on her tongue.

"I'm glad to learn we didn't kill off all the snakes," Jurgen said, "but I'd be happier if this one wasn't poisonous."

"How do you know it's poisonous?"

"See those two big holes? Those are fang marks, where the venom is injected. Question is, what species?" He rehearsed the possibilities as he labored up the slope. "Too far north for cottonmouths. A rattler would have made a ruckus. Likely a copperhead." He suddenly turned, and Marn, hurrying after, bumped into him, then immediately pulled back. "Could you tell," he asked, "was it brownish, with darker bands, or creamy with copper bands?"

Marn trembled. "All I saw was like a rope lashing out. I didn't notice color."

"Well, open your eyes." His gaze, dark and rough as the stones he had been heaving, glared at her, then swung away. He continued on up to the sycamore, where he slumped against the piebald trunk. His outstretched legs in their muddy coveralls looked like two more knotty tree roots. He tilted the arm for inspection.

Marn approached cautiously, afraid of Jurgen, of the snake, of the repulsive wound. "Shouldn't we go back?"

Again he laughed harshly, his chin thrust up by pain. "If that bastard could survive our poisons, I can survive his."

"We need the medicine kit."

"I'll be okay as soon as I rest a minute." He tilted his head back against the trunk and loosed a full-throated bellow.

Was this how the poison worked? Marn wondered. She hovered uncertainly before him, feeling too small to budge him unless he cooperated. "Come on, Jurgen. We've got to go back."

"If there's snakes, what else might have survived?" His eyes, already squinting from pain, squeezed tighter in his effort to recall names. "Fox. Deer. Turtles. Eagles. Salamanders. What else? Bears. Beavers. Owls. Why not coyotes? Maybe even cougars."

The terror Marn had felt when she first peered out through the hole in the pipeline now swept back over her. It was madness to have left Indiana City. Stifling or not, life back there was at least safe. Nothing could lash out at you, leap on you, bite you. Her skin crawled. "Jurgen," she said as calmly as she could, "get up. We're going back to camp."

"Right," he grunted. But instead of moving, he gazed at his wounded arm. The flesh was turning purple, the skin from elbow to wrist was swelling. "Imagine—snakebite!"

"Jurgen," she pleaded.

"Just get my pins under me." His legs jerked, but failed to lift him. "Dizzy."

His weakness frightened her now, as his strength had frightened her before. "Should I go for help?"

Jurgen shook his head. "No. I can walk. Give me a hand." He raised his good arm.

Without letting herself think, Marn grabbed his thick hand with both of hers, braced her feet against a root, and tugged with all her might. Slowly he rose to his feet. Once upright, he staggered a few steps. "Can't see. Fool legs won't work."

Again without thinking, Marn slipped an arm around his waist and cased her shoulder against his side, bracing him. They lurched ahead. He was massive and his weight seemed to grow with every step. But she would not let go, not even when he reeled and his beard rasped her forehead. She could feel his panting against her ribs, and she found herself panting in sympathy.

By the time they stumbled into the dome she was too weary to fret about their twined bodies. But the startled expressions with which Hinta and Sol greeted them brought back her confusion.

"A snake bit him," Marn explained, short of breath.

"A what?" demanded Sol, shrinking back. Even Hinta raised her gloves, palms out, as if to shove them away.

"Help me lay him down."

"Are we there?" Jurgen's voice rose brokenly. The good fist rubbed his eyes. "Can't see a thing."

That snapped Hinta and Sol out of their daze. Together with Marn they lowered him to his cushion. The swollen arm, mottled scarlet and purple, made Marn nauseous. She pushed her feelings aside and bent over him, covering him with his sleeping bag. Sol ran to call the others, while Hinta powered up the medicine console.

Marn was trying to cut Jurgen's sleeve with scissors, to ease the swelling, but the arm kept jerking. "Jurgen," she spoke close to his ear, "you're going to be all right. But we've got to touch you. You'll forgive that?"

His answer was mumbled. "Sure, sure. Go ahead."

A point of fear glinted from his black eyes. His shivering made the cushion tremble. Marn finished cutting the sleeve, then drew the cover to his chin, leaving only the puffy arm exposed. "Hurry," she whispered to Hinta. "He's in shock."

"Snakebite?" Hinta called. "Are you sure?"

"Yes, I'm sure. Copperhead. Code it in, see if there's an antidote."

Hinta slipped off her gloves and typed the implausible message on the console. As Marn watched the lithe fingers dance on the keys, desire uncoiled in her. She yearned to make her first contact with this brisk woman, so easy in her body. But instead here was Jurgen stretched out beside her, his body cumbersome and rough.

"It says lower the arm," Hinta read from the screen, "bind it above the elbow, slit the skin at the fang marks, suck the venom out, administer antivenin."

"Can we make that?" Marn asked.

Hinta tapped the keys, paused, shook her head, the milky hair swirling. "Idiot machine synthesizes antidotes for every toxin we ever invented. But for natural poisons—nothing."

Jurgen broke into delirious babbling. "Snake, by God. Thought they were all dead. Wolves. Bears. Ghost bite."

"Easy," Marn whispered. It seemed callous to touch him through clumsy gloves, so she drew them off and pressed her bare hand to his cheek. The shudder of that contact ran through her body. But she had no time to savor it.

Hinta passed her the antiseptic swab and scalpel. Worry swept aside all of Marn's inhibitions, made her scrub and then slice the skin, exposing red flesh. Meat, the same as any animal. "Now the syringe."

"I'm looking for it."

Marn waited. Jurgen trembled under her hands. "Hurry."

Hinta rummaged in the medical chest with angry clacking noises. "It's not here. Maybe somebody took it for collecting samples."

Marn let her body think for her. "Quick, check if the venom is a stomach poison."

"Why do you—"

"Just do it."

Clicking of keys. "No," said Hinta, "it's a blood poison."

Marn looked down at Jurgen. Only the whites of his eyes were visible. His mouth was a wheezing hole in the beard. The skin around the wound seemed ready to split. The fang marks oozed.

"You're not going—" said Hinta in a panic.

Marn waved her away. It was like bending steel to force her mouth down to the festering wound. Her lips met his hot skin. She sucked, and the first trickle of fluid on her tongue made her gag. She reared back and spat violently into a bowl. Then she bent once more to the wound.

By then the others were crowding into the dome, simmering with questions, carrying with them the smells of wood and dirt. Marn heard the word *snake* hissed repeatedly, as if it were an incantation. She kept sucking, gagging and spitting, until they were shocked into silence, kept sucking until nothing more would come, then she leaned back, mouth sticky, an acrid taste on her tongue. She glared at the ring of faces. "What are you staring at? You'd rather he die?"

They drew back from her, as from a sparking wire. Marn stayed by Jurgen, her hand on the black spittle-soaked fur of his jaw. She felt a connection with this man, as if in pressing her lips to him a circuit had been closed and power had surged between them.

"We don't have the antidote," Hinta explained to the others.

Their whispers took up again the hiss of *snake, snake.* It was as though, in felling Jurgen, a legendary beast had struck at them all. What did any of them know about the wilds? School had taught them little, merely filled them with dread of the outside. Videos and holos showed only deserts, sulphurous volcanos, blank oceans, and miles of blighted emptiness. You could learn about this forested and rivered world only by hearsay, through the old folks, or through tedious hours in the archives.

Marn stroked Jurgen's hair, which felt as springy and resilient as the soil in the forest. His mouth sagged open, breathing hoarsely. His naked arm, bloated and discolored, lay at his side.

"The question is," Hinta was saying, "do we take him back inside or not?"

"And give it all up?" The acid-scars on Jolon's cheeks reddened with indignation.

"No, absolutely not," said Coyt.

Voices jumbled together too quickly for Marn to sort them out. The sensations from her hands commanded all her attention—the wiry mat of his beard, so strange, and the stuttering pulse in the bend of his elbow. Could a heart pump so fast, through so huge a body? He bulked on his cushion like a fallen tree.

When Marn could separate voices again, Rand was saying, "It would take a pair of us to haul him back through the pipe. Or we might locate a health patroller."

"And the Overseers would be here in half an hour with cages and chemmies," Jolon pointed out. The ruddy scars on her cheeks, the tension in her body, the balled fist on either knee proclaimed that she had no intention of going back.

Heads nodded in agreement. Marn knew they were right. Any contact with Indiana City would end the experiment and land them in quarantine, most likely for the rest of their lives. But she wanted the choice made clear: "And if he dies?"

No one answered. Except for the strain in their faces, they might have been meditating, or drugged. Marn recalled the vows she had taken with them back in that echoing oil tank—to live outside for a year, a cycle of seasons, before voting to stay or return. And if they returned, to do so in secret. She remembered how Jurgen had always been the first to shove aside every obstacle. Jurgen, with sawdust on his beard, proclaiming to all the astounding properties of wood. Jurgen, stinking with sweat, laughing when the others wrinkled their noses at him. Jurgen, ripping away his mask, spreading his hands on the Earth.

Marn spoke deliberately. "It's not worth his dying. Nothing's worth it."

Sol pinched his upper lip. "We knew there'd be accidents."

"That's why there are nine of us," Coyt added. "Redundancy."

Marn could not connect their words to this body panting beneath her hand. She kept hearing him cry out in pain, kept seeing those mitts claw at his inflamed eyes. Her own vision began to blur. The others' faces merged, until they all seemed like clones of the same hostile person. For the first time in days she longed for her mask, to hide herself.

Then she heard Hinta's voice, and recognized once again the silky hair, the high cheek-bones: "I don't think he'd want us to go back inside."

Her blue eyes, which usually made Marn think of sky, now made her think of ice. "Look," said Marn, "this isn't a broken machine. It's Jurgen, don't you see?"

"We know, Marn, we know," Hinta soothed. "We're not forgetting him. He's why I'm here, and why I'm going to stay."

"I say we vote," Jolon insisted.

"Vote, vote," cried the others.

"All right, then," said Hinta. "Do we take him inside?"

Like the others, Marn curled one hand in her lap, thinking furiously. Thrust one finger up—or a closed fist? That was the computer's binary choice, yes or no, too stark for human questions. How could she let him die, the first person she had ever touched? And yet this was why they had come outside, to get back in touch. Return to Indiana City would be death of another kind.

"Time," Hinta called.

As Marn lifted her arm, the fist closed of itself, squeezed tight as if to keep hold on something. Around the circle were eight balled fists, eight refusals to go back.

Marn closed her eyes. Beneath her fingers Jurgen's hectic pulse raced on and on, against all reason.

The others padded away to the hatch, where their boots and tools waited for them, a few pausing beside Marn on their way, glancing at Jurgen, whispering in sober tones. If the largest one of us could fall so quickly, to a beast we thought was extinct, what might happen to the rest of us? That is what Marn heard in their whispers, what she read in their taut faces as they withdrew again to the day's chores.

Only Hinta stayed behind. Her eyes, no longer ice, had become sky again, a softer blue. As she lowered herself beside Marn, she sighed. Their shoulders brushed. Neither drew back. "So we wait," Hinta said.

"We wait," said Marn.

"He might live. Just to spite the city. Show them he can survive outdoors, do without their fancy medicines."

Marn wanted to bury her face in that springy hair. But her lips were still gummy with Jurgen's blood. Beneath her hand his pulse shredded away the minutes.

After a while Hinta stirred. "Come on, you need a break from this." Rising with a sensuous unfolding of her legs, she went to the dome's entrance and whistled.

Moments later, Sol ambled in. "News?" he asked.

"No," said Hinta. "He's the same. Would you sit with him, keep him warm, spoon him some cardio if he comes to?"

Marn caught the small word—*if*.

"Sure," Sol replied. "You going out?"

Hinta drew on her gloves, tucked her hair into the collar of her worksuit. "Marn and I want to go clear that spring."

"No," Marn insisted. "The spring can wait."

"He's unconscious. He doesn't know you're here."

"But I can't just leave him."

"Your staying won't do him any good. You'll only make yourself sick. And we need you, we need everyone." Hinta waited by the airlock holding a shovel, one hip thrust out in a challenge Marn could not decipher.

"Go on," Sol urged. "We'll come get you if there's any change."

Marn knelt beside Jurgen, hesitating. Her wrist tingled from his breath. The pulse seemed to be growing stronger. A crescent of black iris showed under each eyelid. What if he should wake, now, and find her fingers on his throat, her hair brushing his face?

Confused, she lifted her hand from the warm skin, stood up, backed away, and followed Hinta outdoors.

The rock-strewn spring, which had seemed a kilometer distant this morning when she was helping Jurgen back to the dome, was only a few minutes' walk away.

"Look at the lovely blue flowers," Hinta said.

"Bluebells," Marn told her. "And that's a sycamore," she added, pointing to the gigantic piebald tree.

"Such odd names. Sounds like Jurgen's teaching."

"Yes." Marn took the shovel from Hinta, saying, "In case mister snake is still around." Then she scooted down the bank amid the nodding blossoms, her boots gouging the mud.

And mister snake was still around, slashing at the shovel as soon as Marn disturbed its lair. There was the same blur of movement, like an end-knotted rope snapping, and the click of teeth against metal. The two women leapt back, and the snake withdrew. Furious, Marn realized now why she had come. She pried the stones apart with the shovel, tumbled a few, and then out the creature slithered, gliding with sinuous ease. Its wedge-shaped head was the color of copper, and its length was ringed by coppery bands. It might have been a limb off the sycamore, cast down and set moving. Nothing she had ever seen rivaled it for grace. She watched, fascinated, as a forked tongue licked out between the fangs, tasting the air.

Only when the snake lowered its head and began writhing away did she remember Jurgen lying unconscious. Hatred ran like acid in her veins. Hefting the shovel she advanced on the snake, tightening every muscle to crush it. But even before she heard Hinta crying, "No, no, let it be!" she was easing the handle onto her shoulder. The hatred passed, dissolved away by an emotion she could not name, as she watched the creature until it glided out of sight into weeds.

"He belongs here," Hinta said. "This is his place."

Marn nodded, half mesmerized. Now that it had vanished, the snake seemed almost legendary again, too beautiful and supple and quick to be real. She tugged the gloves away to wipe her eyes.

Hinta removed her own gloves. Without a word, she took Marn's hand.

＊　＊　＊

That night, when Jurgen muttered in his sleep, "Marn? Where's Marn?" she rolled over, pulled the sleeping bag up to his throat, rested a hand on his forehead. No fever. She touched his wrist, and was reassured by the slow, steady pulse.

Relieved, she crept from the dome and into the bewildering night. The darkness buzzed with clicks and cries. From the woods came a hooting sound that might have been an owl. Was that possible? Scraps of moonlight rocked on the lake. In the water there might be more snakes, or other beasts for which she had no names, but she would go in anyway. Shrugging free of her clothes, she waded in with muscles tensed, breath held, then splashed forward as she would in a pool. But this was no sanitized water; this was whatever the lake gathered from land and sky.

Marn lay on her back and floated. The air was rank with the smell of weeds and mud. The water licked the salt from her skin, washed away the dirt, but it could not scour away the taste of Jurgen's blood or the feel of Hinta's fingers.

The night was the coolest she had ever known, as the day had been the hottest. This was what it meant to live in weather, shivering and sweating by turns.

Lit from inside, the dome appeared like a faceted globe. Marn could see the dim shapes of the others preparing for sleep. Someone would be checking on Jurgen, giving him water, making him comfortable. I should be doing it, Marn thought. But she could not yet look into his stone-dark eyes without confusion.

Afloat, she let her thoughts spread out on the water and dissolve.

Sometime later a voice called her name, and she opened her eyes on darkness spangled with stars.

"Marn! Are you all right?" came the voice. It was Hinta, her lean silhouette on the bank.

"I'm fine," Marn answered. The water sluiced along her ribs, her thighs, as she swam toward shore.

"I saw you go out," Hinta said. "I started to worry."

"Time seemed—" Marn began. But she could not tell what had become of time, or of her fear. She stood up in the shallows, and could see her nakedness register in Hinta's startled gaze.

"Here's a towel," Hinta offered.

Marn's feet sank into the muck without moving. "I'm not ready to come out yet."

"Isn't the water cold?"

"Come see."

For a few seconds, Hinta did not move, a slender column of darkness. Then she wriggled free of her clothes and eased into the shallows beside Marn. "Brrr," she said. "It *is* cold."

"Swim out with me," Marn answered, "and you'll soon warm up." Touching the other woman to keep contact in the dark, Marn led her away from shore.

Eros Passage

On the morning of his thirteenth birthday, Hoagy Ferris woke to find an eros couch installed in his bedroom. He had been hoping for a more advanced model. The screen was small, the stimulus rating low. But the Freud, as his mother called it—or the Orgasm Express, as his friends called it—was potent enough for a beginner.

The eros couches Hoagy had used in friends' apartments and public arcades came loaded with sexual fantasies for every taste, but this one required the user to create fantasies of his own. Undaunted, he buckled on the helmet and soon learned to mesh his brainwaves with the simulator, using biofeedback techniques he had learned in an effort to manage his epilepsy.

At first the video stars and nubile schoolmates he summoned onto the screen were fully clothed, their images blurry. With practice, he sharpened the focus. Undressing his heroines took longer, since his knowledge of female anatomy, after four years of sex education, was still entirely theoretical. Too shy to get down to business, he carried on long conversations with his primly dressed sirens. "Do you have many friends?" he might ask.

"Not many," the current beauty would confess. "I get awfully lonely."

"Does your mother understand you?"

"She's forgotten what it's like to be young."

"And your dad?"

"I never had one."

"Me neither."

Emboldened by these chats in which he dictated both voices, eventually Hoagy allowed a strap to glide from his heroine's shoulder, a streak of thigh to show through a slit in her gown. Once the disrobing began, it hastened forward until she lolled on the screen as naked as the sun in a cloudless sky.

Tanya Ferris had been assured by the psychiatrist that the Freud would not ply her son with fantasies but rather would train him to orchestrate his own desires. By learning to direct the flow of neural impulses, he might be able to control his epilepsy without the use of drugs. Indeed, within a few months after installation of the eros couch, Hoagy's seizures had all but ceased, and the few he suffered were mild, allowing the doctor to wean him off medications. Still, Tanya wondered if she had done the right thing by enrolling him in the timeshell experiment, with all its risks. Yet how else could she have secured treatment for him? She could never afford even the cheapest Freud, let alone the psychiatrist's fees. As it was, she and Hoagy were barely getting by on the pension she received as a retired surrogate mother. Even to buy him a new pair of shoes required weeks of scrimping.

In the evenings, after he had finished his homework at the kitchen table, he retreated to his room. Tanya often paused outside his shut door and listened, hearing muffled dialogue, one voice recognizably Hoagy's, the other one higher-pitched, girlish. Even with her ear pressed against the door, she could not decipher the words. When sharp laughter or urgent moans broke out, she hurried on down the hall.

✳   ✳   ✳

Hoagy soon lost interest in the girls who trailed perfume down the corridors at school or flashed their bare legs on the sidewalks; now he could conjure up women more desirable than any female he had seen in the flesh. The prim, chatty maidens of his early scenarios were succeeded by strumpets cavorting in negligees, then by lascivious nudes. Their breasts and buttocks defied gravity, refusing to sag, and their skin was unblemished silk. Their limbs assumed any posture he chose, including ones that would baffle a yogi. Their eyes said only what he wished them to say.

One red-haired temptress haunted him for weeks. Delicate blue veins showed through her translucent skin. Her jade green eyes, fixed on him, gave back a tiny image of his face.

"Where do you live?" he asked.

"On the fifth planet of Epsilon Eridani," she breathed. "Come find me."

He summoned her back again and again, surrounding her with a landscape of ancient forests, rolling prairies, wildflower meadows aflame with butterflies, rivers teeming with fish and skies with birds. Such riches were no longer available on Earth. But why not on the fifth planet of Epsilon Eridani, or on some other habitable world?

By the time Hoagy received a more powerful eros couch at age fifteen, all his projections had grown otherworldly. No longer rushing him to orgasm, as they had in the early days of acrobatic postures and lacy lingerie, now his beauties entranced him for hours at a stretch. As settings for his trysts, he fashioned gardens riotous with flowers and brimming with fruits and thronged by magnificent beasts. Sometimes he postponed climax for days in order to refine his visions, like an alchemist in search of gold.

While his friends were vibrating to sex like struck tuning forks, rubbing one another's ticklish bodies, conceiving and aborting the occasional baby, Hoagy kept to himself at school and divided his time at home between the eros couch and his computer, where he studied exobiology.

Though the psychiatrists had warned her, Tanya was not prepared for the transformation in her son. He scarcely spoke to her anymore, unless she prodded him with questions. At meals he would stare off into space, forgetting to eat. He became alarmingly thin, his cheeks gouged by shadows. Fret lines appeared at the corners of his mouth.

One night, as she tiptoed down the hall, she noticed his door was ajar. Glancing in warily, she saw he was at his desk, studying a screenful of data. Relieved that he was not on the Freud, she slipped into the room. "What are all the numbers?" she asked.

Without looking up, he said, "Coordinates for E-type planets in our galaxy."

"E-type?"

"Planets sufficiently Earth-like to have the potential for supporting life as we know it."

She squinted at the rows of numbers. "So many?"

"On the order of ten million identified so far."

"How many have we explored?"

He snorted. "A handful. And those only by drones."

"Imagine all those planets. There might be creatures we've never dreamed of."

"Or creatures we *have* dreamed of," said Hoagy. Hunched over, his face reflecting the glow of the screen, he withdrew his attention from her as firmly as if he had thrown a switch.

Tanya studied the boy, her ninth birthing, whom she had been allowed to keep because of his unforeseen epilepsy. He was no more her genetic offspring than the previous eight had been. Only the Fertility Board knew whose egg and sperm had been implanted in her womb, knew what couple had refused to accept this flawed child. By rearing Hoagy, feeding him, helping him learn to crawl, to walk, to speak, she was bound to him by a link deeper than genes.

He did not glance up or speak when she wished him good night and closed the door.

Shortly before Hoagy's eighteenth birthday, when the time came to replace the Freud with a state-of-the-art model, Tanya brooded once more on the decision she had made years earlier to sign him up for the timeshell experiment. From his earliest schooldays, tests had shown him to be gifted at remembering complex images in precise detail. After glancing at a page of print, he could recite every word without error; after glimpsing a picture, he could draw an exact replica. Eidetic vision, the examiners called it, possibly a side-effect of his epilepsy. The gift was so rare that a Project VIVA psychiatrist, learning of Hoagy's case, had persuaded Tanya to enroll him in the program. The eros couches were designed to wean him away not merely from earthly women but from Earth itself. The psychiatrist put it bluntly: Your son will give up the chance of leading a normal life for a chance to overcome his disorder. Better he should pay this price, Tanya reluctantly decided, than die of a seizure. If he could contribute to science in the process, all the better.

What the psychiatrist did not tell her was that her son might go mad. Project VIVA, the program for mapping life in the Milky Way, had been stymied by a difficulty no one had foreseen in the pre-warp days: matter, including human bodies, passed through the timeshell without harm, but minds were deranged. When the early warpships returned at all, their crewmembers were insane. Nothing, it seemed, would protect the astronauts, neither drugs nor freezing nor hypnosis. Many scientists began calling the timeshell an impassable barrier, as the speed of light had been described in the twentieth century.

Just when the International Space Agency was on the point of shelving the project, declaring the human costs too high, the seventh flight brought back the hint of an answer. Officials approved for the trip a woman who was a paranoid schizophrenic. She returned just as insane as the rest of the crew, just as incapable of reporting her observations, but with her psychosis undisturbed. Her paranoia had passed twice through the warp without altering.

If some fixation less crippling than paranoia could be induced in the astronauts, perhaps it would preserve their sanity through the warp. Subsequent flights bore crews trained with mantras and mandalas, meditation and prayer. The returning astronauts were mad in novel ways, but mad nonetheless. Again there was a curious exception—a twenty-year-old Zen adept. Although he raved most of the time, he also had lucid spells in which he could describe the lava-spouting planet his flight had orbited. He was the youngest person ever to breach the shell, the youngest to be trained in fixation.

Perhaps, the psychiatrists reasoned, adults were the wrong candidates for training. Perhaps adolescents, with their fierce cravings and attachments, were more likely subjects. And what craving was fiercer or more easily manipulated than sex? Cautiously, after prolonged debates in scientific and governmental circles, Project VIVA was commissioned to test the idea.

After more than a thousand interviews, eight couples and four single parents were persuaded to enroll their adolescent children. If this experiment succeeds in revealing how to break through the timeshell, the parents were told, your child's name will be honored alongside those of Lindberg and Armstrong, Gagarin and Chi. The parents were not allowed to visit the hospital in Santa Fe where survivors of earlier flights dozed under heavy sedation or slouched in chairs, drooling. Imagining the dangers their children might face, Tanya Ferris and the other parents thought only of mild phobias, a stutter, a twitch. The risk seemed worth taking in exchange for the possibility of fame.

On the afternoon of his eighteenth birthday, Hoagy returned from the Institute for Exobiological Research to find in his room a top-of-the-line eros couch. Instead of projecting images onto a screen and synthesizing odors and sounds, this model directly stimulated the occipital and cerebral cortex and limbic system. The helmet pressed electrodes against his skull, the webbing cradled him as in a hammock. Lying in the machine's embrace, mind absorbed by the tingling sensations, Hoagy immediately entered a trance. Whatever he envisioned in this spellbound state became more vivid to him than anything in the waking world.

Fantasy women still drew him into his visions, with their silky bellies and exquisite feet, their hair spun from starlight. But now his desire expanded beyond these goddesses to conjure up entire planets, lush and pristine. Making love with such women, in such places, required him to leap beyond the confines of his own chemistry, to merge with an alien ecology.

Even when not strapped into the couch and helmet, he carried the images with him. By comparison, his actual surroundings seemed ugly and crude. He shuffled between home and the Exobiology Institute in a perpetual daze of desire. His teachers had never come across anyone so insatiably curious about extraterrestrial life, so relentless in his studies. The curriculum that should have kept him busy for seven years he finished in three. By age twenty-one he was working on the frontiers of the discipline.

He became a leading proponent of the view that wherever conditions were suitable for carbon-based life such life would inevitably appear, and if given enough time it would evolve and diversify, producing more and more complex organisms. The possibility that any of these organisms would be humanoid was vanishingly small, of course, but not zero. In a galaxy with tens of millions of candidate planets, there might be thousands on which species akin to Homo sapiens had evolved, and somewhere among them he might discover the infinitely desirable women who tantalized him in daylight and dream.

＊　＊　＊

Hoagy's link to the everyday world had grown so tenuous that he felt only mild surprise when his application to become an astronaut for Project VIVA was promptly accepted. He was more surprised by his mother's delighted response when he told her the news over breakfast.

"You're not upset?" he asked.

"Why should I be?" she said. "You were born for space. I've seen you headed there since you were a boy."

"You're not worried about the dangers?"

"Everything worth doing is dangerous."

"The timeshell—" he began.

"Wouldn't you love to be the one to break through?" she asked eagerly. "You'd be a pioneer. They say you've got the ideal mind for it. And you've prepared so well on the Freud."

The fervor in her voice rattled Hoagy. He shoved away from the table and retreated to his room and slammed the door. Prepared so well? *Prepared*? He paced back and forth, scowling at the eros couch, this luxurious and treacherous dream machine. All these years, his mother had let him believe these devices were only therapeutic, training him to govern his epilepsy. But that had never been their real purpose. They were designed to groom him for warp flight.

Suddenly furious, he flung the couch on its side, ripped the harness loose, tore out the electrodes, and stomped on the helmet until it cracked.

The door swung open and his mother stood there, appalled, gazing at the wreckage. "What are you *doing*?"

"Cutting the puppet strings!"

"What puppet strings?"

He kicked the helmet and sent it spinning across the floor. "This machine has been pumping me full of junk."

"Your visions?"

"The psychiatrists' visions!"

"They're yours, sweetheart."

"No." He shook his head doggedly.

With hands on hips, she glared at him. "The Freud only picked up your longings."

He slumped on the edge of the bed and waved a hand in front of his face. "Okay, they're my stupid longings. But they've been used to manipulate me."

"That's not true, and you know it. What you've imagined came out of your own mind."

He sat in silence for a moment before saying, "Then I'm a monster of desire."

"You're not a monster." She sat next to him and curved an arm around his waist. "We all have strong desires. I wanted a husband. I wanted a college degree. I wanted to be an artist. I've run out of chances for any of those things," she said, tears brimming. "But you have a chance to satisfy your longings. You have a gift. Your vision is so strong it can deliver you."

He let himself relax into the curve of her arm. "Even if I survive the warp," he said quietly, "my chance of finding a planet and a woman to match my vision is slim."

"Slim is better than nothing," she said. "It's better than I ever had."

For the first time in a long while, he looked searchingly at his mother, chastened and surprised by her grief. Her cheeks were splotched, her eyes red from crying, her lips crimped tight. Instead of dwelling on his own unappeasable hunger, he felt hers.

"Alright," he muttered. "I'll try. If I break through without going crazy, maybe I can find my heart's desire."

His mother picked up the shattered helmet. "But won't you need the Freud?"

"Not anymore. The vision never leaves me now."

Training for warp passage took three strenuous years. While Hoagy's conscious mind was absorbing the technicalities of flight, cross-species communication, bio-surveys and the like, his unconscious mind was elaborating the details of his visionary planet. The VIVA engineers who lectured about safety systems, the linguists who explained computer translation, and the neurophysiologists who monitored his brain were a blur to Hoagy. He took in their lessons, but otherwise ignored the instructors. The only people who captured his attention were his two partners, Jaffa Marx and Blake Polo. The three of them made up Alpha Trio, the first mind-conditioned group selected to pass through the timeshell.

Soon after the three had been introduced, Hoagy asked the others, "How old were you when you started on the eros couch?"

"Fourteen," answered Blake, a dark and doughy man, fluent in a dozen languages, expert in semiotics.

"Twelve," said Jaffa. She was an astrophysicist, tall and slender, with pale skin, lilting speech, and a bright, inquisitive manner.

"How long before you were—" Hoagy let his voice trail off.

"Possessed?" said Jaffa, her green eyes glinting. "I was hooked within a few months, first on guys, then on wild landscapes, and finally on a gorgeous planet."

"I followed the same path," Blake said, "only it took me a year to work my way from lovers to planet."

"This place you've imagined, does it feel like your real home?" Hoagy asked.

"Yes," said Jaffa, "like a garden I've been kicked out of."

"Exactly," Blake said. "I feel I'm in exile here on Earth."

As they compared their visions, they gradually realized they were all imagining the same planet, right down to the contours of cliffs and smell of hot stone and taste of springwater.

"Maybe the VIVA psychiatrists implanted the image," Blake suggested.

"That's what I used to think," Hoagy conceded. "But there's another possibility. Maybe our vision is a genetic inheritance, passed down from ancestors who lived on another world before they brought the seeds of life to Earth."

Jaffa snapped her fingers. "I've had the same thought."

"So myths of paradise aren't inventions—" Blake began.

"They're species memories," Hoagy said.

"Eden, Elysium, Shangri-La, nirvana," Jaffa chanted, "all of them glimpses of an actual place, somewhere out there."

"Yes," Hoagy said. "One of those tens of millions of E-type planets."

"But what are the chances of finding it?" Blake asked.

"And if we do," said Jaffa, "will it still be a paradise?"

And so the trio spoke excitedly, finishing one another's sentences, merging ideas they had conceived in solitude. Blake held that language forms a cosmic net, which all living things are weaving with their manifold speech. Eventually, consciousness will be able to journey from galaxy to galaxy on a web of signs. Consciousness already pervades the universe, according to Jaffa, who speculated that stars and quasars were manifestations of mind, with a subjective interior as well as a physical exterior. "Matter thinks," she said flatly. "Just look at the brain. If the brain, why not a nebula?"

Why not? Hoagy thought, even as he realized that he and his partners might only be spinning theories out of a need to believe they could actually reach the world they longed for.

✳   ✳   ✳

The sense of being in exile from their true home bound the Alpha Trio closely, further estranging them from ordinary people. Hoagy found it difficult to speak even with his mother, when she called two weeks before the launch to wish him well.

"You must be excited," she said.

"Yes," was all he could answer.

"This is the last call I'm allowed to make until after . . ." Her voice broke. On the screen her face was a white smear, which he could not bring into focus.

"After I'm back?" he suggested.

"Right. After you're back." When he said nothing, she pleaded, "Hoagy?"

"I'm here, Mom."

"Sweetheart, if I was wrong to get you into this . . . if anything happens to you . . . I'll never . . ." Again she faltered. Her face on the screen crinkled with pain. "I'm sorry," she added hastily, and hung up before he could think of anything comforting to say.

* * *

During the final week before launch, the members of Alpha Trio were kept apart, each one training in a mock-up of the warp chamber. Murmuring through headphones, psychiatrists coaxed them into deep trance, then urged them back to ordinary consciousness. "Mind sprints," Jaffa called the exercises.

Hoagy entered trance with ease, but struggled on the return. Hearing "T-state now," he swiftly conjured up his garden planet. Earth dwindled away behind, until he could no longer feel its pull, as he raced toward his beautiful, sumptuous globe. He recognized the oceans, the green continents, the mountain ranges, the sinuous rivers. Nearing the surface, he smelled the ozone from waterfalls, the pheromones from mating animals, the juices of burgeoning plants. He ached to land. But an instant before he touched down, the voice rang in his ear: "R-state now!" Return was torture. He had to fight against the lure of his vision, wrenching himself free, until he tumbled back into real time and found himself once more in the warp chamber. After a brief rest, he was told how many seconds he still needed to shave off his re-entry time. Then came the order, "T-state, now!" and the cycle repeated.

He was always tempted to ignore the peremptory voice that called him back. But he knew he must delay consummation, for he needed the full psychic charge of desire to keep his mind from whirling apart as he passed through the temporal dislocation of warp.

Beginning three days before launch, the training schedule was relaxed. Nutritional supplements brought Hoagy's body up to peak strength, and injections of neurotransmitters revved his brain to a dazzling clarity. He could not help wondering how much of this treatment had been given to those earlier astronauts, who had returned broken and mad.

✳ ✳ ✳

On the morning of launch the Alpha Trio were reunited in the warp chamber. They nodded at one another, lips tight. Once harnessed in, shoulders nearly touching in the cramped space, they went through pre-flight checks. They confirmed the targeting instructions: fourth planet of K-47 in the Great Globular Cluster of Hercules, 25,000 light years away. Time elapse, .001 seconds. For reasons the physicists still could not explain, zero-elapse passage disintegrated machines as well as minds, while times longer than a thousandth of a second accelerated the rate of metal fatigue. So the meter was set at .001, and each of the astronauts read the setting aloud.

While Hoagy listened to final instructions from the mission controller, he ran his gaze over the interior of the warp chamber, its rows of gauges and switches, its hard surfaces and warning labels. With a pang, he thought how much of his life he had spent encased in machines. If he survived this trip, maybe he would go outdoors more often. Earth must still have a few wild places. Nothing to rival his vision, of course, but small pockets of beauty here and there.

A faint whine told him the warp projectors were ramping up. Instinctively, he braced himself for super-G acceleration, even though he knew the force he was about to encounter would be nothing like gravity.

"Ready to center. Counting from sixty."

Hoagy glanced at his partners. Blake squeezed the armrest until his knuckles turned white. Jaffa's fingers spidered in the air, playing among life-fields only she could detect.

"Prepare for T-state," the controller said.

The projector's whine grew louder, and a shock sizzled along Hoagy's spine as the warp vector strengthened.

"T-state—now!"

Warp chamber, partners, everything vanished as he leapt into trance. Immediately he was buffeted by turbulence more violent than any seizure. Gales ripped at him, twisted and tumbled him. He could feel his center loosening, giving way. It would be so easy to let go, to be torn asunder. But he clung fiercely to the vision of his garden planet, filled his mind with its glory, and at length he passed beyond the turbulence, the winds relented, and he realized the ship had passed through the timeshell. He returned to real time without being summoned.

There on the monitor was a blue planet, which the sensors confirmed as their target. Of course, it wasn't the ancestral world that he and Jaffa and Blake had imagined, but it was lovely enough, marbled with clouds, burnished by light from its orange star. The reward for their ordeal would be to land there and search for life.

Blake's voice came through the earphones. "Are you back?"

"Yes," Hoagy muttered. "But it was a rough passage."

"Jaffa hasn't come around yet."

Hoagy looked in alarm at Jaffa, who twitched in her harness. He laid a hand on her arm and squeezed, absorbing her tremors. Presently she grew still. Her eyes slicked open. At first only the whites were visible, then the green irises. He leaned close. "Are you all right?"

"What?" Her head swiveled, surveying the warp chamber. "Where are we?"

"The other side," Hoagy said.

Her face lit up with a smile and she grabbed his hand. "We really made it?"

"There's our gem," Blake said, pointing at the monitor. "Covered in liquid water, as promised. If it isn't brimming with life, then nature missed a good chance."

Jaffa came fully alert as she gazed at the lovely blue planet. "There's life down there."

"Let's hope so," said Blake.

"There is. I can feel it. You'll see when we land."

Hoagy eased himself away from her. His hand burned where she had touched him. "First," he said, "we have to persuade the computer we're still sane."

They took the psychometric exam, to prove they had survived the warp with faculties intact. When each one earned a green light, they cheered.

According to the flight plan, now the engines should ease them down into the atmosphere, with Hoagy piloting them on the final descent. Instead of hearing the sizzle of plasma, however, they heard the start-up whine of the warp projector. An instant later the ship computer buzzed in their headphones: "Five minutes until transfer."

"Destination?" Hoagy demanded.

"Earth," the computer answered.

"Why?" said Jaffa. "Is there something wrong with our tests?"

"You have passed the tests. Now you will be returned for study."

"But we're supposed to land!" Blake roared.

"The bastards," Jaffa said. "They lied to us."

Hoagy slammed his fist on the instrument panel, where the clock was ticking down. "They never intended for us to explore. All they wanted was to see if we could pass through the timeshell without going nuts. We're just a source of data."

"Three minutes," droned the computer.

"Lab rats," Blake muttered. He said it again, louder, then he howled and his eyes rolled up and he thrashed in his harness.

Hoagy grabbed him by a shoulder. "Blake, snap out of it. We're going to jump."

"We can't let him go through warp like this," said Jaffa.

"I don't know if we can stop it." Hoagy scoured the instrument panel, but he could find no switch that would override the computer, which had clearly been programmed to carry out an immediate return.

"One minute."

Between bouts of laughter, Blake muttered in languages they had never heard.

There was no time for coaxing him back.

"Thirty seconds."

Hoagy and Jaffa exchanged despairing glances. He grasped her hand, curling his own thick fingers around her delicate ones, which could trace life's energy in thin air. Loud enough to be heard above the countdown, he called to her, "I need you to be whole when we get back."

Her reply was a shout. "And I need you!"

Those words and Blake's gibberish were the last sounds Hoagy heard before leaping into trance.

The agonizing spiral back to real-time was familiar, but instead of emerging in the warp chamber, Hoagy found himself in a blazing white room, strapped to a table, with a scanner swinging back and forth over his skull.

"Tell me your name," said a voice he recognized as that of the VIVA psychiatrist who was in charge of the timeshell experiment.

With brusque impatience, Hoagy responded to that query and to many more, until the doctor seemed satisfied.

"How are the others?" Hoagy demanded.

"Don't worry about the others."

"Damn it, tell me. Is Jaffa okay? Is Blake?" A pinprick in the hollow of his elbow soon washed away his questions. This trance was a chemical one, insipid, blank.

✳ ✳ ✳

When he was allowed to place calls the following day, Hoagy spoke first with his mother, who sobbed when she heard his voice. "I'm fine," he assured her.

"Oh, honey, I was so worried."

"Really, Mom. Everything's okay. They checked me out."

"You sound groggy."

"They shot me up with drugs when I got back. But my mind's clear."

"That's what the doctor told me," she said. "But I needed to hear it from you."

Unable to bear her crying, he said, "Gotta go, Mom. There's a big meeting."

"I'm so happy," she breathed as he ended the call.

There really was a meeting, a debriefing session in a seminar room crammed with a couple of dozen VIVA staffers by the time he arrived. He took a seat near the door. A moment later, Jaffa sidled in and sat next to him. "Zero damage," she confided.

"Same here," he answered, noticing her smell, as of mint tea.

Neither mentioned Blake.

The Director, a stern, fast-talking woman, opened the session by apologizing for having deceived the Alpha Trio with the promise of landing. "We were afraid no weaker motive would carry you through, yet we couldn't risk losing you to some mishap on the planet."

With that formality over, she ignored Hoagy and Jaffa and proceeded to explain what the mission had revealed about the psychology of warp transfer. The lights in the room dimmed. Projected onto a giant wall screen, a graph displayed three data lines, showing changes in brain chemistry and neuronal activity in each of the astronauts as they passed twice through the timeshell, once on the way out and again on the way back. Although the data lines were labeled simply A, B, and C, it was clear which one belonged to Blake, for on the return passage the line spiked chaotically, like the seismic trace of an earthquake and aftershocks.

Using a laser, the Director pointed out that in the two records where no damage occurred, and in the outgoing phase of the third record, the peak moment when mind slipped through the timeshell coincided with a precise mix of catecholamines—principally serotonin, dopamine, and epinephrine—and a corresponding neuronal firing pattern. A murmur spread across the room as the doctors, neuroscientists, and behavioral engineers took this in.

"We should be able to reproduce this effect in any healthy brain," the Director said, to rousing applause. She then set up two teams, one to work out the chemistry, the other to map and program the neuronal activity. "I want compounds and devices we can test on subjects within six months," she said. "And I want astronauts prepared for safe warp travel within a year."

The two teams gathered at opposite corners of the room and began buzzing with plans.

Hoagy leaned close to Jaffa and said, "So much for finding our planet."

She gave him a surprised look. "You don't think we'll get to go out again?"

"You might, but not me. Now that they've figured out how to send healthy people through warp, why send an epileptic?"

"But your seizures are under control."

"I've had two since we returned."

Jaffa laid a hand on his cheek and searched his face with her jade eyes. "If you don't go, I don't go."

Hoagy returned her gaze, feeling heartache for abandoning his visionary planet and gratitude for what she was offering. "I've been thinking there must be some wild places left here on Earth," he said.

"There must be," Jaffa agreed. "Let's go look."

The Audubon Effect

Keeva heard the eerie, strident hooting and felt the air tingle with their approach moments before she actually spied them. In a straggly V they climbed above the horizon of Aton-17, carving the violet sky, their wings blazing white as they banked over the ocean. Waves of energy rippled before them, like the advance of a storm.

"There," she whispered, pointing a slender arm.

"I don't see anything," said LaForest, who crouched beside her in a thicket of reedlike stalks, peering through binoculars. The muck of the shore smelled like a salt marsh on Earth, fecund and sour, as Keeva imagined the original broth of life might have smelled.

"They're headed straight for us," she told him.

LaForest crouched lower. Though his elbows and knees bent at painful angles, he was so lanky that his coarse brown hair rose above the water plants like an abandoned nest. His gawky height made people stare at him from a distance, but few exchanged looks with him at close quarters, for he had penetrating eyes. Keeva was among those few. She delighted in his searching gaze. It shielded her from the empathic signals that flowed into her from every living thing. Where she pressed against LaForest, there in the shallows, his limbs felt like tensed springs.

Taking his bearded chin in hand, she turned his face toward the approaching V. "See how their wings catch the light?"

Under the binoculars his lips drew tight from concentration, then parted with astonishment. "Yes," he murmured. "My God, they're like fire. Must be a hundred of them. And hear those high-pitched calls?"

The reeds quaked from his trembling. Keeva circled an arm around his waist, fingering the bones of his hip through the taut fabric of his shimmersuit. "Be still," she whispered. "I sense they're coming down."

They did come down, wings tilted, plowing to a stop and floating majestically in the calm waters of the cove, their black-billed heads lifted high on long white necks.

"What in the world *are* they?" Keeva asked. She recognized the bio-fields of thousands of creatures, but these were new to her.

LaForest lowered the binoculars, a flame of excitement in his cheeks. "If we weren't sixty-four light-years from Earth, I'd say they were tundra swans."

"Which they can't be?"

"Of course not. They aren't even birds, really."

The improbable creatures were feeding, tipping forward and thrusting their regal necks into the water, then bobbing upright and swallowing captured morsels. Between bites they ran their bills along their wings, preening. Born twenty years too late to have seen any species of living swan, Keeva possessed no feeling-print for them. But she had studied museum specimens and videos of swans, and in these elegant white beauties, afloat on Aton-17 like scraps of sunlight, she could see nothing alien.

"The resemblance is amazing," she whispered.

"But that's all it is, resemblance. This place differs from Earth in only a few parameters. It's a case of similar environments selecting for similar organisms." He drew the netgun from his pack. "Let's get one to scan."

He fired. The net settled on a gleaming body and held it firmly, wings folded and head erect. The others paddled around the immobilized one in nervous circles, long necks periscoping, on the alert. As LaForest began reeling in his prize, they broke into raucous chatter. Keeva sensed their panic, and her stomach knotted in sympathy. Suddenly there was an explosion of white bodies kicking and flapping, wings swatting the water, as the creatures scrambled for take-off. In seconds they were airborne, beating away out of sight, all except the specimen LaForest had snared.

"Got one of them, anyway," LaForest said.

Keeva put a hand on his shoulder, to keep him from rising. "Wait. I feel something else . . . flying . . . huge."

They searched the sky. She quickly spied an immense gliding shape with stiff wings, cruising toward them along the coast. In the otherworldly daylight, its underside was cobalt blue, and its wings and back, visible as it wheeled about, were an even deeper blue, like the smoky depths of mineshafts. A crested head with sword-like beak slowly turned, surveying the water.

Keeva shrank down among the reeds. The beast's aura made her think of caves, crevasses, deep sea rifts. "Some sort of raptor," she whispered. "It's ravenous."

LaForest nodded, a wag of beard. Stealthily he continued reeling in the net, its captive bobbing on the waves. The motion must have caught the hunter's eye, for the great head ceased pivoting, the wings drew in, and the massive body came hurtling down like a fallen swath of sky. LaForest dropped the reel and tugged at the line hand-over-hand, grunting, but it was too late. An instant before the raptor struck, its wings flared out and taloned feet swung down, then it snatched the animal, net and all, and began to climb.

LaForest leapt up, roaring, "Let go of my swan!" He yanked on the line and the talons opened, dropping the torn and bloody prey.

Gasping for breath, Keeva watched the predator ride a thermal up into the glare of Aton's star. The beast's hunger had nearly smothered her. When LaForest waded back through the shallows cradling the limp creature, the anguish in his face made her feel a stab of jealousy. "You called it a swan," she said.

"I was excited." Lifting the body, he rubbed his cheek against the downy breast.

Keeva took the black-billed head gently in her palm. The ebony eyes had glazed over. "It has the face of a swan. The same feathers, the webbed feet."

He shook his head doggedly. "All it lacks is the right history on the right planet."

LaForest held the tattered creature in his arms, its blood smearing his suit, as Keeva piloted the shuttle back to the warpship, which was anchored a few kilometers out in the bay. She and the other five members of the survey team had spent the previous week cooped up in that ship, studying maps, swallowing detox pills, running tests. The tests confirmed what the drones had shown: Aton-17's atmosphere was not only hospitable to humans, it was rife with flying organisms. LaForest had spent much of the week pacing the ship, eager to get outside. In studying most exotic creatures he was self-possessed, even coldly rational; but anything resembling a bird sent him into a frenzy. Keeva had seen him wade through swamps, crawl through briars, dangle in harness from shuttles, for the mere glimpse of a flying creature.

After remaining silent during the brief flight, his mind clearly churning, as they docked at the ship LaForest muttered, "This bird can't *be* here. It can't be *any*where. The last tundra swan was shot in 2049."

"What about that blue nightmare with the six-meter wingspan?"

He went on obliviously. "There were swans on the arks they sent up in the thirties. But those were real-time ships, and even if one had been aimed this way, it would take another five or six hundred years to get here."

"Did those ships carry raptors?"

"One puzzle at a time." He staggered to his feet under the swan's ungainly weight. "Let me get this to the lab. There's got to be an explanation."

Keeva opened the hatch and stood back. As he passed, the gleaming neck jounced languidly from his arms and one lustrous wing brushed her thighs.

Inside the ship, Gomez and Tishi were seated at the galley table, dictating their logs. Evidently they had just returned, for their shimmersuits were still muddy. Between log-entries, Tishi was sucking a drink through a straw, her thin lips puckered into a kiss. Gomez fondled a handful of glistening baubles that resembled clams. The two gazed up open-mouthed as LaForest hobbled through the galley with his burden.

Tishi's eyes widened. "What's *that*?"

"I don't know yet." LaForest stilted past them into the lab.

"It looked like a bird," said Gomez, face screwed up in puzzlement.

"It felt like a bird," Keeva said. With delicate motions of her fingers, she sketched in the air the creature's feeling-shape. But of course Tishi and Gomez, unable to sense bio-fields, could not read her gestures. The imprint of the huge soaring hunter she would not even try to draw, for it was too hideous.

"We saw plenty of flying organisms near our survey spot," Gomez said. "But we were busy studying the river"—he displayed his handful of iridescent baubles—"and we never dreamed those fliers could be anything like Terran birds."

"What was the largest wingspan you saw?" Keeva asked.

"Oh, a meter or so, I'd guess," Gomez replied. "Why?"

"There's something a lot bigger cruising around out there."

"How big?" Tishi asked. A frown accentuated the slant of her ink-black eyes and the upward strokes of her brows.

Keeva scrutinized the diminutive figure. Would she weigh even forty kilos? "Big enough to haul away a Japanese exobiologist."

Tishi smiled cautiously. "How about our plump friend here?"

"Me?" proclaimed Gomez, smacking his ample belly. "There's too much of me for one flying monster to haul off. It would take a flock."

"Wait until you see it." Keeva popped a detox pill in her mouth, washed it down with distilled water. "Yuck. The price we pay to thwart the local microbes." Rising to join LaForest in the lab, she turned, uneasy. "Are Minsk and Wodo still up in the hills collecting plants?"

While Gomez put in a call, Tishi sat very still and fixed those dark eyes on Keeva. "You are not teasing about this giant?"

"I wish I were."

"They're on their way back," Gomez announced.

"Any problems?" said Keeva.

"Something attacked their shuttle and knocked them around pretty good, but nobody's hurt. And they're bringing a few surprises for LaForest."

The two brightest regions in the lab were the wall screen, which displayed anatomical drawings of the tundra swan, *Cygnus columbianus*, and the table where LaForest was dissecting his baffling specimen. His gloves were stained with blood the same rusty color as his beard. He glanced up as Keeva entered, his face radiant with curiosity. "How could one of our extinct species turn up on Aton?"

"It's the same bird?" she replied.

"Genetically identical, according to the scanner."

She drew close to him. His hair still smelled like the muck of the seashore. Keeva felt roused by that smell, by his obstinacy, by the pale queenly presence of the dead swan. "Could it be parallel evolution?" she suggested.

"The odds against it would be astronomical. Think of the billions of accidents that led to this species. They couldn't be duplicated on two planets."

"What if they're not accidents?"

"You know I don't believe in cosmic design. Evolution is like water running downhill, cutting a channel, and no two paths are ever the same."

"Do you really think life's that simple?"

"I think it's blind, that's all. It blunders into shapes that work in a given habitat. I don't believe there's a preordained set of possibilities."

"But sometimes I feel patterns." She plucked the air, as if playing a harp, searching for words to convey her intuitions. "There are only so many states an electron can occupy, so many ways a crystal can form. Organisms might be like that, except the number of possible states is far greater."

"You and your Platonic forms." His face softened and he put a finger to her cheek. "The tundra swan can only happen once. And so can you."

He leaned down to kiss her. Through the bloodied suit she traced his collarbone, touched the hollow at the base of his throat, felt his pulse. Life danced everywhere—in the violet skies of this planet, in the deeps of space, in this man. She felt him trembling, as he had shivered while watching the swans, and she trembled with him.

Boots sounded in the passageway and the lab door slid open. Tishi hurried in first, then Gomez. Wodo came next, with several catch-nets dangling from his brown fists, each net holding a lump of feathers.

"Fliers for the bird man!" he cried, hoisting the specimens.

"And here's more," said Minsk, who sidled in after Wodo, bearing another clutch of nets.

LaForest stooped excitedly over these new discoveries. One of the feathered tufts squirmed in its web and emitted a frail peep. "They're all alive?" he asked hopefully.

"Of course," said Wodo. "We knew you'd skin us if we snuffed any."

For their first survey they had chosen to botanize—as Wodo liked to say—up in the hills in a stand of tree-like plants. From each trunk at a height of four meters or so, limbs rayed out like spokes, each limb joining onto a nearby trunk, so the branches formed a scaffold. The wilderness came alive in Keeva's mind as Wodo and Minsk reported their findings. They described phosphorescent vines weaving through the lattice of limbs. Fungus-like growths sprouting from flinty soil. Lavender tubes writhing to catch the filtered light. Everywhere a chattering and buzzing. Furtive shapes darted in the shadows. When Minsk and Wodo climbed up into the canopy, they found the air thronged with fliers—swooping, twittering, winging dizzily, a fever of motion.

"So we caught a few for our bird man to study," Wodo said.

"And the raptors?" said Keeva. "A pair attacked you?"

Wodo frowned. "We were flying back when they hit our shuttle. It took all the juice we had to drive them off the hull."

Ivory-billed woodpecker, demoiselle crane, bower bird, Carolina parakeet, dodo, crested ibis, passenger pigeon, blue bird-of-paradise, and half a dozen more—LaForest called out their names as the scanner analyzed the chemistry and anatomy of each specimen. He wore an expression of stunned amazement, the same look he wore during warp-jump or love-making, Keeva thought, as if the muscles of his face were numb from an excess of emotion. Only his eyes burned.

She had met him six years earlier, when he approached her at a VIVA conference with a song sparrow in his hands, inviting her to hold it. Even without his rangy good looks, his passion for birds would have attracted her. Since childhood, she had yearned for companions who shared her gift—or affliction—of sensing biological fields. Oh, to meet a St. Francis, Thoreau, Leopold, or Carson! Such people, uncommon at any time, were exceedingly rare in her own age, when humans lived inside the Enclosure, never leaving the network of travel tubes and domed cities, wandering among their own artifacts like joy-seekers lost in a labyrinth of mirrors.

So when LaForest invited her to hold the tiny sparrow, his face aglow, Keeva had felt a tremor of recognition. Soon they were members of the same Project VIVA team, then survey partners, and eventually lovers. His bio-sense proved to be weaker than hers, but his reasoning was more powerful. Their complementary skills made them a brilliant survey team—Keeva locating the organisms, LaForest fitting them into the scheme of near-galaxy life. In their first five years together, they produced bio-maps for seven E-type planets. By the time video arrived from drones sent to Aton-17, showing skies filled with bird-like creatures, she and LaForest were in a position to choose their own survey locations, and of course they chose to go investigate these flying wonders.

This was the dream, she knew, that sustained him through the arduous training for Project VIVA and the ordeal of warp-jump, this dream of finding, somewhere among the millions of E-type planets in the Milky Way, creatures analogous to the avifauna that once flourished on Earth. Now he had found not merely analogies but exact matches.

LaForest gently placed the last of the captured birds in a mist cage. Bending near, he made cooing sounds, more like a doting father-bird than a sober scientist. "So now we have two mysteries," he said.

"How they got here and—what?"

"Why they all belong to species that are extinct on Earth."

She contemplated the rainbow of birds. "*All* of them?"

He nodded. "Every last one. Extinguished."

"How long ago?"

"Most of them since 2020. A few earlier."

She bent over the warbling turquoise bit of fluff which LaForest had identified as an indigo bunting. It was like a bright scrap torn from the enormous predator that had killed the swan. "When did this one disappear?"

"Around 2050."

"And this one?" She pointed to a small, streaked bird with a cocked tail and down-curved beak.

"Yucatan wren, last sighted in Mexico about 2040, soon after Enclosure."

Keeva gazed at the chittering, posturing, preening birds. Who, seeing such beauty, could bear to have it erased? Had her ancestors ever imagined it this concretely—a chorus of vibrant, singing creatures banished forever?

"Of course," LaForest mused, "our sample may be skewed. We may have stumbled onto the only pocket of birds on the planet. Or there may be hundreds of other species that are nothing like Earth's." He smoothed his beard with fingers and thumb. "We've got to find out how they blundered into these familiar shapes."

"Life doesn't *blunder*," she said. "These aren't accidents."

"You think some deity collected them on Earth and planted them here?"

"Of course not," she said defensively. "It's just a feeling I get from the birds, a note common to all of them."

"A feeling—"

"Something familiar, something I've picked up before—"

"On Earth?"

"I'm not sure where." Eyes closed, tracing the energy field radiating from the caged birds, she tried to name that elusive overtone.

✳   ✳   ✳

Each morning the survey teams set out in their shuttles to study the planet. They found bizarre vegetation, colonies of clicking bugs, legless ground-wrigglers, inflated water-skimmers—nothing even faintly earthlike, except for birds, and birds they found everywhere. Some they netted, but most they merely scanned, for the ship was soon crowded with specimens.

Even the most improbable of the birds—ones with bills like hatchets, wattles bright as neon signs, feathers in more zany colors than a clown's wardrobe—proved to be identical with species that had once flourished on Earth but were now extinct: whooping cranes, emus, auks, an array of hummingbirds, three kinds of eagle, nine owls, leggy herons, bald vultures. Born into the desolate age of the Enclosure that followed the Great Extinction, Keeva found it hard to imagine her home planet had ever held such bounty.

Here on Aton-17, birds appeared to occupy the top of the food chain. The lattice-work forests abounded with small creatures, none of them quick or powerful enough to prey on adult birds, but perhaps they kept the avian population in check by raiding nests.

For the next few days, nobody sighted the menacing raptors. Every time she glanced at the sky, Keeva nerved herself for that huge silhouette and its blast of hunger. Then one afternoon, as she and LaForest were returning to the ship with a cargo of birds, a wide-winged shape glided onto the shuttle screen, wheeling overhead.

"Uh, oh," she said.

"What's the matter?" said LaForest.

Before she could answer, the creature dove. Keeva threw the craft into a roll but could not evade the raptor, which slammed into the shuttle. The captive birds screeched. Keeva jounced in her harness, clinging to the joystick. There was a scrabbling sound, talons raking metal, wings buffeting the roof. She fired a mild voltage through the hull, but the jostling continued. She upped the voltage. A crested head loomed in front of her and hammered on the cockpit window. Finally she amped the charge to maximum and the raptor loosed a piercing shriek and spiraled up and away.

Keeva pulled the shuttle out of its dive. The birds cowered in their cages. LaForest looked stricken.

"Whew," she said. "You all right?"

Between gasps, he muttered, "Now I know how the swans felt."

The following day, Tishi beamed a breathless call from the nearby canyon where she and Gomez were surveying. "One of those raptors is prowling around upstairs," she told Keeva, who was in the ship logging data. "I think it's measuring us for supper."

"You'd only make a couple of mouthfuls," Keeva said.

"Don't joke. You should see this thing."

"I've seen one. Listen, you two get in your shuttle and put a scan on it. We'll fly over there and dart that bruiser."

"Too bad we can't just *kill* it."

"Now, now. Remember the code. Get under cover and sit tight."

Keeva had to wake LaForest, who was bone-weary from hours of wading in marshes and climbing pseudo-trees. When he understood what they were going after, he came swiftly alert.

In a few minutes they were nearing the canyon, and could see the other shuttle, sleek and fan-shaped like a stingray, with Tishi and Gomez inside. The raptor circled above, wings motionless for long spells, then it flapped languidly, swiveling its great crested head. Its hunger made Keeva throb. The wheeling flight left a burning afterimage in her mind. Whatever it was, it clearly ruled these skies.

"Some kind of dinosaur," LaForest murmured, glassing the beast. "Early in the transition to birds. No sign of feathers. Wings covered by membrane. Scaly legs."

"I'll try to get close enough for a dart," said Keeva. "You figure the dose."

While they spoke, the hunter pumped its wings and climbed rapidly.

Focusing the scanner through the cockpit window, LaForest said, "Don't lose it. I'd love to get some DNA. But I need at least a clear scan."

"Okay. Here goes." Keeva donned the guide-helmet, so she could steer with her eyes. The predator's hunger drowned out all other sensations. Finger poised on the throttle, she warned, "Hold on."

The shuttle rose swiftly to pursue the soaring hulk. Its long tapering wings stroked the air. Suddenly it banked, and plunged toward the canyon. Keeva watched it steadily, and the shuttle rode the beam of her sight, diving with giddy speed. The raptor leveled out a few meters above the canyon floor and raced between the sandy walls. Then it swerved up a side canyon, the great wings nearly raking stone, and with a sickening tilt the shuttle hurtled after, down ever narrower gulches. Keeva was scarcely breathing. The hunt possessed her. Suddenly a bluff loomed ahead, the raptor swooped up and over, Keeva jerked her gaze after it, and the shuttle, lurching, barely cleared the stone rim. In the few seconds it took the craft to right itself, the raptor escaped.

Keeva spun the shuttle, searching the sky. She wanted to chase down that beast, pounce on it, tear it apart, her training forgotten in a rush of adrenalin.

Beside her in the cockpit, LaForest wheezed, "Enough."

She was shaking. "It can't have gone far."

"No, please, let it go. I got a good scan."

She forced her eyes away from the arid landscape, toward her partner. His face was drained, skin drawn tight.

"I never saw you so fierce before," he said. "It was like blood lust."

She released a long breath, pulled off the guide-helmet, shook her hair loose. "I never felt a bio-field like that before. It was monstrous, ancient, like some primordial enemy."

The scanner identified the creature as *Quetzalcoatlus alleni*, a pterosaur from the Cretaceous, with a wingspan up to twelve meters, best known from fossils discovered in the 2020s.

The raptor's aura still haunted Keeva as she roamed among the mist cages feeding and watering birds. The air was thick with trilling. The flood of sensations made her dizzy. That familiar overtone, part of a melody she could not quite remember, played above the roar.

Tishi and Gomez were hunched over microscopes, examining plants. LaForest was analyzing scans of *Q. alleni*. The skeletal view glimmered on the screen when Minsk and Wodo trooped into the lab with their day's catch of birds and data.

Keeva groaned. "Where are we going to put more birds?"

"Hang them from the ceiling," answered Wodo cheerfully. Gesturing at the screen, he said, "We saw four of your raptors flying down the coast."

"Keeva and I saw two on our way back to the ship," LaForest said.

"I wonder how many of those brutes there are," said Minsk.

"I'm waiting for an answer to that," LaForest replied. He had fed to the drones orbiting Aton-17 information on the pterosaur's wingspan, flight pattern, and infrared print, enough metrics to distinguish it from other avifauna. Now he keyed in a request for a global census. A schematic of the planet flashed onto the screen, and black dots began appearing, each one marking the position of a giant raptor. Eventually, skeins of dots encircled the globe, sweeping along coasts and mountain ranges, all converging on a volcanic island near the equator.

"There are *thousands*," Tishi breathed.

LaForest scratched his beard. "Why the devil are they congregating?"

Keeva imagined that fearsome gathering. "We stirred them up, and they're swarming like bees when you disturb a hive."

Fingering the spot on the globe where the flight trajectories came together, LaForest said, "Let's move the ship there and see what they're up to."

No one objected. If the crew members had craved safety, they would never have joined Project VIVA, never left the Enclosure. The jump was quickly made, and the ship materialized on a lava field near the center of the island. Dozens of raptors spiraled overhead, casting great patches of shadow. More glided over the horizon, gathering from all points of the compass. By nightfall, several hundred smoky shapes whirled in that vortex.

✻   ✻   ✻

Next day, while the others ventured out cautiously in their shuttles to continue surveying, LaForest and Keeva stayed aboard ship to observe *Q. alleni.* He inscribed their data onto a warp chip for transfer back to Earth, and she kept watch through the domed roof. All day the sky darkened as flight upon flight of predators arrived. She had expected to be overwhelmed by their hunger. But instead she sensed a different craving. For what?

"Why send back data before we have any idea what they mean?" she asked LaForest. "What's Control going to think when they read that the dominant bio forms on Aton-17 are extinct Terran birds?"

"They'll probably think I want to see birds so badly that I'm conjuring them out of thin air," he admitted.

"Could you delay the report long enough for me to test a hunch?"

He turned abruptly toward her, bumping one of the suspended cages, which set off a chorus of alarm calls. "What's your hunch?" he cried above the din.

She waited for quiet, then said, "You know that terrible hunger I was picking up? It isn't coming through anymore."

"So they've gorged themselves."

"Exactly, as birds do before they set off on migration. And they're milling around, like a vast dynamo, charging up for some move."

He gazed at the funnel of birds. "What sort of move?"

"I can't tell from inside the ship. Too much shielding."

Although he objected, she slipped out through the hatch. Immediately, the full force of the raptors' energy surged through her. Tears sprang to her eyes.

In a moment the hatch swung open behind her and LaForest's bushy head emerged. "This is crazy. Come back in here."

Barely able to speak, she growled, "I'm all right."

"At least carry a stunner."

"They're not interested in me."

"Keeva, please—"

"Go back inside. You're disturbing the field."

After a pause the hatch clicked and she was alone. Standing amid the rubble of cooled lava, with thousands of pterosaurs circling above, Keeva felt as if she were in the eye of a cyclone. She glanced at the ship. It looked frail, like an exposed egg. How presumptuous, she thought, for Earth to fling these bubbles into space.

The hatch opened and LaForest called out, "They're all here. The drones show every single one on the planet has arrived."

"Quiet, or I'll lose them."

Again he withdrew. She pressed a palm against each temple, intent on the vortex of raptors circling above, building power. Their yearning swept everything else from her mind. As night fell the ominous forms merged with the darkness, their craving sharpened, and suddenly she recognized the shape of their desire. She screamed.

An instant later the sky was empty.

Even with eyes shut, Keeva realized from the serenade of birds that she was in the lab. When her eyes blinked open, she discovered five anxious faces peering down at her where she lay on a bench.

"We thought they'd snatched you away," said LaForest with a tense smile.

"No danger of that," Keeva murmured. "They were too intent on traveling."

"Traveling where?" LaForest asked sharply.

"To Earth." Keeva sat up with a groan. The others drew back, as if fearing she might flail about. "Just before they took off, what they were longing for came into focus—the image of Earth—and their desire swept over me. It was more than I could bear. That's why I screamed."

Above her, the others exchanged worried looks.

"Lie back down," said LaForest, who was gripping her shoulder lightly. "Give your head a chance to clear."

"It *is* clear. Everything finally makes sense." His gentle pressure forced her down onto the pillow. She did not really mind. There would be time to explain. She was exhausted, yet the energy of that blue cyclone whirled in her still.

"No animal can fly sixty-four light-years through a vacuum, not even with a twelve-meter wingspan," LaForest said patiently.

Keeva was unwrapping herself from the blankets in which he had bundled her the night before. She felt restored, except for the aching sense of loss which the departure of the great hunters had left in her. "They didn't fly," she said.

"Then how did they go?"

"They warped." She sat up with blankets snarled about her waist, hair frizzed. The mad empath in the morning, she thought.

LaForest eyed her warily. "We're talking about pterosaurs, sweetheart, not ships."

"I'm telling you they went through warp. I saw where they were going, I felt them slip through. I've passed through too many times myself to mistake the feeling. And every bird in here," she said, gesturing at the twittering cages, "gives off some trace of warp passage. It's in them, in their genes. That's the overtone I've been trying to identify since we netted our swan. From at least as far back at Q. alleni, they're descended from creatures that migrated through warp."

Years of collaboration had taught him not to dismiss her intuitions, but his reason balked. "How could they have learned to warp?"

"How did they learn to fly?"

"But humans have understood the principles of space transfer for only a few decades."

"So? Birds have had millions of years to figure it out. Think of all the methods they use to orient themselves in migration—sun, stars, magnetic field, landforms, wind. Who knows what else? We still can't navigate as well as a homing pigeon."

He shook his head. "Birds can't warp. They just can't."

"Trust me. I felt them go."

His bewilderment touched her. His mouth sagged open, as it had when he first spied the tundra swans blazing like white fire above the ocean. She knew he was turning over the idea, to see what it might yield.

"All right, for the sake of argument, let's suppose they *can* go through warp." He began pacing among the cages, the birds tracking him with their glossy eyes. "Let's say the ancestors of all these birds traveled here from Earth. To avoid extinction back home, they all fled here." Suddenly he stopped, snagged by a memory. "Maybe old Audubon wasn't so demented after all."

"Audubon?"

"There's a passage somewhere in his *Lunatic Journal*, the one he wrote in his final years, when he was demented. Let me find it." He punched in a query, and a page came up on the screen. "Here. Listen. 'Extinction of species has ever mystified the naturalist. As for birds, perhaps those that vanish are merely slaughtered. Or perhaps cruel nature has extinguished them with ice or fire. Or perhaps, when sorely pressed by men or circumstance, birds undertake a grand migration, to the moon or farther planets.'"

"Maybe he wasn't so demented," Keeva said.

"Maybe not." LaForest stood dead still among the birds. A parrot thrust its enameled bill through the mesh of its cage and took a nip at his shoulder. With mounting excitement, he said, "If Audubon's guess was right, and some threats on Earth drove these birds here, could some disturbance here drive them back?

Did *Q. alleni* flee because we challenged their dominion over Aton?"

Keeva hugged the blankets about her knees. She gazed at the captive birds, large and small, gaudy and plain, each one the exquisite outcome of millions of years of evolution. "Just think, if all these beauties went back home."

He considered the idea, then said quickly, "No, the code won't allow it. We can't tamper with whole ecosystems."

"Then we'll have to leave, won't we? Otherwise, we may trigger more migrations." When he hesitated, she asked, "Are you going to say anything about it when you send that data?"

"I transferred the chip an hour ago," he said. "Control sent a reply, but I haven't had a chance to look at it."

Curious what earthbound scientists would think about news of tundra swans, indigo buntings, and other extinct Terran birds, Keeva thumbed a button to display the message:

> *Very funny, LaForest. Were you sampling Aton-17's mushrooms when you made that report? Now please send real data.*
>
> *Speaking of birds, here's a puzzler for you. Hong Kong reported an aerial attack this a.m. We sent a drone to check and it came back loaded with the body of a flying monster, which had crashed into the dome. Huge blue thing. The scans show it's a pterosaur known from fossils dating to the Late Cretaceous.*

LaForest reached out for Keeva's hand, like a man surprised in sleep groping for a light. "So they really are going home."

"Home," she echoed. "I wonder what they'll think of Earth."

The Land Where Songtrees Grow

On all that forsaken planet, nothing moved but the searchers. Their boat glided through the swampy forest, slipping over mats of water plants, around hummocks smothered in ferns, beneath the arching roots of songtrees. Vines looped from branch to branch, gnarled lavender ropes like crude streamers left from a party. Far overhead the canopy of purple leaves formed a lacework roof, admitting needles of daylight. The glassy still water divided at the prow of the boat, gathered at the stern, and in a moment turned again to glass.

The rescue party had quickly found the desolate basecamp. Leaving their warship in orbit around Memphis-12, they had flown down in the shuttle, following locator signals that kept beaming out from the orange dome of the camp like the wail of an abandoned child. Inside, the dome was a shambles, with tools and clothing scattered about, mud caked on the floor, papers and disks and bits of plants jumbled together, the air fetid with the smell of corrosion and rot. Careful examination of the mess revealed no clues to the scientists' disappearance. They could not have gone far, for their boat, a bright red inflatable like the one the rescuers used, was tethered near the dome.

For three Memphis days, which were just over thirty E-hours long, the searchers had scoured the swamp, working outward from the dome in widening circles. Their boat skimmed the water, driven by an electric motor that purred quietly. Otherwise, the silence was broken only by their own voices and, for a spell each dawn and dusk, by the clamor of the trees. Now and again a crew member would cry out, having seen in the murk what looked like a grimacing face or lifted hand, but every alarm proved false. By their fourth day of threading the watery maze, they had grown sick of peering through the gloom for any sign of the missing exobiologists. Eyes ached, throats rasped from the steamy air.

Their fatigue was obvious to Kyle Benton, leader of the five-person team. But he was a stickler for schedules, and so he would keep them looking until songtide. They could rest for the hour or so while the trees howled and screeched, then the search would resume. In every direction the songtrees rose on scaffolds of roots, like muscular arms propped on splayed fingers. Benton could not shake the feeling that, behind his back, the trees kept shifting, their knobby roots astir in the muck. Everything was a purple tint, shading from violet through lavender and mauve to near-black. Returning to camp this evening would be a relief, if only to see the bright orange dome, its geometrical curves defying this vegetable disorder.

When the trees began the creaking and groaning that preceded songtide, Benton called a halt. Though the team had encountered nothing on Memphis-12 that could upset the boat—no wind, no current in the inky water, no beasts—he ordered that the craft be moored. It paid to follow routines; they kept a man steady in face of the unexpected. That was why he set one dial of his watch to Pacific Time, no matter where Project VIVA sent him on rescue missions. Obeying routine had kept him and his crews alive and sane through two decades of hunting for scientists who had run amok or gotten lost or died in dozens of ways on dozens of worlds.

"Okay," Benton called, "we knock off for an hour."

"May we swim, Captain?"

The question was from Megan Kerry, a cyber engineer fresh out of Chicago, with the reckless energy and curiosity of a first-timer. Her genius with electronics had persuaded Benton to take her on, in spite of that dangerous enthusiasm and her Irish good looks. She had pestered him about swimming since the first day.

"Why are you so eager to get into that filthy soup?" he asked.

"I want to hear how the music sounds in the water."

"Music?" he scoffed. But she was so unjaded, so eager, that he relented. "All right. Go ahead and swim. But take detox."

Kerry tucked a loop of sandy hair behind her ear. "We have to wear helmets?"

He wished the woman would either chop off her luxuriant hair or tie it back in a knot. "Yes, you have to wear helmets. I don't want any skin exposed to that swill."

She obediently swallowed the medicine and sealed her bubble helmet to the neck-ring on her yellow shimmersuit. Then she plunged over the side, her sleek body sinking into the lavender broth. A moment later she surfaced, glistening like a seal. The pleasure on her face unsettled Benton. He was reassured to see that Seth Cummings, the doctor, was also taking detox and donning a helmet. Ingrained caution had enabled Cummings to survive thirty missions. If he would entrust himself to those scummy waters with only a pill and a suit for protection, Benton could stop worrying.

Mary Zee, the communications tech, also went swimming, which left Benton alone in the boat with Reynaldo Valdez, the pilot, a droopy man in his forties who never exerted one joule of effort more than was absolutely necessary. Without a word, Valdez leaned back and closed his puffy, red-rimmed eyes.

Benton endured the bellowing and caterwauling of the trees with gritted teeth. Whoever had named them songtrees must have possessed a tin ear. For that matter, the burly growths with their vaulted roots and purple canopy were not really trees at all, any more than the spiky fans bristling from every hummock were ferns or the rafts of scum were algae. How many of these organisms had the biologists named before breaking off contact with VIVA Control? Labeling things seemed to be mostly what researchers did on these E-type planets. Benton never stayed long enough on any world to learn the exotic names, so he called things by whatever terrestrial analog they brought to mind.

The scrawking of the trees grew louder, like a crescendo of voices in a madhouse. He glanced at his watch. Another half hour or so, and then the breathless calm.

A splashing caught his eye and he jerked. It was Kerry, backstroking from one songtree to another, her knees and arms churning with each stroke. Inside the helmet her mouth was open wide, as though panting or singing. Had he ever felt so exuberant, even as a child?

Eventually the high-pitched squeals gave way to mutterings, and then to silence. The craft wallowed as three dripping figures climbed aboard, the young woman last. She pulled the helmet away and gave her head a vigorous shake, the long hair whipping out in russet curls. "You should try it, Captain," she said. "The singing makes you tingle all over."

"I'll leave the tingling to you," said Benton.

She turned away abruptly and moved to her seat.

"Cast off the lines," he commanded, "and let's get moving."

In the stern, Valdez yawned, and reached for the throttle. They swept another circle through the bog, Kerry and Zee sharing the middle seats, Benton and Cummings the bow, on the lookout for movement in the mazy stillness, for a break in the monotonous purple.

"Their bodies couldn't just vanish," Benton muttered to the doctor. "The suits would have kept them afloat."

"If they're dead," said Cummings, always the hopeful one. At fifty he was the oldest of the crew, with a squat body and a face as round and blank as a plate. He never ceased to expect good news, no matter how many times he stumbled upon disaster.

Benton ducked as they passed beneath the arching roots of a songtree. "Two months without logging in to Control? Their boat tied up at the dome and their camp a pigsty? Of course they're dead."

From behind, Kerry said, "I understand why VIVA wants the data and gear, but why are they so intent on collecting the bodies?"

"Because nobody wants to rot alone and forgotten on some stinking planet," said Benton.

"When I die, Captain," said Zee, a thickset woman with the abrasive rapid-fire voice of an auctioneer, "just chop me up and dump me in the fish tank."

"I'll do that, Zee."

"It's getting too dark to see," Valdez called.

"It's light enough," said Benton. "We'll finish this circuit and then head back to camp."

Again he checked his watch—midday back in Oregon, which he still thought of as home, although he visited there only briefly between missions. On Memphis-12 it was late evening, but in the perennial gloom you could only tell it was nightfall because, here and there, phosphorescent stumps began to glow. To some eyes, he thought, the twilit swamp might almost appear beautiful.

※　※　※

Sleep had always seemed to Benton a bite of emptiness out of the day, and he got by on as little as possible. Long after the others had curled up in the antechambers that encircled the dome, he sat at the main console listening to the biologists' log.

". . . synchronous variables for sound contour in lower registers . . . songtide enunciation period . . . mimicry blended with improvisation in the mocking-trees . . ."

Skeins of jargon. He punched the fast-forward, released it, heard a rattle of numbers, punched the control again, heard a buzz of polysyllables. He kept skimming the record, without finding any clue to the disappearance of the nine researchers. Toward the end, the log became fragmentary, days passing between entries; he detected a note of boredom, almost of lethargy, as if the ponderous rhythms of the swamp had invaded their blood. But the substance of the entries remained the same—numbers and jargon—so perhaps the boredom he heard was his own.

He shut off the log, rubbed his eyes, then peered through the console window. He imagined the vegetation out there seething, roots groping through the mire. The darkness was broken only by those glowing stumps. On Earth their pale light would have been called foxfire, a kind of fungal decay. No telling what it should be called here, or what caused it.

Startled by a shape blurring the edge of his vision, he swung round. Kerry's wiry figure, clad in a sleepsuit the color of mint, swayed toward him on bare feet. Her eyes were closed, her lips moved, and her body undulated to whatever music was playing through her headphones.

Benton stood up, hesitated, then grabbed her shoulder and gently shook her.

Her eyes blinked open, dreamy, gray. She removed the headphones, setting her curls jouncing. "What?"

"You're walking in your sleep."

She looked about in confusion, then crossed arms over her chest. "Oh, my."

"You aren't on anything, are you?"

The confusion in her eyes gave way to indignation. "I'd never touch a chemmie during mission, sir."

"You'd better not, or I'll warp you straight home." Her lips crimped into a hard line. A twitch beneath his hand made him realize he was still clutching her shoulder. He lifted the hand casually, as if no longer feeling the need to steady her. "What were you listening to?"

"Recordings of the songtrees." The contour of her lips softened. "They're lovely."

"Lovely? They sound like bedlam to me."

"But there are melodies, subtle ones. Sometimes you can almost make out words." She combed fingers through her sandy hair, clutching a handful and letting it fall over her shoulders. "If you'd go in the water when they're singing, you could hear."

"I don't give a damn about moaning trees. I want those nine bodies."

"If it's not rude to ask, sir, do you get any pleasure from exploring new planets?"

He considered a moment before replying, "I get pleasure from finding things."

"Things?"

"Equipment, tools, people—whatever's lost." He felt unaccountably defensive, here in this pocket of light, surrounded by the impenetrable swamp, confronted by a woman still warm from sleep. He added, "I hate for things to be lost."

"A place for everything and everything in its place?"

He looked sharply at her. Was she mocking him? Her cheeks, he noticed, were lightly freckled, her lashes as pale as gauze, her rosy Irish face unlined. So young—twenty-three, was it? twenty-four?—too young to understand how easily things fall apart. "You'd prefer chaos?"

"No, sir. Of course not."

"Because that's how everything trends, don't you see? Toward increasing disorder, maximum entropy. Everything we've made is fragile. If we relax, it will collapse."

"Is that why you're out here? To push back chaos?"

He shrugged the question aside. "Back to bed, Kerry, and don't go wandering."

Her hand rose in a gesture of apology, but he refused to acknowledge it. She backed away, placing her bare feet carefully as if she were approaching the brink of a cliff.

* * *

If the instruments had not assured Benton that each sweep
of the boat covered new territory, he would have sworn they kept
circling over the same path, for on all that soggy planet there were
no shorelines or mountains, no lakes or rivers to mark boundaries,
nothing but hectare after hectare of swamp. At dusk and dawn he
called a halt during songtide, for he did not trust his crew to keep
a watchful eye during that nerve-grating din.

Valdez took advantage of these respites to catch up on his
sleep, as if he were compensating for a lifetime of wakefulness. Zee
and Cummings sometimes played chess, sometimes sat reading on
the upthrust knees of songtree roots, sometimes floated lazily in
the water. Kerry always swam. Too often, Benton found himself
watching her. He would be seated in the bow, mapping search patterns or writing in his log, when the sleek figure would hook his
attention and drag his gaze along.

Catching him at this once, Valdez commented drowsily, "Bit
of a distraction, isn't she, Captain?"

"I'm worried about her, is all," Benton said. "I keep wondering
if there's something in the muck that detox won't handle. I can't
afford having anyone get sick."

"No, indeed, sir," Valdez replied with a skeptical smacking of
his lips. "Still and all, she livens things up."

On the sixth day the scanner guided them to a concentration
of metal, which proved to be the nine survival belts, concealed in
a hollow stump. Some of the tools were missing, but each belt still
carried its locator. Instead of beaming out signals, however, the
transmitters were silent.

"They've been jammed," said Zee. "That took some doing."

By reflex, hands touched the locators at the rescuers' own waists. Immune to almost any accident, these devices were like amulets guaranteeing eventual return to Earth, dead or alive.

Kerry studied the heap of belts, her face pensive. "They didn't want to be found."

Benton turned to the doctor. "You still think they're alive, Cummings?"

"Well, sir, there've been cases—"

"Save it. I don't want to hear any miraculous survival tales. Let's just find them and get off this filthy planet. They can't have gone far without equipment."

Piece by piece over the next few hours they turned up the missing tools. Everything the scientists brought with them had now been accounted for, except for the scientists themselves. Equipment was easily found, thought Benton, but the human body could be damnably elusive; it dissolved into the landscape. An empath could locate a living body, but not a dead one, and even a live one was hard to find if the competing life-fields were strong. He had brought an empath along to Memphis-12, but after one day in the swamp the man had been driven frantic by the waves emanating from the songtrees. Never fully trusting empaths, who seemed to wear their nerves outside their skin, Benton sent him back up to the orbiting ship. Eyes would have to do.

That night when Kerry stole into his pool of light her eyes were open. Earphones dangled like a necklace about her throat. For a minute after sensing her presence Benton did not look up from the map he was studying. At length he said, "What is it?"

She hesitated, the minty sheen of her sleepsuit flickering at light's edge, like a specter on the threshold of materiality. "I couldn't sleep, sir, for thinking about those songs."

"Isn't listening to them morning and evening bad enough?" he asked. "You've got to listen to recordings half the night?"

"I'm sure I can hear words in the singing."

"You don't hear anything of the sort."

"I *do*, Captain. Human speech. There are words in French and English and Chinese. Maybe some Russian, too."

What was her game? She knew perfectly well the missing scientists included native speakers of all those languages. He studied her. She was awake this time, the gray eyes open wide, the fair face bright with excitement. Her voice and gaze were too fresh for someone on chemmies. "Don't hang back in the dark," he urged. "Come, sit down, tell me about it."

She edged closer. The overhead light cast shadows beneath her chin, her breasts. Without sitting down, she said, "They're sort of like nursery rhymes. Or nonsense poems."

"Such as?"

She withdrew a notepad from a pocket and began to read: "Pop, popcorn, pickle, participle, pumpernickel, pharmaceutical—"

Benton cut in. "You heard this in that squawking?"

"And a lot more," she replied, riffling the notepad.

"Strings of words beginning with 'p'?"

"That's just a sample. The mocking-trees seem to love rhyming. Their words run in streaks, with a thread of sound stitching them together. 'Raw, rarity, rhomboid, rib—'"

"I get the idea."

Kerry sat down next to him, pressing palms together between her thighs and rocking nervously. "I noticed it the first time I went swimming at songtide. No, I thought, I'm just putting human words to alien music. But every time I swam, the impression grew stronger. I'd keep my head underwater, listening, and pretty soon I recognized words in the singing."

Indulging her, Benton asked, "How do you tell these mocking-trees from the other kinds?"

"They're the ones with the shiny knees," she explained, rubbing her own knees for illustration. "Kind of like cypress. Half the recordings are of mocking-tree arias. Like in opera, only in three or four languages, rhyming every way you can imagine." Unclasping the headset from around her throat, she offered it to him, saying, "Here, listen."

Reluctantly he took it, hoping to put an end to her raving. The pads against his ears were still warm from resting on her throat. She punched a button and the pandemonium of songtide crashed in on him. He tried to hear something intelligible, but could not. She watched him expectantly, her face uncomfortably close, the freckles a dusting on her cheeks. Her lips were parted, fleshy, pink. He imagined breath eddying in and out. He found himself inclining toward her, only half conscious of the babble in his ears.

Recovering, he tugged away the headset and pulled back. "It's nothing but noise."

She stood up in confusion. "You didn't hear—"

"I heard bleats and warbles and screeches."

"The words *are* hard to make out. It takes patience—"

"I have nine corpses to find and a crew to deliver home safely. So forgive me if I don't have energy left over to decipher gibberish in the middle of the night."

"But, sir—"

"That's all."

He listened to the scuff of her bare feet. He tried looking at the map, but a pang of guilt prompted him to call after her. "Kerry?" The scuffing halted. She was a slim silhouette in the lighted passage. "I know you're trying to help," he said. "You could help me a lot more by forgetting this nonsense and sticking to your duties. Understood?"

Her reply was barely audible. "Whatever you say, Captain."

During the next day's search, Benton noticed that some of the jutting roots did appear shinier than the rest, like knees gleaming with oil. He could not help recollecting how Kerry had rubbed her own knees while telling him about the mocking-trees.

Valdez broke into the memory. "Do we stop, Captain?"

Benton craned round and blinked at him. "What for?"

"The trees have been singing for several minutes now."

The noise washed over Benton. How could he have failed to hear? The others were staring curiously at him. "Songtide," he muttered. "Of course. Tie up here."

As usual, Kerry was first in the water. Cummings and Zee followed her in, as they often did. But when Valdez forsook his nap in order to join them, Benton began to feel uneasy. The four of them drifted through the swamp, floating on their backs, legs scissoring languidly, eyes shut in the bubble helmets. Their lips were moving and their faces wore a drugged expression of delight. Had they all caught some alien fever?

The clamor of the songtrees kept him from thinking clearly. In the din he fancied he heard a guttural "broom, doom, gloom," then a rhyming chant that might have been Russian. He cleared his throat irritably. It was only noise. Imagining one heard words in that racket was like seeing shapes in clouds or beasts among the stars.

Kerry floated serenely by. Beneath the helmet her lips never stopped moving.

Benton sat rigidly at his post. He endured the songtide as he would endure any pain.

Once back on board, the four swimmers whispered among themselves, their voices like the scrabbling of insects. Before the craft had proceeded far, Benton spun round. "What are you all mumbling?"

Cummings turned on him that round, pasty face, which even the bloodiest mess could not perturb. "Nothing important, sir."

"In the water your mouths were gaping like fish and now you're muttering. What *is* it?"

"Oh," said Cummings, glancing at the others, "we were just discussing what we'd heard in the singing."

"And what did you hear?

"Some old video jingles," said the doctor.

"Opera for me, sir," said Valdez.

"I heard show tunes," Zee confessed.

Kerry clenched her jaw and said nothing.

The boat drifted through the glassy water, the calm air, the unbroken stillness of the drowned forest.

"Listen to me," Benton said carefully. "You're all sick. You've caught some bug from swimming in that filth. It's causing you to hallucinate."

The doctor's face cracked with a smile, like a flawed plate. "Begging your pardon, sir, but I'd say we're perfectly healthy. We just like the music. Nothing wrong with that."

Benton checked his temper. If he lost control, they might all become bait for yet another rescue team. "Cummings," he said in level tones, "by now even you've got to realize those poor bastards are dead. Their camp's a mess. Their food stores were left open, as if they'd given up eating. They abandoned their ship, their tools, their survival belts and locators. The log dwindles away into incoherent fragments, and finally to silence. Now *why*?" He fixed each of them in turn with a sober stare. "I think they went mad from listening to those damn trees."

The five sat utterly still. Out in the bog, stumps had begun to glow, the only sign that purple dusk had fallen.

At last Valdez admitted, "Maybe you're right, sir. Maybe it's a sickness that makes us hear things."

"I'll give everyone a thorough exam," said Cummings.

Zee added regretfully, "No more swimming, I guess."

"No more swimming." Benton hunched his shoulders to ease the tension in his back. "No one goes in the water. And during songtide we wear earplugs and helmets to block the noise."

The others nodded agreement, but with a show of reluctance.

Later, as they were finishing their last sweep in the lavender twilight, Kerry sidled up and crouched next to Benton. Her nearness quickened his breathing. "Yes?" he said.

"Sir, if we're deluded in thinking we hear words—"

"There's no 'if' about it."

"Then why does the impression grow stronger as we approach a particular sector?"

"Listen—"

"I think if we follow the sound gradient we can trace the words back to wherever the mocking-trees are learning them."

A sandy tress curled below her chin. He had to make an effort to keep from brushing it away. "Kerry, the mocking-trees aren't learning words."

"With all due respect, sir, they are. In four languages."

He looked at her with a feeling close to despair. The delusion had penetrated her so deeply that it had the intensity of a religious conviction. Her flushed cheeks and burning eyes were those of a woman possessed.

*　*　*

Before songtide next morning Zee spied, across the water on a fern-covered hummock, a splotch of Day-Glo yellow, which proved to be nine shimmersuits tied in a bundle.

"The fools," said Zee. "Why would they take them off?"

"That means the bodies could sink," Benton grumbled.

For once, Cummings found nothing hopeful to say.

Benton glowered at the mirror-slick water, spiky vegetation, gnarled trunks, and stilt-like roots. The bodies could be tangled anywhere in those murky depths. The prospect of returning empty-handed oppressed him. VIVA scientists did not seem to worry overmuch about dying; but they wanted someone to know where and how they had died, as if their death were a crucial piece of evidence. He understood that desire to return, to be put back in place, if only as a corpse.

As the trees began uttering their preliminary croaks, he sensed Kerry hovering near his shoulder. She said, "I think I might be able to find them, sir."

"We will find them. But with our eyes. Now sit."

"But, sir, we're close. The words are getting clearer. If you'd let me swim during songtide, I could track them to their source." She trembled with eagerness to be in the water.

Benton felt an impulse to squeeze his hands over her ears and preserve her from this intoxication. He told her firmly, "No."

"You all could stay on board with your ears plugged, and follow me in the boat."

"I said no."

"Sir?"

"No. Sit down. Shut up." The trees were piping louder. Turning, he shouted, "Earplugs and helmets everyone."

He followed his own orders and watched to make sure the others obeyed. He could not tell which possibility bothered him more—there being no pattern in the songtides, or there being a pattern he alone could not hear. He closed his eyes, hoping to shorten the wait by drowsing.

A jostling of the boat was followed swiftly by a tap on his shoulder. Benton looked up to find Zee pointing excitedly off the bow toward a froth of lavender bubbles. He whirled. Kerry's seat was empty, except for the helmet she had left behind. He flung off his own helmet and pulled out the earplugs, wincing at the crash of noise, and yelled at the swimming woman. He could barely hear his own voice, and she did not slow down. With a slash of his arm he signaled for Valdez to follow her. The boat nosed along in her wake.

She swam powerfully, dodging roots, churning up spray, then she drifted, swinging her head from side to side, before setting off on a new tack. The russet hair flowed over her shoulders. The songtrees were deafening. And yet words seemed to rise above the chaotic roar like rainbows above a storm. *Fire, free, forest, forever.* Benton found his lips moving, a sugary taste on his tongue.

The boat gave a lurch as it raked a stump. He flinched, then sat erect and struggled to block out the noise. They were closing on Kerry. When she rolled onto her back to breathe, her face wore a look of voluptuous pleasure.

"Faster, Valdez!" he yelled. "We've got to pull her out."

But Valdez could not hear, of course. No one could hear except Benton. The three faces in their sealed helmets gazed stupidly at him like bottled specimens. He gestured angrily, and Valdez, perhaps thinking a snag lay ahead, throttled back on the motor.

"Catch her!" Benton stabbed his finger in the direction of the entranced swimmer, who glided away through the tangle of roots and vines.

Valdez lifted his eyebrows in bafflement.

Without giving himself time to think, Benton clambered over the side, keeping his head up as he bobbed in the water. The chanting of the songtrees poured through him like an electric current. He nearly gagged at the shock, the scum, the tremors. But thinking of the look on Kerry's face, he fought down panic and swam after her, neck arched and head high.

He gained on her quickly, for she had stopped kicking. His frenzy on hitting the water had given way to a surge of ecstasy. It was all he could do to keep from crying out. Only a few strokes ahead, Kerry pulled herself up onto a cluster of mocking-tree roots, shook out her wild hair, and sat there roaring with song.

"Stay there!" he yelled. "Stay out of the water!"

She ignored him, her mouth stretched by song, eyes closed to slits. She reached for the tab at her throat and quickly unzipped the shimmersuit from neck to belly. Benton reached her before she could pull her arms free. He grabbed her about the waist with one arm and with the other clung to the vaulting roots, struggling to keep her from sliding into the water. She writhed against him, like a sleeper caught in the web of dream. The songtide kept pouring through him a charge of bliss. He longed to let go and sink alongside her into the purple depths. Yet he clung to the root, to the air, to consciousness, and would not let go.

Presently the boat drew alongside, hands reached out and laid hold of Kerry, and he let them drag her to safety. Almost reluctantly, he crawled in after her. She lay slumped against Zee, who was tugging at the suit to cover her. A seam of pink skin showed where the zipper parted over her belly, reminding Benton of a baby's translucent eyelid.

Cummings held a small bottle under Kerry's nose. She jerked, her flailing ceased, and her eyes slicked open.

Above the diminishing racket of the songtrees, Benton could barely make out what she said: "It's so beautiful, so beautiful. That's why they're here."

"Who's here?" he asked.

"The singers." She lifted an arm and pointed to starboard.

Feeling a chill of premonition, Benton looked where she pointed. A few meters away, in a placid expanse of water, the bodies floated just below the surface, naked, with only the faces exposed to air. The mouths were open. Lank hair wavered out in a halo about each head. Roots and tendrils had grown through the bodies, piercing the skin.

Benton stared for a minute before he realized they were singing. Or more accurately, song was emerging from the gaping mouths, although the lips did not move. Chants, jingles, nursery rhymes, pop lyrics, love babble, arias. Nearby mocking-trees caught the sounds and toyed with them, improvised, spun jazzy variations. More distant trees repeated the chants in garbled form, so the songs pulsed out through the swamp like rings of rumors passing through a crowd. In spite of the horror, he felt joy—as if he were a child again learning to speak.

With the passing of songtide, the voices dwindled, and as if at the stroke of a baton the mouths closed. For a minute or so the neighboring trees sustained the music, then they too subsided, and trees more remote fell silent, ring beyond ring, until all was still.

For a long while, none of the rescuers moved.

Then Kerry said, "I didn't mean to cause trouble. I just wanted to help find them."

"You did find them," Benton said. "The important thing is, you're safe."

"I suppose so," she replied in a muted voice.

No one else spoke. To break the stillness, Benton said, "Pull ahead, Valdez."

Without answering, the droop-eyed pilot nudged the boat closer. The bodies were stitched together in a solid mat of roots, five men and four women. The men's faces were bearded, the women's heads were encircled by coronas of glistening hair. Violet threads enmeshed their skin, as if they were bound up in cocoons, with only their serene faces bare.

"Can we cut them loose, Cummings?" Benton asked.

The doctor stared at him dazedly. "Cut, sir?"

"Can we get them out of there without killing them?"

Cummings surveyed the raft of bodies. "I'm not sure they're alive, sir."

"Of course they're alive. How else could they sing?" Benton shoved a hand into the water and grasped a sinewy wrist. It belonged to a woman of thirty or so, with black hair and sharp features. Through the mesh of tendrils that covered her skin he could find no pulse. He checked a second body, a third, a fourth, with the same result.

He pulled his hand from the water, held it dripping above the surface, as if it were a loathsome fish he had caught. "How could they make all that noise without a heartbeat?"

"The songtrees make the noise, drawing patterns from their brains," Kerry said.

"So the trees are parasites?" Benton asked.

"Not parasites," she insisted. "The relation is symbiotic. Both sides benefit."

Benton felt a surge of revulsion. "What are the corpses getting?"

"Rapture. And they're not corpses. They're a living part of the forest. You can see they're contented. We should leave them alone."

No one spoke for a while. They had all been touched by that rapture, even Benton. At last he said, "They're not going anywhere for now. Let's dismantle the camp and get it ready for shipment home. Tomorrow we'll decide what to do with our singers."

*　*　*

The slovenly camp, the abandoned shimmersuits, the data disks and instruments were stowed in the scientists' shuttle and launched on automatic back up to the warpship in orbit. That left only the rescue shuttle for sleeping. The five of them stretched out as best they could in the cramped quarters.

Benton lay awake thinking about that hideous tangle of flesh and roots and the hypnotic music. Feeling smothered, he wriggled out of his sleep-pouch and lay on his side, head propped on one bent arm, gazing through the window at stumps glowing in the lavender twilight.

He lost track of time. When he heard a faint singing, he thought at first it was the songtrees warming up for their cruel serenade. Then he realized the voice was single, frail, arising nearby. He sat up stealthily. The three nearest pouches were sealed. The fourth, at the far end of the shuttle, was open, and Kerry's upper body lay visible—sandy hair, milky throat, bare arms flung negligently to either side.

Benton rose and picked his way over to her. He knelt close. Her eyes were shut and the song leaked out in a slur: "Owl and pussycat went to sea in a beautiful pea-green boat." She heaved a sigh, shifted drowsily, and resumed: "They took some honey, and plenty of money, wrapped up in a five-pound note..."

Abruptly the voice died away and she opened her eyes, staring at him in panic. "Don't," she hissed, "no, don't! We'll drown!"

Benton laid a hand on her cheek. "Easy now," he whispered, "easy. You were singing in your sleep."

Coming fully awake, she asked, "I was?"

"Something about an owl and a pussycat."

"Oh, that." She smiled. "I learned that in third grade."

"How does the rest of it go?"

Her lips turned down. "You're making fun of me."

"No, please," he whispered. "I want to hear it."

"I'm not sure I can remember all of it."

"Sing what you remember."

As if suddenly noticing her arms were bare, she folded them across her breast. "I don't want to wake the others."

"They're zipped in their pouches."

Her gray eyes searched him for a moment before she murmured, "All right, bend down." He leaned close enough to feel her breath on his ear. In a voice that broke from the effort of quietness, she sang,

They sailed away for a year and a day,
To the land where the bongtrees grow,
And there in a wood a piggywig stood,
With a ring at the end of his nose.

"What on earth are bongtrees?" Benton asked gently.

"That's what brought it back to me. Bongtrees, songtrees."

"And what's a piggywig?"

"Oh," she said uncertainly, "it's a kind of farm animal they used to have." With a wave of her hands she sketched a fat shape in the air, and ended by flinging her arms wide, as if, had a piggywig waddled, in, she would have embraced it. She could have embraced him as well. His face hovered a hand's-breadth above hers. After a moment's hesitation, she let her arms fall.

He sat up, retreating into the shell of his rank, his role, his years. "What a strange thing to remember in the middle of the night."

When he made to rise, she grabbed his hand, saying earnestly, "You're going to let them stay here, aren't you?"

Her grip was firm, hot. "Should I?"

"Yes, oh, yes. They'll die if you cut them loose."

"Cummings might be able to patch them together."

"No, leave them. Please."

"But I have to take them home. I'm a rescuer. My duty—"

"Is your duty more important than their desires? They want to be right where they are."

"How can you be sure?"

Her nails dugs into his hand. "Aren't you tempted? To throw everything away, strip yourself bare and sink into that music? Aren't you?"

He did not know what to answer. But he would have to decide soon, because the songtrees were tuning up for their dawn chorus.

Travels in the Interior

The two brothers landed by parachute on a spongy red turf they would call grass, in a field encircled by thick somber growths they would call trees. They staggered a few paces, drew in the lines of their chutes, and flattened the billowy fabric. Each one checked to see that the other was all right before giving a thumbs-up to the hovering shuttle. The shuttle dropped their pallet of gear, waggled its wings, then swept back up to the warpship in orbit, leaving Graham and Carl alone on Amazon-7.

"Yo, bro!" Carl shouted, waving his big gun at the end of a meaty arm. "You good?"

"Right as rain!" Graham shouted back.

Without needing to speak further, the brothers fell into their roles. Carl began unpacking the gear and setting up a base camp, while Graham walked the perimeter of the field and studied the encircling wall of vegetation. It was as dense as any jungle on Earth, yet looked nothing like those Terran thickets. The landscape would do, Graham thought, assuming they could stir up something scary. Sensations poured into him—the musty smell of rot, the crackle of red grass under his boots, a metallic clinking from the ash-gray trees, the bloated orange of the local sun, a rancid taste in the air, the wind on his neck hot as a dog's breath.

Graham's own breath came in shallow puffs. The atmosphere was supposed to be as close as damn-it to E-normal. Yet no human lungs had ever breathed here, so he kept bottled air handy. Before leaving the warpship, he and Carl had been dosed against toxins and alien microorganisms. Against larger organisms, they would have to use their wits and their weapons.

"No trances, nature boy," Carl hollered from the camp, where the dome had begun to rise. "Keep your eyes peeled."

"Wide awake," Graham answered. It was the condition of his sport, his art, his job, this adrenalin rush. If he ever lost that edge, he would be finished. The heightening of perception that kept the brothers alive also kept them employed. The studio paid their salaries and the enormous costs of warping them to unexplored worlds for the sake of Graham's raw sensations, which even now, as he scanned the jungle, were being picked up by a recorder at the base of his skull. The stronger the sensations the better, for they would be made into yet another *Wild Cosmos* feelie to divert the city-bound dwellers on Earth, who had an insatiable appetite for virtual danger. For Carl and Graham, the danger was real.

Left to himself, Graham would forget to eat, as he would forget to pitch his tent or charge his gun. So as usual Carl cooked, and when supper was ready his voice boomed across the field. "Come and get it!"

They ate in the faceted green dome. Although tripflares and mines had been set in a ring around the camp, the brothers kept rising from their meal to stare out the windows, leery about what might be stealing up on them from the forest. Reinforcing mesh in the windows imposed on the view a grid of lines, giving the illusion of order. But the planet had never been mapped; its life forms had never been catalogued. Videos from orbit showed a continuous land mass wrapped in a belt around the equator, separating the polar seas. This lone continent bristled with vegetation that was broken only by rare clearings, such as the one in which the brothers had landed, and by gashes that could have been riverbeds or game trails. Nobody knew if there were any animals to make trails. Nobody knew much at all about Amazon-7, which was what appealed to the brothers, and what made Graham's sensations worth a few million to the studio.

"So how far to those mountains?" Carl asked.

"Five days," Graham answered, "maybe seven. Depends how mean the bush is."

The videos had shown a series of white peaks strung out along the equator, rising like teeth above the rust-dark jungle. Planning a feelie called *Journey to the Crystal Mountain*, the studio wanted the brothers to hike to and from one of those peaks, with gritty adventures along the way. While descending in the shuttle, Graham had taken a bearing on the nearest shining mountain. What made it gleam? he wondered. Not snow, at this latitude. Stone? Volcanic glass?

Carl tilted up his mashed fighter's nose, hairy nostrils flaring. "You trust this air?"

"It'll do. I'm not lugging tanks, even in point-nine G."

"Risk it, right?" Carl thumped him, hard, and filled the dome with rowdy laughter. "My daredevil bro."

Graham was older by two years, but Carl was taller by a hand and heavier by thirty kilos. He was large and steady, slow to excite and slow to calm down, like a boulder resisting changes in temperature. The older brother picked his way around obstacles, while the younger one bulled his way through. The elder sensed patterns, nuances, details; the younger tuned in on threats. And so in their treks they had fallen into complementary roles, Graham leading them into the uncharted zones and back again, Carl keeping them in one piece.

After supper, Carl began methodically packing their two rucksacks, checking the food, the clothes, the stove and fuel, the lights, especially the guns and explosives and flares.

Unsettled by the silence that came on at dusk, Graham kept pacing from window to window, staring out at the mazy woods. No movement, no glint of eyes. Abrupt and final as a wall. Somehow he must find a way through that tangled mass to the dazzling mountain. He trembled. Unless you could die from going there, no place was truly wild. On Earth, death had retreated to the intensive-care wards. Off Earth, it could meet you anywhere.

"Ease up, bro," said Carl.

"I'm loose. You don't think I'm loose?"

"You're wound tight as a top."

Graham knew it was true. But the excitement was sweet, the tension of standing on a cliff's edge.

Their shimmersuits were opaque in the early light, clinging to them like brown pelts, and their packs bulked high above their helmets. It was the twilit hour when nighttime predators yield to those of the day. Nothing stirred.

"Point the way, big brother, and let's move." Even though Carl whispered, his voice sounded huge in the stillness.

"I'm looking." Graham always savored this moment on the threshold of a wild zone, deciding where to enter. At length he ducked under a limb and stepped into the russet woods.

They moved slowly at first, cautiously, then more quickly as Graham picked up the grain of the land, Carl lumbering behind with stungun in hand, the two swinging along in tandem like a four-legged beast, rarely talking, rarely needing to talk. Beyond the palisade of trees at the jungle's edge, the undergrowth thinned out. Light from the orange star speckled the ground. The spongy soil yielded beneath their boots, preserving the faint mark of their passage.

In the first few hours, they paused only for Graham to sight back along the way they had come, memorizing the gestalt of trunks and limbs so that days from now he could lead them back out. Then as the shafts of light from the local sun tilted toward vertical, the brothers halted as if on signal. They shrugged free of the packs and sat on their helmets.

Graham took a pinch of dirt and held it to his nose. Must, mildew, iron. From overhead came that metallic clinking, as of jangled keys. "I can't figure out that noise."

"That's my gears seizing up from this heat," said Carl, mopping his broad face. The gun lay in his lap. "Melt me to a puddle of grease, at this rate."

Graham surveyed the jungle. The leaves and vines and fernlike fronds were in shades of red, the solid trunks nearly black, creating an impression of embers and ashes. The trees rose about three times a man's height before branching horizontally. Wherever they touched, the limbs of neighboring trees interlaced, and the joints blazed with gold and blue growths like bright flowers. Dead trees, their trunks rotted through, dangled from the lattice of branches, and creepers looped down in festoons. The canopy appeared so tightly woven, Graham imagined a person could walk up there. Animals certainly could. "You see anything move yet?" he asked.

"Negative," Carl answered.

"Better not be all plants. No animals, no action."

"I figure they're here, just back deeper in the woods."

On their next halt, Graham asked the question again, and Carl answered, "Nothing to sweat about."

"What? I didn't see anything."

"You notice those things like gray bags hanging from the trunks, spikes all over them?"

"Those are animals? I thought they were epiphytes."

"They move. Tree-burrs, I call them." Pointing overhead with the gun, Carl added, "And those snaky dudes that slither through the roof I call branch-weavers."

Graham peered long before making out a gliding shape, like a scarlet rope, moving through the web of limbs. Having detected one, he saw them everywhere. The canopy was in fact crawling with these snake-like animals, which seemed to be lacing the branches together, binding twig to twig.

"Want a closer look?" said Carl. "Give the gawkers back home a thrill?"

Before Graham could protest, Carl fired a quick burst up through the canopy. Three of the branch-weavers clattered to the ground and lay still, like hanks of rusty chain.

"You and that gun," said Graham.

"It won't hurt them. Give them a minute, they'll be squirming again." He turned over one of the scaly bodies with his boot.

"Check out that armor. See how these plates mesh? And look how this gooey stuff seeps out between the joints. I figure they smear that on the bark and glue the whole mess together tight as a net."

"To catch what?"

"Anything that's crawling around up there."

Graham studied the scaffolding of limbs. He would have to climb up there eventually to get a bearing on the crystal mountain. But he was in no hurry. He shouldered his pack, pulled on helmet and gloves, yet he did not want to leave until the branch-weavers revived. As the seconds passed, and the bodies failed to stir, he grew uneasy. "Maybe you gave them too high a charge."

"It was nothing. A tickle." Carl prodded the motionless bodies, the plates clicking. He snorted. "Well, crap. I do believe the suckers are dead. You wouldn't think anything this tough on the outside could be so weak on the inside."

"Too weak for you to go blazing away with that damn gun."

"I wasn't blazing away. What I shot them with wouldn't have stopped a rat back home."

"Well, we're not back home."

"I noticed. So don't get us lost."

They had walked only a few paces when there came a snarling and scratching from behind. Wheeling, they saw a pack of many-legged animals the size of cats tearing the ropy bodies of the branch-weavers to shreds. In less than a minute, the beasts had stuffed the scraps into pouches along their flanks and were scurrying into burrows under the roots.

Carl whistled. "You talk about hungry."

"And quick," said Graham, disturbed by the scavengers, yet doing his job, filling his senses with the oily smell, the scrabbling sounds, the bitter tang of this first kill. There would be others. Every year, Carl became more trigger-happy, firing at anything that was even vaguely menacing, as if he feared their luck was running out.

They swung into motion, Graham at point, Carl behind. Their shimmersuits took on a ruby sheen from the heat. They sauntered easily, a pace they could maintain all day, if need be, for days on end, for weeks, like caribous migrating. Now and again Carl would whistle, gesturing at the canopy or the undergrowth, and Graham would stare and stare before seeing a camouflaged beast. This was always the way of it: Graham had an eye for the still pattern of things, Carl had an eye for anything that moved, and each brother was nearly blind to what the other could see. "If it can't run or jump, it can't hurt you," was Carl's slogan. "If it moves, you can't find your way by it," was Graham's counter.

Because the local day was little more than twenty E-hours long, the afternoon passed quickly, shafts of light piercing the jungle at lower and lower angles. They pitched camp beside a creek. After shaking a slug of the water in a toxi-vial, to make certain it was safe, Carl lay down and plunged his face into the stream. "I'll set up," he said, chin dripping water, "you remember."

While the encampment took shape under Carl's big hands—domed tent blossoming, sleep-mats inflating, supper brewing, tripwires unfurled around the perimeter—Graham sat on the bank with his bare feet in the creek, recalling the day's trail. He retraced their steps until he reached the beginning point in the parachute field. Then he turned about and worked his way forward to this creek, then back again, as if he were winding and unwinding a ball of string.

When he opened his eyes, Carl was serving out the stew. It tasted of catfish and potatoes, but it was the same high-energy confection that would wear other flavors on other nights. Graham swallowed some, then spoke about what had been troubling him: "Let's not do any more killing than we have to, okay?"

"The feelie crowds love it," said Carl.

"I know they do. But I hate it. I'm sick of it."

Carl did not reply. A movement in the vault of limbs had snared his attention. "Visitors," he grumbled.

This time Graham easily spied the beasts, inky blobs against the darkening sky. There were ten or so, arrayed in a circle above the camp. Two more joined them, then two more and two more. They kept arriving in pairs until their bodies formed an unbroken ring. The limbs creaked under their weight. They were larger than the scavengers that had torn up the branch-weavers, as large as wolves, but thick and slow-moving.

"Ring-watchers," whispered Carl, naming them.

Graham placed a hand on his brother's arm. "Don't shoot."

"You want to sleep with that party upstairs?"

A tremor passed around the circle of bodies, setting off harsh grating noises in the network of limbs.

"Let's see if the light will scare them off," said Graham.

With a grunt, Carl switched on the perimeter flare. There was an explosive release of gas, and the camp was haloed in a blaze of light. Guttural cries sounded in the branches, then a jostling of sluggish bodies. "Go on, you hairy bastards," Carl shouted, "find somebody else for supper."

Graham watched uneasily as his brother shuffled in a lumbering, triumphant dance.

Twice in the night Carl wriggled out of his sleeping bag, hissed, "Relax, I got this," disappeared outside, and in a few minutes returned, breathing heavily. Come daylight, Graham found two ring-watchers sprawled near the entrance of the tent.

"They got too curious," Carl explained. "I could hear the pack of them nosing around. These two crossed the flare."

Graham set his mouth. Death, always more death. This, too, he must absorb. He turned over one of the carcasses, revealing a cluster of many-jointed legs surrounding a hole that was lined with spikes, a lethal opening large enough to swallow a man's head. A knobby skeleton bulged under the pelt, which was silvered like that of an aged gorilla. It smelled like rotting fruit.

"Pretty, eh?" said Carl. "I figured you'd want a look."

"Did they attack you?"

"Not what you'd call attack. Moseyed up. Wouldn't stop. I hit them with about the right dose for a dog. And thump, down they went. Not a kick." He grasped one of the ponderous sacks of bones with gloved hands. "Here, grab hold of this thing."

They heaved the bodies out through the barrier of light, which still blazed yellow against the orange dawn. While the brothers ate breakfast, the humpbacked scavengers dismembered the carcasses, then withdrew under the shadowy roots, gorged and swaying, leaving behind only a solitary bone.

"Six minutes flat," said Carl. "Hide and hair and giblets."

"I'm going to look at what they left." Putting on gloves and slipping out through the light-barrier, Graham squatted beside the bone. It was hammer-shaped, the color of old piano keys, dimpled with sockets. He lifted it gingerly, testing its weight and hardness.

Suddenly there was a frantic scuffling and a wave of scavengers came rushing at him and tumbled him flat under their swarming weight. The bone turned in his grasp and jerked violently away. A moment later he was sitting up dazed, Carl beside him with gun at the ready, and not a beast in sight.

"You hurt?" Carl asked.

Graham shivered. He felt as though twenty fists had landed on him, but landed gently, as if tapping a message. "No, no."

"Did they bite you?"

"I don't think so."

The brothers inspected Graham's suit, but could find no rips in the tough fabric.

"God damn," said Carl, "they were all over you before I even saw them. I thought they'd tear you to pieces."

Rubbing his neck, remembering the furious weight, the bone twisting from his grasp, Graham said, "I bet they could have, if they'd wanted to. But all they seemed to want was that bone."

"What in hell for?"

"Who knows?" said Graham, his voice quavery.

"Don't mess with their booty, man, that's the lesson."

"Maybe they won't eat anything unless it's already dead."

"Which is what I figured you were. Lunch meat."

They broke camp in silence. Pathfinding came hard for Graham that day. The more he thought about the attack, the more his fear tainted every other sensation. Again and again he found himself at a standstill, up against a river or thicket or swamp, uncertain how to proceed.

By mid-morning he realized he must overcome his dread and climb up into the canopy to get a fresh bearing on that mountain. Leaving his pack with Carl, he shinnied up a tree, grabbing vines for handholds. A scampering broke out overhead, then receded. As he rose, the light grew brighter, and as he surfaced above the web of limbs the full dazzle of daylight made him squint.

"See anything?" Carl shouted.

Graham blinked water from his eyes. "Oh, my Lord, yes." Strewn with those blue and yellow flower-like growths, the canopy spread away in undulating plains. In the distance, dark, shaggy herds were grazing, with here and there a lone beast skulking around the edges. He thought of bison and wolves. The only break in that rolling prairie was the mountain, gleaming against the horizon. "There it is," he called down to Carl. "We're right on course."

"Good. Now move it," Carl hollered. "I've got company."

Before Graham could put away the binoculars, from below came the stungun's whine. He gave a shout and scrambled down through the branches and hit the ground with pistol drawn.

A few paces away, Carl stooped over a gray hairless mass of flesh. "Check it out, bro," he said. "Another ugly brute."

Graham studied the body. It had a bear's bulk and a segmented torso, with a dozen or more legs jutting from the sides, each one ending in a pad of flesh as broad as a dinner plate. The skin was ash-gray mottled with black, like the tree bark, and it was perforated with hundreds of slits that oozed a sweet-smelling liquid.

"What are these holes for, you figure?" Carl pried open one of the slits with his knife.

Graham winced. "Don't. I've seen enough." He scanned the woods. "Was it alone?"

"Naw, they're all over." Carl stood up from the ashen body. "See the bulges halfway up that tree? Greasy shine on them? The whole bunch came at me. Not fast, kind of like trucks in low gear, grinding along. When I nailed this one, the others split."

The descent from the flowered canopy, with its glimpse of the shining mountain, to this grisly scene left Graham shaken. He slid the pistol into its holster, without fastening the flap.

"Come on," said Carl, hefting his pack. "I don't expect they'll stay scared for long."

All that afternoon the ashen creatures trailed them, slinking along the fretwork of limbs. The brothers made good time, because Graham now had a clear sense of direction. But no matter how fast they walked, the shadow-creepers—as Carl named the beasts—never fell behind.

That night, relieved to be inside the tent with the light-shield arching overhead, Graham said, "Maybe they're just curious."

"Want to interview us, you think? Or see how we taste?" said Carl from his sleeping mat. "You volunteer to find out?"

"No, but I can't help thinking—"

"Thinking what?"

"About those scavengers, the way they snatched that bone, then let me go. Like they were being careful not to hurt me."

Carl laughed. "You didn't smell dead enough."

"But what about those others—the ring-watchers and branch-weavers and that gray bag of guts you shot. If they meant to kill us, why did they creep up in full view instead of charging? Maybe they're only trying to drive us away, or find out what sort of animals we are."

"Next time I'll give them a questionnaire," Carl said.

"You don't hear what I'm saying," Graham muttered.

"I hear, I hear. You're saying, don't snuff the bastards. But I was only trying to stun them. How was I to know they'd die so easily? A little poof, and their circuits go haywire."

"That's the problem. That's what eats me up. We don't know anything. We're pig-ignorant. We never stay in any wild zone long enough to learn the first thing about it. We're always pushing on, out and back, soaking up new sensations."

Carl fixed him with an amused glare. "You tired of the wilderness, nature boy? Want to pack it in? Live in the cities?"

"No, it's just—"

"You rather live in a box, ride around in a box, work in a box? Count me out, chum. I want to keep seeing things I never saw before, go places nobody's ever been."

"But every time we land, we're like babies waking up, without names for anything. It's all a buzzing, swirling mystery."

Carl sat up on his mat and said earnestly, "If you couldn't budge until you understood everything, you'd never get out of bed. You'd sure never get away from Earth. Never see that roadway of limbs up there, or your white mountain."

"Or the butchered animals."

"What's the big deal? A few beasts dead?"

"There's more of them every trip," Graham said sharply.

"That's because we keep going to wilder places. What do you expect, a picnic?" Carl seized a boot and slammed it on the tent floor. "All you've got to worry about is filling your senses and watching the trail. Fine. I couldn't do it. I'd get lost in an hour. But I've got to protect your ass. You're the star. I'm the bodyguard." He loomed over Graham, gesturing with the boot. "And if you wandered off by yourself, something would get you, no matter what your tender heart tells you about the wilds."

Graham did not answer. He stared through narrowed eyes at the luminous barrier that arched above the camp. Would it keep out beasts? He lulled himself to sleep by summoning up his vision of that pale, tranquil mountain.

Whenever the brothers paused for a rest, for a drink, for Graham to climb up through the canopy to scope the mountain, the beasts closed in. What did they want? There was no way to find out, no language for putting the question, no time for asking. Usually Carl shot the boldest animal, and the others drew back. Sometimes he had to shoot several. The scavengers, following in droves, pounced on the kills.

"I don't see how they can still be hungry," said Graham on the morning of the third day, watching a band of scavengers at work on a carcass, remembering how the pack had swarmed over him with that odd gentleness.

"I expect there are fresh ones coming along all the time." Carl watched the ferocious feast with stony eyes. "The news gets out through the woods. Like sharks sniffing blood."

Despite the frequent kills, the number of pursuers kept swelling. At night the beasts were visible outside the light-dome as a shadowy crowd encircling the camp. They might have been ambassadors gathering for a parley, or warriors defending territory. Or like moths they might simply have been drawn to light. Staring out at them, the brothers rarely spoke, and then only in whispers. Graham kept doing his job, soaking up sensations, remembering the path, but understanding little.

"So much for your peaceable kingdom," said Carl, after a day of almost constant battles.

There was nothing Graham could answer to that. Weary and appalled, he was trying to hold himself together, keep the doors of perception open, until he reached the mountain and could turn back. The glistening peak seemed so out of keeping with this dark and murderous jungle that it had become in his imagination a kind of mecca, a reassurance.

On the fourth day they encountered an even larger beast. They could hear it coming, for its weight set off a sharp crackle through the woven branches as it swung ponderously toward them. Its body was like a huge jackknife with pincers at each end, the sullen red skin gleaming as if smeared with oil. It held on by one set of pincers, snapped forward until the other end could seize hold, and so whipped along like a trapeze artist. In face of this newcomer, the lesser animals beat a hectic retreat.

"Trouble with a capital T," said Carl, shrugging free of the backpack and bracing himself to fire.

For once he was too slow on the trigger. The creature swung over them and dropped, its body spreading like a fan, heavy ribs unfurling. Graham leaped clear. Carl fired a burst, and was smashed to the ground and buried under a thick blanket of flesh.

Graham cried out, and began tugging furiously at the greasy hulk. But the muscle was rigid, the ribs would not give. Too heavy, too damn heavy. The thing was dead weight. Again he shouted. No sound from Carl, no motion, a lump under the smothering blanket. Spots of panic danced in Graham's eyes. He drew his knife and began chopping a hole through the stinking flesh, hacking away until he could see a boot. Then cautiously, to avoid cutting his brother, he sliced the muscle and pried the ribs apart. Carl was stunned, but he managed with a tug from Graham to crawl out through the raw sopping hole.

The brothers caught loud gobs of breath without speaking. Then Carl raised his battered face. "You can put that away."

Graham stared at the fist holding the knife as if it belonged to a stranger. The knuckles were still blanched from the fierceness of his grip. His sleeve was smeared black with the creature's juices. Slowly he relaxed his fingers, cleaned the blade against his pants leg, and sheathed it again. A darkness of utter revulsion came over him. "Let's turn back," he said, trying to keep the tremor out of his voice.

"What for? It was a close call, but no harm done." Carl thumped himself on the chest. "Nothing broken. And think how it'll play on the feelie. The fans will eat it up."

Twitching uncontrollably, Graham said, "I want to go back."

Carl gave him a searching look. "What's to get worked up about? Nobody's hurt, right? Next time one of those hombres comes along, we'll bag it before it gets close."

"No. No more killing. I don't want any more killing."

"Ease up, bro." Carl rested an arm on Graham's heaving shoulders and spoke soothingly. "What say we hike on a ways, leave this pile of meat behind, and set up camp? Unwind a little? Things will look better in the morning."

Graham could not stop trembling. But he was glad to clear away from there. As they left the mutilated hulk, which the scavengers had already begun to rip apart, he was aware of the knife hand dangling at his side.

The fray must have alarmed the stalking beasts, for that night the woods outside the ring of light were still. Yet Graham slept poorly, troubled by suffocating dreams.

In the morning things did not look better, and he said so.

Carl growled, "You going back and wait for the shuttle, stare at your belly button? The studio would love that. Look, how much farther is it to this blessed mountain?"

Graham did not care. The mountain had lost its allure. "A long day. Maybe a day and a half."

"So if we go double time we could make it by nightfall?"

"I tell you I'm not going. I've had it."

Jumpy with anger, Carl said, "I'm the one who got smothered under that hunk of meat, and you don't hear me bitching. You quitting on me? You hanging it up?" He seized Graham by the arms. "Because, listen, bro, if you turn back now we're done. Finito. The studio wouldn't send us across town. You hear me? And we'll be stuck earthside in boxes forever."

Graham shook all over. "It's not worth it."

"Not worth what?"

"The cost in lives." Carl let out a scoffing breath, but Graham pushed on: "I'm not thinking only about last night. I'm thinking about everything we've killed—here, other planets. A road of corpses."

After digging his fingers into Graham's arms, Carl released him. "So where can you go and not hurt a fly? Tell me that. Where can you go without killing? Where? Not Earth. The job's already finished there. An asteroid, maybe. Or some desert planet. But if you go anywhere that's got life on it, you're going to have to kill some of it to make room for yourself."

Hoisting the rucksack, Graham faced back in the direction from which they had come. "I'm sorry, Carl. I can't. I'm burnt out. I don't have the stomach for it anymore."

Carl swung his own pack into position, and set his face in the direction they had been traveling. "Go, then. And to hell with you. I'm going to that damn mountain."

Neither moved to take a step. They stood side by side, eyes averted. Finally Graham said, "You don't know the way back."

"I can still read a compass. I'll get there."

"But I've got the trail in my head."

Carl spat in the dirt, then scraped his boot across the stain. "You worry about saving your ass from those beasts you feel so sorry for. I'll worry about the trail."

They touched hands roughly. Carl glared at him with eyes bruised by a sense of betrayal. Graham took the first step, and soon heard the receding clump of his brother's boots.

After less than an hour of hiking, while beasts prowled around him in a tightening circle, Graham staggered to a halt, overcome by the weight of ignorance and fear. He shoved his back against a tree. At least nothing could lunge at him from behind. What did they want? Just food? With so many, they would get a mouthful apiece. Or did they merely want to touch him, speak with him through their pincered and padded limbs? If he let them swarm over him, as the scavengers had, perhaps they would be satisfied and go away, leaving a message imprinted on his body.

"Scat!" he shouted. His heart was clenching and unclenching like a fist.

They crept nearer, bristling, giving off a sour hot smell, their spikes clattering, their bellies scraping the dirt. Even now he was doing his job, soaking it in.

Stupid brutes. He suddenly hated them with a pure white hatred. They had made him abandon his brother. Carl would never find his way back—he didn't carry the path in his head—he trusted Graham for that.

"Leave me alone!"

The stalkers clotted into a solid dark mass in the branches overhead. Graham picked up a heavy stick and flung it at them. It clattered on the underside of the canopy, and the knot of animals broke apart, then regathered like murky water.

He roared. The watchers did not move. Above, below, every direction he looked, stealthy shapes closed on him. He drew the pistol, but was shaking too hard to aim it. What did it matter where he aimed? He wanted to spray the forest with death, murder everything, drive it back, clear a path. His finger jerked and he fired wildly, wherever the gun happened to point, squeezing off burst after burst. Bodies tumbled from the canopy, slumped in the shadows, floundered among the roots, a hail of bodies, and still he kept firing, blasting away until nothing moved, no least quiver of flesh. Then he stopped, lowered his arm, horrified.

Within seconds, the scavengers began hustling out from the tangled roots to clean up his leavings. He nearly fired on them as well, but held back. Blind with shame and loathing, sobbing, he wanted to drop the gun and rucksack, strip away his clothes, wander into the woods and give himself to the beasts.

But no, he had to find his brother, had to lead him back out. Carl would be lost without him. That was a reason to keep going. Carl would be lost. Carl needed him.

Facing about, Graham set off at a jog. Immediately he felt better, as if a wound had begun to heal. He soon arrived at the place where they had separated, then he rushed on, stooping now and again to search for the faint traces of Carl's boot prints, his breath coming in rags, oblivious to the shadow-shapes that were stalking him. Several times Carl had stopped to climb a tree— no doubt to make sure he was headed toward the mountain—so Graham, who did not need to climb, kept gaining on him. By late afternoon the trail was so fresh that the trampled grass was still unbending, and boot prints in the sand of a creek were filling with water.

Dusk was gathering like smoke among the trees when Graham finally glimpsed his brother, standing motionless in a clearing up ahead, his brawny silhouette dark against a radiant white slope. The gun was cradled in his arms. He seemed to be contemplating the mountain, from which the lamp on his helmet struck brilliant reflections.

Knowing it would be suicide to steal up on him without warning, Graham ducked behind a boulder, slipped free of his pack, and gave a shout.

Carl whirled, hit the dirt and lay on his belly, gun and lamp aimed in Graham's direction.

"Carl! Hey, I've come back!" Because of the light, Graham could not see his brother's face, but he stood up anyway, arms lifted. "Carl?" he repeated, stepping into the clear.

"Bro!" Carl shouted in a jubilant voice. Flinging down the gun, he surged to his feet and came running. He seized Graham in a hug and lifted him off the ground, yelling, "Nature boy! My broody bro! And still wearing your skin!"

Laughing, hooting until the woods rang, they held one another, rocking in a clumsy dance. After a while they pushed away to arm's length. Carl grew sober. "Come here," he said quietly, "you've got to see this."

It was now quite dark. The brothers followed the jiggling beams of their helmet-lamps toward the clearing. While they were a distance from the slope, Graham still could not guess what made it shine. Not snow, not minerals, not metal. Then, drawing close, he realized what it must be.

"Bones," Carl murmured, "a whole mountain of bones."

Graham stared in awe at the glistening pile. The forms were strange—curlicues, sprockets, hoops—but the color was a familiar calcium sheen, polished by wind and rain.

"Where'd they come from?" he whispered.

"Our hungry buddies drag them here." Carl aimed his lamp up the scree of bones at a scurrying shape.

Transfixed by the light, one of the slinking humpbacked scavengers paused in its ascent. Loose bones gleamed from the pouches on its flanks. One of my kills? Graham wondered. He remembered the bodies swarming over him, the bone twisting in his hand. How long had they been building this mound? And why? Was it a temple? A cache? A shrine? A dumb clutter like a magpie's hoard? He thought of elephant graveyards, lemming suicides, antler heaps, whale skeletons near Inuit villages, mass graves from Roman and Nazi and Frontine holocausts—but nothing earthly would explain this glimmering peak.

Presently the scavenger resumed its climb, rousing a faint clatter. The brothers watched it labor up beyond the range of their lamps, up into darkness.

Graham released a hiss of breath. "And there's a whole string of these mountains. Think of all the deaths it took."

"Damn near every last one on the planet, I'd guess."

They fell silent, their lamps playing over the white slope.

Then suddenly both brothers talked at once, Carl saying, "If you hadn't come back I was a dead man. Lost. Had no idea which way was home. Bro, I was scared," and Graham confessing, "I freaked out. Went crazy. Just started killing. I wanted to blow everything away, erase it, clear the jungle."

Again there was a silence. What they had to tell one another would take a good deal of saying, and much of it could never be said in words.

At length, Carl asked, "You want to hang around and see it in daylight?"

Graham frowned at the vast pile. "I'd like to sit down and think and not budge until I could make sense of it. But I'm afraid I'd go mad."

"We wouldn't live long enough to go mad. They'd be dragging our bones up there before morning. The studio told us to come here, and we came here. Now I say we head back. What do you say?"

Graham nodded silently, never taking his eyes off the gleaming slope. He knelt and fingered a bone. It was cool, slick, resistant to his touch. Above him the scavenger turned, crouching as though to spring. Graham dropped the bone and stood back. "Let's go."

"Right." The straps of Carl's pack creaked as he put it on. "Can you see well enough with lamps to find the way? Maybe go a couple of hours, to give us a little breathing space?"

Graham took a last dazed look at the ivory mountain. He had been coming to this place for a long time. Dozens of scavengers were hauling new trophies up the slope, the talus of bones shifting beneath them. Enveloped in this rustle of bodies, each with its shiny offering, the mountain possessed a terrible beauty. Was it beauty born of instinct, like a termite hill or bird nest? Or was it born of intellect, like pyramids and cathedrals? And if the work of mind, what did it mean? He did not know. A lifetime here would not answer the question.

"Yes," Graham said, "I can find the way."

He guided them unerringly. Perhaps because they moved so swiftly, or because news of their slaughter had spread through the forest, the brothers were rarely stalked on the return journey, and they left no more casualties in their wake. The trek into the wild zone had taken them six days; they reached the base camp in four. They had done their job. The studio should be satisfied, able to make from Graham's impressions another safe and stirring feelie about an unknown world.

The shuttle came for the brothers within hours, lifting them away from the field of red grass, the circle of ash-dark trees, the necklace of white peaks. Even aboard the ship, even after the recorder had been unplugged from his skull, Graham could not rid his mind of the mountain of bone. The peak rose in his memory, up and up, a glistening monument without inscription, as blank and unreadable as ice.

Dancing in Dreamtime

The shamans are dancing, their beads clicking and feathers swaying to a music I cannot hear. I can scarcely hear myself think, they
are making such a hullabaloo. Circling my console, they laugh,
gibber, stamp their feet, and shout in a babble of languages. A few
have been drinking their private brew since we parked in orbit, but
most appear to be high on the dance itself. How am I supposed to
navigate in the midst of this pandemonium?

Fortunately, there is little navigating to be done until the
shamans begin searching out the dream paths—whatever those
might be. So I am free to sit here and observe as they whirl about
me in their furs and masks and clattering ornaments. They are
old, their faces weathered like driftwood. If they notice me at all,
they must think me dull, an unpainted young woman in a gray
jumpsuit, blond hair cut short, seated before a monitor, fingers
curled over a keyboard.

For simplicity, I think of them all as shamans, yet among their
tribes they go by many titles: faith keepers, witch doctors, sorcer-
ers, magicians, wizards, healers, soothsayers, prophets. There are
sixteen of them, nine graybeards and seven crones. In their great
age, some plump and others withered, they seem to have passed
beyond gender, into a sexless twilight. Their costumes and skin
tones are as varied as their titles. The Pygmy is the darkest, a dusty

charcoal, closely rivaled by the lanky Bushman and Aborigine. The reindeer herder from Lapland is the palest, the color of moon-lit snow. Between those extremes of dark and light, the Siberian and Mongolian nomads are the Earthy ginger of the steppe, the Hopi is the roasted brown of her own pottery, the Inuit is the am-ber of old scrimshaw—and so on through the spectrum of flesh.

During launch, strapped in seats and cloaked in pressure suits, they looked like ordinary passengers. They might have been a load of tourists, or physicians heading to a symposium in orbit, or bu-reaucrats on a junket. But once the simulated gravity kicked in, they shrugged free of the suits and emerged wearing loincloths, patched blue-jeans, sequined skirts, fur-trimmed parkas, with necklaces and bracelets of bones or copper amulets. These bi-zarre outfits wheel about me now like figures on a carousel. One man wears an iron helmet and decrepit tuxedo. A woman wears a feathered headdress and a coat stitched with gleaming seashells. Snakeskins trail from ankles, bird-wings flap from shoulders, tails wag from bare haunches. The exuberant faces glisten with sweat. Most of the stamping feet are bare, but some are shod in mocca-sins, others in boots, sandals, or sneakers.

Aside from me, the only person in the cabin who doesn't dance is the major-domo for this expedition, a bulky, sun-roasted Australian named Patrick Johnson. "I'm a humble servant, not a leader," he told me when I met him before launch. "Merely a facilitator, an oiler of gears." It is hard to see where he will find the oil, because his manner, like his flesh, is so dry. "Then who *is* the leader?" I asked him. He pointed a forefinger at the sky, saying, "The Great Spirit." I assumed, from the glint in his ice-blue eyes, that he was joking.

Now, through breaks in the circle of dancers, I catch glimpses of him lounging in the front row, his ruddy face beaming, oblivious to the uproar. He wears a grass-green caftan with a large rufous eye painted on the chest.

As a steadying contrast to the ruckus that flows in through my right ear, the voices of the crew reach me through the plug in my left ear, reciting numbers, formulas, and procedures, mixed with occasional barbs.

"Do they have you wearing feathers yet, Connie?" says the captain. He and the copilots remain forward in the cockpit, the engineers remain aft, all of them amused that I must ride in the passenger cabin. The shamans need to study the images of Earth on my screens as they choose the routes to follow, so my console has been moved from the flight deck and socketed here next to the area cleared for dancing.

"No feathers yet," I tell the captain. "But I'm tempted by these bear-tooth bracelets."

"Warn us before you go native," he says.

To play along for the crew, I say, "You never know what lurks back there in the genes. My triple-great grandmother was a full-blooded Lakota named Hawk Soars."

"No kidding?"

"No kidding. According to family stories, she was a fierce woman. At the Battle of Little Bighorn she castrated seven soldiers."

"Dead ones, I hope."

"The stories don't say."

There is a chorus of male groans from the engineers, and a female snigger from one of the copilots.

"Was this ancestor of yours a witch doctor?" the captain asks.

"I wish I knew."

The dancers whirl about me, grunting and hollering. When I glance at Patrick Johnson, the rusty eye on his chest appears to wink.

☀   ☀   ☀

The ship has been leased by the World Indigenous Peoples Fund to carry seventeen passengers—the shamans plus Johnson—for a week in orbit. It is a small party to run upstairs, but otherwise there is nothing unusual about the arrangements. We are to fly wherever our customers ask us to, as we would for a load of joy-riders or eco-artists, or officials wishing to see with their own eyes the expanding deserts and dwindling forests. Never before, however, have I been asked to navigate according to the dictates of our passengers' dreams. The point of the trip, outlined in our briefing paper, is to heal the Earth with dance and song.

To keep from going gaga, I slip between a bear and a wolf in the circle of dancers and make my way to the cockpit, an arena of meticulous order and subdued voices. It is like escaping from a whirlpool into a calm lagoon. My face must betray my relief, because Lillian Riggs, a copilot whom I know from previous runs, asks me, "Pretty wild back there, Connie?"

"Bedlam."

"It's the screwiest bunch I've ever hauled," says Captain Blake. "Just look at them."

The sound has been muted on the cabin monitor, so the outlandish figures wheel in silence on the screen.

"I have the feeling they're still warming up," I say.

The captain strokes his kempt beard. "You mean they'll get crazier?"

"Why do they need a ship, anyway?" says Lillian. "Couldn't they just fly on their own?"

Magical flight is only one of the powers attributed to the shamans in our briefing paper. Supposedly the spry old coots can visit the underworld as well as heaven, dive to the ocean depths, converse with animals, pass unharmed through fire, travel outside their bodies, stab themselves without bleeding, cure all manner of sickness, and raise the dead.

"Maybe they can put me in touch with my dear departed wife," the captain muses.

"Why not have them bring her back?" says Lillian.

The captain frowns. "She wasn't that dear."

All this while, the other copilot, a solemn trainee named Sonya Mirek, never utters a word. Tall, custard-skinned, with lank hair cut ruler-straight across forehead and neck, she must be twenty-five or so, half a dozen years younger than I am. Seated stiffly erect at her instrument panel, she runs a light pen down a checklist, as though to declare her devotion to duty while the rest of us joke around.

Perhaps sensing her rebuke, the captain says, "Well, we'd better earn our fat paychecks."

I return to my station at the heart of the whirlpool.

A spell of quiet. The drums and rattles are still. The shamans are resting, a few in seats, most on the floor, squatting or sitting cross-legged or lying down. A graybeard in a turban balances on his head, his gown drooping to reveal scrawny shanks. A kneeling crone draws a landscape on the deck with colored sand. Stewards wheel through the crowd, taking orders for food and drinks. Their translation programs have been severely tested by these polyglot passengers, whose voices sound to me less like human speech than like the racket of nature.

The one human servant the shamans brought along seems to have precious little to do. Patrick Johnson cleans his fingernails with a penknife, picks lint from his grassy sleeves, stretches and yawns. The eye on the front of his caftan droops. At length he ambles over to my console, his body moving with a horsy weight, his sunburned face cracked by a smile.

"All serene there, mate?" he says to me, the Aussie accent as thick as his neck.

"Smooth sailing," I reply.

"How do you keep track of all those screens?" He nods at my console, where half a dozen monitors currently show views of Iceland, Greenland, and the Arctic Ocean.

"It takes a while to learn. Like a musical instrument, I suppose."

"Only thing I ever learned to play is a harmonica, and that fair rotten."

I glance sidelong at him. In the right setting—a desert, say, under a broiling sun—he might look good. Big as he is, at least he'd offer shade. "First time up?"

"First time in a ship."

I want to ask how else he came up, if not in a ship. Then I remember the claims about magical flight, and let it pass. Instead I ask, "How did you meet your friends?"

"This lot?" He jerks a thumb at the shamans. "By accident, the way I tumble into most things. I was collecting Aborigine songs for my thesis, when this bloke from the WIPF hired me as a guide. Wanted to visit the dawn of time. Learn the wisdom of primal peoples. He talked like that! Funny Pom, he was, with bags of money. Pretty soon I was guiding him to oases in the Sahara, huts on the Amazon, temples in the Himalayas, Pueblos in the American Southwest—anywhere the old Earth-religion survived. Eventually, he persuaded all these folks to fly up here and see what they could do for the planet, and paid me to ride along."

"There must be lots of squabbles," I say, "with so many different beliefs."

"Oh, it's all the same religion."

I survey the cabin. The sand-painter still broods over her artwork, the turbaned elder still balances on his head. Horns and feathers show above the seats. "One religion?"

"Oh, they dress bloody strange," Patrick concedes. "Look at my own getup!" He plucks the blousy waist of his caftan, causing the rufous eye to blink. "But don't judge by costumes. Underneath, we're all the same forked animals, living on the same planet."

"Do you believe all of it? The shamanic flights? Spirit trances? Dreamsongs?"

"I believe they believe it."

"That's not what I asked."

"I heard what you asked, and it's what my mum calls a rude question."

I blush, feeling stupid. "So it is. I'm sorry."

"No need. My hide's as thick as a kangaroo's."

Jaw clamped tight, I fiddle with dials, stare at screens, pretending to be busy.

"Ah, now, don't go all glum," he says. "Here, I know what you need."

I look up from my console only when I hear the music. His grin is as wide as the silver case of the harmonica. His cheeks puff, his blue eyes narrow to larky slits. He does indeed play rottenly. The shamans rise once more and begin to shuffle.

✳   ✳   ✳

Shutters descend over the windows to give us night, and eight hours later they open to give us dawn. I wake with scraps of a dream caught in my throat: a hooked claw, a baby, a knife. I sit up in fear, slither from my pouch, check the screens, do fifteen minutes of aerobics. Gradually, the lump in my throat dissolves. When I go aft for my shower, the engineers call me Hawk Soars and check my shoulders for the buds of wings.

By the time I return, the shamans have gathered in a ring to discuss their own dreams. Patrick Johnson hunkers down among them, translating, a globe in his lap. Now and again one of the shamans crouches beside him and points with a gnarled finger at some geographical feature. The others nod their heads, as if the same location appeared in their own dreams.

After a while they break their circle and approach my console, pushing Patrick ahead.

"They're spooked by your flame-colored hair and your electronics," he says, "so they want me to do the talking."

"The electronics part I can believe." What a dizzying leap it must be, from grass huts in the bush to our ship hurtling through space. "So where do they want to go?"

"All business, eh? Right-o, then. Here's the first path." He traces an arc on the globe from the Ross Ice Shelf in Antarctica, over Tasmania, New Guinea, the Philippines, and China, to the highlands of Mongolia.

"Then where?" I ask.

"Won't know until one of them goes into a trance."

I relay this to the cockpit. "Bizarre," Captain Blake sighs into my earphone. "Trances, dreams! But you punch it in, Connie, and we'll cruise it."

As I set the coordinates, the shamans crowd closer, smelling of incense, musty fur, sweat, and grease paint. I hear the rasp of breath, clack of bracelets, tinkle of bells. Patrick explains to them in signs what I am doing.

A tall, thin, dignified old man in a red loin cloth and bowler hat startles me by asking in impeccable English, "Can you speak with spirits through your device, Missy?"

To cover my surprise, Patrick says, "Allow me to introduce Luke Easterday, from Shark Bay, Western Australia." The old man bows, his white beard mashing against his chest, which is streaked with yellow paint in the zigzag design of lightning bolts. "Luke holds a degree in classics from Cambridge," Patrick adds. "He's translating Ovid into his Aboriginal tongue."

Regaining my own tongue, I say, "No, I don't speak with spirits."

"What a pity," the old man observes.

Patrick says, "Luke owns this first path, so he'll do the singing."

We get the okay from ground control and fly the arc from Ross to Mongolia. The others dance, but Luke Easterday squats beside me, watching the Earth pass on my screens. Every now and again he grunts, as though recognizing some landmark. The grunt is followed by a few minutes of singing, without any melody I can decipher. Then more watching, a grunt, a round of singing. I have no idea what it means, and the old crooner's grave manner keeps me from asking.

While we're crossing over the Gobi Desert, the Hopi woman slumps to the floor, twitches violently, and looses a high-pitched cry. The shamans bend over her, but do not intervene.

She's had a stroke, I'm sure, but as I reach for the alarm, Patrick seizes my wrist. "Not to worry," he says. "It's a visionary trance. They all have 'em. Like epileptics, except they're in control."

With an effort, I shut the stricken woman from my sight. Luke Easterday keeps watching the screen and singing. Presently, one of the wizards speaks to Patrick, who relays the message to me: "We've got path number two."

We fly that second route, then a third, a fourth, each one dictated by an entranced shaman, each with its own singer. I understand nothing. The shamans caper and cry, seeming to gain energy by the hour. Long before the shutters come down for sleep, I am wrung out.

"They're singing about how Earth was made," Patrick tells me on our third day in orbit.

I tilt him a wry look. "They know how Earth was made, do they?"

"You'd be surprised what the old codgers know." He looms over me in his green caftan with its cunning eye. "They don't tell the same stories that astrophysicists do, I'll grant you. What they tell about is the Dreamtime, when Creator made the stars, the sun and moon, the Earth and all its creatures."

"And us?"

"Us, too. We came last, when Creator had bestowed all but one gift."

Despite my skepticism, I'm intrigued. "What was that gift?"

"Singing. Telling stories. Our job was to keep the world alive by traveling across it and recalling how everything was made—the rain, the rocks, the oaks and orcas, bears and ferns."

This mythology appears in the briefing paper, but Patrick's account makes it sound less like raving nonsense. "So when the shamans sing, they're renewing places down below?"

He pats my back, a light touch for a heavy hand. "Exactly. Mountains forget how to be mountains. Rivers tumble out of their beds. Animals lose their desire to bear young. Plants become muddled. The songs remind things of how they were in the beginning, the Dreamtime, when everything was fresh. Like tuning up an orchestra. Putting the Earth back in harmony."

"You say all this with a straight face."

"It's a lovely vision."

"But is there any truth in it?"

He grins. The teeth look stunningly white in his scorched face. "There you go again with your rude questions. Let's just say my mind's open. I don't know if they can mend the blooming Earth. But I've seen the old bastards do amazing things."

"Such as?"

"Just wait, and you'll see for yourself before this journey's over." His ruddy face darkens, as if shadowed by a passing cloud. "Actually," he says, "the hardest thing to believe is that our sweet planet's gone all crook."

"Crook?"

"Sick. Out of whack. Because of us, who were supposed to care for it."

I cannot argue with that. On my screens, Earth looks perfectly hale, a blue-and-sandy ball iced with clouds. But I am not deceived by this semblance of health, for I have flown hundreds of research missions with scientists who document the planet's ailments.

✳   ✳   ✳

The engineers cannot resist teasing me about my drop of La-kota blood. They pretend to see a few black strands in my pale hair, a tinge of cinnamon in my vanilla skin, a hint of Asia in my cheekbones. Their hands tarry on my shoulders. So I avoid them, and spend my breaks up front with the pilots. The others work in four-hour shifts, but I am on call to the shamans around the clock, like the purring stewards. Lillian offers to spell me. "Spell her?" the captain mocks. "Why, Connie's like a firefighter. Only works in emergencies. Most of the time she loafs."

The shamans themselves loaf all the fourth day. They play cards, finger their beads. They squat in the aisle and chew nuts, scattering hulls that crunch beneath the stewards' wheels. They mend their costumes, which have grown tattered from three days of dancing. Amid their gibberish, I catch a word or two of English. Crooked lines. Love medicine. Eternal return. Their bursts of madcap laughter make my head spin.

Patrick spends the day weaving a belt from brightly colored threads. In the morning he pins the knotted end to the arm of his seat. By afternoon the weaving has grown so long that he removes one of his sandals and loops the end of the belt around his big toe.

It makes a grotesque image—the robust man and frail threads. He has exchanged his caftan for a tie-dyed dashiki. His wayward hair is stuffed into a white skullcap. He gives no sign of realizing how preposterous he looks. The whole lazy day, he ignores me and I ignore him.

During a break the next morning, I am in the cockpit, basking in the orderly atmosphere, when his Aussie drawl pours from the speaker: "We've got a new path for you, mate!"

Lillian rolls her eyes at me. The captain grumbles about chasing wild geese. Sonya Mirek sits rigidly at her post, scowling at her instruments, ignoring me, as if she fears I carry the germs of disorder.

"Back into the lions' den," I say.

No lions, but an elk, wolf, bear, and eagle flash by. I leap between the whirling dancers to reach my console, where Patrick waits, cradling the globe. I strain to hear him above the rattle of amulets and thunder of drums and roar of leathery throats. "This is a powerful path!" he shouts.

"Show me the route!" I holler back.

His thick finger arcs over the globe from Sri Lanka to Madagascar and the tip of Africa, crosses the South Atlantic, and stops at Tierra del Fuego. I reach for my light pen, find it floating above the desk, grab it, and start tracing coordinates. A moment later the strangeness hits me. We're not in zero-G. I lift the pen, let go, and it hangs there. I glance up in confusion.

Patrick shrugs. "It happens!"

A playing card spins between us, a seven of hearts. Inside the ring of dancers, the air is awhirl with chess pieces, feathers, peanut shells, wads of paper, and quivery blobs of water. The din of drums and voices and feet is deafening. "No, it doesn't happen!" I shout.

"Side effects! Not to worry!" The skullcap floats above his sun-blanched hair, which stands out from his scalp like the spines of a sea urchin.

When I feel my thighs lifting from the seat, I buckle my harness. Calm down, I tell myself. Do your job. Figure it out later. I punch the coordinates, reassured by the precise clicks of the keys.

As we swing onto the dream path, the Inuit woman leaves the dance and waddles up to me. She is bowlegged and squat, wearing a sealskin tunic decorated with appliqués in the shapes of birds. "Now I sing," she says. The others hush. She launches into a tremulous wail, peering into a drum that hangs upside down at her waist. Presently she cries, "They come!"

Patrick stoops over her, whispering calmly, "Catch them, Marie. Hold them."

The drum emits a resonant thud. The old woman cannot have struck it, for her palms are lifted above her head. "Stay there!" she cries. She resumes wailing, shivers, breaks off, and again the drum booms. Seven times this happens. I give up trying to understand and simply watch. After the seventh boom, she reaches into the drum and draws out two egg-sized rocks, smooth and gray, like beach cobbles, and begins rubbing them together. They make the gritty sound of bare feet scuffing over a sandy floor. Pebbles ooze from her fingers, then coil in the air like a swarm of bees, forming the same teardrop shape now glowing on my screen: Sri Lanka.

I shut my eyes and hiss into the intercom: "Are you guys watching this?"

"Quite a trick," the captain says. "How does the old gal do it?"

"I have no idea."

"Connie, are you all right?" Lillian asks.

I take a deep breath. "I just needed to hear a sane voice."

"Two more days," says the captain.

When I open my eyes, the pebbles have swarmed into the shape of Madagascar. Chanting, the Inuit woman squeezes the cobbles against her temples. Patrick looms behind her, arms spread. Soon the pebbles reform as the islands of Tierra del Fuego. My hands rise from the keyboard, buoyant, and I force them back down. She yells again, cracks the stones together, and the pebbles go rushing into her fingers like bees into a hive. The drum pounds seven times, so loud my teeth clack. The old woman goes limp, and Patrick catches her. The sudden hush is broken only by the ticking of coins and pencils and chessmen settling to the deck.

Objects do not float in one-G. Pebbles do not pour out of fingers or swirl into the shapes of landmasses. I know this, yet I also know what I saw.

The crew studies the recording, but even in super slow-motion we can't unmask the trick. "Amazing," says the captain. "That dumpy old gal could play Las Vegas."

Sonya Mirek refuses to look at the replay. Bent over a training manual, she says curtly, "It's all rubbish," one of the rare times I have heard her speak.

"If you'd been sitting there beside her, you wouldn't be so sure," I reply.

"Hocus-pocus. Mumbo jumbo. Only a child or a savage could be taken in."

Her smugness infuriates me. "Which am I, child or savage?"

"You decide."

The captain breaks in sharply. "That's enough, you two."

I glare at Sonya's rigid spine, her mousy hair chopped off straight. She never lifts her gaze from the manual.

✻   ✻   ✻

One sandal off, one sandal on, Patrick slumps into the seat next to me. Hoisting his bare foot onto the console, he attaches the half-woven belt to his toe and resumes work. "You look like you could do with a cheer-up," he declares.

"I do, do I?"

"Bit gray around the gills."

"Nice of you to say so."

His booming laugh reminds me of the drum that resounded without being struck. "Must be the lights," he says, squinting at the ceiling. "They'd make a parrot look dull."

I brush the taut strings of his weaving. "Pretty belt."

"It's called a rainbow snake. Learned the pattern from Tina Cactus Owl, my Hopi sweetheart back there." He swings his chin toward the shamans, who doze in their seats or mosey up and down the aisle, muttering.

Objects lie down now, obedient to our simulated gravity, but I remember the air flurried with castles and jokers. "What did you mean about side effects?" I ask.

"Odd things happen when the old fellas get their power cranked up. Like the way stuff floats about. I've had these blokes singing in my kitchen when the fridge lifted off the floor and shimmied."

He weaves delicately, holding the bright threads between his thick fingers. My own fingers, half as thick, feel clumsy on the keyboard. "But that Inuit woman—"

"Marie? Isn't she a wonder?"

"What was she doing with the drum?"

"Catching her helpers. She sings their names, coaxes them with sweet talk. Seal and raven. Whale, polar bear, snowy owl, arctic fox. Did you hear the bloody great thumps as they fell into the drum? She catches them, and gets them to help with the healing."

"But those pebbles?"

"That's how she does the healing." He pauses to unsnarl the strings. "The pebbles show how things should be, as they were in the Dreamtime."

"Where does she hide them? How does she control them?"

"You've got me, mate."

"Doesn't that drive you nuts, seeing without understanding?"

He ties off a thread and severs it with his teeth. "Used to. Not anymore. The longer I'm around these old bastards, the more I accept that reality's bigger and stranger than my brain."

The shamans dictate three paths on day six. I do my job, reciting the coordinates in my head, clinging to the certainty of numbers. With each path, the dancing becomes more delirious. The cabin fills with scudding shoes, candy wrappers, spoons. The dancers straddle their drums and ride them like horses, leaping, whirling. Their energy is phenomenal. When the Pygmy croons his dreamsong, the banging of his tiny foot on the deck sends a tremor through the ship. Luke and Patrick hold onto him, yet he shakes them like rag dolls. When the sorceress from Borneo sings, butterflies burst from her mouth and flutter about the cabin. Their wings brush my cheek. I navigate. I recite numbers. When the Lapp sings, antlers sprout from his head and grow until they rake the ceiling, and owls glide in to perch on the tips. Snow begins to fall.

Through my earphone come excited voices from the cockpit. Loudest of all is Sonya Mirek, who screeches over and over, "Savages! Savages!"

The herder of reindeer completes his song. The antlers shrink back into his skull. He stumbles away, dazed, supported by Patrick. The snow flurry ceases, and the melting flakes leave drops on my lashes. I fumble at the console. The switches and gauges make no sense.

Hands settle on my shoulders, and under their calm grip I feel myself trembling. "Easy now, Missy. Easy."

I twist round to see Luke Easterday's dusky, wrinkled face, his scraggly white beard, the ruff of wild hair escaping from his bowler hat. He is ancient, ages older than I will ever be. I let my head fall against the yellow zigzags of lightning on his chest, and I whisper, "I'm scared."

"I know," he murmurs. "You are wise to be frightened. The Dreaming is powerful. It keeps the whole universe going. We catch a pinch of that power in our machines and think we are gods! Hah! We are like spray flung up from the ocean."

Shuddering, as after a long cry, I say, "I don't understand."

"The Dreaming does not explain itself to us, Missy." His fingers stroke my forehead. "Now rest. You need to be strong for the last day."

The seventh day begins with a smothering silence. Not a snore, not a whisper, no clink of talismans or tinkle of bells. After

I open my eyes, a dream lingers: Inside a teepee, an old woman in doeskin dress hunches over a fire and stirs a pot with a knife. Her silver braids hang down like vines. A baby is strapped to her back with a shawl, its naked feet exposed. I realize they are my feet. The baby flings out an arm, and my arm twitches. The old woman raises the knife from the pot and slicks the blade across her tongue, tasting. I peer into the pot and see fingers, kidneys, ears. The baby wails, and I hear my own voice bawling, "Grandmother!"

Yanked out of the dream, I catch the reverberations of my cry in the still cabin. I cover my mouth. Too late. The shamans begin to stir. Patrick flinches upright on his foldout bed. His blanket slips away, revealing a brawny chest matted with blond hair. "What is it?" he mumbles.

"Nothing," I say hastily. "Only a dream."

"Uh oh." He plants his big feet on the deck, rubs his eyes. "Better tell it to me."

I shake my head. "No. It's ugly. It's stupid."

"Come on, then. Out with it."

The shamans approach me, led by the gangly figure of Luke Easterday. "You must not hide your dreams, Missy," he says. "They are given for all of us."

They fix their glittering eyes on me. I swallow, bow my head, and quietly describe the teepee, the old woman, the pot. The shamans huddle close as Patrick translates my words in sign. When I finish, there is a sizzle of whispers, followed by dead silence. Luke eyes me soberly for several seconds before saying, "A black shaman has come for you, Missy."

"She was brown," I insist, realizing how irrelevant my words are as I utter them. I also realize whom I met in sleep. "It was Hawk Soars."

"Yes," Luke says. "Your Lakota ancestor. It is not her skin that is black, but her power."

"She's evil?"

"Not evil. She is hurt. She wants revenge."

"What for?"

"The slaughter of her people, the stealing of their land."

"How do you know that?"

"Because we feel the same about our own people, our own land. But instead of revenge, we seek healing."

Suddenly furious, fed up with these feathered, beaded, posturing fools, I cry out, "It's got nothing to do with me. I'm a navigator. I want no part in your myths."

The shamans crowd around Patrick, jabbering at him, waving their arms. After they quiet down, he gives me a rueful look. "Trouble is, Connie, you may be dangerous."

"Because of a dream, for God's sake?"

"Because that knife-happy ancestor of yours is boiling mad."

"She means us harm," Luke says. "She may force you to lead us on the wrong path."

"That's ridiculous!" I turn for reassurance to my console. The switches are gleaming teeth. The monitors are roiling pots, filled with hands, livers, and hearts in green broth. I bite my lip to keep from screaming.

The shamans erect a slender, white-barked tree on top of my console, with its base clamped in a metal stand and its tip grazing the ceiling. Seven branches, tufted with dry leaves, curve out from the trunk.

"A birch," Patrick says. "A holy tree in cold country."

"What's it for?" I ask.

Overhearing me, Luke points to his navel. "The doorway," he explains.

"Doorway to where?"

"The depths and heights," says the old man. "The roots go down to the underworld. The branches reach the sky."

Our final path is a pole-to-pole orbit that will sweep out a sinuous curve over the spinning Earth. I punch the coordinates carefully, yet in my cross-checks I find a mistake that would have led us astray by several degrees, enough to spoil the shamans' plans. I look up, and find Luke's flinty black eyes and Patrick's icy blue ones intently watching me.

"Problem?" says Patrick.

"No, I've almost got it." Shaken, I repeat my calculations.

"Missy," Luke says, "if the grandmother comes back, tell me, and I will deal with her."

"I'll do that," I reply brusquely.

"If she invites you to go with her, you must refuse. You must."

"Whatever you say." I touch the keys with exaggerated care, as if I were disarming a bomb. Satisfied at last, I notify the captain. "Ready when you are, sir."

"Good," he replies. "Let's get this monkey business over with, and go back downstairs."

My right ear fills with the sober voices of the crew. No wisecracks from the engineers, no sarcasm from Captain Blake. Lillian plods through a systems check. Sonya Mirek is mum. My left ear fills with the racket of the shamans, who form their motley ring and start prancing. They are even more gaudily painted, and they bristle with more feathers, more clattering ornaments. As they circle, the air thickens with floating debris. My skin tingles.

Once again wearing the grass-green caftan with its rusty eye, Patrick settles in the chair next to me. The newly woven belt inscribes a rainbow at his waist. The playfulness has gone out of him. Now he is watchful, like a lion-tamer inside the cage with his beasts. Close though we are, we must yell to be heard above the drums and bells and moans. "Hold tight!" he shouts.

I am already clutching the edge of the console, my knuckles white.

As the shamans leap and sing, the atmosphere in the cabin becomes charged, as before a storm. The seven old women spiral in toward the center, brushing me as they pass, then they all sit down, forming a smaller ring inside the wheel of dancing men. The women begin slapping their thighs, which makes the men leap higher, cry louder.

The Bushman staggers out of the ring, throws back his head in a high-pitched wail, and flames gush from his mouth.

Fearing he'll die, I cover my eyes with my hands.

"He's all right," Patrick assures me, peeling my hands away and holding them firmly in one big paw, where I let them stay.

The slapping of thighs accelerates. The men cry sharply, and in their frenzied circling they begin to glow, their chests and faces burning like embers. A headdress smolders. Where are the alarms? Why don't the extinguishers spew foam? The cabin reeks of singed fur.

The blood slams in my head. My muscles twitch. Craving some bit of order, I count the graybeards as they wheel past. Only nine, yet they seem like a mob. I count the seated crones, whose arms thresh the air. Eight? There should be seven. I count again. Eight. Suddenly, the crone nearest to me rises. Her face is cloaked in a bird mask with a hooked copper beak. Silver braids sway against her doeskin dress. Over her shoulder, a raven-haired papoose squints at me.

"Come home with me, daughter," the old woman whispers. Her voice is soothing, like water over stones, washing away all other sounds.

The bird mask and peeping child crowd out all other sights. "Where, Grandmother?"

"You know the place." She rakes a finger across my brow.

An image rises in me of stony crags, blowing dust, the moon caught in the limbs of a leafless tree. I do know the place—the Black Hills, where Hawk Soars hid while soldiers killed the rest of her family. The old woman nods. "Fly us there," she says.

Power surges through me. I tug my hands free from the grip of a hulking man with a giant eye on his chest, and fling him aside. My fingers find the keys. I start to punch in coordinates for the Black Hills, when my wrists are seized by a scarecrow with lightning on his chest. I try to lift my arms to shove him away, but his strength is greater than mine. He squeezes my wrists and bends down as though to kiss me. Instead, he puffs air into my left ear, then my right, and noise comes crashing in on me again, my vision widens to take in the cabin, the chanting women, the whirling men, and I see Patrick with an astonished expression picking himself up from the floor. My mouth fills with the tinny taste of fear.

"She came, and you did not warn me," Luke tells me sternly.

"I didn't realize who it was."

"She tried to make us crash."

"But why? Why would she hurt us?"

"She does not want us to sing Earth back to health. She wants to hasten the end, wipe out the two-leggeds, clear the land of those who mined and paved and poisoned it."

"She'd condemn everybody, even the innocent?"

"The innocent would be reborn on a new Earth. Her tribe and all the tribes that never caused harm to Earth would be reborn, along with all the animals and plants." He says this with the fervor of a man who has been tempted by the same vision.

Patrick slouches up, rubbing his ribs. "What did you hit me with?"

"It wasn't Constance," Luke says. "It was her ancestor. The black shaman."

I shiver, counting the crones. Seven. None wears a bird mask or carries a papoose.

"She will try again," Luke warns.

The dancing men and drumming women put out a fierce heat, yet I keep shivering.

"Why doesn't Connie move to the cockpit?" Patrick suggests.

Luke shakes his head. "She is our link with Earth, which she holds inside her."

"How?" I ask, startled.

Luke points at my screens. "It pours in through your eyes."

I look, and see India spreading away toward the rumpled quilt of the Himalayas. The sight is more familiar than my own bed. *Do I carry the Earth inside me?*

"While I am gone," Luke tells Patrick, "Constance must not use her machine."

"How can I stop her?"

The old man plucks the rainbow belt at Patrick's waist. "Catch her with this."

The arms of the women blur as they pound their thighs. The men whirl so fast their feet scarcely touch the floor. There is a banging on the hull and the squeal of tortured metal. In the earphone I hear Sonya Mirek shrieking and the engineers shouting and the captain bellowing for silence. The ship is breaking up, I feel certain, yet I am oddly calm.

From the inner circle, the Inuit woman, Marie, struggles upright and stumps over to me on her bowed legs. Placing a hand on my neck, she pushes me gently forward until my cheek rests on my crossed forearms atop the console. "Be still, young one," she tells me. "You must hold us up and welcome us back." The fat old woman clambers onto my shoulders, light as a child. With my upturned eye, I watch her grab the birch trunk and climb nimbly up. When she reaches the tip of the tree, a hole opens in the cabin roof and she vanishes through it.

Why aren't we sucked into space, with our precious air? I am too astonished to feel afraid. Next comes the woman from Borneo amid a cloud of butterflies. Once again, child-light feet tiptoe along my spine, then up she climbs to the top of the tree and disappears. One by one, the other women follow her through the hole, taking the sound of their clapping with them.

I glance at Patrick, who watches me, the rainbow belt tightly balled in his fist. The sunlight has drained from his face. "It's dicey," he says, "but they may pull it off."

The hull groans. The panicky voices of the crew swell in my ear.

The Pygmy skips in from the ring of men, stamping his feet, yet when he pounces on my back he weighs less than a cat. Up he goes, vaulting from my shoulders to the tree and on up from branch to branch and through the opening. Next the antlered herdsman, then the Siberian with his clanging copper amulets, then the immense Mongolian in his iron helmet and tuxedo, nearly weightless, all of them, skittering up my back. As each man vanishes, the cabin grows quieter.

Last of all comes Luke, in his bowler hat and red loin cloth, his face solemn above the white beard, the lightning streaks on his chest flashing. He glares at me. "You must not move, Constance. You are the threshold, our way in and our way out." Then he climbs swiftly, and just before disappearing calls down, "Mind her, Patrick!"

The hull ceases to groan. The crew hushes. I hear only the thudding of my heart. Then a creek-water voice pours over me, calling, "Daughter! Daughter!" I lift my head, and feel the prickle of hot skin as my cheek peels away from my sweaty forearm.

"Hold still, Connie!" Patrick's voice is muffled, as though he shouts through layers of cloth. "You'll trap them out there!"

His hand on me is a fly I shrug off. "Grandmother," I whisper. Her brightness dims the air. The bird mask is thrown back and her face is webbed in wrinkles, the mouth cinched tight with bitterness. Her silver braids gleam. In place of arms she has russet wings, folded now, and her toes are talons. The papoose gazes over her shoulder with my face.

"Come away, Daughter," the bird woman murmurs.

There is a resistance in me, but it gives way before the pressure of her stare. I gather myself to rise, ignoring the man's fumbling efforts to hold me.

"Come, child, I will take you to the soul's country." She opens her wings. The undersides glow with the soft luster of a full moon. The papoose gazes at me with my own eyes.

I am drawn to my feet. The wings open wider, and I step toward them, but a serpent coils around my waist and yanks me backward an instant before the wings can embrace me.

"Daughter!"

"Grandmother!" I wail, clawing at the rainbow snake that binds me, and I tumble backward, knocking the man down, but he pins me to the deck and keeps tightening the belt.

"Connie," he hisses, "wake up!"

Suddenly I recognize the voice. "Patrick, you're hurting me."

"Is she gone?"

I gaze wildly about, but can no longer see Hawk Soars or the baby. I nod, sobbing.

Patrick loosens the belt a little. "Crikey, you're strong when she gets in you."

Between sobs, I say, "Why won't you let me go with her?"

"And kill my wizards and crash the ship? I'd sooner throttle you." As though to demonstrate his willingness, he picks me up and sets me roughly in my seat at the console. "Now put your head down, just like before."

As my cheek touches the console, there is a sharp high whistle, and the cabin goes dark, the ventilator quits, my screens black out. The stewards grind to a halt. Gabble roars from the earphone, Sonya Mirek screeching, the captain barking orders, then static, then dead air. I hear a scuffle from above, a pounding on the hull, then nothing but my own gasps. The lights flare as the back-up power kicks in, then dim and go out. We are left in utter darkness.

Her strength is in me. The ship may die, but I can soar without it. I snatch the rainbow snake from my waist and fling it away. I smack the hand loose from my neck. I could snap this man like a twig. He pants, his voice gone small and fearful. "Listen, Connie. You've got to put your head down, or you'll kill them. You're their way back in."

In the darkness I hear the scrape of talons on the floor, feel air move from the slow beating of wings. She waits for me. I can crawl onto her shoulders, become the papoose, fly with her. Or I can stay here in this life, puny, mortal, and walk on my own legs.

I stare into the gloom, unable to see her. Why doesn't she grab me, force me to go with her? Why leave me this choice? Seconds pass, like bubbles swelling and bursting.

"Grandmother?" I whisper. No answer.

"They'll die, Connie," the man cries. "We'll all die."

In the darkness and silence, I hold the spinning Earth inside me, the sheen of oceans, the continents with their snowy mountains and meandering rivers, the forests and prairies, and the host of living creatures, sadly diminished, battered, but beautiful still. At last I choose. "No, Grandmother, I will not leave."

There is a rush of air, the sharp high whistle of a hawk, and she is gone.

The cabin lights flicker on, the ventilator hisses, stewards purr, monitors glow, and the earphone sputters with talk. The captain announces that Sonya Mirek has been sedated. All stations report systems normal. The ship appears to be undamaged.

I bend over the console and lay a wet cheek on my crossed arms. I weep and weep. Patrick strokes my hair.

Presently, a dusky foot appears through the hole at the top of the tree, then two bony legs, then the entire scarecrow figure of

Luke Easterday, who eases down from branch to branch, steps on my back, and hops to the floor. "You frightened us, Constance!"

"Leave her alone," Patrick says.

"The door was locked."

"I said leave her alone. Can't you see it tore her up?"

The old man grunts. The other shamans descend the tree and scramble over my back, heavier now, their trinkets and beads jangling. They encircle me, charged with triumph from their journey, chattering in their many tongues. Patrick translates for me. They have spoken to the powers, tuned the cosmic strings, sung the melodies of Dreamtime.

Have they truly? I don't know what to believe. When I go back to my home on that miraculous, exquisite globe, I must walk in the woods, wade in creeks, hunt for wildflowers, search for birds and butterflies, foxes and frogs, to see if Earth has begun to heal.

No longer a stepping-stone, I rise and stretch. Every joint aches. I gaze at the spot where the hawk woman stood in all her splendor. Two long russet feathers lie on the deck. I pick them up and place one behind each ear. Noticing, Patrick smiles and runs his palm over my cheek. I have been wrenched out of a world I thought I knew and thrust into a bewildering new one, unsure what I have lost, what found.

Credits

Earlier versions of the stories in this collection were originally published in the following periodicals and books:

"The Audubon Effect," "The Circus Animals' Desertion," "Dancing in Dreamtime," and "Travels in the Interior" in *Omni*; "The Land Where Songtrees Grow," "Sleepwalker," and "Terrarium" in *The Magazine of Fantasy and Science Fiction*; "The Anatomy Lesson," "The Artist of Hunger," "Ascension," "The Engineer of Beasts," "Mountains of Memory," and "Clear-Cut" (under the title "Tree of Dreams") in *Isaac Asimov's Science Fiction Magazine*; "The First Journey of Jason Moss" in *Poet & Critic*; "Quarantine" in *Habitats*, edited by Susan Shwartz; "Eros Passage" in *New Dimensions 11*, edited by Robert Silverberg and Marta Randall; and "Touch the Earth" in *Edges*, edited by Virginia Kidd and Ursula K. Le Guin.

"The Engineer of Beasts," "The Circus Animals' Desertion," and "Mountains of Memory" were later adapted for the novel *The Engineer of Beasts*. "Terrarium" and "Quarantine" were later adapted for the novel *Terrarium*.

Author's Note

Most of the stories in this collection behaved themselves and quit haunting me after they were finished. One of the exceptions was "Terrarium," which kept stirring my imagination long after I had written the final scene. I wondered how Phoenix, this cautious man, would find the courage to abandon the Enclosure, the only world he has known, and escape with Teeg into the wilds. I wondered how Teeg acquired her daring, and her passion for nature. Would these seemingly mismatched lovers go outside alone, or with fellow conspirators? If there is a conspiracy, how was it formed? How would they escape? How would they survive in the wilds? Would the security forces discover them, and, if so, what punishment would follow? Has Earth begun to recover from the ecological breakdown that forced the move into the Enclosure? What species have survived the pollution and climate disruption, and what ones have perished? Is there any prospect for reconciliation between the human and natural worlds?

As I wrote my way toward answering such questions, the stories "Quarantine" and "Touch the Earth" emerged, and eventually the tale of Phoenix and Teeg grew into a novel called *Terrarium*. To give you a taste of the novel, which is also available from Indiana University Press, here are two sample chapters. In chapter 4, while outside on a repair mission, Teeg surveys a bay on the Oregon shore as a possible site for a colony. She tries to imagine what her mentor, Zuni Franklin, a designer of the Enclosure and an advocate for moving humankind inside, would make of the plans for an escape into the wilds. In chapter 10, Teeg takes Phoenix to a meeting of the conspirators, in hopes that he will pass their test and be accepted as a member of the group. With or without him, they will make their move soon.

CHAPTER FOUR

On the beach at Whale's Mouth Bay, amid boulders and sea gulls, Teeg lay roasting in the sun. Against her naked back and rump the sand felt like a thousand nibbling flames. Salt-laden wind fanned her hair. Even through the breathing-mask she could smell the ocean. Between repair missions, when she was required to stay inside the Enclosure, more than anything else she missed the feel of sun on her skin.

During this trip she quickly finished her assigned job—replacing fuel cells on a signal booster atop Diamond Mountain—and had three hours left over for scouting. Most of the time she used for discovering how hospitable a place the bay might be, testing for radiation, toxins, soil nutrients, the quality of water. These last few minutes of her allotted time she lay basking in the sun, as a celebration for having found the right place at last. She would have to make sure Whale's Mouth had been omitted from the surveillance net. It probably had, since no tubes or laser channels or signal avenues passed anywhere near the place. Just another piece of real estate long since erased from human reckoning. She hoped so. Phoenix could tell her for sure. And she would need to spend a week here, later on, to run more tests on plants and microbes and air before she could assure the other seekers that this was indeed the place for the settlement.

Phoenix's maps had led her straight to the bay, her shuttle flying low and coasting along on compressed air to avoid the patrollers and the sky-eyes. On each repair mission, stealing time to explore locations for the settlement, she was more and more tempted to stay outside alone. But whenever she wavered, all she had to do was close her eyes, think about the plans for the settlement, and the faces of the seven other conspirators would rise within her silence. She was one of them, a limb of their collective body.

Lying there on the beach, she felt the sweat gathering in her navel, between her breasts, on the slopes of her thighs. The crash of surf against the volcanic walls of the bay sent shudders through her. Occasionally an eddy in the wind snatched the odors of fir and alder from inshore and filled her with the pungency of green. Thoughts swung lazy as hawks through her mind.

A sound pried her eyes open. Two gulls squabbling over a fish. Life was creeping back into the land, the ocean, though on nothing like the scale her mother used to tell about. Her mother. Dead up north in Portland. Murdered. Will I ever gather the courage to go there, Teeg wondered, and look at the place where they killed her?

The cliffs surrounding the bay bristled with young trees and bushes. Life reclaiming the land. The plants seemed hardier than animals; they recovered more quickly, perhaps because they had evolved in an atmosphere even more toxic than the present one. She had noticed on this flight that there were fewer scars of bare soil in the countryside. Perhaps, as Zuni always insisted,

Enclosure had been the only way of halting the energy slide, the famine for materials, the poisoning of the planet. If it *was* halted. An oceanographer had confided to Teeg (one did not say such things in print or on video) that it might take another fifty years for all the toxins to wash off the land masses into the seas, and perhaps another fifty years before the oceans showed whether they could survive the poisons. "We might already be dead and not know it," he had whispered. "Or then again, the ocean may surprise us with her resilience."

Resilience. She liked that, the springing back of nature. She smeared the sweat across her belly, enjoyed the springiness of her own flesh. Womb inside there, where never babe did dwell. Enclosure. The great domed cities, wombs spun of glass and alloy and geometry. Mother helped provide the materials for them. Zuni and Father helped provide the designs. And I? I want out.

She propped herself on elbows and surveyed the bay. Yes, this was the place to build a colony—hills shouldering down to within a few hundred meters of the shore, then a meadow traversed by a sluggish river, and then the beach of black sand and black volcanic boulders. The north arm of the bay was a massive headland, topped by the ruins of a lighthouse. There was even an abandoned oil pipeline running along the old roadbed nearby, connecting across eighty kilometers of ocean to the tank farm in Oregon City. Ideal for smuggling out equipment and supplies.

When she had first visited this place as a child, on one of those rapturous holidays with her mother, the pipe had still carried oil and the shoreline had been half a kilometer farther west. Snags of the old coast were still visible as gray outcroppings, great broken teeth, farther out in the bay. On one of their recent outings

Phoenix had assured her that the polar icepacks had stopped melting. "One more benefit from the transition to solar living," he explained. That meant the new coastline would probably remain stable for a while.

A strand of marsh grass blew along the sand, clung to her ribs like a green wound. She peeled it away and wrapped it about her left thumb. Will Phoenix decide to come out here with us? she wondered. The grass made a vivid ring on her sun-pinked flesh. Sitting up, she hugged her knees. Can he shake himself free of the city? And will the others let him join our circle?

A bank of clouds shut away the sun, and the air grew chill. Teeg rose, slapped sand from her legs and buttocks. Cleaning grit from her back would have to wait until she took an air-shower at the sanitation port. Despite the chill, her body still felt atingle from the sun. She slithered into boots and shimmersuit, tightened the breathing-mask over her face. Through goggles the bay still looked beautiful. Running shadows marked the passage of clouds across the knobby black walls of the cliffs. Surf exploded rhythmically on the boulders. She wanted to make love with that roar in her ears.

Aloft in the shuttle, Teeg hovered for a minute over the beach, before heading inland toward the nearest port. She skimmed across the meadow, sun winking in the river, then she climbed the foothills at a height some ten meters above the tips of spruce and hemlocks. There was joy in balancing the tiny craft on its cushion of air, riding the thermals like a falcon. From above, the slopes looked solid green, a carpet of moss, as if you could walk from treetop to treetop without ever touching the ground. Some patches still showed brown where the last clear-cuts had not yet mended, or where toxins had concentrated. But everywhere the forest was coming back. The oceans provided cheaper substitutes for cellulose, without all the mess of lumbering.

Between the first range of hills and the somber mountains, she could just make out stretches of the old coastal highway. Scraps of concrete and tar showed through the weeds. In places the ocean had backed into valleys and covered the roadbed. A charred clearing beside the road and a scattering of rubble marked the location of a dismantled town, probably some fishing port. The map Phoenix had given her mentioned neither road nor town, identified nothing but landforms and the frail web of tubes.

From the peak of the next range she spied, away down in the mountain-shadowed Willamette Valley, the glowing travel-tube. Its translucent glass pipes, frosty white and glittering like an endless icicle, stretched north toward Vancouver City and south toward the clustered domes of California. Whenever she glimpsed the tube system or the domes from outside, she was amazed at their grace, and she thought of her father. Whatever shape you could reduce to a mathematical formula, he would weep over. But that was the only beauty he had ever learned to see.

While Teeg watched, a freighter poured its flash of blue lights through the northbound tube.

She let the shuttle skip lightly on the updrafts along the far side of the coastal range, dipping down into shadows. The valley stretched away north some two hundred kilometers to Portland, her mother's place, the place of death. Teeg shivered, trying to shut the scene back in its mental cage. Yet I must go there, she thought, go and face whatever remains of her.

In the shadowed valley she looked for the yellow beacon that marked a gateway to the Enclosure, her thoughts drifting, as they often did, from her mother to Zuni, who had grown up in one of the lumber towns on these slopes. Sheep used to graze in this valley, Zuni would tell her, and the hills were green with mint, and fruit trees covered the terraces like ornate stitchery. Teeg had always been surprised, the way the older woman's eyes would soften when she told about the Willamette Valley.

Can I tell her about Whale's Mouth Bay, about the settlement? Teeg wondered. No, no, she decided, it would be madness to confess this hunger for the wilds to the mother of the Enclosure.

Fly the shuttle, she reminded herself. There must be no mistakes on reentry. Each time she returned from a mission she feared they would demand proof that all her time had been spent making repairs. But the insiders who staffed Security never dared go outside, so they grew more ignorant of the wilds each year. With no idea how long a repair job should take, they let the wildergoers alone.

At the junction of the Willamette and McKenzie Rivers she spotted the yellow beacon of the sanitation port. Come here, the beacon seemed to promise, come here all you who have wandered from the human system, come and we will purify you, bathe you in artificial light, admit you once again into the charmed circle of the city.

CHAPTER TEN

In boots and hoods and ankle-flapping capes, with masks drawn close to hide their faces, Teeg and Phoenix walked among the circular oil stains of the tank farm. Behind them, the gamepark flung its riotous colors toward the nightdarkened dome, and farther behind, near the city center, buildings heaped up in pyramids and honeycombs of light. Ahead of them loomed the dark knobby shapes of the few remaining oil tanks.

"What if I can't—" Phoenix began.

Teeg shushed him quickly. "You *can*. Now be still and keep your mind centered. No doubts. You've got to be clear."

They passed between two partly demolished tanks. Where lasers had cut through the triple-hulled walls, cauterized edges gleamed with a dull luster. This might be the last ingathering here, Teeg realized, for the wreckers were gnawing their way each week nearer to the tank where the seekers met. The pipeline leading from here to the mountains near Whale's Mouth Bay had already been severed. Phoenix had to pass the test tonight, for there might not be another chance.

Teeg climbed the ladder first, feet quiet on the rungs, and when Phoenix joined her on the roof of the tank she motioned for him to slip off his gown and streetmask. They added their garments to the pile beside the entrance valve, pried off their boots. Turning, with Phoenix between her and the distant glow of the gamepark, she could see for the first time his actual shape, hugged in the fabric of his shimmersuit. The months of training had drawn his body tight. She touched him lightly on the chest, felt the quiver of muscle, then trailed her fingers downward over ribs to his waist.

"I'm afraid," he whispered.

"Of course."

Through her bare feet she sensed the hum of voices in the tank below. As she cranked the valve open the hum grew louder, then separated into distinct and familiar voices. Jurgen's gruff baritone, Hinta's soothing purr, Sol's gasping with the sound of blood in it. They were discussing Phoenix, wondering aloud if his light would merge with theirs.

"You follow me," she whispered to him. "And relax, keep yourself clear."

His silhouette blocked out a man-shaped chunk of inner-city lights. "But am I ready? Maybe I need more—"

"You're *ready.*"

She lowered her feet through the cold jaws of the valve, swung down from handhold to handhold. Before her feet kissed the floor the voices hushed. She bowed deeply. Grave faces nodded at her: the lovely rainbow shades of skin, cinnamon and plum, olive and cornsilk—the colors of growing things. A moment later Phoenix swung down beside her, looking self-conscious in his silvery shimmersuit and naked face. She had never before seen him scrubbed perfectly clean of paint. His cheeks were the color of peaches; descent through the valve had left one of them smudged with grease. As the conspirators stared at him, he shuffled his feet nervously, and that little stagger caught at her heart.

"Phoenix Marshall," she announced.

"Peace," murmured several voices. Each person raised the left hand, palm exposed. Although the backs of the hands were the color of salmon and copper and chocolate, a mixture of races, the palms were all yellowed with calluses. They carried this imprint of the outdoors with them always, this thickening of the skin from work.

After bowing, Phoenix licked his lips and carefully pronounced the formula she had taught him. "I am seeking the light. I ask to join your circle."

Hands waved him to the mat which had been made ready. Teeg lowered herself onto the mat next to his, and the circle was gathered. She noticed Sol and Marie staring across at Phoenix, sizing him up—curious, probably, to see what had attracted her to him. If asked, she would not have known what to say, except that something in her leapt up to answer the yearning she felt in him.

When at last the two old spirit-travelers lowered their eyes, Teeg did the same, and immediately power began to flow around the circle. There was a roaring like the joining of rivers inside her, and then stillness began trickling through her.

Open up to us, Phoenix, open up, she chanted over and over to herself.

After several moments she realized her back was tensed and her jaw was clamped tight. She was trying to *will* the coming together. Gradually she relaxed, let go, made herself into a gauzy sail that winds of the spirit could shove along. And the winds set her quivering, caught and spun her, leaf-light, across the waters. Presently she drifted up against some barrier, could not break through. She was conscious of her skull, an enclosure trapping her, and then the walls of bone evaporated like mist and she floated outward, nudging against the curved walls of the tank. Those also gave way, and after them the walls of Oregon City, and then the vaporous envelope of the planet, and so on outward past solar system and galaxy, always adrift, until her frail craft burst through every last barrier and coasted into the center of light. Here all was a dazzle and a blazing stillness, a burning without movement, a chorus without sound. A fierce energy gripped her, spinning her round, and yet she felt calm.

Against the dazzle at the center shone fainter lights, like dim stars set off against the awesome fire. The lights formed a ring, and with her last shred of consciousness Teeg knew which light was her own and which Phoenix's. The ring drew inward, the ten lights merged into one and that light merged with the fire, and Teeg was

Phoenix was Jurgen was Hinta, Teeg was all the other seekers, and she was God, and she was herself. There was no wind anymore, for she was at the source of all winds, and no time passing, no urge to go anywhere else; there was only abundance and peace.

After a while the breeze caught her, shoving her away from the center, back toward the two-legged packet of flesh called Teeg Passio. The walls thickened around her again, walls of galaxies, walls of bone, shutting her up once more within the confines of her own self. Yet as she roused from the trance she brought with her glimmers of that inner blaze. She held her fingers close to her face and bent each one in turn, feeling the joints mesh, the blood flow, the billion cells flame with their sparks of the infinite burning. Each time, coming back from the center, she was more amazed by life, by this flame leaping in the meshes of matter.

She reached out to left and right, found Marie's hand on one side and Phoenix's on the other. Hand joined to hand around the circle and the shudder of return passed through them, like the involuntary shudder after a bout of crying or lovemaking. Following a spell of quiet, to let the ecstasy settle in them all, Jurgen said, "Peace."

"Peace," said Teeg.

"Peace, peace, peace," Phoenix murmured. His cheeks were slick.

"Welcome, new one," the others said.

Phoenix gazed at them, letting the tears come. He sat there with a look of baffled joy on his face while the seekers approached him, each one in turn pressing palms to his palms and forehead to his forehead. Marie came last. Her shaved head glistened. She beamed down at Phoenix with all the intensity of her weathered and finely wrinkled face. "Now you know where we truly are," she said, brushing her forehead against his, "and don't you ever forget."

"That's where we are," Phoenix echoed her. "And all this," he said, gesturing at the other people and the oilsmeared walls of the tank, "all this is illusion?"

Marie's gleaming head wagged side-to-side. "No, it's not illusion. It's performance. We're all performing the history of God, all of us, men and women and trees and pebbles, each one carrying bits of fire."

She withdrew to join the others at the far side of the tank, leaving only Teeg beside him. His lips parted as if he were going to thrust out his tongue and taste the air.

"That's Marie," Teeg said. "She and Sol have taken the longest spirit journeys, so we listen to them. Sol's the one over there with skin the color of ripe plums." Realizing Phoenix had never seen a plum, she pointed. "There, see, the one kneeling down and unrolling the map."

Phoenix nodded sleepily, but his eyes were not focused. It was no use telling him the names of the others tonight; he was too dazzled to see their faces. Their voices chattered on about dates, routes, meetings, about plans for escape from Oregon City. Contrive a water accident, make Security think the entire crew had drowned, then boat to Whale's Mouth—that was the gist of it. Teeg was not paying close attention to the talk, for she had this joy to share with Phoenix. She kept his fingers laced in her own, giving him time to come down, to come back. Let him giddy about on his own inner winds for a while longer. She remembered her own first ingathering, the sense of coming home at last to the place she had been seeking all her days. Rainwater rediscovering the sea. Sexual orgasm was delicious, but it could not rival the splendor of that homecoming.

At last his fingers came awake in her hand, and this time when he looked he really saw her. "Now I know why you gave up trying to describe it," he said.

Later, walking back with him through the ruins of the tank farm, after the crew had worked out all the details for escape, she asked, "Was it what you expected?"

"The test?"

"The journey inward."

He lifted both arms, hands cupped domeward. "How could I ever dream of a trip like that?"

"Of course you couldn't." She skipped gaily, boots scuffing on the metal floor. She felt like a gauzy sail again, blown along.

"Is it always like that?" he said.

"Is sex always spectacular?"

"Is sex—what?" he stammered.

"Spectacular. Like fireworks."

"Do you mean—"

"I mean sometimes loving is magnificent, sometimes it's okay, and sometimes it's just a sweaty thumping of bodies. And the sky's not always perfectly blue and the crocuses don't burst through the soil every day. There's rhythms to these things." She couldn't stop using the speech of natural things, even though she knew it meant little to him. Soon it would mean a great deal to him, once he was outside. "Things come clear in their own sweet time. We just prepare, open ourselves, and wait."

"So it was special?" he said.

"Rare, very rare. We'd never been that close to the center before. Some of the others might have, privately—Sol, maybe, or Marie, even Hinta. But as a group, that was a whole new . . . intensity. Maybe you were just the bit of chemistry, the trace element, we needed."

"And you think they accepted me?"

"You were there, weren't you, in the fire? What other proof do you need?"

He didn't need any other, for he seized her by the hands and danced her in circles, their gowns kiting outward, their boots clumping. Gravel skittered away over the gray metal floor. They were like two stars orbiting one another, drifting closer as their spinning slowed, until they danced to a stop with hips and breasts and lips pressed together. For once his body felt easy against hers, yielding, as if the glacier that had built up in him during years of emotional restraint were melting at last. This time, when his cock bulged against her, he did not turn away. He kept his lips on hers, his hands on the curve of her rump. They stayed that way for a spell, with the scraps of cut-up oil tanks heaped around them, with sirens and delirious shouts rising from the nearby gamepark. Then Teeg felt the chill slowly coming over him again, the glacier accumulating, the cold spreading through his body like crystals of ice. And finally he pulled away.

"I lost control," he said with an abashed tone. She could see him ticking over in his mind the articles of the mating code.

"What you lost were those stupid shackles, for about half a minute." She kicked a chunk of gravel, sent it clattering. Patience, she reminded herself. He had already come a long way in a few months. He had become a walker, an inward exile from the

Enclosure. Did she expect him also to become an uninhibited lover so quickly? "I'm sorry," she said. "I keep forgetting. And we'll have time, outside. We'll melt the polar icepack if we need to."

"Polar icepack?"

"Never mind. Let's go, before the healthers come sniffing after us."

She led the way cautiously through the outskirts of the tank farm, avoiding the rings of oil. The crew had decided not to meet again in the doomed tank, but still, it would not do to give the place away. Properly booted and hooded with streetmasks over their faces, Teeg and Phoenix skirted the last heap of scrap and emerged into the many-colored illumination of the gamepark. The noise was deafening. People shuffled from one buzzing electronic box to another, climbed in and out of bump-cars, stood howling in the laughter booths. The loudest shouts came from the eros parlors, long anguished cries of pleasure, as if the customers were releasing in a single burst all the pent-up emotion of the day. Around the chemmie dispensers people hopped on one leg or flapped their arms, eyes rolling, or crowed with heads thrown back, or skittered about on all fours.

Teeg drew the gown tight at her throat, made sure the mask snugged down over her jaw. Beast time, she thought. A few minutes of licensed animalhood to relieve the dread they carry with them all day. She stopped short to let a man slither past on his belly; his painted face lunged at invisible targets in the air, jaws snapping. Before he left the park he would swallow a capsule of eraser, and never know he had played lizard.

"Hurry," Phoenix hissed over her shoulder. "I can't stand this."

No one paid any attention to them as they passed, quickly, through the park, their pace as frantic as the revelers'. At the gate, where pedbelts dumped the rigid bodies of new customers and carried away the limp exhausted ones, Teeg hesitated. She turned for a moment to look back the way they had come, across the riotous glow of the park toward the squat oil tank where so many ingatherings had taken place. She could not actually see the tank—which was just as well, since she would go there no more. The crew would remain scattered until the next call for emergency work, and that call, if the weather and the sea cooperated, would carry them outside the city for good. Sometimes, even here inside the dome, she thought she could detect shifts in the weather, as if some antique portion of her mind had never fully submitted to life indoors. This was one of those times, standing there at the gateway of the amusement park with Phoenix. A stirring in her marrowbones, a tingling along her spine, told her of storms brewing outside.

Turning back around, still holding onto Phoenix, she stepped on the slick black river of the pedbelt and let it carry her away.

Book Club Guide

1. Critics have debated whether to describe these stories as science fiction, speculative fiction, magic realism, or fantasy. What label, if any, would you use to describe them?

2. Some of these stories, such as "The Artist of Hunger," are satirical, and laced with humor; others, such as "Land Where the Songtrees Grow," are somber and brooding. Do you find yourself drawn more to one type than to the other?

3. The English poet Samuel Taylor Coleridge claimed that fantastic tales require from the reader a "willing suspension of disbelief." The degree of strangeness in these stories increases over the course of this book, from stories set on Earth in our own day, to ones set on Earth in the near future, to ones set on distant planets. Do you find yourself willing to accept the fantastic elements, or do you find yourself resisting?

4. A number of the stories extrapolate features of contemporary American society into the future, as if to make them more visible, and therefore more available for examination. What extrapolated—or exaggerated—features do you notice?

5. Sanders appears to lament the increasing separation between humans and nature. Do you see evidence of such a separation in America today? If so, does it trouble you?

6. In his memoir, *A Private History of Awe*, Sanders has written about his youthful fascination with rockets and space travel. How does that fascination show through here?

7. Sanders often draws on science in his nonfiction, as a way of understanding the world and as a source of metaphors. What role does science play in these stories?

8. What trends in technology appear to worry Sanders?

9. What do you think of the way "Clear-Cut" explores the sources of human dreaming?

10. *Déjà vu* is the apparent inspiration for "Sleepwalker." Have you experienced *déjà vu*? If so, how have you interpreted it?

11. What motifs from folktales and fairytales do you find in "The Anatomy Lesson," "Ascension," "The First Journey of Jason Moss," or any of the other stories?

12. What present-day forms of sexuality might have inspired "Eros Passage"?

13. A global "Enclosure," consisting of domed cities linked by travel tubes, provides a setting for a number of the stories. Why have humans moved inside the Enclosure?

14. What do the Enclosure stories suggest about the ways that attitudes toward the human body might be influenced by the banishing of wild nature?

15. "The Engineer of Beasts," "The Circus Animals' Desertion," and "Mountains of Memory" gave rise to Sanders' novel *The Engineer of Beasts*. Likewise, "Terrarium," "Quarantine," and "Touch the Earth" inspired his novel *Terrarium*. If you have read either book, what changes do you notice between the stories and the resulting novel?

16. This book is dedicated to Ursula K. Le Guin, a distinguished writer of science fiction and fantasy. Her parents were celebrated anthropologists, and her work has been described as "anthropological science fiction," because of the way she creates imaginary worlds as lenses through which to view our own world more clearly. Do you see a similar impulse in "Travels in the Interior," "The Audubon Effect," or any of the other stories?

17. Look up an on-line description of the Australian Aborigine concept of "Dreamtime." Why would such a concept appeal to a storyteller, such as Sanders?

18. In interviews, Sanders has described his debt to writers such as Mark Twain, Ursula K. Le Guin, Kurt Vonnegut Jr., Gabriel Garcia Marquez, Italo Calvino, and Jorge Luis Borges. Insofar as you may know the work of any of these writers, can you see their influence in these pages?

19. If you have read any of Sanders' nonfiction—books such as *A Conservationist Manifesto, Earth Works,* or *Hunting for Hope*—what parallels do you see between his concerns in those works and the concerns expressed in these stories?

20. Has the reading of these stories prompted any fantastic imaginings of your own?

SCOTT RUSSELL SANDERS is the author of twenty books of fiction and nonfiction, including *Hunting for Hope, Earth Works*, and *Divine Animal*. Among his honors are the Lannan Literary Award, the John Burroughs Essay Award, the Mark Twain Award, the Cecil Woods Award for Nonfiction, and fellowships from the Guggenheim Foundation and the National Endowment for the Arts. In 2012 he was elected to the American Academy of Arts and Sciences. He is Distinguished Professor Emeritus of English at Indiana University. He and his wife, Ruth, a biochemist, have reared two children in their hometown of Bloomington in the hardwood hill country of Indiana's White River Valley.